The Language of Bears
Book I: The Polyps of Christ

John Eidswick

This is a work of fiction. Names, characters, organizations, places, events, and incidents are either products of the author's imagination or used with fictional embellishment. Any resemblance to actual persons or animals, living or dead, or to actual events, is purely coincidental.

Cover Art: *Desembarco de los puritanos en America* (1883) by Antonio Gisbert

For Hiroko and Seiji, my reasons.

The devil can deceive the human fancy so
that a man really seems to be an animal.
　　　—*Malleus Mallificarum*

They paved paradise
Put up a parking lot
　　　—Joni Mitchell, *Big Yellow Taxi*

PART ONE

Chapter One
The Fall of Adam

If on that Autumn morning someone had visited the cabin of Adam Green, the timid young northland farmer whose uncle grew giant apples, to tell him that his life was about to get ripped apart, that his humble patch of land would soon be saturated with blood, oil, and smoke, he might have jumped off a cliff. All he ever wanted was peace and all life had ever given him was horseshit.

The family cabin atop Green Hill was slightly ramshackle, and bore the stamp of generations—a long porch, thick logs well-trodden, a tribe of rough-hewn chairs, a change of wood color on one side where extra rooms were added to accommodate new children. When folks passed on the way to town, wagons heavy with harvest from the grangelands, they often commented, a touch of pity in their voices, on how large this cabin was now for only a solitary farmer. The glassless windows were shuttered against encroachment by bears.

The front door opened and Adam stepped onto the porch. Adam Green was muscular and lean, a step or two into adulthood. His hands in the pockets of his leather breeches, his shaggy brown hair moving with the breeze, he walked across the clearing to the edge of the hill.

It was a modest hill. You could descend to the base, where Mills Trail snaked between the hill and the Forbidden Forest, in less time than it takes to draw water from a well. Yet Adam could see the whole world from here.

To the north and east, as far as the eye could see, the vast woods descended in a series of furrowed terraces, shrinking and darkening into the distance until they disappeared on the horizon. To the south and west, the forest rose. The land climbed steadily into a chain of mountains with rocky peaks that were white all year round and rose halfway to the top of the sky.

From the top of humble Green Hill Adam could see in one direction the planet drop away into magnificent green and brown swells, like the cascades of some unimaginable river, then turn around and see the world rise to breathtaking, unreachable heights.

About a hundred yards to the south was the other farm on Green Hill. Adam's uncle was in his garden, stooped under his famous apple tree. This year the apples were even more gigantic, bigger than human heads, and with a lush sheen on the skins that bespoke an intoxicating deliciousness. Adam's sister Daisy was circling Uncle Walt, hopping around on one foot in her green smock, her red hair flying from under a sky-blue bonnet. She didn't remember any of it, the deaths of their parents seven years before. Seven years since their aunt and uncle took her in like their own infant, and seven years since Adam had refused, out of some principle of adolescent stubbornness, to move with her.

To Adam, it seemed much longer.

He went behind his cabin and approached the barn to feed his horse. His wagon was out, the hitching rod on the ground. He noticed a wheel leaning askew. He crouched in front of it. A spoke was split. A crack ran along one side, deepening toward the center until light showed through at the place where the rod vanished into the rusty iron core.

A noise in the clearing made Adam jerk his head around. A sort of hissing squeal that ended so abruptly he wondered if he'd heard it at all. He started in to looking at the wheel and the sound came again. Then stopped.

He walked around the house and crossed to the edge of the clearing. All was quiet. Below him, at the base of the hill, the trees were the same as usual. The curving wall of the forest had been there since Adam's earliest memories, the same endless star-flicker of leaves in the breeze.

Adam scraped the ground with his foot and the sound came again, louder. Damnedest thing he'd ever heard, like a cat hiss. This time it didn't stop. He sidled down the slope.

Mill's Trail marked a separation between the peopled land and the forest that was as stark as the meeting of oil and water. He stepped across the trail and reached the the woods. The noise was now stronger and higher, an unchanging, sibilant hiss.

He stopped at the first trees, uncertain. The forest was dangerous. Tribes of carnivorous bears. Treacherous soil that appeared safe but turned to broth when stepped on and sucked you into the earth.

Fighting the urge to flee, Adam pressed his face into the leaves and squinted. Through the dimly-lit tangle of branches and twigs came the heavy odor of mold and water and rich, moist soil.

To the right, low to the ground, an odd shape. "Somebody there?"

As if in answer to his voice, the tone jumped higher. The thing, whose outline he could begin to make out through the gloom and tangled branches, was square and squat, crouching twenty feet off.

It was moving.

Adam took a deep breath. The thing didn't shift from its place. The movement came from within the creature itself, at its center, like the desperate thrashing of the legs of a great insect caught on its back. The motion possessed the same quality as the trickling vibrations of light that dappled the leaves, but tighter, more controlled. Adam was dazzled by the strangeness of it.

Then he understood. Of course. Adam let out a sigh of relief. A bee's nest.

He took a few steps down. He found a small clearing through the outer trees where it wasn't so dark, the light leaking through the canopy. The trees around the perimeter glowed a curious pale green, as if underwater.

Adam spread the top branches and pushed himself through the wall. His foot caught on something and he fell.

On his knees. Red ants scrambled up and down the blades of grass near his face. Beyond, there were two oak trees, one small and one large. Their branches were scorched from a lightning strike. One had a fractured branch bent up against its burned trunk. The trees leaned together, propping each other up.

The thing was between them.

It wasn't a hive. There were no bees. The noise was not of many small things but of one big thing.

It was trilling frantically from within, thousands of tiny dots prancing and skittering in—on?—the creature's middle. Gnats? Adam grabbed at the thought, trying to find anything to explain the impossibility in front of him.

The body of the creature was the strangest of all, devilishly unnatural, squared off like a dough box, black as the scars of the scorched oaks, fine-angled as saw teeth.

Adam, rigid, sweat dripping off his cheeks. His breath came in gasps. With each gulp of air he felt his panic recede a little, boil up again.

The dots vanished. They didn't fly away, didn't go anywhere, yet they were gone. And more unfathomable was that in their place another thing appeared, all pink and familiar and smiling through the leaves.

It was a human head. And it spoke to him.

Chapter Two
Something Unholy

The Auberon family farmhouse had grown much over the years. From a single-room shack thrown together by a forgotten ancestor, with a cooking hole on the dirt floor, the Auberon stead sprouted three bedrooms with a large common living area between. Along a wall in the central room wall was a wide fireplace with a chimney. On cold evenings, the family —Henrietta and Walt, their son Richard and his wife Clarissa, and little Daisy—sat around the fire and told stories.

The square openings next to both front and back doors had shutters that could be latched to block the rain and wild animals from violating the interior.

Henrietta Auberon was squatting before the fireplace, stirring breakfast in an iron pot. She was an attractive woman with a lean face, sharp cheeks, a small nose and mouth, and blue eyes that showed intelligence and warmth. She had the fiery red hair that marked all the female members of her side of the family.

Concentrating on moving the spoon through the steaming pot over the fire, she heard the footsteps of Daisy racing from the garden and up the porch. The back door crashed open.

A burst of wind followed the girl in. Daisy Green, a comet of red hair, shot into the room in her blue smock, spun around three times, hopped on one foot to the fireplace. "Auntie," she said, "Uncle Walt's building something by the apple tree, and he won't let me pound the nails."

"That's because the last time he let you," Henrietta responded without looking up, "you pounded them into his foot."

"Not his foot. His boot."

"Foot's in the boot."

"What's for breakfast?"

"Mush."

"What kind?"

Henrietta smiled over her shoulder. "Fox mush."

"Eeeuh!" Daisy gripped her own throat.

"With tomato worms squished in."

"Aach!" Daisy collapsed dramatically, thrashed her feet like an insect in its mortal throes, heaved her final breath, stood up. "Seriously."

"Your favorite. Strawberry butter mush. But you better get washed up first." Daisy had already sprinted to the back door. Henrietta hollered, "Don't forget your face."

High-spirited, Henrietta thought. The girl has a spirit of fire, just like her mother did. After Henrietta's sister Hattie died that horrible night seven years ago, and took her husband with her, Henrietta took on the role of mother for the girl. Hardly a day passed since that she wasn't startled by how similar Daisy was to Hattie. Both as sweet as angels when it suited them and wild as cougars when it didn't.

From a bowl, Henrietta took three spoonfuls of butter and added them to the brown and grainy mix of wheat, oats and water. She put in a pinch of salt and a spoonful of sugar, continuing stirring to soothe out the lumps. She removed from one of the pockets of her apron a sack of strawberries. She'd picked them from the garden before sunrise, finding the ripe ones by feel.

The fat, red fruits exhaled a wonderful scent. Henrietta pressed her face close to the opening of the sack, closed her eyes, and took a deep whiff.

A man screamed.

Henrietta dropped the sack and ran to the window. Clarissa appeared at her bedroom door, her baby pushed to her breast. "What's wrong?"

Henrietta opened the door. "It's Adam, tearing up the hill." She ran out to the porch. Clarissa's husband. Richard, chopping wood out back, came running around to the front yard, gripping his axe. Daisy pranced up behind him.

Walt waddled up after them, his pudgy face befuddled. He held an iron adze in one hand, and a half-adzed hunk of oak in the other. "What's going on?" he said.

Adam was halfway across the clearing. He was close enough for them to make out the redness of his face and the wild look in his eyes.

As they rushed out, Adam stopped, bent forward, and put his hands on his knees, gasping. Everyone crowded around.

Adam's voice came in pieces. "I saw something down there." He pointed weakly over his shoulder. "A ghost!"

He collapsed. Richard leaped forward and caught his cousin before his head hit the ground. He carried him inside the house as easily as Clarissa carried their baby. With his enormous arms and legs like the trunks of trees, Richard was one of the strongest men in the land.

He carried Adam into his parent's room and laid him on their bed. Daisy ran out and returned with a cup of water from the barrel in the kitchen.

The family stood around the bed. Walter dipped his finger into the cup and splashed water on Adam's face.

The young man groaned. He opened his eyes and saw the half-circle of faces looking down on him.

"Where am I?"

Walter said, "You're in our bed. You had a spell."

Henrietta touched Adam's forehead. She spoke tenderly. "You hurt anywhere?"

Adam felt terrible. His right leg was torn in a couple of places. His shoulder and face were burning from scrapes suffered when he fell in the brambles. His head felt like it was splitting apart.

"I'm fine, Auntie."

"What happened? You said you saw a ghost," asked Walter.

Adam threw one of his arms across his face. "Don't know if it was a ghost or something else. I don't know how to explain it. It was the awfulest thing, like something from Hell."

"I'm scared." Clarissa said. She pressed the baby closer to her breast and stroked its head protectively. "There's something unholy in this room."

Daisy pushed her head between the adults to see her brother. She sneered, "You're just a dainty petunia, Clarissa-missa. Tell us what you saw, Adam. I ain't scared."

Adam took a deep breath. He described the thing in the woods. He faltered sometimes and shook his head, like he couldn't believe his own words. As they listened, Walter and Richard struggled to keep their faces impassive. When Adam came to the part about the head talking, Clarissa gasped. Henrietta whispered, "Lord Almighty."

Daisy clapped her hands. "I want to see it!"

"Adam," said Richard. "You sure about all this?"

"Course. What do you mean?"

"Well, I mean, you said you fell down. Maybe you hit your head on something and..."

"No."

"Cause what you're telling us, well, it don't make any..."

Adam glared up at his cousin. "Richard, this was real."

"Show us then."

Adam pulled himself up in the bed. Henrietta told Clarissa to keep Daisy with her in the cabin. Henrietta, Walter, Richard and Adam moved from the bedroom and out the front door. When Daisy tried to follow, Richard pushed her back through the door, where Clarissa, still holding her baby in the crook of one arm, grabbed her with the other and pulled her in.

They stood on the porch, looking across the clearing to the edge of the hill.

"We got to be real careful not to let this spread to town," said Richard. "That bitch Wandabella'll sling the gossip at every customer in her store."

Henrietta placed her hand on Adam's shoulder. "Honey, you sure you don't want to stay here?" After her sister's death, Henrietta had sworn an oath to do her best to lavish upon the poor orphaned boy enough maternal affection to compensate for what she saw as the cruelest of fates.

Adam looked pale and weak. Although he was gazing in the direction of the forest with fear in his eyes, he mumbled, "I'll be okay."

From the base of Green Hill, they could no longer see the farmhouses. A few clouds in the midmorning sky cast oblong, fast-moving shadows across the green and brown slope.

Adam pointed ahead to a space along the pass where the trees were especially thick. "See that gap in the branches? That's where I fell in."

Richard raised his axe. "I'll go." He tried to look into the trees. "Too dark." He jabbed the axe blade into the trees, pried open the tangle of branches and stuck his head in.

"What do you see?" Henrietta demanded.

Richard yanked his head out. "Adam, you sure this is the place?"

"What do you mean?"

"Ain't nothing in there."

Adam ran to the trees and looked. The black box was gone.

"It was here!" Adam cried. He broke through the wall of trees, fell again, and crawled to the place where he'd found the thing. He could hear the others following him in. He whipped his head around. "Look here." Richard crouched next to him. Adam moved the tip of his finger along the perimeter where the box had been.

"See? The grass inside is crushed."

Richard cleared his throat. "Adam, you made that square now with your finger...."

"No!" Adam yelled. The two men jumped up. Adam shook his fist at his cousin. "I didn't make nothing!"

Henrietta slipped her lean body between them. She glared up at her nephew. "Put your hands down," she ordered. Adam dropped his fists. Henrietta stabbed her finger toward the trail.

Adam climbed from the forest, his head drooping to his chest like a perishing bloom.

Walter emerged next, followed by the others.

"Now," said Henrietta to Adam, gesturing at the line of trees, "you sure this is the spot?"

"Damnit." Adam's face was red.

"Just tell me if you're sure."

"I'm sure. Oh, you all gotta believe me!"

No one knew what to say. Richard snatched up his axe and started up the slope. Walter and Henrietta trudged after him. Adam followed far behind.

Chapter Three
After the Trees

When Walter Auberon shifted his weight in his chair, the ancient floorboards creaked. The porch, which straddled the slope of Green Hill on the south side, was one of the improvements made to the building generations back to accommodate the Green family brood. Henrietta's great great great grandfather used slabs of oak to build it, hewing the trees and cutting them into rough boards, lashing them together atop columns of raw stone. The porch was constructed at a dim point in history after, according to family legend, an even earlier, more primitive version of the cabin burned down and was rebuilt as a well-ventilated structure with an elevated foundation that kept the family dry and, during heavy rain, safe from plummeting over the side of the hill.

A fortuitous byproduct of the porch were the chairs Henrietta's ancestors had made to put on it. Within moments of their creation began the tradition of sitting on the porch in the evening and chewing the fat.

When Walter, a man with no living family of his own, married Henrietta, he moved himself into the house and brought the surname of Auberon. He now sat upon one of the chairs on his wife's distant ancestor's porch, sipping tea. The night sky was spotted with clouds, luminous bruises spread over the stars. From the backyard came sounds of Henrietta doing the supper dishes at the well. Clarissa and Richard were in the living room, tending their infant.

A single candle burned in a window of Adam Green's cabin. From this distance, it looked to Walter like a fleck of starlight, cast down from the sky.

A breath of chilly air hurried past Walter's face, a dashing spook. Adam had refused to stay with them that night, refused to discuss the incident in the woods any further.

"Uncle?"

Walter jerked. Daisy was an expert at slipping up on people, silent as a mouse.

"Let me up."

She climbed into his lap. She rested her face against his chest. He sipped his tea.

"What's the matter, Sprout?"

"Couldn't sleep."

"Afraid of the dark?"

Daisy flashed him an offended look. "I am *not* afraid of the dark."

"Sorry. How was school?"

"Okay, except for that stupid Bobby Dunkel."

"Boy from the swamplands?"

"He stuck a spider in Hildie's hair. So I punched him in the nose."

"Daisy, what did I tell you?"

"But…"

"No buts. You don't hit."

"Uncle?"

"What?"

"Is Adam okay?"

"Nothing to worry yourself about."

"Why doesn't he let people help him?"

"What do you mean?"

"Auntie tried to bring him dinner tonight and he wouldn't take it. And every time you tried to help him take in his corn last week, he wouldn't let you."

Walter nodded. "You know, honey, Adam's a good man."

"He's the best brother I've ever had."

"He's the only brother you've ever had."

"He's the best brother in the world then."

"Hattie and Jed—your ma and pa—both passed on when he was only a little older than you. And you were just a baby."

"And I moved here with you and Aunt Henrietta 'cause Adam couldn't take care of me, I know. And Adam didn't move here because he wanted to be alone. You think my ma and pa killed themselves 'cause they were witches?"

Walter choked on his tea. "Daisy, don't say things like that!"

She yawned. "Why not?"

"Where did you hear that?"

"School."

"Bobby Dunkel?"

Daisy shook her head. "Fred Fodder."

"No one knows exactly what happened. It's a big shock, for someone that age to lose his parents."

"Uh-hm."

"Especially in that way."

"Mm. So they weren't witches?"

After a long pause, Walter said, "Ain't no such thing as witches."

"Reverend Branch says there is."

"Reverend Branch has a colorful way of speaking."

"And Mary Lena was a witch."

"Daisy!"

"Well, she was."

Mary Lena was the former schoolteacher who had gone mad. She had torn through the town one Autumn afternoon, shrieking that the mice in her garden were talking to her.

"She wasn't a witch, Daisy." Walter tapped his skull with his forefinger. "She was broke in her head."

"Everyone says she was a witch. Clarissa says so."

"Clarissa says that 'cause the Reverend's her kin, and she grew up hearing it. Just 'cause people say things don't make them things true."

"So Clarissa's wrong?"

Walter considered. "Clarissa's a good woman, and a good wife to Richard."

"You're not answering my question."

"And Clarissa's...religious."

"And you didn't answer my question about Adam either."

"Some folks ain't treated him so good...on account of their superstitions...because..." Walter felt queasy. He'd known for a long time that the baby they'd inherited from Henrietta's sister would eventually grow up enough to hear the rumors and to ask about them. But he'd thought he had a few more years.

"Listen, Daisy. You're too young to be hearing about such things."

"Adam wasn't much older when all that happened to him. They say at school that people were calling *him* a witch."

"Those were bad times. Too bad for little girls to hear about."

"Come on, Uncle, tell me what happened. I ain't scared."

Walter looked at his little niece. No bigger than a radish shoot, but absolutely fearless. Like her mother.

He sighed. "After your mama and papa passed on, some folks, like you said, were saying these foolish things about witches. Just a lot of nonsense, but for some reason it sounded reasonable to Reverend Branch, and he said a few things there in his church, and that kind of brought these folks together into one noisy group. Now, you know, Sprout, when you get a group of people together to do something good, they can work real miracles, and do a lot more good than they can working separate. But the opposite is true too. Get a bunch of folks with some bad ideas teaming together, and the results can be terrible, and it only gets worse if that bunch is also led by a man of God. Anyway, yes, there were some stupid people who thought that Adam was a witch, because they thought that Adam's parents were witches, and they believed things like that are passed in the blood. And they wanted something bad to be done to him." Walter wiped a hand across his forehead as though to force away the unpleasant memory.

"Who were they?"

"Daisy, it ain't important."

"Come on, Uncle, tell me."

"Nothing happened. Mayor Gladford—not the Mayor William Gladford we have now, but his papa, Increase Gladford—stood up to Reverend Branch, said Adam Green was a fine young man, and all this talk of witchery was just poppycock. And in the end, they let Adam be. And people got on with their lives."

"So that's what makes Adam the way he is?"

"It's left him people-shy."

Daisy yawned.

"You oughta get to bed."

"I ain't sleepy."

"You're yawning."

"Uncle Walt?"

"Yes?"

"What's out there?"

"Out where?"

"There." The girl pointed into the gloom.

"In the forest?"

"Yes."

"Now, Sprout, you don't need to worry about that business with Adam today. It was just the light playing tricks on his eyes."

The girl snuggled against him. "I worry about him. He's hardly got nothing."

"What do you mean, honey? He's got his farm, and his wagon, and his horse. And his cow and pig. And he works at the Grange."

"He only works there sometimes, and he's only got one cow. And only one pig. And they're not food, they're pets."

"We'll help him with food if he needs it."

"He'll say no."

"Your aunt'll make him say yes."

"He ain't got no friends."

"He's got Virginia. He's got George."

"They don't come around no more. Ain't seen George around here in a year, probably."

Walter shifted uncomfortably in the chair. "Hear George is busy on the ranch."

"On account of his mean, fish-face father."

"Daisy, don't talk about people like that."

"But Uncle Walt, he really does have a fish-face. And he really is mean. Especially to George. And George is getting mean too, because of it."

"You don't need to be talking about people."

"Uncle Walt?"

"Yes?

"What else is out there?"

"In the forest?"

"No, after the forest."

"What do you mean?"

"There's lots of trees out there."

"Uh huh."

"What comes after them?"

"After them?"

"If you go past them, what's there?"

"More trees, of course. And you can't go out there, told you a thousand times. It's called the forbidden forest for a reason. Those woods are dangerous. Filled with bears."

"Adam went in them."

"He shouldn'ta."

"Skinners go in them."

"They're different."

"Uncle?"

Walter took a deep breath. "Yes?"

"After the trees, there are more trees?"

"Uh huh."

"What's after those trees?"

"More trees."

"And after those?"

"More."

"And what about the mountains? They get taller, and taller, the farther we can see. What's after them?"

"After them? Taller mountains, of course."

Daisy spoke patiently. "There can't be taller ones than the ones we see, Uncle."

"Why not?"

"If they were taller, we could see them."

"Maybe they aren't taller. Maybe there're shorter mountains behind the tall ones. Like children, standing behind their parents." Walter added the last sentence with a kind of poetic flourish.

"But you don't know."

"Well…I don't need to know," Walter decided. "There're some things that ain't none of our business, like Preacher Branch says."

"Uncle?"

"What?"

"Out there, are there others?"

"Other what?"

"Other people."

"Other people?" Walter was shocked.

Daisy lifted her head up from his chest and stared up at him earnestly.

"Other people."

"Daisy, where do you get these strange ideas?"

"But…"

"No buts! The only people is us, right here. The rest of those mountains and trees is not us, and not for us. And none of our business!"

"But Uncle," Daisy persisted calmly, "Preacher Branch said our people came from somewhere else, a long time ago."

Walter laughed. "Oh, that. Well, somewhere way back when, at the time of your great, great, great great grandparents, folks was living in another part of the forest. It was bad there, they say, on account of wild animals. Practically around every corner was another killer bear or poison snake. So they packed up and moved on. And after many encounters with all manner of monsters in the Forbidden Forest, and their faith tested severely, the Lord saw fit to lead them to this peaceful valley. And they named this place Arcadia." Walter finished his story with a far-off look. "Reverend Branch used to tell that story every week in church, in those very words, so many times I remember them perfect. Then he stopped."

Walter braced himself for her next question, but the girl remained silent. She snuggled up on his chest. Soon, her breathing deepened.

Walter took another sip of his tea. Great swathes of the sky were now swallowed up by clouds. The inky splashes let only a few stars shine through. Walter looked toward where the trees were huddling in darkness and wondered what was out there.

Chapter Four
A Particle in the Body of God

Little Victor was moving through his Saturday deliveries, perched on the splintery riding board of his old cart, his small body wobbling with the pocks of the trail. His stubby fingers were twisted around the rope tied to his donkey Ewell. The animal was melancholy as usual, head lowered, dragging his hooves morosely along Mill's Trail as though it were a river of mud.

The day was looking to be unusually warm for autumn. It was Victor's Saturday route, starting near Broke Ranch in the south, moving north to the grangelands, making stops along the way to pick up and drop off deliveries. Sometimes folks would ask him to repair something—a broken farm implement, a fence, a wagon wheel. That night, he would set up camp in the north, rise before daybreak to follow his route back again, arriving in the south late at night. He worked mostly for farmers who didn't have time to do repairs or ride far to trade with other farmers. Mayor Gladford also paid him to bring food from the communal stores to the elderly or injured.

With a tug, he turned Ewell off Mill's Trail and onto the meetinghouse road. He was bringing sacks of grain, flour, tea, and smoked pork to Reverend Calvin Branch. It was Victor's favorite delivery, for the reverend was a true man of God, one of the last.

He took out a handkerchief and wiped sweat from his forehead. Victor had a huge, barbed nose that jutted from a tiny face whose eyes were separated by several inches and whose long, pointed chin bent oddly to the right. His waxy brown eyes were set deep in his head, within craterous sockets the width of crabapples. This deformity made it hard for Victor to lower his eyelids, and gave him the appearance of constantly goggling in surprise. Victor's skin seemed to be the wrong size for his distorted skull, stretched too tightly here, hung too loosely there, giving the impression of a man who was different ages at the same time.

He wore a huge hat that swallowed up his tangles of red hair and fell halfway over his face.

He squinted at the sky. A glorious, bright, and beautiful day, the cloudless sky wide open. A day for giving thanks to Jesus, yet the morning had left him with an ugly, crawly feeling, like that time he woke up in an infested haystack with fleas in his flesh.

Lunchtime, he'd dropped by the two most popular merchants in town, Shrenker's General Store and Hanker's Barrel and Pub. The gossip at both was more frantic than usual. Wherever Little Victor went, the topic alighted before him like mice in a field: Adam Green, that strange farmer out on Green Hill, went mad yesterday, screaming he'd seen a ghost in the forest.

At Shrenker's, a dozen ladies were gabbing about how unfashionably dressed Henrietta Auberon was in church the previous Sunday. A customer threw in the information about Adam Green, Henrietta's nephew, having come bolting from the woods claiming he'd seen a ghost. Wandabella Shrenker, the store's owner, grabbed onto the news with slobbery glee and started in on it, embellishing it, her spidery fingers doing a dance in front of her bony face as she spoke. By the time Victor left, the dozen ladies were in heat over this new scandal.

A few paces down the road at Hankers, Victor joined men gathered around a barrel, heads lowered in discussion about what was the worst kind of folks.

Joss Hankers stomped up to the table, a tray of pewter tankards propped on her big shoulder. With her booming voice, she weighed in: "I think the worst folks is those too cowardly to do the right thing when the right thing needs doing. Remember how Ole Brock wouldn't get himself out of bed to help rebuild after that fire at Widow Hutch's? That's the day I stopped serving him, the lazy snake. If a body can't do right when right is needed, a body's got no right to live."

The men thought on what she said and someone raised the subject of the incident with Adam Green, but the others hadn't heard about it yet. The topic of conversation instantly changed and gossip surged like a fire on dry hay.

Wherever Little Victor went, they started in talking about it, and soon they couldn't talk about anything else. Adam Green, whose mother and father had already scandalized everyone seven years back by taking their own lives in the Forbidden Forest, the couple who even now folks whispered might have been servants of the Devil, had finally gone over the edge himself. Malicious old rumors, near-extinguished by the passage of years, found new fuel. Could Adam's seeing a ghost be a sign that he had inherited witch-blood from his parents?

Victor was glad to get out of town. The trail climbed, rounding Staff Hill. Here Victor could look out on larger pieces of sky and land: the central plains with the southern mountains rising behind them; the jagged clay-iron of the Grey Mountains to the east, the green and brown checkerboard patterns of the grangelands and northern valleys behind them. All this beauty made Victor feel connected to the grandeur of things, like he, despite his small stature and deformities, was part of something greater, a particle of the body of God. It was a feeling he rarely had when with others of his species.

At the top was the community meetinghouse. Farmers still attended the reverend's Sunday services, but in dwindling numbers. The Reverend Calvin Mathers Cotton Makepeace Branch lived behind the meetinghouse in his windowless, shutterless cabin. A sole wooden chair, its back straight as a hitching post, separated the preacher from the stone floor. When he slept, he did it on a pile of coarse hay.

Little Victor too spent most nights sleeping in hay. He felt it was one of many qualities that bonded him with the reverend. Within the cold morass of cruel humanity on whose periphery the little man existed, only a handful of people was kind to him. The schoolteacher, Miss Dorothy, offered him regular treats from her kitchen, and the mayor was tolerable enough polite. Virginia at the bakery almost treated him like a normal human being. However, Reverend Branch was the only person Victor really trusted.

While some found in the old man's stormy face and ice-blue eyes an antique and terrible Puritan zealotry, Victor saw only wisdom.

He tapped Ewell with the reins to bring the wagon to a halt in front of the cabin. Reverend Branch, tall and thin, a few white hairs clinging stubbornly to his skull, emerged from behind, where he was tending a small vegetable garden. "Victor!" His eyes twinkled above his frown. "What did you bring me today?"

"Brought something special, Rev."

The little man, his distorted body bobbing awkwardly to one side, reached into the back of his wagon and pulled out a couple of filled burlap bags with the word "corn" scrawled on them. The bags were much larger than him, yet he hoisted each easily over his shoulder and laid it on the ground. Victor then burrowed into the recesses of his wagon and dragged out a wooden box. He removed the box so gently, he might have been lifting a newborn baby. He held it up to the Reverend. "Got these today from the southlands."

The old preacher lifted the lid and cried out in delight. Inside was a bunch of tiny grapes. On their purple surfaces, sunlight broke into a spray of enchanting white stars. "Victor, they're magnificent!"

The small man flushed with joy. The reverend nodded his head enthusiastically. "Bounty from Heaven, for certain. What did I do to bring down the Lord's blessings on me this day, I wonder?" The reverend looked up to the sky.

You treated a man like me with respect, thought Victor.

The reverend smiled down on him. "I thank you, sir. And how are you today?"

"Can't complain, Rev."

Calvin Branch looked at the donkey tethered to Victor's cart. "I see Ewell is down in the spirits, as usual."

"Seems to be his nature, Rev."

"Maybe his bones hurt, like mine. Getting on in years."

"Was thinkin' maybe of taking Ewell to see Doc Midland, maybe get'im a powder for his sad moods."

Reverend Branch's countenance darkened.

"I think the last thing you should do is take your poor donkey to that ungodly charlatan."

"Sorry, Rev. I forgot you and Doc don't get on."

"Doc Midland has forsaken Christ. It's as simple as that. He is a practitioner of Natural Philosophy and has no shame about it. He comes from a long line of practitioners of alchemy and apothecarial arts. I know he denies it—I've endured his protestations on too many occasions—but these endeavors are the handiwork of the Devil. There is no room for dispute. Rather than consuming devilish herbal powders, Ewell would do better to treat his melancholy by embracing his condition of original depravity and accepting the Lord Jesus into his heart."

"Okay. I'll try to convince him."

Victor threw a huge sack of grain over his shoulder. He staggered dangerously under its weight, but the reverend didn't offer to help him. Victor would assail even a man of God with kicks and bites rather than allow him to shoulder any of his responsibilities. As he moved the sacks of grain, the casks of cider, butter, and other stores into the house, he continued talking, as the reverend walked alongside.

"Did you hear about that Adam Green?"

"No. What happened?"

Victor paused in mid-stride, a barrel of apples balanced on his back.

"Don't know how to talk on this without sounding downright, excuse the word, Rev, *witchy*."

"What do you mean?"

"This morning, seems Adam Green came screaming out of the Forbidden Forest, mad as a bear. He ran to his aunt and uncle, you know? They first thought a snake bit him, but it were a lot worse."

Victor lowered his voice. "He says he found a box, in the woods, that had a human *head*—with no body— inside. And he says the head *talked* to him."

The reverend's face grew very serious. "Are you sure?"

"Sure as rain, Reverend."

"Where did you hear this, Victor?"

"I heard it," Victor paused to think, "At Shrenkers Store." He screwed his eyes upward in their deep sockets. "Then I heard it again when I was delivering to Hankers Barrel."

"Who did you hear it from at Shrenker's?"

"Them fancy-dressed ladies was talking it up, Rev."

"Where did they hear it?"

"Think it were from Wandbella Shrenker."

The reverend nodded. "That woman is a most fearsome gossip. Did she start this rumor?"

Victor shook his head. "No, she weren't the first to tell it."

"Where did she hear the story?"

"Think she overheard some man talking about it. Lot of men drinking over at Hankers."

"You too said you heard men talking about this at Hankers, Victor. Was there one man in particular who was telling this story? I'm very curious to know."

"Men was talking. I didn't really look at'em close."

"Did you speak with these men?"

"I was working."

"Did you hear which of the men told the story *first*? I want to know who started this rumor. Think hard, Victor." The old man's eyes were blazing down at him. Sweat began to drip down Victor's cheeks.

At last Victor squeaked, "Oh, yes. One of the men at Hankers said he heard the story somewhere else. And then he told the story to the men at Hankers."

"What was the man's name?"

"I get names all confused, Rev."

The reverend took a deep breath. "Where, Victor, did this man say he heard the story?"

"From the ladies at Shrenkers."

For a long, terrifying moment, Reverend Branch looked like he was going to reach down, and wrap his long, gnarled fingers around Victor's neck. Then all at once, he instead burst into laughter. He patted the little man on the head.

"Victor, God bless you for bringing simplicity and honesty into our tawdry human proceedings."

"Thank you, sir."

"What I wouldn't give to have such trueness to the Lord even mimicked by our citizens such as you radiate naturally from your very being." The reverend heaved a sigh. "Like the old days."

"The old pur'tan times, Rev?"

Calvin winced. "Please don't say 'Puritan', Victor. It's a vulgar designation given to us by heathens. We must call ourselves the People of God."

"Okay."

"Victor, do you realize there used to be Sabbatical Laws?"

"No, sir."

"Well, there were. We had Sabbatical Laws. And *everyone* needed to attend church. And there was none of the free and easy sinning we have today."

"Really?"

The reverend smacked the palm of his hand with his fist. "No working or drinking on the Sabbath, no hayrides, merrymaking, laughing, none of that." The old man swiped his open hand through the air like a sword. "On the Sabbath! When people weren't in church, listening to my father preach, they were at home."

"What were they doing at home?"

"Praying, Victor! Thinking about the Lord!"

"Oh, my!"

"My, indeed!"

"But Rev."

"Yes?"

"If they wanted to do their merrymaking, what could stop them?"

"We had constables, Victor!"

"Constables? What's that?"

"Constables were men who stopped people from breaking the Sabbatical Laws. Why, my father spoke of one young man and woman who were caught holding hands. Holding hands, yea, even *kissing,* on the Sabbath!"

"Oh?"

"Yes," the reverend smiled. "And those big constables grabbed those two sinners and shoved them into pillories and whipped them bloody. And all the townsfolk turned out to pitch rotten apples at them. Some even threw stones."

Reverend Branch gazed into the distance, his features pacified by nostalgic recollection. "That's what we need now," he said. "We need someone who can make the old ways come back, *force* them to…"

"What are pillories?" asked Victor.

"Pillories, yes, um…" The reverend stammered, then said, "Victor, it's of no matter."

"Just last Sunday, I saw a couple of folks kissing," said Victor conversationally. "Under the smooching sycamores."

"The what?"

"Smooching sycamores."

"What are they?"

"Some trees, by Silver Stream. Couples go there to smooch."

Reverend Branch stabbed his finger at the air.

"That's what I mean, Victor! No one has any respect for God anymore!" Victor nodded. "Now why don't you put away that thing, before you fall down the hill?"

Victor looked up at the big barrel still perched on his shoulder. "I forgot." He finished carrying the goods to the house. The reverend took from his breeches a leather pouch jingling with coins.

"Victor, coins are okay today? Or would you prefer provender in trade?

"Coins, Reverend, if it don't put you out."

"You know, Victor," he said as he fished out coins from the pouch and handed them to the little man. "You too would be welcome at my services. I wouldn't pillory you if you came." Reverend Branch said it with a twinkle in his eye.

Victor looked down. "I do come to church. Every Sunday."

"Really? But I don't think I've ever seen you."

"After everyone's inside, I listen at the window."

"You are a good man, Victor."

Victor pocketed the coins and climbed into his wagon and bade the reverend farewell. He rode down the hill, pondering. Life was so hard. He didn't like lying to him about where he'd first heard the story of Adam Green. He hated not telling him the truth about the fact that it was he, Victor himself, who had spread the rumors about Adam at Shrenkers and Hankers.

He wouldn't have done it if small, ugly men like him didn't need to earn money from unholy sources too.

Chapter Five
A Spark of Memory

Victor went off down the trail in his squeaking cart, his despondent donkey trudging in front. Calvin Branch smiled and waved back.

The instant Victor was gone, the smile dropped like a rock from the reverend's face. He ran to the barn and pulled open the door. He was already wheezing from the exertion. He hobbled to where his mare was slumbering in the shadows.

Suzie peeled open her eyes and blinked with geriatric irritation. She grew more agitated when Calvin, straining so hard that his voice was squeezed through his throat in a strangulated whine, threw a saddle onto her back. The reverend hadn't run the horse in years, for fear of abrasions to his dilapidated buttocks. Suzie was a pastured decoration of the church, a plaything for visiting children.

He floundered to get himself atop the horse and heard his breeches tearing. He managed to grip the saddlehorn and flip himself to the summit and did it so awkwardly the tail of his smock wormed under the saddle. Sensing the snag, he jerked his body hard in the opposite direction and nearly fell off the horse.

Perspiration breaking from his pores, he righted himself. Suzie snarled, tossing her head back and forth.

Reverend Branch put his mouth next to the mare's balding ear. "Old girl, sorry to wake you, but something of great importance has arisen. We must hasten ourselves to Mayor Gladford's house immediately or all is lost!"

Perhaps it was the alien presence of the man atop her, or maybe a spark of memory from her days as a filly, but the horse gathered her most ancient strength, trotted creakily to an overgrown trail behind the cabin, and took off like lightning.

Chapter Six
An Approaching Coil

Mayor William Orwell Gladford was a pudgy man with a warm smile, merry blue eyes, and a long white beard. His chief loves in life were, after his wife, tending his vegetable garden and fishing. He did all three, and everything else too, with the same easygoing cheerfulness that made him well loved by the community.

He'd just sat down for his mid-morning tea. He ran his fingers thoughtfully through his beard. Although the day was as fine as a day could be, William felt something troubling him, a mysterious nagging in his gut whose origin he couldn't quite pin down.

The view from the porch was especially fine this time of year. From this humble vantage could be seen the whole of the vast plains of central Arcadia. Under the cloudless blue sky, the grasses were changing color and the land lay in a patchwork of browns, yellows and oranges, climbing and falling gently toward the horizon, where it encountered a ragged line of dark green, the outer pines of the Forbidden Forest. Decades before, William's father, Increase Gladford, the first mayor, tore up logs to build their home here. Because there were no trees in this area, Increase had carted in the logs himself. He chose the expanse of rolling, grassy hills southeast of the town to construct the cabin for his wife and child because he felt the region, populated by more rabbits than plants, would be safe from fire.

Before his death from an accident, Increase Gladford had earned near-legendary status among the community as a man of superhuman strength. Single-handedly, William's father had changed Arcadia from the primeval region it had been, where the line between the woods and the land populated by settlers was not clearly drawn, and where dangerous animals emerged from the forest to prey upon the helpless, to what it was now, a land where everyone, regardless of ability, was kept safe from hunger and peril. It was Increase Gladford who established the elaborate system that allowed their society to run smoothly with only moderate effort from everyone, including his sole son who inherited his position, and it was also Increase Gladford who shepherded the necessary forces to separate the wilderness, with its poisonous snakes, demonic wolves and monstrous bears, and the territory inhabited by humans. How exactly he had accomplished these feats was a thing of distant history and largely lost to memory, even to William's, who was only a small boy during that revolution. What remained vivid in the public consciousness was the reputation of the man, the great Increase Gladford, who was widely revered as a hero.

Perhaps the only person who didn't place William's father on a pedestal was William's old friend, the Reverend Calvin Branch, and that was because the crusty preacher discerned in the honoring of any human the handiwork of the devil. That, and Reverend Branch had bitter memories of how Increase Gladford had publicly humiliated Calvin's own father, the Reverend Titus Josephus Branch.

As William sat sipping his tea, nagged by vague anxiety, looking over the Arcadian landscape, he thought it strange that so much pain and turmoil had occurred in a place so apparently peaceful and serene. His father Increase had humiliated Titus Branch two times, actually. Each act of humiliation had to do with clashes between the two men over witchcraft. The first was over Titus's handling of the Mary Lena affair. The second concerned his response to the deaths of Adam Green's parents.

While Reverend Calvin hadn't necessarily agreed with his father's actions in these two incidents, he still had enough loyalty to his father that, even when joined now in a conversation with people who praised the memory of Increase, Calvin would always maintain a careful silence, neither praising nor criticizing the man who had both brought prosperity and peace to the land but also made his father look like a fool.

The disagreements between Titus Branch and Increase Gladford were so passionate and so public that they had created a schism between these two men, who had once been close friends, that never healed. In the first clash, William's father had promoted the scientific idea that Mary Lena derived her delusions about talking mice from a perfectly natural causes, whereas Titus Branch saw her claims as a clear-cut case of witchcraft. Increase Gladford said the poor woman needed rest, in a secluded place, and advocated that she be allowed to live in a remote cabin, where she would be provided nourishment and care. Titus Branch, on the other hand, said the woman should be burned at the stake.

Each man had his fervent followers, and something akin to civil war was on the verge of breaking out in the peaceful land of Arcadia, before the issue was finally resolved in Increase's favor when he called together a town meeting whereat he delivered a thrilling speech that smashed to smithereens each argument put forth to support the idea that Mary Lena was a witch. Increase unveiled evidence that the younger male members of the Fodder clan had, as a joke, hidden in Mary Lena's garden on a number of occasions and, by means of eerie whispers and chirruping mingled with half-comprehensible sentences, had driven Mary Lena to believe these preposterous things about mice.

Titus never forgave Increase for that public humiliation, but the acrimony he felt for the elder

Gladford might have manifested itself even more sharply if it weren't for the affection he felt for his son, young William, and the lengthy friendship between William and Increase's son, Calvin Branch.

Long before, Titus had taken William under his wing to teach him how to fish. It was one of the few things Increase Gladford had little skill in. Titus had developed a fondness for the young man and had maintained a close relationship with him throughout the decades.

Increase Gladford and Titus Branch had avoided each other for at least a decade when another disruption rattled the land. One full-moon night, Adam Green's parents walked, of their own volition, into the Forbidden Forest. They didn't come back out.

For a few days, it was believed the couple had been devoured by bears, for what else could be the outcome for civilized humans entering the forest at night? Everyone knew the only people able to survive in those evil woods were the skinners of the east, that clan of wildmen, scarcely human at all, who made their living from killing animals and sawing off their skins.

Then came the sightings. The first was from Wandabella Shrenker. The gossipy owner of the General Store said that while she was gathering blueberries near Merlin Grove, she saw a real bear at the forest wall, walking along casually with Adam's parents. That was stunning enough, but Wandabella claimed that the couple seemed to be companions of the bear, and even that—horrors—Hattie Green stroked the huge paw of the beast with affection. Wandabella claimed that when she overcame her shock and found her voice, she called out to the couple. Hattie! She cried. Hattie Green! And at the sound of her name, Adam's mother turned and gave her a look, and in the woman's eyes was not a hint of humanity, just pure beast. She had the eyes of an animal.

Wandabella's story ended with the three leaping together straight into the forest.

Wandabella dramatically told the story again and again to customers in her store. It wasn't long before other sightings were reported. The wife of a farmhand at the Grange said he witnessed the Greens, their clothing so tattered from forest life that they were in a state of shameful nakedness, at the bank of a stream knocking trout into the air, catching them in their mouths, and chomping them down raw. Some children walking home from school said they were chased by a bear-like creature whom they recognized as Adam's father by his familiar beard.

Reverend Titus Branch returned anew to his pulpit with tales of doom. To him, the visitations of Adam's parents in the company of bears could mean only one thing: witchcraft. He was of the opinion that witchcraft was a kind of contagion of the soul, which could be passed down biologically through one's children, a theoretical orientation that implicated the offspring of the Greens. Looks of suspicion and fear began to be leveled at Adam Green, so young then his voice had scarcely begun to change, and even at his baby sister Daisy. Over the course of a several Sunday sermons, Titus whipped up the superstitious fear of Adam and Daisy. He reached a point where he was suggesting openly that the children should be, for the safety of the good Christians in Arcadia, tied to posts and burned alive. And while a large number of sensible folks were dubious, yea, even appalled, by Titus's proclamations, they were also cowed by the reputation of the preacher, whose position as spiritual leader afforded him a great deal of respect in the community, and also by the ferocity of his more passionate followers, whose faith in every word the reverend spoke was unshakeable.

It was only through the brave intercession of William's father Increase that the children were saved from the madness. As he had with the case of Mary Lena, he called a town meeting and again talked sense, using incontrovertible arguments, delivered calmly and eloquently, into the majority of the community. Many were grateful for his courage and sobriety in the matter. And many, William suspected, still harbored secret resentment against his father, even though he was now dead, and against himself.

William recalled these events wistfully as he now sipped tea on the comfort of his porch. His father had died a few years back while searching on the cliffs for some farmer's runaway pig, The great Increase Gladford, to the end, trying to help someone. Still honored as a hero. Unlike his mediocre son. William was in some ways like his father: calm, friendly and reasonable. Always willing to help. But he knew that his accomplishments as the mayor of Arcadia paled in comparison to his father's. If his father had been an eagle, he was a hummingbird.

William turned toward the cabin. The door was propped open with a log. "Annie?" he called.

Whenever William thought about his father, he was struck with awe. How could any one man do all the things he'd done? In the face of his father's bravery, power, and intelligence, William felt cowardly, weak and stupid. His father's rescuing of Adam and Daisy Green was so amazing by itself that it was easy to forget that the incident was only one of a broader swathe of tragedies fortune had visited upon the land during that era, and that his father had handled all those other tragedies too with the same awesome dexterity.

Those horrible nights. The fire at the Bakers that killed Virginia's mother. Then only a few months later, that bizarre night that brought another tragedy. At the

Broke Ranch out south, an accident involving Obadiah Broke and his experimental tanning liquids, that had fried every hair from his body and turned his skin permanently the color and texture of trout flesh. The bizarre accident happened not only on the same night, but at about the same moment, when Adam's parents killed themselves. And Doc Midland was unable to help with one catastrophe because he was already occupied with the other.

"Are you okay, William?"

The mayor looked up. Annie was standing at the door.

"I'm sorry, dear. My thoughts were wandering."

"How is the tea?"

Just looking at his wife melted away his anxiety.

The mayor smiled. "You make the best in the world."

Anne Gladford sat in the chair next to him, holding a cup of her own. Even after all these years, he still felt a flush of emotion at the sight of his wife. Like himself, she was stooped with age, waddles of flesh dangling from her face, but she was still his lovely Anne, just as beautiful as that day so many decades ago when he first saw her at a barn dance and nearly keeled over at the sight of her.

"What's that?" she said.

William looked in the direction she was pointing and perceived, on the far end of the plains, a thread of brown coiling up in the distance.

Fear jumped in Anne's voice. "A fire?"

"I think it's dust."

The hazy brown dot swelled until they could make out the galloping horse causing it.

"That looks like Reverend Branch."

"Calvin? He doesn't ride."

They stood up. Soon horse and rider were close enough to see it was indeed Reverend Branch bobbing wildly atop his old mare. Man and animal clattered up to the porch.

The preacher fell as he tried to dismount, grabbing onto one of the stirrups just in time. He flipped upside down and dangled. William and Anne helped him to the ground.

"Calvin, what's happened?" asked William.

To the astonishment of William and Anne, Calvin's eyes were filling with tears. When he spoke, his voice trembled. "William, has little Victor come here today?"

"No."

"So you haven't heard?"

"No. What is it?"

"I fear the end is near."

Chapter Seven
Splotched

Walter Auberon was on his knees, tending his apple tree. He was digging out small holes around the base of the huge trunk, taking care to space them evenly. The holes were intended to spread water more efficiently to the roots and the compost Walter had already spread evenly around the sunny side of the tree was intended for the same purpose.

Walter plunged in the spade again and pulled out the black dirt with jerks of his arm more vigorous than necessary.

What a goddamned bad day, he thought. The worst day they'd had in years.

Adam! Walter jabbed the shovel in again and twisted side to side. Please, Lord, he pleaded in his mind, almost saying the words out loud, don't let us go back to those bad old days.

After the incident with the specter in the forest, Adam had fled to his cabin and refused to come out or even answer the door.

Walter sighed. He looked up into the boughs of the apple tree. He knew the efforts he made to care for the tree were probably not needed. The tree had always pretty much taken care of itself, especially after its miraculous growth spurt seven years before that tripled its height in only a week. It had vaulted practically overnight from a scrawny sapling to a mighty tree whose towering form dwarfed all others within sight

The apples were big too. This year, they were bigger than ever. Walter had already picked a few ripe ones. Carrying even one to the house was like carrying a large stone. The full crop would be too copious for the Auberons to eat, and Walter planned to give away most to co-workers at the Grange.

Richard came through the back door and walked over. He had his axe slung over one of his huge shoulders. His face was fatigued. They'd been up much of the night worrying about Adam.

"Clarissa's still mad, Pa."

"About Adam?"

"She's spooked. She don't want him near the baby. I don't blame her."

Walter opened his mouth to scold his son, then shut it. Trying to defend Adam from Richard's contempt was a battle with no hope of victory. The feud between those two had started in childhood. Some long-forgotten rivalry. Personalities on different trajectories. Richard, short on brains but a muscular powerhouse who could tear trees from the ground with his bare hands. A ferocious temper. Adam his opposite, shy as a mouse, kind as a saint, and, when he could rise out of himself enough to share his thoughts, smart as a whip. The rancor between the cousins was manifested most dramatically by Richard, who never was shy about showing his anger and was cowed by no one except Henrietta.

Richard folded his arms and screwed his face into a sneer.

"He's hiding in his cabin again. Won't even take breakfast from Ma."

Walter shook his head. "Feels like all that trouble is coming back."

"What the hell is wrong with that boy?"

"I don't know, son."

"It's like he's so shy he can't talk to people at all any more. And then he makes up these crazy stories to get attention…"

"I know, I know. But he ain't bad. He's just…shy."

"Shy, my arse. He's a coward and a liar."

"That's enough," Walter snapped, and for a moment, father and son glared at each other. Then Richard bowed his head. "Sorry, Pa."

From the other side of the cabin came the sound of approaching horses. On the trail, coming from the direction of Merlin Grove.

When Walt and Richard came to the clearing, Henrietta had already emerged from the house. Daisy was hopping behind her on one leg.

"Who is it, Mama?"

"Don't know. No one's supposed to come today."

Walter pulled the brim of his hat low and squinted across the clearing. The sun had climbed in the sky, bringing out the yellow in the dying grass.

"Virginia?"

"No," said Henrietta. "She delivers a couple days from now."

In one big thrust over the ridge, the wagon came into view. It was one recognizable to everyone in the land. No one else had a wagon as big and fancy, and no one else harnessed their wagon to four horses.

"Obadiah Broke," muttered Richard.

Henrietta glanced nervously in the direction of Adam's cabin.

"Fine time to come. Why is he here?"

Richard spit. "Just like last month. Trying to buy us out."

Henrietta commanded, "No one say a word about Adam and his ghost. We can't have that getting to town."

The wagon thundered up. The big wheels were rimmed with iron forged at the Broke Ranch. The carriage was shiny and black, like the shell of a beetle. The huge man in the front of the two rows of black leather seats yanked the horses to such a sudden halt they skidded, slinging up a cloud of grit.

"Hallooo, Walter, Henrietta."

Obadiah Broke was an enormous man with a boulder head, squinting eyes and a hooked nose. Seven years before, an accident with tanning chemicals had left his skin completely hairless and horrifically scarred. Every inch of his body was slathered with blue-green splotches.

"Howdy, Obadiah," Walter said. "You're a long way from home."

"Yep. Left before sunup."

Walter raised his face toward the cloudless sky. "Going to be a warm one."

"Yep. What you all looking so scared about?"

"What do you mean?" asked Henrietta.

"You're pale as pig bellies."

Daisy shouted, "Adam saw a ghost yesterday."

"Daisy, hush," hissed Henrietta.

Obadiah squinted down at the girl. "That so?"

"In the woods. It was a head inside a…"

Henrietta gripped her daughter by the shoulders and spun her around. "Inside. You got chores."

"But…"

"*Now.*"

Moping, Daisy limped back to the porch. She offered her parents an expression of unendurable injury, then entered the cabin.

Obadiah's blue-green lips spread into something like a smile. "Adam saw a ghost?"

Henrietta laughed nervously. "Oh, don't pay her no mind. She's got an imagination that won't stop."

"So, Obadiah," said Walter. "What can we do you for today?"

The rancher's gaze moved northward across the landscape and settled on Adam's cabin across the clearing. He smacked his lips.

"Came to see Adam again about the offer I made him. Is he't home?"

Walter scraped his boot in the dust. "Obadiah, we already said we ain't interested in selling."

Broke chuckled, a slobbery sound pushed up from some wet cavity in his barrel chest. "Reckon he might want to move to a different place, seeing how he's got ghosts in the woods here. You too. Same offer holds for your farm as for his. I'll buy'em both off you and pay you handsome. Y'all don't want to live in ghost country, do you? Mighty dangerous, 'specially with that little girl running around."

"We ain't interested."

"The farm I really want is Adam's, not yours. He's got himself a nice view."

"Adam don't want to sell."

"Now, Walter. It seems like what Adam wants to do with his land is his business, not yours."

"We're kin. We can speak for him."

"I can see why you can speak for little Daisy, seeing how she's still a child. Even though she ain't your *real* daughter." Broke paused meaningfully. "But Adam's full grown."

"We already know his answer on this."

Obadiah's blue-green lips started worming against each other, like he was chewing agitatedly on something. "Seriously, now. You don't want children around ghosts, do you? Lord knows, you all have already had enough trouble with that damned forest. Ain't you worried about what people will say when they hear about this ghost story of Adam's?"

None of the Auberons responded.

"Have you forgot what they tried to do to Adam and Daisy the last time?"

Henrietta opened her mouth to speak, but Walter cut her off, saying, "we're fine where we are. That's the end of it."

"Maybe my last offer was too low. I'll give you *seventeen* head for the house."

"Obadiah." said Walter.

"And I'll up the pigs from forty to fifty. And throw in a hundred chickens. A hundred!"

"We ain't selling."

Broke's damaged cheeks were shimmering with sweat. "But you can buy ten farms for that much!"

"Obadiah, my wife was born in that house. And our son was born there too. And Clarissa had my grandbaby inside them walls. Daisy, if she don't move off, will have hers in there." Walter inhaled deeply. "That's our *home*."

"You're being pretty cold to me, Walter," said Broke. "Seeing's how we used to be friends."

Walter's face tightened. "That was a long time ago, Obadiah."

"And Adam?"

"Stop, please."

"He was just a little boy, but you couldn't get him to move over with you. You let him live all by himself, even when the whole town wanted to kill him."

"This ain't the time."

"Now he can't even take care of himself. Got no friends, says he sees ghosts…"

"Stop, Obadiah."

"Someone needs to give him a good ass-kicking, or he'll never grow any balls."

"Stop."

"Probably no one will ever want to marry him."

"Be quiet."

"He needs a real man to talk to him. Suppose I just go over there and…"

"Suppose you don't."

It was Henrietta who said it. Her shoulders were ratcheted up and her eyes were blazing, She snatched the axe from Richard, hoisted it onto her shoulder. "Suppose I give you ten seconds to get off our land before I chop your goddamned head off."

Broke stared at her. Then his lips stretched into a grin. He climbed back up onto the riding board and uncoiled his bullwhip.

"Guess we know who wears the pants around here, eh, Walter?"

He cracked the whip and jolted the horses into a quick trot that swelled to a gallop as the wagon disappeared down the hill.

Chapter Eight
Something Fishy

From her seat at the end of the dinner table, Daisy watched her family with keen attention.

After Obadiah Broke had rumbled down the hill, Daisy could hear through the cabin doors Aunt Henriettta explode into a storm of forbidden words. By the time she came inside with Walt and Richard, the three adults had composed themselves to behave as if nothing unpleasant had happened. And they refused to answer Daisy's questions.

That night, Henrietta conjured up a delicious stew, an old family recipe passed on through generations stretching back past recollection. The finest ingredient was juice pressed from one of the mammoth fruits of Walter's famous apple tree. She mixed it in a marinade with a savory mix of herbs from her garden, filled a bucket with it, and inserted the rabbit, steeping the meat for ten hours before boiling it with carrots, onions, and potatoes. They ate the stew with cups of fine apple wine and a loaf of Virginia's magic bread.

Despite the wonderful dinner, it was clear to Daisy that the family was ailing. Walter and Richard were lost in dark thoughts and not touching their food. Henrietta jabbed at them with her spoon. "Eat up! You're insulting the cook!" But it was clear the cook was also troubled by something and forcing herself.

Clarissa was absorbed with her baby and seemed too busy to pay attention to the heavy atmosphere. She was seated in the rocker on the other side of the room, the infant snuggled to her breast.

Daisy observed them carefully while acting like she wasn't. She chattered on as though unaware of the sickened mood of the adults, but she was taking in every detail: Uncle Walter frowning at the table and stirring his stew without lifting the spoon to his mouth: Richard squeezing the edge of the table between his thumb and forefinger, making his big arm muscle flex, affecting an expression of stony irritation, as though to keep more delicate emotions under wraps. And Daisy noticed the mournful gaze her aunt directed toward the north, where Adam lived.

Daisy prattled on while she watched them, adding new entries to the catalogue of outlandish tales she'd already told at previous meals. She claimed to have seen a rabbit that afternoon wearing a tall black hat and a silk tie. The rabbit, she said, barely able to keep from bursting into laughter, spoke to her.

"This rabbit looked at me and said…" Daisy made her voice deep and important. "'…I must hurry, I'm late!' And he ran down a rabbit-hole."

After a pause, she sighed. No one was listening. When Daisy had heard the story that Adam had told the previous day about a human head inside a box talking to him, every inch of her body burned with the wish to know more. She was torn with frustration when her aunt, uncle, cousin, and brother returned from the forest and responded to her frantic questions by telling her, *lying to her,* there was nothing down there, and forbidding her to go near the place.

The first chance she got, she'd slipped away to the forest and went to the place. Heart racing with excitement, she had peeped through the branches and was tormented to find nothing.

Something fishy was going on. She wondered if that creepy Obadiah Broke had something to do with it. "Auntie," she said, putting on her nicest voice, "why is that Mr. Broke so angry all the time?"

Henrietta jerked at the question, as though waking from a deep sleep. "What? Which Mr. Broke, Daisy? Obadiah or George?"

"You know. George's father. The one who was here today, with the ugly fish face."

"Daisy, don't speak like that. You shouldn't judge people by their appearance."

"I'm not judging him, Auntie. I'm *identifying* him."

Henrietta's face tightened. "Obadiah Broke's got lots of worries, I guess."

"Worries," sneered Richard. He rapped the table with his knuckles. "He'll have plenty more worries if he comes around here again. He's got a lot of nerve, talking about how you and Pa take care of Adam. He treats his own son like a whipping post."

Henrietta touched her son on the arm, giving him a don't-say-that-around-Daisy-because-she's-too-young look.

"Well, it's true, Ma. We don't need to put up with a man like that around here, even if he is rich. That man's plain mean."

"He wasn't always like that," said Walter with a trace of sadness. "He used to be one of the kindest men around."

A loud knock at the front door startled everyone. Henrietta gripped the collar of her smock. "Who could that be, this time of night?"

"Maybe Adam finally came out," said Walter.

They all went to the door, and Richard opened it.

A pudgy man with a long white beard was standing outside. Daisy started bouncing with joy.

"Mayor Gladford!" she cried.

"Mayor, what on Earth are you doing out this time of night? Come in, come in," said Henrietta.

The mayor took off his hat and bowed, saying, "Hello, Henrietta, Walter, Richard. Good evening, Clarissa. Sorry to disturb you."

Daisy slapped the mayor on the leg. "You forgot me!"

William put his hat back on and bent down. With both hands he lifted Daisy so high her head nearly touched the logs of the roof. "And good evening to you, pretty Daisy Green!" Daisy shrieked with laughter. The second she was returned to Earth she demanded to be lifted again, but Walter interceded.

"Daisy, go sit at the table. The mayor must have some business, coming out so late." Daisy trudged back to her chair and pouted while Mayor Gladford was ushered to the table.

"I came out here to talk about what happened with Adam yesterday in the woods," said Mayor Gladford.

Henrietta gasped. Walter and Richard exchanged shocked looks.

"How did you know?" asked Henrietta.

"The whole town is talking about it." The mayor glanced uncertainly at Daisy.

Henrietta said, "Daisy, it's time for bed."

"Oh, Auntie," bellowed Daisy. She threw up her hands in a tempest. "I'm not sleepy."

"It doesn't matter. Go on back and wash up, then get your night smock on. I'll come tuck you in."

"But, Aunt! Uncle!" Theatrically, Daisy held her hands to her heart.

"If you don't get to bed now, I won't tuck you in."

"But…"

"And you'll be doing Richard's barn chores tomorrow."

Without another word, Daisy walked obediently out the back. She shut the door behind her, and stomped loudly down the steps of the back porch, in the direction of the well. She reached the ground, turned around and tip-toed back up. With the silence of a mouse, she brought her ear to the door.

Chapter Nine
A Little Squeal

Walter collapsed against his chair. "Musta been Obadiah told everyone. He was out here, trying to buy our place again, and Daisy said things."

William frowned. "When was he here?"

"This morning."

"They were already talking about it in town by then, so I doubt it was him. Besides, for all his faults, Obadiah Broke isn't the gossiping sort."

"His sister sure is, though." Everyone at the table nodded. Obadiah's sister Wandabella Shrenker, who ran the General Store, was said to be so aggressively loose-lipped that she could spread word of the birth of a baby before the news reached its mother.

"But Obadiah stopped talking to Wandabella. They hate each other."

"I don't know exactly what happened," said the mayor. "All I know is Calvin Branch came riding out to my house and told Annie and I about it. He had heard it from little Victor, and *he* heard it from folks downtown." William looked over his shoulder at Clarissa. "Clarissa, your uncle is in rather a pother over this event. He actually thinks the world's ending. Thinks the Lord sent Adam a sign of the Doom to Come, because we've all been such sinners."

Clarissa showed no response except for a slight widening of her eyes.

"If they're talking about it in town, then it's starting again," Henrietta moaned. "You know what they're going to be saying about Adam."

"I thought we'd gotten past all of this, but now it looks like it'll never stop," said Walter. He looked exhausted. "Damnit, mayor, the last time, they were ready to hang Adam. Or tie him to a stake and… If it weren't for your daddy…"

"Why don't you tell me exactly what happened?" said William.

They told the mayor everything they could remember about Adam's seeing a ghost in the woods. When they finished, the old man ran his fingers over his beard thoughtfully.

"A head inside a box, you say? Talked to Adam? What did this head say?"

Walter and Henrietta looked at each other.

Richard said, "Mayor, we didn't ask him about that. It don't matter. Adam made the whole thing up."

"Don't you dare talk about your cousin that way!" Henrietta snapped.

"But Ma, there was nothing there!"

"Why would Adam lie about such a thing?" asked the mayor.

"To call attention to himself, probably."

"Well, whether a lie or the truth, I'm still interested in knowing what Adam claims this thing said to him."

"Do you think it's important, Mayor?" Clarissa's soft voice came from the shadows. The lantern light barely reached the corner by the door.

William draped his arm behind the back of the chair. "It might be, Clarissa."

"I don't agree with my husband on this. I think that Adam really saw what he said he saw. He saw a wicked spirit." Clarissa smiled down on her baby.

Henrietta nodded. "Think she's right. Adam really saw a ghost."

Richard scoffed.

"Shut up, Richard. You don't know what you're talking about."

"Ma, one thing I know is that I had to put up with people not talking to me at the Grange for a whole year. Don't you remember? Remember how them Fodder boys threw rocks at our cabin?"

"That weren't Adam's fault."

"But they did it because of him."

"It weren't his fault then, and it ain't his fault now."

"Mayor," said Clarissa, "I do not want to know what the thing said. If a ghost, or a witch, or a demon, or some other malevolent spirit speaks, the last thing a person of God needs is to understand the message, lest we be seduced by it. Great Uncle Calvin said so recently in a sermon."

"Well…" said the mayor.

"And do not we read in Job that God stores up punishment not only for the sinner, but also the sons of sinners? And didn't Great Uncle Calvin say also in another sermon that the Lord Jesus bestows the shame of it unto their offspring, father-to-son, just as sure as blood flows from the chopped neck of a rabbit and gushes onto the chopping block, yea, even for generations onward, and stains the wood long after the rabbit is gone? Aren't you a pretty baby?" Clarissa cooed to the infant. Her voice retained its angelic tone, even while the contents of her words became more violent. "And that cleaning the bloodstains on this wood is not a thing possible by any human act with the exception of fire, which would consume the wood and turn it to ash?"

Henrietta cleared her throat. "Clarissa, don't forget. Adam's your kin."

A look of disgust appeared on Clarissa's face. "He's *Richard's* kin, Mother Auberon. He's no kin of mine."

The mayor said, "We can't be certain Adam Green's seeing witches or ghosts, can we? There are other possibilities, like boys playing a prank, like they did with Mary Lena. Or maybe Adam fell down and hit his head. That can make a person see things that aren't really there."

Clarissa settled back into her rocking, nursing her child. The curved slats creaked out a slow rhythm under her feet. "Time will tell," she said.

The mayor stood. "I believe I should pay a visit to the boy himself."

"Maybe I'll be over to join you later," said Walt. At the door, they bade the mayor a good night.

Clarissa continued to nurse their infant, her face toward the far wall, her back to the family.

Chapter Ten
His Great Great Great Grandfather's Chair

According to faded notes in the Green family Bible, Adam's favorite chair had occupied his porch for five generations. Adam had a hazy memory of his father, Jedediah, telling him of a foggy recollection he himself had from early childhood of Adam's great grandfather, Jacob Green, sitting on that chair, bouncing him, Jedediah, on his lap. Jedediah described Jacob as a craggy old man with a briny odor, a slow voice, and vaporous wisps of hair on his bony head, who described to Jedediah how his own grandfather, Adam's great great great-grandfather, the legendary Abraham Green, had built that chair by intertwining branches foraged from around the original homestead. They said Abraham Green died searching for a favorite pet pig who'd wandered into a cave on the boulder-covered slopes adjacent to the Green homestead.

Abraham made the chair as a birthday present for his only son, Ebenezer Green, Adam's great great grandfather. It was an adult-sized chair, meant for a little boy to grow up seated upon.

Abraham must have built other chairs, of course, for himself and his wife. There were rumors of twin daughters with hair blindingly red who did not survive to adulthood and they must have sat on something from time to time.

Ebenezer, in dutiful tribute to his father Abraham, had gone on to build a chair for his sole son, Jacob, and Jacob begat a chair for his only progeny, Samuel, and Samuel Green made a chair too, for his son, called Jedediah, who was Adam's father. Samuel was a muscular and spirited man. They used to tell stories about his climbing jagged cliffs in the Grey Mountains, battling gargantuan mosquitoes near the swamplands, and playing with grown bears as fearlessly as one would a mouse. The Auberons still had a family artifact, a petrified tooth, six inches long, that Grandpa Samuel had discovered while exploring a cave. No one knew what animal the thing came from, but Henrietta liked to take the old fang out and show it to people. Samuel Green was late in getting around to building his son's chair, putting it together after Adam was born. Adam could remember Grandpa Samuel shaping the wood with an axe. "This is your daddy's chair, boy. Someday, you'll have a chair too."

On the porch, there were four chairs, ordered in degree of age and decrepitude, belonging to Adam's great great grandfather, his great grandfather, his grandfather and his father, the result of a family tradition of generational chair-building whose purpose was, to Adam, an utter mystery.

Adam's father had never build him a chair.

Adam was grateful for the refuge of the quiet evening sky. In good weather, he sat sipping tea on the porch every night, on his great great grandfather's chair. The oldest chair was also the roughest, a blunt slab of wood with latticed branches for a back, but it was Adam's favorite.

Tonight he was especially relieved for the solitude of the porch, the rootedness of the ancient chair, the indifference of the night sky. These past two days were as bad as could be, about as bad as the time his mother ventured out under a full moon in only her night smock and walked straight into the Forbidden Forest, and his father silently followed after her.

Adam twisted his fingers around the surface of the tea cup. The sky was splashed with stars. To his right, hanging round above the poplar grove, the moon was bile-yellow.

There was a time in Adam's memory when this house was a home. His father worked the farm and returned in the evening, a smile booming on his shaggy face. He'd take his wife in a bearhug when she ran to him, and patted little Adam on the head as the boy hugged his leg. It wasn't until years later Adam understood how strange his father was.

Father. The mere word sent worms of trepidation crawling through Adam's insides. He wondered if fatherhood caused men to break somehow. Most fathers he was familiar with were brutes, cowards, or madmen. Adam's childhood friend George Broke was sired by a man who seemed a combination of all three. And although Adam could recollect in their childhoods a time when Obadiah Broke was a kind and loving father, that man was lost to eternity when he began experimenting with brain-tan solutions and one day, seven years ago, sniffed deeply from the tanning cauldron and brought a catastrophe to his body the likes of which no one had ever heard of before.

The accident left Obadiah splotched with defects, of both the soul and the skin, and his kindness toward his son and wife, along with every hair on his body, vanished overnight. Most people believed little George when he said the bruises on his face and arms came from falls from horses, but Adam knew the truth.

That horrible year. So many losses. Virginia lost her mother. Adam lost his parents. George's father lost his mind.

Pretty Ginny. Adam leaned back in his chair and regarded the stars, his heartbeat quickening. Virginia Baker. Yet another one with a flawed father and a saintly mother. Hugh Baker, craven and mirror-obsessed, was more concerned with the fillip of his golden blonde hair than the happiness of his daughter.

Adam's own father, of course, was the worst of all.

Adam's earliest memory of comprehending his father's eccentricity came during a sermon. They were gathered in the Meeting House for the Sunday oratory of Reverend Calvin Branch.

Jedediah Green's presence in church was itself an oddity. Like many men in Arcadian society, he avoided the Sunday pieties like a lightning storm, preferring to leave organized study of the Lord's words to the womenfolk while he reposed at a prime fishing spot. But Papa that day had something on his mind, and he was not his usual cheerful self. Adam remembered how strange it was in church that day. Tension was in the air. People were muttering and scowling, and an ominous silence gripped the room. Little Adam knew something was wrong, but couldn't understand what.

It wasn't usually that way. People coming to the Sunday services were usually smiling and chatty and were always nice to Adam, which was why he, as a little boy, loved to go to church. Dorothy Rivers, the sweet new bosomy, flaxen-haired schoolteacher who had replaced Mary Lena, always gave Adam an oatmeal cookie. Church was fine, except for Reverend Branch's sermons, which never failed to terrify Adam and give him nightmares. The scary old man's speeches were filled with words about how people were filthy rodents doomed to eternal fire.

That strange day in church, when people were grumpy and troubled about something, Reverend Branch delivered his sermon as usual. When the reverend was finished and started to walk off the stage, a man's voice roared—not spoke, but roared—*Reverend Branch!*

Adam shivered as he remembered watching dozens of faces turning toward the origin of that voice, which was the man standing next to him, his own father.

For a second, Adam imagined that his father was just calling out a greeting to the reverend, although it would have been odd to do so, but when he saw Calvin Branch's face braced with rage—the jaws tense enough to bring out the points of the bones under the weathered skin, the furious eyes set firmly toward the exit door—as he tried to ignore Adam's father completely, there was no doubt that something very bad was happening. All hope was lost when his father shouted, *Don't you walk away from me, you son of a bitch!*

Adam forced himself away from the memory. He tilted backwards in the old chair and, rocking slightly, he decided to never become a father. Truly respectable men, such as Mayor Gladford and Doc Midland, were childless. Jesus Christ himself hadn't had kids.

The full moon blanketed the clearing with anemic blue light. Adam could discern the outline of the circular nub of his well near the fence, and the wooden frame above it. The bucket seemed like a head hanging from a rope. Beyond it, the long smear of dead black where the summit of Green Hill gave way to the slope that ended at the forest fifty feet below. A spark of anxiety shot through his chest. He gripped the cup tighter. Again, the flat face of the forest, alive with darting shadows. He could smell the rotten foliage where he fell and, right before his eyes, there it was, the upright head grinning at him from the black box, with the shiny black hair, the lips red as fire, the teeth white as new snow, a pair of bizarre eyeglasses with rims black and fat and gleaming, made of some material the world had never seen.

Adam put the cup on the ground. He held out his right hand and, with all his strength, slapped himself on the face.

The pain dwindled and the night full of stars was back. He picked up his cup and sipped.

To chase away the awful picture, Adam had been slapping himself all day.

Soon, he needed to go to town to get supplies. What if the people there found out? A terrifying thought. Whenever there was news worth gossiping about in Arcadia, it had a way of getting spread, no matter what you did. If that happened, Adam realized with a shudder, Virginia would know too.

What would she think? The baker's daughter, whose magic bread was a staple in every home in the land, was Adam's oldest friend. Maybe his only friend.

When Virginia and Adam were children, Virginia's parents still lived in the north, only a short walk up Mill's Trail from the Green farm. Virginia's family had grown oats, wheat and barley in a modest cluster of fields and also owned the only mill in the northlands. Virginia's mother Mary Baker was famous for her magician's hands with the art of making bread. People came from far and wide to purchase the steaming loaves from her stone hearth. Little Virginia would help her put the bread in burlap sacks for the customers to take home.

As children, Adam and Virginia played together constantly, dashing up and down the hills and through the groves in the spring and summer, flying kites and collecting fire-colored leaves in autumn, and sledding in winter.

While sometimes they included other northland children in their play, Virginia and Adam were most comfortable when together, just the two of them, where they could share their most private thoughts. The other children teased them, because she was a girl and he was a boy, but they didn't care. All Adam and Virginia wanted was to continue playing happily up and down those hills for the rest of time.

Then, just as they were peeking through the door of adolescence, the great fire broke out on the Baker farm. It started in the wheat fields, in the middle of the night. Hugh Baker, Virginia's father, woke to the smell of smoke. He told his wife to stay in their bedroom while he went outside to investigate. Moments after he left, Virginia's mother spied from her bed a halo of orange swelling at the window, and stood to encounter a tongue of seething flame that licked through the window and encircled her like a spiraling red serpent.

When Hugh came screaming back into the cabin, she was already gone. The couple's room overflowed with a roiling black-orange mass that was already crumbling the roof.

Virginia's room was also being consumed. The little girl's bed was an inferno, but Virginia saved herself by hiding underneath the frame. Hearing her screams, Hugh, in an uncustomary act of bravery, flipped over the bed and carried her away.

Although Hugh and Virginia survived, the fire and the loss of Mary Baker devastated their spirits. Virginia changed overnight from a happy girl bursting with energy to an ashen wraith that hardly spoke. Hugh was worse. For months he could scarcely feed or dress himself.

Adam's parents took Virginia and Hugh in. His mother fed them while his father, grinning crazily, repeatedly gave them the same cryptic advice he gave everyone for improving difficult situations: *Look up!*

After a month, father and daughter showed signs of recovery. Virginia smiled and Hugh spoke. Another month, and Hugh made a deal with Obadiah Broke to start a business downtown, in the new three-story building Broke had just built there.

In a deal whose details were not made public, Hugh sold the charred remnants of his mill and fields to

Broke, and the Bakers moved into the town to open a bakery. Hugh knew nothing about selling or making bread, and counted on the skills his wife had passed onto his daughter for the business to succeed.

Not wanting to move away from the countryside and Adam, Virginia resisted the move with all her might, but at last succumbed, collapsing under the weight of her father's hangdog expression. Obadiah Broke's hand in the arrangement was apparent in the name on the big painted sign above the store: *Broke Bakery.*

Six months later, Adam's parents walked as if enchanted into the lethal woods to be eaten by bears. And Adam was so stricken with horror and grief that he locked himself up in his parents' cabin and, despite being little more than a child himself, refused to move over to his aunt and uncle's farm next door. He boxed himself away in the cabin and stopped communicating in the language of humans with anyone.

It was Virginia who brought Adam back to life. She persistently visited him at his farm every day, refusing to leave even when he shouted through the door for her to do so. She nursed him with her bright smile, her gentle voice, and her magic bread. And during that awful time when some people were calling Adam a witch, Virginia was the one of his loudest supporters.

The young teenagers were very close, but over the ensuing seven years, the distance between them grew. Adam was a country farmer, Virginia a town baker. Their circles of activity rarely overlapped. Also, adulthood had brought with it feelings of a biological nature that were embarrassing to Adam to the extent that he could barely talk to Virginia. On those rare occasions when he rode into town and bought bread from her, they exchanged nervous glances across the bakery counter that he felt were more meaningful than the forced small talk they engaged in. He thought she felt it too.

A sound interrupted Adam's musings. He was amazed to see an old man with a long white beard , mounted upon a horse, emerge from the darkness. Mayor Gladford!

Adam jumped up. Mayor Gladford dismounted.

"Evening, Adam," he called.

Adam stood up quickly and gestured toward another chair on the porch. "Please, sir, have a...take a rest off yourself."

"Glad to." The mayor sat on the chair of Adam's grandfather. He leaned back and inhaled the night air.

"How are you, son?"

Adam sat down and stared straight ahead into the dark. "Okay, sir."

"Seems like forever since we talked. About the only chance I get to gab with you folks out north is at church, but I haven't seen you there for..." The old man leaned his head back and observed the starry sky. "How long has it been?"

Adam cleared his throat. "Some time. Been so busy with the farm. And I work most days on the Grange."

The mayor nodded. "Reckon that's so. I know it's been hard on you these years, since your father and mother went to the Lord."

Adam fiddled with his cup. "Mayor, do you want something to drink?"

"I just visited with your aunt and uncle, and my cup is still running over from their hospitality."

They sat silently for a time that to Adam seemed eternal. Then the mayor said, "I heard from the reverend something happened to you yesterday. In the woods. Something about a box with a head inside?"

"What? From the reverend?" Adam was sputtering a little, shocked by the mayor's knowledge of the incident.

"I heard it first from Reverend Branch. He heard it in town."

"In town? But how—?"

William stopped him with a gesture. "Let's take this slow. Everything's going to be alright. Tell me what happened."

Adam looked off into the night. His heart was racing. *Everyone knows.* He took a deep breath and told the story again. He shut his eyes as he related the last moment, the talking head.

"What did this, uh, head say to you?" the mayor asked.

"Say? It was strange. The…head…told me to dry my beans."

The mayor squinted. "Pardon?"

"He said, 'dry your beans'."

The mayor gazed at him. "You been eating jimson weed, boy?"

"No, sir!"

"Do you even grow beans?"

"Some, sir. But mostly I grow corn."

The mayor leaned back in his chair. He ran his fingers along the edge of his beard.

"You generally dry your beans?"

"Most of them, sir. Sometimes I sell them fresh too. Or just eat them myself."

The mayor stared into the gloom. "Maybe you heard wrong."

"Maybe. Mayor, I was so scared." Adam looked at him earnestly. "Scareder than I ever been."

"Adam, I need to ask you a question. You must give me a straight answer. I can read dishonesty on a man's face like I can tell smoke from fire. Will you tell me honestly?"

"Yes, sir!"

"This story about the head, do you swear you are telling me the absolute truth?"

"I am. I swear. I don't know what that thing was, but every word about it I said is the Lord's truth. I don't understand and I'm so scared, Mayor." Adam placed his face in his hands.

The mayor patted Adam's shoulder. "Don't worry, son. I believe you."

Adam looked up. "Really, sir?"

The mayor smiled. "Of course. I'm still confused about what really happened. Could this've been a prank? Say, by them Fodder boys?"

"Don't think so, Mayor. That face was like a grown man's, not no boy's."

"Hello!" hollered a voice in the clearing. It was Walter, approaching across the divide.

The mayor waved back. "Evening, Walter. Come over and sit with us."

Walter settled himself in Adam's father's chair.

"Adam and I were just talking over what this thing might've been yesterday," said the mayor.

"One hell of a mystery," said Walter. "Can't figure it out. Sure wish Adam's father was around now."

"My father?" Adam said.

"Yes," the mayor agreed. "If anyone could've figured this thing out, it would've been him."

"*My* father?" Adam repeated, pointing at himself.

"You sound surprised."

"It's just that he…"

"What?"

"Well, sir, my father wasn't really no good to no one."

"No good? Where do you get an idea like that?"

"Sir, he was strange."

"Strange? You mean because half the people in the land were stupid enough to believe all that nonsense about witches?"

"No, sir. I don't mean that." Adam squinted down at his boots, scraped at something on the boards.

The mayor patted him goodnaturedly on the shoulder. "Well, what then?"

Adam smiled slightly. "When I think back to when I was small, I have good memories of him, but later, he started saying crazy things nobody understood. And he did that thing in the church. He called...he called Reverend Branch a...a..."

The mayor laughed. "He called him a son of a bitch. I remember. Adam, I'm an old friend of Calvin Branch's, and I can tell you that, despite being reckoned justifiably as the spiritual cornerstone of our community, the man sometimes really is a son of a bitch. Everyone with any sense knows that, and your father was the only one who had the guts to say it out loud's, all."

Adam dropped back against his chair with a sigh. "But, Mayor, he wasn't right in the head. He must've said to me a thousand times, 'Adam, if you ever find yourself in trouble, *look up!* If that don't work, *look down!*' If I asked him what he meant, he'd go quiet, and stare at me long and hard, with this little smile."

Walter chuckled. "Indeed, he was peculiar. But that man understood the world better than anyone in this land. He could read it like a book."

Adam's uncle rubbed his hands together. "I remember once, he came over to our cabin all wild-eyed excited and he tells Henrietta and me to get all our harvest underground, to get all the animals locked up, and to run the whole family underground too, 'cause there was a tornado coming." Walter gestured at the surrounding forest and mountains. "Can you believe it? A *tornado*. In October, no less. The sky was blue! Well, nothing could get that man to change his mind. He was running around, hollering for everyone to get underground, and we were laughing at first, and then we got a little afraid, because your father was so serious. So we finally did everything he said, just so's it would give the man some comfort in his mind. And we got into our big pantry under the house, your mother was there too, and so were you, but you were just a baby and too young to remember. Your mother was as confused as we were, but she went along with it, because she went along with everything he said, she was such a good soul. Anyway, we all got underground, and we were all huddled down there in the candlelight, wondering what we should do next, and then it come. The biggest tornado ever hit this land."

Walter pointed his finger toward the north and swept it across the clearing in front of them. "That twister blew right through here and left a trench seven feet wide. These houses, yours and ours, were knocked half to splinters. About the only thing left was your pigpen and these chairs we're sitting on." Walter looked Adam in the eyes. "Because of your dad's special ways, we're alive today."

The mayor nodded. "It's true."

"There were other things like that through the years. Don't know how he did it. Said things came to him in dreams."

"Sad thing, though," said the mayor. "On account of your pa being that way, he made some folks uncomfortable."

Adam closed his eyes. "I don't want to talk about this no more."

The mayor leaned back and looked off into the dark. He ran his fingers over his beard. "Let's get back to what we were talking about before. I'm trying to understand what could've made you see a thing like that. Did you get hit on the head lately?"

"Don't think so. Oh, wait. Yes sir, I did bung my head the other day. In the barn. Rosenlee's saddle fell down from the wall, and I went to pick it up and jostled a shovel from its hook, and it fell and hit me on the head." Adam touched his scalp. "Hurt like I can't say. Seems alright now, though."

The mayor laughed. He slapped Adam on the leg.

"That's the story! Isn't it, Walter?" Walter was nodding but looked confused.

"He didn't see a ghost!" explained Mayor Gladford. "And he didn't make anything up. Adam, you got yourself a head injury and your vision got jangled. Could happen to anyone, right?" Adam nodded uncertainly.

The mayor was speaking fast. "We just need a couple of days to spread this news around and…subdue…fake news. Listen carefully, I want you first thing tomorrow to ride to Doc Midland's and have him check your head. You tell him exactly what happened and do what he says. He's going to tell you to take a vacation from the Grange, to get your head well."

"How do you know Doc Midland tell me take a vacation?"

"When you know someone as long I've known Doc, you know what they'll say before they say it. And you obey him, you hear? You come back to your cabin and stay put until I tell you to do otherwise."

"Okay, sir."

"Yes, yes, yes," Mayor Gladford said, leaning back and patting his stomach contentedly. "That takes care of everything."

Adam picked at a thread dangling from his shirtsleeve. Beyond his arm, he perceived movement. At the edge of the porch, where the wood slats ended, a brown nub wiggled. It was there for a split-second, then jerked away.

"What are you looking at?" William asked.

"A mouse."

"A mouse?"

The creature poked its head over the precipice again. It peeped up at them. Its little black eyes filled with wonder. It hesitated for a couple of seconds, then climbed onto the porch. It stood on its hind legs, whiskers twitching.

"Strange to see one out so late in the year," said Walter.

"Been getting lots of them," said Adam. "Found six yesterday in the house."

Walter frowned. "They's after the food, Adam. You better start cleaning your cabin better or there'll be hell to pay from your aunt."

"They weren't after food. They weren't in my pantry."

"Where'd you find them?" ask the mayor.

"In my bed."

Both men turned toward Adam.

"Your bed?" asked William.

"Yes sir." Adam's eyes were still fixed on the mouse. "When I woke up, they were all snuggled up next to me, asleep."

The mayor surveyed Adam for any signs of joshing.

"What did you do with them?"

"Nothing. Just got out of bed carefully so's I wouldn't hurt them."

William cleared his throat and stood up. "Well, looks like you've got yourself an adopted family. I'm going to head on out now. Adam be sure to see Doc early tomorrow morning."

Walter also stood. "I think I'll head on back too."

The mayor climbed on his horse and Walter waddled off toward the Auberon cabin. Adam waved at Mayor Gladford as he galloped away down the hill.

Their departure left a heavy silence on the porch. Adam hunkered inside his coat and pressed himself against his chair, felt the rough slabs of ancient wood against his spine.

A trickle of icy air moved across his face. He took a sip of his tea. It was cold. Soon, the candlelight in his uncle and aunt's window snuffed out, and the house was swallowed by the night. Adam suddenly was conscious of being very alone.

Even the mouse was gone.

Chapter Eleven
An Awful Presentiment

After Mayor Gladford left Adam's farm, he coaxed his horse down the winding path from the top of Green Hill. The instant they reached Mill's Trail, the mayor urged her to top speed. The slab of wild pecan trees that separated the northlands and central Arcadia, called Merlin Grove, was not exactly a part of the Forbidden Forest, but was still hazily connected to it. It was so densely overgrown that even by day it allowed almost no light to pierce through its canopy and reach the swathe of Mill's Trail that had been cut through it.

At night, it was as dark as an underground chamber. William drove his horse Lizzie to a full gallop straight into the black hole entering the grove. Although he couldn't see a thing, Mayor Gladford trusted his horse to find the way and complete the run through the grove fast, even in the dark. Like any rational person, he did not want to spend a second longer in those woods than was necessary.

Like his old friend Calvin, William was a man of God. He read his Good Book daily. He reckoned the form of every shadow, the plummet of every sparrow, the direction of every breeze, to be conscious, ongoing decisions of the Almighty. Like others of his generation who still clung to the old beliefs, he found divine import in the places crows landed and the directions toward which they stared; alterations of the moon's shape and hue signified important things: the future fecundity or frailty of a crop, the timing of a calf's birth, the duration of winter.

William differed from Calvin in how he responded to these ethereal insinuations. Unlike the preacher, who saw in each of God's decisions evidence of holy retribution against the total depravity of the human soul, the mayor saw every earthly event as a source of joy, for in each he saw the miracle of God's handiwork. God had created a nice place, this world in which they lived, so relax and enjoy it, was William's summary judgment of reality, and while he suffered private twinges of remorse over his lack of accomplishment in comparison to his father, he was for the most part a contented man. Only rarely did he encounter natural occurrences that he interpreted as portents of destruction.

William and Lizzie emerged from the grove. The starry sky opened above them. Now that she was free from the oppressive tunnel, Lizzie slowed her pace. A short distance on, they passed the homestead of Doc and Claire Midland. In the vaporous glow of the moon, Mayor Gladford could make out the front cabin. It was in that small building that Doc healed wounds and Claire helped babies enter the world.

All was dark. The mayor had stopped and talked to Doc earlier that day and spoken with the couple. He explained Adam's situation. Doc and Claire were expecting Adam's visit in the morning. They agreed to tell Adam everything William requested. It was fortunate that Adam had hit his head on something. It made the story all the more believable. But even if he hadn't, William's plan was for a physical condition of some kind to be offered to the community as an explanation for Adam's seeing a ghost, and for Doc to provide a professional opinion supporting it. Doc, who had lived through all the witchcraft madness seven years before, was more than willing to lie to prevent a recurrence of it.

William had visited others too. It had been a day of visits, as he worked to put his plan into action. He had gone to town and dropped in to talk to Hugh Baker at Broke Bakery, Joss Hankers at Hanker's Barrel, and Wandabella Shrenker at Shrenker's General Store. He found a worker from the Broke Ranch, and asked him to deliver a message to Obadiah Broke. All these visits had the same goal: to request attendance at a meeting early the next morning to discuss Adam Green, with all the most influential members of the community in the same room.

William pulled his horse to a stop to get his bearings. He knew the turn-off to his own farm was nearby. A chill wind was blowing from the north. Snow would come early this year, he thought, and the winter would be especially cold. Special care would need to be taken to protect food stocks from the cold and community volunteers from the Grange would need to visit shut-ins. Like Adam was becoming again.

William finally recognized where he was. The turn-off was only minutes away. He brought his horse into an ambling trot.

Adam Green. From the beginning, that poor boy had been threshed by misfortunes whose origins had nothing to do with him. Nothing would ever make sense of why Mary and Jedediah Green had wandered into the woods to be eaten by bears that moonlight evening seven years before, but the reasons for Adam's subsequent problems in adjusting through adolescence were clear as could be. That damned group of fools in town. When William thought of Wandabella Shrenker and that crowd, he felt a surge of unaccustomed anger.

That gang of superstitious, mean-spirited, low-minded fools! They had spread the worst kinds of rumors about the newly orphaned boy, and Calvin's father, Titus Branch, the reverend back then, had used his pulpit to disseminate them. It wasn't long before the gossip started flowing so overwhelmingly that even those favorably disposed to Adam and his remaining family started thinking of the Greens and even the Auberons as a suspicious, even dangerous tribe. They started attributing Jed's well-known eccentricities to witchcraft, and some suggested Jed and Mary Green had even used their diabolical powers to survive in the bear-infested woods. And then some folks started saying they had seen the couple, still alive, in the company of bears. *Fools*.

William's father had put a stop to all that, and things gradually improved for Adam and the Auberons. Adam's reputation had gradually improved over the years, mainly because people's memories were short and he had shown with his every action that he was a hardworking, honest and decent young man, even if he was a bit aloof. With this new incident in the woods, Adam was in peril of losing everything he had gained. William was determined to prevent that from happening. Maybe he could rise to fill his father's shoes after all.

William was grateful for the familiar trudge of Lizzie's hooves on the ground. Soon he would be home. Relax with Anne a bit, have something to eat, get some sleep before the big meeting in the morning.

The land descended steadily. It wasn't long before the foliage turned brushy. Thick patches of brambles grew on either side of the path. On the left, another trail opened, leading from the direction of the Meetinghouse, a couple of miles northeast. It must have been the one Calvin had taken to ride to William and Anne's the other day.

The horse stopped. She did it so abruptly the mayor almost fell off her. Lizzie threw her head back to the left and right. Even in the dark, William could see her eyes wide with fear.

"What's wrong, girl?"

Then he heard it. To the left, where the bushes were the thickest, an immense body was tearing through the scrub. Before William could react, the border broke in an uproar of cracking branches and a bear moved onto the trail.

It was the largest animal William had ever seen. At least twenty feet long, from tail to snout. When it pushed itself through, its shaggy brown fur tore at the leaves like thousands of small blades. From the great snout came a cavernous hiss as it snorted at the dirt. The claws, as long as gut knives and bone-white, clacked at rocks in the path. The tar-black eyes were two flashes of moonlight.

William went rigid, his breath chopped in his throat.

The bear stopped, sniffed at the air The fur on its back swelled into a bristled arc between its shoulders. Its jaws rolled under the fur. The head came up and swiveled, eyes searching, until the animal found William.

He ached to wail and kick at Lizzie, to gallop her to safety, but it was no use. Nothing could outrun the great bears. William thought of praying but the only thing that came to mind was his wife. Goodbye, Annie. Goodbye, my dove.

The bear continued to watch him, motionless except for the flaring of its nostrils.

The animal turned. With a single, awesome leap, it vanished into the brush.

It took a full minute for William to understand he was safe. With a shaky hand he wiped his forehead. His sweat was icy. He had to kick Lizzie hard in the flank to get her to move. Every few seconds, he glanced back to make sure they weren't pursued. Before long, He found the turn-off, and not long after that, he saw the lights of his home twinkling in the distance.

He stopped outside the barn. He climbed off and patted Lizzie on her side. The poor girl's ribs were trembling under his fingers. He brought her into the barn. He checked the bolt on the door twice before heading to the house. Through a curtain over the window, the glow of fire in the hearth.

William moved up the porch steps and reached his hand to the door. He was struck by an awful presentiment. The impact of it nearly knocked him down. It was so horribly real. He could see himself in this same position on the porch, his hand on the same door handle, but the building was cold and empty, leeched of color, and the land around him in every direction, as far as the eye could see, was a scorched wasteland where nothing, absolutely nothing, was alive.

It took all his strength to push open the door and greet his wife with cheerfulness that betrayed nothing.

Chapter Twelve

Twitching All Over

Wandabella Shrenker was next to her stove, preparing dough. She was springing happily up and down on her spindly ankles. She'd started the fire in the oven-box, and the flames crackled up and snapped out of the hole in the iron sheet. The sour nauseating odor wafting from the head-sized hunk of dough squatting within the dough box did not trouble Wandabella.

She was so happy! What a wonderful day it had been! First, Little Victor had dropped by and told her the stunning news that Adam Green, that cursed boy out north, had gone shrieking through the northlands about seeing a ghost. As if that wasn't good enough, the mayor of Arcadia visited later to ask her permission to use the store for an important meeting the next morning.

Wandabella was a stringy woman with spiked fingers and a nest of grey-brown hair that clambered from her head like creeping hoary mugwort. She was a fantastically nervous woman. She was like a person who'd once been struck by a bolt of lightning that had supercharged her with malignant energy that had yet to fully dissipate.

Her happiness at the day's events charged her with even more energy than usual, prompting her to plunge her sharp fingers into the dough and knead it with jabbing thrusts of her arms. She yanked her fingers out and rubbed her hands together. Dough fell from her fingers in wormy pieces.

Earlier that day, the story of Adam Green had ignited a bonfire of lovely gossip in the General Store, breathing life into what for Wandabella was turning out to be a weak gossip season. It was her routine to stand behind the counter all day, surrounded by a coterie of friends, orchestrating the conversation. The group, composed from the sliver of Arcadian society that didn't need to work for a living, used its abundant free time to discourse about the bad fortunes of others. It was always a challenge to dig up suitable targets in a land where fortunes were almost always good, and where even the worst habits—such as those of Charlie Glump, the town drunk—were not really so bad. It was always a jewel to come across an act of noncomformity so outlandish that it required no embellishment to make it look scandalous. Adam Green's head-in-the-box story was the most gossip-worthy news she'd encountered since Mary Lena and her talking mice, or the deaths of Adam's parents.

It was all connected. Just thinking about it prompted Wandabella to tap the blades of her hands in a little improvised syncopation on the bread dough. Adam Green. For seven years ago, after the wicked behavior of Adam's parents, a movement had broken out, a group of brave citizens, led by the elder Reverend Branch, who demanded in a town meeting that something be done about Adam. If his parents were witches, the thinking went, so was Adam, because these things were passed on through the blood. Wandabella had been passionate about joining the reverend's group, but at that moment in history she was abruptly drawn up into The Great Dream. That became such a distraction that she didn't commit herself sufficiently to the social and physical destruction of Adam Green, didn't strike while the iron was hot. Then former mayor, Increase Gladford, had stepped in and defended Adam, and the movement to burn Adam at the stake for witchcraft went to hell.

Afterwards, it became unfashionable to talk badly of Adam. Wandabella kept the fire burning as best she could in the gossip sessions she conducted assiduously in the General Store, but it wasn't the same, because everyone knew that Adam had been publicly vindicated, and most people, even those who had howled for his blood, felt in retrospect that he'd been treated to some degree unfairly. So Wandabella had largely held her tongue about Adam Green for the past seven years. She instead indulged in mean-spirited gossip about others, and in The Great Dream. It was still a problem, The Dream, because she needed to keep it a secret. She had never mentioned it to her husband or to her daughter Hildegard or to the gossipy gaggle of girls who stopped by her shop every day. If she had, she knew that the community might start to think that *she* was a witch.

A zig-zag grin opened on Wandabella's face. She sank her nails into the dough and twisted them around. With this meeting in the morning, she was being given another chance to gossip Adam Green to death!

Not only that, but Wandabella had been asked to *host* the important meeting. The most influential people would be there, the upper crust of Arcadian society. The invitation reinforced Wandabella's notion, her hopeful notion, her desperate notion, that she too was an influential person, that she stood out from the common herd. Wandabella suffered fits of anxiety over the suspicion that people, especially in the populous northlands, those hordes of smelly peasants who did manual labor on the Grange, those ill-bred yahoos, those pigs, thought of themselves as superior to her and were laughing behind her back because of the new line of clothing she'd designed and was trying to sell in the store.

She squished some dough between two fingers, sniffed it, and winced. Since the most connected people in the land would be at the meeting tomorrow, it was a chance for her not only to destroy Adam Green but to impress them with her superior skills at cooking and her cultivated sense of fashion.

The lady's garments that Wandabella had designed sold well among the small clique of friends who loitered at the store, but hadn't caught on with the far more numerous farm wives. Wandabella Shrenker was fond of birds and flowers, and she decorated her sartorial creations with enormous, wildly colored fakeries of both. At the meeting, she planned to model some of the clothing and dazzle Mayor Gladford.

William Gladford! Now there was a man! Those keen brown eyes! That handsome white beard! That manly protruding belly! If only he weren't married. Then again, in regards to her fashion line, his being married was precisely why he was valuable. After he was dazzled by her clothing, he would mention them to his wife, who was friendly with many of the lower farm women and could inspire them to buy her clothes. And he would certainly be entranced by her baking skills, and mention that to her wife too, and she would encourage more customers to come to her shop and buy her clothes and her bread. That would destroy that haughty Virginia across the street! That would allow her to add more floors to her building! That…was all part of The Great Dream.

Wandabella wiped spittle that was dripping from her lips. Then she spasmed at a movement by the window. She narrowed her eyes. There. On the sill. A mouse.

It was gazing up at her, its whiskers twitching.

She snatched a cleaver from a hook on the wall and brought it down on the creature. In the nick of time, the small animal darted out of the way. By the time she pulled the cleaver out of the wood, the creature had disappeared. Wandabella pouted and looked out the window. Across the way was the Broke Bakery, the foul edifice subsidized by her brother and harboring that Virginia Baker, that horrible girl who everyone found so enchanting and whose disgusting bread everyone thought was so delicious.

Broke Bakery. Her goddamned brother, Obadiah Broke, he was the one that financed the construction of that unnaturally tall building and tricked that ugly girl and her empty-headed father Hugh to move in and start baking the bread that destroyed Wandabella's monopoly on baked goods and humiliated her in front of the town. In Wandabella's opinion, her brother deserved every bit of the ostracizing he got because of his deformities, his hairless and wrinkled body, his monstrous fish face. Served him right for playing around with chemicals and for making her look so bad. Obadiah would be at the meeting tomorrow, Wandabella realized with a twinge. She hadn't spoken to her brother since he'd opened the bakery almost seven years ago, and she sure wouldn't talk to him tomorrow even if he decided to break his silence and speak to her.

She would ignore him.

She laughed nervously and swatted at a phantom insect on her check. She started pummeling the dough. It was a tough one this time, a grey-green mass of compressed wheat, water, salt, flour and baking powder that was already strong enough to patch wall-cracks. She had added extra baking power because at first the dough had slipped from the dough-bag queerly, wobbly as a pudding, then split straight in half, as though an invisible, knife-wielding hand had cut it in two.

Wandabella ground the knuckles of both hands into the dough. The substance only gave an inch.

There it was again. That mouse. It was in the same place on the windowsill. Wandabella leapt to the window, grabbed the mouse with her left hand while lifting the cleaver with her right. She threw the animal on top of the dough and chopped it in half.

The legs on both halves twitched a few seconds, running nowhere, then the portions collapsed on their sides. The mouse stretched its front paws toward the candlelight.

Wandabella reached out with the cleaver and touched the head lightly. She raised the cleaver again and slammed it into the mouse. It caught the back section, chopping it in half. "Three," she whispered. She brought the cleaver down again, again, a dozen more times, converting the animal into a splash of red and brown nuggets. She pulled down a butcher knife from its hook on the wall and minced the mouse even finer, then brought out a potato hammer and ploughed the body through the dough. When she stopped, gasping for breath, the material had softened to a point where she could separate it into balls and bake them.

Chapter Thirteen
An Emergency Meeting

William rode his horse into town as first light was starting to glow behind the Grey Mountains. Arcadia the town was comprised of a dozen or so buildings that had been tossed up in the area where trade roads—Mills Trail, the Meetinghouse Road, Paradise Path, Broke Forks—converged on their separate paths to different places in the land of Arcadia. Of course, few called that cluster of stores, or the wide region in which they lay "Arcadia" because to do so would imply the existence of other towns, and other lands, and to these people, that would be absurd because other towns, lands, and people didn't exist.

It was turning out to be a magnificent autumn day. The sun was easing peach-colored light onto the faces of the largest businesses: Hanker's Barrel and Anvil, Cobble's Boots and Moccasins, Broke Bakery, and Shrenker's General Store. The premonition of doom William had had the night before after his encounter with a bear was starting to fade and he was feeling more confident. He tied Lizzie to a hitching post in front of Shrenker's. The store's shutters were still closed. The mayor stood for a time, going over his plan again.

It was simple. The danger was that Adam Green would be accused of witchcraft again. The mayor's solution was that he wanted to get all the community leaders together in a room and get them all to agree not to spread rumors about Adam Green. And to get them in turn to put a stop to anyone in their various places of business to spread lies that he was a witch. He didn't think he'd run into any serious opposition. Of the five people coming to the meeting, only two of them were potentially inclined to spread rumors that Adam was dabbling in witchcraft. One was Reverend Calvin

Branch, and the other was that horrid woman Wandabella Shrenker.

He had already spoken at length with Calvin and, while his old friend seemed to be in a state of terror over the dire implications of Adam's sighting of the "head in the box," the mayor had convinced him that Adam himself was not to blame for whatever he saw. And Calvin seemed to at least accept the possibility of some natural phenomenon causing the vision, although he still fundamentally believed that the Devil was paying them a visit and it didn't bode well for Arcadia.

As for Wandabella Shrenker, well, William knew she was not so much a fervent believer in witchcraft as a fervent lover of gossip. Such people were highly vulnerable to flattery, and very sensitive to their public reputation, and it was with these qualities that the mayor was planning to prevent Wandabella from spreading any scurrilous lies about Adam Green.

William knew he could count on the strong support of most of the others at the meeting. Joss Hankers and Dorothy the schoolteacher would both be on his side. Hugh, less interested in other human beings than in the condition of his wavy blonde hair and gleaming white teeth, was perhaps shallow and weak-willed enough to join with any anti-Adam forces, but his daughter Virginia and Adam had been close friends in childhood and were still quite fond of each other.

The last person to consider was Obadiah Broke. Obadiah was a mystery to the mayor. He had once been a kind, decent man, a good husband and loving father, but after his accident with tanning chemicals, he had changed. He had become obsessed, bizarrely, with making money, which no one in the history of Arcadia had ever cared all that much about before. Why would they? Everyone had everything they needed already, and didn't fear not having enough in the future. The land would always provide. The community would provide. God would provide. Still, no one could deny Obadiah's generosity. He didn't keep his wealth all to himself. Obadiah had also, it was rumored, turned into a devoted believer in the part of the Good Book admonishing parents that sparing the rod was spoiling the child, but in his case, it was not only spoiling the child, but also the wife and all the many farmhands he'd taken on since he'd dramatically expanded his huge ranch. Still, the mayor thought he'd go along with the plan to nip the gossip in the bud, because his son George and Adam had been close friends as children.

William tapped on the door of Shrenker's General Store. It instantly swung open. Wandabella Shrenker stood beaming at him. "Mayor!"

Mayor Gladford's eyes moved instantly to the apples that decorated Wandabella's dress. There were five or six of the fruits painted about her stalky frame, cut from some deep red, vaguely shiny fabric. The apples were huge, each at least a foot in diameter. They were jarring in relief to the white fabric they were sown into. An eyesore, he decided, and he forced his gaze onto Wandabella's head, which, with its great tangles and tendrils of grey hair coiling out chaotically, like dozens of tiny bleached snakes escaping a fire, was equally disturbing.

Wandabella touched his shoulder. He flinched. "Mayor Gladford, it's ever so nice to see you. Come on through to the back." She batted her eyes at him.

The store was a single, spacious room lined with shelves where products were displayed. To the side, there was a small wooden counter with a moneybox. On the floor to the right and left of the counter were sacks, piled ceiling high, of corn, barley, oats, and rice. She led him through to another room, this lit by an open window. A long table was set up, a dozen chairs around it.

Wandabella had set out teacups in front of each chair and put a couple of teapots on the table that were wafting out a foul odor.

On the wall nearest the door hung the severed paw of a bear. It was an old thing, William recalled, a relic of the Broke family. Wandabella claimed the appendage was originally attached to an animal killed by her own great great great grandfather, Armada Broke, when he'd first settled this land. The bear had leapt on Armada from a tree, Wandabella told everyone who would listen, and her superhuman ancestor had killed the beast with his bare hands.

"Sit anywhere you…" started Wandabella, but she was interrupted by the sound of heavy boots tromping through the store. A second later, Obadiah Broke appeared at the door. Wandabella's face tightened. She silently took her brother's hat, which he held out without looking at her.

"Morning, Mayor," Obadiah said. The rancher was dressed in a black coat that made the blue-green swirls and patches on his gnarled face and hairless head even more flagrant. That face, William thought. Every time he was confronted it with it, he had to push from his mind how good-looking Obadiah used to be. Broke took a seat across from William.

"What's all this about, William? Is it about that witch boy out north?"

The mayor raised his eyebrows. "It's about Adam Green. But he's no witch. All that happened is he got hit in the head with a shovel last week. The injury jangled his senses. Doc Midland can attest to this."

Wandabella entered. With a flourish, she gestured at the door and announced, "Miss Jocelyn Hankers."

The big woman in overalls who entered had short red-brown hair chopped in a blunt bang halfway down her forehead. Joss greeted the mayor in a booming voice.

"Morning, William." Mayor Gladford smiled warmly. "Joss, it's real good to see you here."

A look of discomfort grew on Obadiah Broke's face at the sight of the large woman. Joss grinned at him.

"Obadiah Broke! Long time, no see. How's your wife? And your son George?"

Broke grunted irritably. "My wife is still the same pathetic mouse she always was. And George is still the laziest animal on my farm. Can't seem to teach him the value of hard work."

"Sorry to hear it, Broke." She sat next to the mayor and turned her back to Obadiah.

"And how's Annie, William?"

The mayor beamed. "She's doing fine, Joss, just fine. She's experimenting with growing a new kind of tea leaf. You need to visit us sometime and try it. She calls it 'Boston'."

"Boston?"

"Yes. It infuses into a most soothing yet energizing liquid."

"Why 'Boston'? What is that? Never heard that word before."

"She says it came to her in a dream."

Joss sniffed at the teapot in front of her and leaned in to whisper to the mayor, "well, Boston tea's got to taste better than this shit."

Wandabella came to the door and crowed, "I brought more for you." Through the door came a thin, blondish woman with fretful blue eyes who glanced around the room like a mother searching for her lost child. Behind her, looking more bitter and frail than usual, was Reverend Calvin Branch.

Wandabella proclaimed in a shrill voice, "Everyone, our good schoolteacher, Dorothy Rivers and the Good Reverend Branch."

"Good she's here to tell us they're good," Joss whispered to the mayor as the reverend and Dorothy took places at the opposite end of the table from them.

Obadiah Broke drummed his blue-green fingers on the table impatiently. "Can we get this going, Gladford? I got work to do."

"We're still waiting for Hugh."

"Oh, yes." Wandabella smacked her lips disapprovingly. "Even though he lives only next door, Mr. Baker appears to be late. Perhaps he's still trying to teach his daughter how to bake?"

This insult fell on deaf ears, because everyone knew that Virginia Baker's bread was not only delicious, but radiated an ineffable, even magical, influence which enlivened the spirit and, it was whispered in certain corners, had an aphrodisiacal effect on the body.

A man with blonde hair falling across his forehead peeked in at the door. He smiled shyly, showing a mouthful of radiant white teeth. "Am I in the right place?"

The mayor waved. "Come in, Hugh. There's a free chair next to Obadiah."

Anxiety surged in Hugh's handsome face. He crept past Wandabella, who was glowering at him for being late, and slinked over and seated himself next to Obadiah, who was also glaring at him.

"Okay," said Mayor Gladford. I think we can finally get started. After Wandabella sits down."

"Oh, oh, oh," said Wandabella. "We must first have some refreshments…"

"That won't be necessary, Wanda—"

"…Please help yourself to some tea. I made some food for you all too."

Wandabella looked about the room in confusion. Then she glared at the ceiling and screamed, "HILDEGARD! BISCUITS!" She twisted her lips back into a smile, nodded at them all, then looked up again and bellowed furiously, "HILDEGARD! NOW! BISCUITS!" Back came the forced smile as she turned to her guests again. "Children these days," she tittered.

Hildegard Shrenker, Wandabella's tall, skinny daughter eleven or twelve years of age, sprinted in holding a tray. She looked a bit like her mother, but her kinky hair was reddish-brown instead of grey and her green eyes weren't deranged. Her mother snatched the tray from her with a murderous scowl, slammed it down on the table, slung another smile at the guests, glared at her daughter again. She pointed, with a snapping jerk of her arm that rattled her bracelets, toward the ceiling. "OUT!" The girl sprinted back upstairs.

Wandabella smiled sweetly. "Eat up, everyone!" She removed the cloth from the tray. Underneath was a heap of what looked like stones. When she exposed them, an invisible cloud of foul-smelling gas poured into the air.

"This meat?" asked Joss, lifting one with a fist and eyeing it dubiously.

Miss Dorothy lifted one and held it tentatively before her eyes. "What interesting…colors," she said and took a nibble. She smiled weakly and placed the biscuit back on the plate. Joss gnawed off a piece and looked disgusted. Obadiah Broke stuck a whole biscuit in his mouth and chewed it. His face lit up.

"Oh, sister," he said, looking at Wandabella directly for the first time since he'd arrived. "Didn't know you could cook. This is one mighty fine biscuit."

Wandabella stared at her brother in amazement. It was the first time he'd spoken to her in seven years. Shocked, she stepped meanderingly across the room and took a seat in the corner.

The mayor cleared his throat. "Thank you everyone for coming so early. I know by now you have heard about this troubling thing that happened to Adam Green."

"Is the poor boy alright?" Dorothy Rivers asked.

"I rode out there last night and spoke with him in person. He's quite shaken up."

Joss frowned. "Men were talking about it in the pub. Saying all sorts of damn fool things about Adam. I had a mind to throw'em out, I can tell you. It feels like those bad old days again."

The mayor said, in as commanding a voice as he could muster, "Yes, Joss, and the last thing we want is a return to those bad old days. It is for the purpose of putting a halt to any damaging rumors about this incident that I have called you all, the pillars of our community, together this morning." As he spoke, William felt his confidence rising. He could detect his own father's eloquence coming from his own mouth. "I'm sure we are all in agreement that this boy has already been through enough pain and hardship. And that imprudent gossip, based on nothing more than fancy and fear, is exactly the thing that got him in trouble the last time. Of course I know none of *you* would go around gossiping about the boy—you're too intelligent for that." William paused to let his comment sink in. He let his gaze pass over each person in the room, and lingered several seconds on Wandabella, but she was still sitting with her mouth open and her eyes glazed over, gobsmacked by her brother's compliment about her bisquits.

"So I'm asking you to jump on anyone you hear, in your places of business, saying bad things about him, and tell them to stop. Explain to them, calmly and rationally, what really happened."

Joss said, "William, what *did* happen? Most of us have only heard rumors."

Nods of agreement around the table.

William related the story again of the talking head in the box. The narrative provoked a breathless silence.

"I want to make my thoughts completely clear on this," William continued. "I don't think for a second that Adam really saw a ghost. I'm also convinced he wasn't lying. I think there must be perfectly natural explanation for this. At first, I thought this was a practical joke, maybe by those Fodder boys. But this…thing…doesn't seem like something a child could pull off. At any rate, I visited Adam last night and he told me he'd been hit in the head recently by a shovel that fell on him. Said his head hurt a lot. Such injuries are known to cause distorted senses. He is at this very moment visiting Doc Midland, who I'm sure will confirm my suspicions. The boy just needs some rest, so he can recover, then he can go back to work at the Grange with no further problems."

Obadiah Broke scoffed loudly. Everyone in the room turned to look at him.

"Do you have something to say, Obadiah?"

The rancher rubbed his blue-green face with his palm. "I got to hand it to you, Mayor. That's a creative justification for what this boy is doing."

"I don't follow you."

Broke addressed the whole room. "Well, you conveniently ignored the possibility that Adam Green really *is* dabbling in witchcraft."

A murmur moved through the room.

"What the hell are you talking about, Broke?" demanded Joss.

Obadiah held up his hands in a gesture of contrition. "I know, Joss, these are mighty hard words to hear. But someone's got to say them."

"We went through all of that before," said William. "And the community decided…"

"That's exactly my point. This boy's got a history," said Obadiah.

"But…"

Suddenly, Obadiah stood. He said in a raised, authoritative voice, "Now, I ain't saying I agree with what some people claimed about Adam seven years ago. Back then, we had some old-fashioned folks who still clung to those old Puritan ideas from when we first inhabited this land. Following them old Puritan ideas, they felt strongly that Adam's parents were blood witches, servants of Hell, and Adam, being a direct son of Jedediah, was by definition a witch too. And the only thing to do in a situation like that was to follow the Good Book and not suffer a witch to live. I don't agree with those folks. I'm a modern thinking man." Broke tapped the side of his head with a finger. "I think rational."

William looked around the table and saw that while Joss was staring furiously at Obadiah, everyone else was listening to him attentively.

"Obadiah," said William, "all of this talk about…"

"Let me finish, Mayor Gladford. Then you can have your say. Like I said, that kind of old-style Puritan talk ain't rational. What I believe is more scientific. My thinking goes like this. We all know the Devil is out there, always waiting, right around the bend, to tempt us. Ain't that right?" Everyone, even Joss, nodded. "But most of us are strong enough to resist the Devil, so strong, in fact, that the Devil don't even bother with us because it'd be a waste of his time to try to fetch up our souls. Adam's problem ain't that he's willfully embracing Satan's black magic. It's that he's so weak as a man that he don't have constitutional protection against the Devil's temptations. That makes rational, scientific sense, don't it?" Heads around the table nodded. "Now, here's my idea for a solution. People learn to be strong from their fathers. You know that old

saying, 'mothers hug, fathers slug.' What Adam needs is
a good slug in the face from a strong father figure. Lots
of slugs. He needs to spend time with a strong man, a
powerful father figure, to toughen him up. Then he'll be
strong enough that the Devil will leave him alone."

"Um…" William didn't know how to respond. In
the space of a few seconds, his well-planned approach to
the meeting was falling to pieces. So was his confidence.
"I…I…suppose you have some good points, Obadiah,
but like I said, I talked to Adam and he told me that he
got hit on the head…"

"He hit his head last week? Is that what you said?"
"Yes."

"And that's why he's seeing talking heads in the
forest?"

"It's the most likely reason."

"But I passed him on Mill's Trail two days ago.
He was coming home from working at the Grange. He
seemed healthy then."

"Head injuries are unpredictable."

"I agree, Mayor, if there *is* actually a head injury.
But I didn't see no injury on Adam Green's head. No
bandages. No blood. People who saw him at the Harvest
Festival last Saturday say he was fine. I know, because
some of my men were there and I asked them. Adam
was slinking around in the shadows like usual, staring at
people with those big wide eyes of his without talking to
anyone. But that's just normal behavior for him. Some
folks, by the way, would say that behavior is exactly like
what witchy people do."

"Let's hear from others," said William, desperate
to change the direction Obadiah was taking the meeting.
"What do you think, Dorothy?"

The schoolteacher intertwined her fingers, laid her
hands together on the table. She was well into her middle
years, but still showed the beauty of her youth in her

long blonde hair and kind blue eyes. She was a childless widow, but with an aptitude and love for children that surpassed most, she had given over her maternal energies to the Arcadian children since she'd abruptly inherited the job of schoolmaster from Mary Lena.

"I've known Adam Green practically since he was born," she said. "I was his teacher all through school. He's one of the sweetest boys I've ever known. Whatever happened to his parents isn't his fault. If he says he saw this thing in the woods, then he saw it." With a flicker of hesitation, she added. "I hope so, anyway."

"How about you, Joss?" asked William.

She glared at Obadiah. "I don't care how much money Broke has, or how many cows or millstones or forges he's got on that damned ranch of his, he don't have no right saying these things. We went through hell seven years ago trying to save Adam's life from fools. Adam hit his head. End of story. Anyone at my pub says different can get their beer at another establishment."

Obadiah Broke sniffed. "*Miss* Jocelyn, seems Adam Green couldn't'a hit his head *too* hard. He didn't visit Doc about that injury, did he? The thought never even occurred to him, did it? At least not until Gladford told him to go."

William said, "I don't know what you're implying, Obadiah, but I…"

Broke lowered his head. "I admit, I could be wrong," he said in a tone that suggested he didn't think at all that he was wrong. "If I am, I'm sorry. I don't want to imply anything bad. The only thing I want to do is help Adam."

Joss laughed caustically. "A minute ago, you accused Adam Green of witchcraft. Now you're going to sit here and tell us that you want to help him? By becoming his new father or something?"

"First off, I didn't accuse him of witchcraft. I said he was at risk of being seduced by witchcraft. Don't put words in my mouth, *Miss*. Second, in answer to your question, I propose to help Adam by taking him under my wing. Why don't we have him move over to my ranch, where I can keep a good watch on him? My wife will feed him, put some meat on his bones. I'll put him to work, give him regular chores, stick some discipline in him. Send that Devil flying."

"But Obadiah," said the mayor. "He lives next to his aunt and uncle. They can take care of him."

"William, if Adam is jabbering about spooks in the woods, then his family ain't taking care of him. And that Walter? Well, Adam needs a *real* man around, that's all there is to say on that."

"Why…why don't we move this conversation in a more godly direction?" William's spirit was withering away as he listened to Obadiah. He could sense that Broke was turning the group in a direction William didn't want it to go. He gestured now to his old friend Calvin, whom he trusted would stand by him completely and do all that was necessary, as the official spiritual leader of the community, to protect Adam Green. A word from him and all this nonsense would vanish. "What do you think, Reverend Branch?"

Reverend Branch had been sitting with his head bend down, as though in prayer. Now, when he turned to them, his old eyes were wide and darting, like those of a chameleon, and they seemed to not be looking at anyone in the room. He made a growling noise, deep in his throat, before speaking.

"There are two great forces at work. In our fair land, we've been blessed beyond measure. The good Lord has given us so much…" Calvin shook his head miserably. "We have squandered our unearned gift. We discarded the old Sabbatical laws. We've grown weak, soft, and let a nest of snakes birth themselves in the garden."

The old man stretched out a finger and shook it at the people around the table. "You are all to blame! This Adam Green, I don't know if it's witchcraft or not. But the air is charged with something horrible, crawling with unsavory spirits. The sky is darkening with a storm worse than any we've ever had. I feel it in my bones, It's all our fault."

The reverend stood and roared, "At the service this week, I will announce a Day of Fasting and Humiliation."

A couple of people groaned.

"But it's harvest time!" said Joss.

"It's the only way to redeem ourselves!" he proclaimed. "If Adam Green isn't bewitched, then someone else is!"

Reverend Branch fell into a kind of trance, his lips moving but making no sound.

The mayor drummed his fingers on the table. Calvin's announcing a Day of Fasting and Humiliation was the last thing he'd expected. He wasn't sure how to proceed. "Thank you, Reverend Branch, for sharing your thoughts. I want to...understand how all of you feel. With all due respect to Obadiah and Reverend Branch, I stand by my thinking that the boy got himself a knock on the head, and he'll be fine from now on, if we only nip this thing in the bud. I ask you to put some effort, in the places where you each have exposure to and influence with the general public, to stop unproductive rumors about Adam Green. Who agrees with me?"

All raised their hands except Obadiah Broke.

The reverend also failed to raise his hand, but he seemed so lost in his own thoughts he might not have noticed the vote. Wandabella raised her hand haltingly, as though she wasn't sure what she was voting for. Hugh raised his halfway, his limp fingers splayed in the air. He looked long and hard at Dorothy, and Dorothy looked back at him and for a moment, they gazes met and they both quickly looked away.

The mayor nodded around the room. "Thank you, everyone, for your sensibility and help. Together, we can enjoy a happy and peaceful harvest time and prepare well for the winter." This time, even Obadiah nodded. William felt a surge of relief, the same feeling he had when emerging from the dark path that cut through Merlin Grove.

They moved to the door, smiling and shaking hands. Even Broke smiled, making a jumble of horsey teeth stand out of his lipless mouth. He shook the mayor's hand and thanked him with apparent sincerity.

Chapter Fourteen
The Black Space

Adam was having a beautiful dream. It was his home, the same cabin, and his mother leaning over him in his crib, smiling. Red hair fell loosely from under her night-bonnet, the curled locks dangling down to him. Behind her, the room was filling with lovely yellow light. Adam squirmed and giggled. The light made him close his eyes and when he opened them again, the rods of sunlight shooting through the cracks in the oak shutters widened and swallowed his mother up. He blinked back tears, stretching his arms as far as he could into the light, but she was gone.

The cabin went dark. It was like someone had dropped the whole room through a hole in the Earth. Another sort of light moved into the room, prancing flashes of fire, a constellation of candles, flickering from floor to ceiling in a chamber that was otherwise absolutely black.

Out of the shadows heaved forth a grinning female face. A travesty of a woman, matted black hair shot through with slashes of grey, bulbous eyes, neck red and stringy as rhubarb. A spider-shaped tangle of broken veins hung on one cheek. The toothless hole of a mouth opened, and the woman spoke.

Adam opened his eyes and kicked away the blanket and made himself stand. He kicked open the back door and went out to the well and pulled up the bucket. He splashed water on his face and rubbed hard, trying to rub the dream out of his head.

A recurring dream. It was the third night in a row he'd had it.

He fed his pig, his cow, his three chickens, and Rosenlee, his lazy horse. He ate a soothing piece of Virginia's bread, washed it down with cool water.

He stood on his back porch, taking in the northern landscape. His gaze followed the drying stalks of his corn crop northward, to the area past the pigpen, where the poplar grove was. In the place where the trees met the field, bulging up on the line so that the border seemed fractured, was a hill. Adam went rigid.

The day before, the hill hadn't been there.

He blinked a few times, but it didn't go away. His heart knocking in his throat, he forced himself off the porch and across the yard.

It was more like a mound than a hill, about as wide as Adam and half his height. It had the look of the moist dirt that piles up when a hole is dug to take a dead body.

Adam inched his way around the thing, and was relieved to find no grave. The dirt seemed to have been pushed up directly from the earth by some pressure within.

Adam stooped to get a better view. The part of the mound farthest from the cabin was in the shadow of the poplars. Toward the top was an even darker spot, a jagged black splotch.

Every muscle tensed to flee, Adam reached out and touched it. When he brought his finger back, it was covered with an inky liquid.

He sniffed his finger and grimaced. The black water seethed with ancient decay, rotted fish, ripened saltpeter, fermented wormwood. Adam spat. He tried to wipe his fingers on his shirt. To his alarm, they remained black. He stepped back and watched the splotch, half expecting it to grow wider. After nothing happened for a couple of minutes, Adam returned to the house. He considered getting out his shovel and taking a dig at the mound, but the thought of that evil-smelling stuff gushing forth into his yard was enough for him to keep his distance.

Another mystery, thought Adam. At least this one didn't talk to him.

He hooked his horse to his wagon, swung himself onto the riding board, and gently snapped the reins. Rosenlee started to trudge down the trail toward town.

As they passed through Merlin Grove, Adam struggled with the worms of anxiety twisting in his chest. Popular legend held that Merlin's Grove was haunted by a demented old witch-man named Merlin. Children were warned against venturing alone onto the segment of Mill's Trail that passed through it, where the overlying canopy was so thick that sunlight barely penetrated, and even adults felt squeamish passing through.

In fact, Merlin Grove was once a segment of the Forbidden Forest that some intrepid Arcadian, whose identity was lost in the cascades of history, had cut down to plant a pecan orchard. The remnants of the failed enterprise were everywhere by the trail, for the Merlin trees still grew wild and copious in the gloom. At some point in history, the Forbidden Forest had reclaimed the orchard, but, as though out of pity for the original depravity of man, permitted the trail to remain. Humans could ride to town on this peculiar path that was completely clean of encroaching foliage, although it bored through the one of the thickest masses of flora anyone had ever seen. The fruits of those wild nut trees, intertwined now with many other species, were so bounteous that even the squirrels couldn't eat them all. No one dared to eat the pecans because it was said the fiendish Merlin had cast a spell on them. Parents terrified their children with the tale of the rebellious little boy and girl who ate the pecans and were transformed into mice, to live forever fleeing from perils as numerous as the stars.

Rosenlee trotted along. Adam squinted, trying to penetrate the gloom for any sign of the supernatural. He breathed a sigh of relief when they came through the other side and the sunny sky opened above.

A fine autumn day. The land was full of bright colors and delicious smells, and the weather was as splendid as a soul could ask. Despite himself, Adam started to feel better.

To his left, a sweeping landscape. The hills rolled downward into a distant valley, changing colors as they descended. As the hills eased into the base of the valley, they erupted with splashes of vibrant hues of wildflower fields. Two rivers wound through, branching into shimmering tributaries. At its farther fringes, the valley gave way to hills that climbed steadily until they met the sinewy roots of the Grey Mountains. Across it all ambled carefree shadows of drifting clouds.

Soothed by the passing grandeur, Adam clopped onward to the home of the Midlands.

Francis "Doc" and Claire Midland lived between the northern farms and the town. Some forgotten ancestor of Doc had braved the dangers of the Forbidden Forest, cut down the trees there and built a small cabin. A portion of the original structure was still standing, a rickety shack of moldy pegs and fragmenting boards that would have collapsed to splinters if it wasn't attached to the newer, larger building Francis's own father built when Francis was a child. The building faced Mill's Trail. Doc used it to see his patients. Claire used it to deliver babies.

The couple lived in an even newer cottage in the back. The two buildings were separated by a plot burgeoning with botanical life. On either side of the path leading to their cottage, Claire cultivated a jungle of breathtaking flowers that broke the hearts of visitors with their beauty and their delicate perfumes. The variety of colors was beyond count. In his younger days, Doc made elaborate trellises and set up poles for the plants to climb on, so that now Claire's flower garden ascended well above their heads and shoulders.

Adam and Rosenlee brought the cart through the flower jungle. Adam gazed around in wonder. Every kind of flower he'd ever encountered, and more he'd never seen. The scents of blossoms mingled into a soothing elixir that made him slightly dizzy.

When he emerged, he yawned and stretched, as though shaking off an enchantment. Doc and Claire's cottage was nestled under a great oak. The huge tree spread its branches protectively over the mossy roof, and patted them on the roof of the small barn beside it, where the couple's decrepit bay mare, Fidelio, spent her days drowsing.

Adam stopped his wagon in front of the open barn. Rosenlee trotted up to Fidelio. The two touched noses.

The border of the Forbidden Forest wound around the homestead. A nest of old trees protruded from the forest wall. The gnarled trunks leaned toward each other conspiratorially. One of the branches seemed out of place, too straight. Adam found it joining others, horizontal and vertical. A fence.

Adam smiled. They'd put a pigpen back there. Been so long since he'd visited, that wasn't even there before. He walked over to take a closer look.

The fence ran the whole width of the yard. Behind it, a long, narrow tract of land had been cleared. Next to the fence where Adam stood, a second fence was erected to form a pen within the pen. Inside it, an enormous sow was spread out on the ground. A dozen pink piglets scrambled at her belly, emitting urgent squeaks. The mother's eyes were closed and her lips parted in something like a smile. Dozens of other pigs were snuffling through the hay across the pen.

It was amazing how concealed it was. At the eastern end, the road was only a few feet beyond, but the trees hid everything. Adam had ridden right past the pigpen and didn't see it.

For an aging couple like Doc and Claire, this might have been an easy source of food. But the old healers, famous for their love of animals, never consumed the flesh of animals. Adam gazed in wonderment at the porcine congregation and wondered why on earth the old vegetarians had it.

"Morning, Adam." The young farmer was startled to find Claire Midland standing only inches behind him. She smiled up with her bright blue eyes. "Too long since we last seen you, dear."

Although the top of Claire's head scarcely reached Adam's chest, she was large and billowing as a sail. She was wearing a cheery calico dress and an apron with lines of tiny green and blue flowers prancing across. Her warm smile, soothing voice and cushiony breasts implied doting motherhood, but she and Doc had no children.

Doc wobbled up behind her, with his great pointed nose. He took Adam's hand in both of his own and shook it. "Adam, Adam, Adam. Seems like forever."

"Good to see you again too, sir."

Doc was a tremendously tall, thin scarecrow of a man whose almond skin looked like it'd been stretched out, dried under the sun a few days, and stuck back on his bones. A few stubborn wisps of gray hair clung to his skull. With each precarious step he took, his knees creaked.

Despite these infirmities of age, the sparkling glint in Doc's eyes gave him an appearance of youthful exuberance. It was a common observation that Doc Midland resembled another of the elders of the land, Reverend Calvin Branch. The two looked so much alike they might have been twins, like the ones in the children's tale where one brother grew up merry, the other morose. The impression of radically different fraternal personalities was amplified by the ancient feud between the two; Calvin's contempt for Doc Midland was only matched by the hatred Doc Midland held for him.

"I see you're admiring my pigs." Doc nodded toward the pigpen.

"Yes, sir."

Doc pointed at the sow in the smaller pen. "This is Ursa, my favorite." He smiled with a kind of fatherly pride. "Of course, all my pigs are beauties, but Ursa here has a most unusual set of markings. Do you see them, on her flank?"

Adam squinted. On the haunch of the sow, there was a splash of dots.

"Birthmarks?"

"Look at the shape close." They went around to the side of the farrowing pen.

On the flank of the animal, a chain of dots descended from left to right.

"On clear nights, if you look up, you can see it."

Adam's mouth dropped open. "The Plough?"

Doc grinned. "That's it. Some folks call it the Big Dipper."

Adam marveled. "It sure looks like it."

"Each of those freckles corresponds precisely to a star in the dipper."

Claire jerked her thumb at her husband. "I think he loves those pigs more than his own wife."

Doc's eyes glazed over as he stared adoringly at the sow. He moaned. "Isn't she a beauty?"

"See what I mean?"

Doc laughed and rubbed Claire's shoulder. "I'm the luckiest man in the world, and it's all because of *this* girl." She leaned into his side and patted his stomach.

"Adam, William stopped over yesterday and told me you might come. How are you feeling?"

"Okay."

"Let's go inside."

Doc led Adam toward the front building. Claire bobbled off toward the cottage in back.

The building had an extended porch, supported by two broad beams on either side. Through a window, Adam could see a narrow table, behind which were shelves glinting with small bottles. A breeze whipped up as they climbed the steps, sending yellow leaves spiraling around them.

Adam remembered another visit here, when he was a child. He'd fallen out of a tree and landed on an upturned branch. He was howling with pain when his parents galloped up with him in the wagon, his arm struck through with a piece of wood. It was only a few inches long and only pierced a couple layers of his skin, but to Adam, it was like he'd been skewered by a spear. Doc chatted with the boy about hoopball and sleds, and told a funny story about a self-important rabbit who wore a top hat and suit and carried a tiny clock in its pocket and Adam was astonished when the old man finished his tale to find the stick had magically vanished from his skin.

The building was divided into two rooms. Doc led Adam through the first, past the counter with the shelves and bottles.

A window against the far wall let warm orange light flood in. A long table and a couple of chairs rested on the woven rug. Doc directed Adam to sit on the table.

"When Mayor Gladford came by yesterday." Doc continued. "He said you weren't feeling well."

"Ain't so bad, Doc."

"Let this old doctor be the judge of that."

On the opposite wall were several of Doc's animal paintings. One depicted a squirrel in a tree, another a baby bear playing in the grass. Ten were of pigs.

"You sure do like pigs, Doc."

"Of course I do, Adam. Don't you?"

"Guess they're okay. Honestly, sir, I hardly ever think of them past being food."

Doc frowned.

"Sorry, sir."

"Pigs are my favorite, you know."

"Sorry."

The old man sniffed. "It's alright, Adam."

"Doc, sir, why do you especially love pigs?"

Doc's eyes widened. "Why pigs?" he asked, as though the answer were perfectly obvious. "Because, young Adam, of all the wonders of this Earth, not one is more delightful than the noble pig."

Adam wasn't sure if he was joking. "The noble pig?"

"The noble pig."

"Not the noble horse? Or the noble elk?"

"None compare to the glory of swine."

Adam rubbed his nose. "Partial to dogs, myself."

Doc raised his eyebrows. "Not pigs?"

"Pigs are okay. But don't you think they're sort of, well…"

"Smelly?" Doc demanded.

Adam was too frightened by the blaze in Doc's eyes to respond. He was relieved when a smile spread on the old man's face.

"I suppose they are, Adam. Smelly and ugly. But pigs are beautiful too, precisely because their exterior doesn't delight us in the same way as flowers, or…women. Pigs challenge us to see the less transitory beauty that lies beneath the flesh." Doc scratched his nails against the arm of his chair. "You know, Adam, sometimes creatures appear ugly, or bad, or even dangerous, when they aren't. Through no fault of their own, they get a bad reputation."

Adam nodded uncertainly.

"What are you thinking, Adam?"

"Um."

"Don't worry. You can tell me."

"I'm thinking about what Reverend Branch said at church one time about pigs."

Doc's face darkened. "What?"

"He says pigs are the pets of Satan."

Doc pressed his lips together tightly. "That is his Puritanical opinion. At which, we can now change the subject." He leaned forward and patted Adam on the shoulder.

"You haven't been around here to visit in many years, son. What have you been doing with yourself?"

"I work half-time at the Grange, and the other half on my farm."

"You go to church much?"

"Not much."

"Go into town?"

"When I need supplies."

"Talk to anyone out there at the Grange? Or in town?"

"I keep to myself."

"Boy your age should be getting out some. It isn't healthy to be alone all the time."

"I did get to the harvest festival."

"And how was that? Meet any pretty girls?"

Adam laughed nervously. He shook his head. "To tell the truth, I just delivered some corn for the feast and headed home."

Doc looked at the young man long and hard. "Adam, what happened to you in the woods?"

Adam was caught off guard. Stuttering, he related the story again about the talking head in the box.

"Interesting," Doc said. He rubbed his fingers against his chin. "Was there anything behind this box?"

"Couple of burned-out oaks."

"I see. Any chance someone was lying behind the box?"

"No. There was no space."

"Is it possible that the person—the head—who talked to you had the rest of his body buried under the ground?"

"No."

"Why not?"

"No hole was there."

"I was considering the possibility that someone was playing a prank on you."

"Don't think so, sir." Adam leaned closer to Doc. "Sir, I think saw a ghost."

Doc smiled at the thought. "I don't believe I've ever heard of a ghost visiting folks in the—confined— form you describe. I'm given to understand they prefer wafting through open spaces, under a full moon."

Adam whispered, "Do you think I saw a...a...witch?"

"A witch?" Doc bellowed. Adam ducked. He wanted to throw his hands over the old man's mouth to keep him from saying the dreaded word again.

"There are no witches in Arcadia!"

"I just thought..."

"Yes, yes," Doc cut in, chopping into the flow of Adam's words with the sharp edge of his hand, "You thought. If there's anything that would move people to outrage, it would be to have a witch in their midst. And, as you know from your own painful experience, there have been some fools who believed that witches have been in our midst. I hope we have finally snuffed out that plague of stupidity once and for all. It reminds me of a time, a long long time ago, before the Great Migration, some witches were discovered. Our ancestors, mine, yours, theirs," Doc gestured with a sweep of his arm to indicate the entire population, "were in a frenzy of hatred, and a dozen people, men, women, even children, were hung."

"Hung?"

"Hung."

"What's 'hung' mean?"

"Hung." Doc coiled his fingers around Adam's neck and yanked, lightly, upward. "With a rope, so they couldn't breathe."

Adam's eyes widened. "Did they die?"

"Of course they died."

"But...how...?"

"Long time ago, there were these things called courts."

"Courts?"

"Courts were places where they took people accused of doing bad things to decide if they really did them or not."

"Bad things? Like what?"

"Well, like pig-stealing."

"Pig-stealing? But Doc, ain't no one does things like that." Adam was dazed at the thought. The only time he'd ever heard of stealing was in old children's stories, and no one believed in those.

"Now, no one does things like that. But in the old days, some people really did steal things, and worse. The community needed punishments to stop them."

Adam shook his head in amazement. It was the most startling thing he'd ever heard.

"Just be happy we live in a time when people don't do things like that anymore. Cause there's another, uglier side to it. Adam, it was horrible, those witches.

When I was a little boy, I remember it. Hanging up in the air, mouths open, in a row. Left up in trees along the row, to rot."

"Is that bad?"

Doc gawked at Adam.

"I mean, it sounds awful, but they were witches, right? Maybe they deserved that, um, court thing?"

"Oh, Adam. We've gained much in this bounteous land, but we've lost much too. Listen. It was terrible, those witches hanging like that because they weren't really witches."

"But you said…"

"I said what the witch courts were saying, not what really was."

Doc crossed his arms over his chest and stared out the side window. "None of those so-called witches even came close to passing the real witch's test."

"What's that?"

It was Doc's turn to whisper. "Those who understand these things say that there is only one foolproof method of determining if a person is a witch."

"What's that?"

"Men of understanding know that *only* a real witch understands, and can use, the language of bears."

"Huh?"

"You know, Adam, like people, animals have languages. You've heard the chatter of birds in the trees, the low of your cattle, the oinks of pigs, haven't you? Bears have a language too."

Adam exclaimed, "so witches can talk to animals!"

"Not animals," Doc corrected. "Bears."

"Why bears?"

"How the hell should I know?" Doc answered testily. "I probably shouldn't be telling you this anyway. Just old wive's tales." He rubbed his hands together.

"Now, let's get down to the examination. Have you had any agues lately?"

"I'm not sure."

Doc placed his hand on Adam's forehead. "No fever?"

"What's 'fever' mean?"

"Fever's when you feel real hot, like your skin's on fire, because you get sick."

"Like from too much rum?"

"No, a different kind of sick. People used to feel bad, and get real hot, and they coughed and sneezed. And they'd upchuck, just like when someone drinks too much. But people got this kind of sick without drinking anything."

"Why'd they get sick then?"

"No one knows. We all stopped getting that kind of sickness when we came here. After the Great Migration, a lot of things changed."

Adam shrugged. "Don't know anything about that, Doc. Don't feel hot. If nobody gets fevers anymore, why did you ask if I had a fever?"

Doc peered into Adam's eyes. "I have my reasons. You sure are an inquisitive one. Just like that little sister of yours. Speaking of Daisy, your uncle brought her a month ago with a deep splinter. She wouldn't stop asking questions, and all of them started with why. Why this? Why that? Cough."

Doc had placed his fingers on Adam's chest. He coughed a few times and Doc concentrated on the sensations the convulsions brought to his fingertips.

"How does it feel, Doc?"

"Like you're coughing. Stand up."

Adam stood and Doc placed his head against Adam's chest. He smacked Adam hard on the back and listened.

He frowned. "Your heart's beating."

He gripped Adam by the shoulders and whirled him around, then, in a rapid scissoring motion, battered his back with the blades of his hand. He listened again.

"You definitely have a heart, young Adam, and it's a good one. Hold your hands above your head. Turn around, turn around. Spin. That's right. Faster! Okay, sit."

Adam found the table with the palms of his hands and eased himself down.

"You feel dizzy?"

"Yes."

Doc's eyes shined. He nodded importantly. "I see."

"Because you spun me around."

Doc looked closely at Adam's teeth, scalp, and earlobes.

"How much jimsun weed do you smoke?"

"None."

Doc pressed the tips of his fingers against the edges of Adam's neck. He squeezed.

"Ow!" Adam cried.

"That hurt?"

"Yes."

"It's supposed to."

Doc finished the examination. He took his place atop his professional stool. He cupped his chin with his hand.

"Have you had any peculiar dreams lately, Adam?"

Adam perked up. "Well, yes, sir. I've been having the same strange dream every night."

"Tell me about it."

"It's back when I was just a child, like a baby, and I'm lying in a cradle and a beautiful woman's there, a woman with long red hair, and she's looking down on me and smiling."

"Your mother."

"Think so, but then her face changes."

"Really?"

"Into another woman."

"What kind of woman?"

"Ugly. With big veiny eyeballs. Red, spotty skin. And she's got about the longest, stringiest neck I ever saw."

Doc looked at Adam for a long time without speaking. "Do you recognize this woman?"

"No. Never saw her before."

"Did she have any marks on her face?"

Adam tapped his left cheek. "Yup. Right about here's this spider-shaped bunch of veins standing out. Why'd you ask?"

"No special reason. Have you had any injuries lately?"

"Yeah. I told the mayor about it last night. Shovel got me in the forehead."

Doc peered at the place Adam indicated.

"Nothing here now, but when it's your head…" Doc nodded. "Yes, your condition is quite clear to me now. I diagnose you as having bile."

"Bile?"

"Black bile. Loads of it. You are suffering from an excess accumulation of black bile, leaning you toward melancholia and morbid sensical perceptions."

"What?"

"You see, Adam, the human character is governed by an interaction between four basic humors. You've got your black bile, your yellow bile, your phlegm and your blood."

"I know the blood one."

"Problems are caused when one of these humors gets out of balance with the others. That knock on your head encouraged the collection of bile," Doc tapped his forehead, "right here. Your skull is full of black bile."

"I never heard of this."

"I haven't seen a case of it since I started treating people. I remember my grandmother treating people for it, though. It used to be a common thing, but not anymore."

"Is it dangerous?"

"Not if you get treatment."

"What's the treatment?"

"You have three choices. One, I go to the scum pond out back and get a bunch of leeches. Then I attach them," Doc started poking at Adam on the arms and chest. "Here, and here, and here. Let'em suck on you, maybe three hours."

"What are the other options?"

Doc walked to the next room. He returned with an evil-looking butcher knife. He took Adam's hand and held the blade next to his skin. "I can hack here, between the thumb and finger, and give you a good bleeding. It'd take care of things faster than the leeches, but I'd need to cut you about four times a day for a week."

"What's the third choice?"

"That takes longer than the other two. I let you go home, if you promise to do no field work for the next month. Just stay on your farm and rest. Eat good food. Sleep late. Don't tire yourself. Relax. After a month, you'll be good as new."

Doc lifted the blade again, preparing to cut. "So I expect you'll want the fastest way."

Adam had already stood and was making for the door.

The young farmer fetched his wagon. Claire and Doc stood with him by the road to say their goodbyes.

"Adam, dear," said Claire, "you have to come back more often. You went clear through puberty since your last visit."

"Yes, ma'am."

"Wait," said Doc. He handed Adam a small leather sack.

"When you get home, put some of this in water and drink it."

"What is it?"

"Medicine."

"What kind of medicine?"

"The medicinal kind. So many questions, just like your sister."

"Yes sir."

"Go straight home. Rest. Drain that black bile from your skull."

"Yes, sir. I need to go to town first, though."

"No, you don't, Adam. I said you go straight home."

"But, Doc, my grain's low. And I need bread."

"Can't your family do that?"

"Today's my turn to buy. Clarissa and Aunt Henrietta's got to watch the children and cook, and Uncle Walter and Richard, they're at the Grange."

Doc frowned. "Well, okay, just this once. But you finish fast and get yourself home. We don't want any further morbid sensical perceptions, do we?"

"No, sir."

As Adam's wagon was turning the bend toward town, Claire looked up at her husband anxiously.

"He's really going to town?"

Doc nodded. "He needed food."

"Couldn't we have given him some?"

"Not to that boy. He's like his father was. Giving food to some folks shames them so much they can't eat it."

Claire wrapped her hands around her husband's arm and pressed closer to him.

"Pray he gets home safe."

Chapter Fifteen
Broken

Obadiah Broke slammed his foot against the floorboard of his wagon. He cracked his whip on his horse's back. "Go!" he roared. The horse whinnied in pain and pushed itself to gallop even faster.

Broke was a man for whom rages were as familiar as breathing the air, but it was rare he'd felt a rage as furious as this one. How could they treat him like that!

He'd maintained a calm appearance after the meeting. He forced himself to smile at those fools around the table. He even agreed to do his part in support of Adam Green!

Support that weakling? Obadiah ground his teeth together. This anger was a chunk of molten iron sizzling in Obadiah Broke's gut and he wanted to shove it into something and twist it. He gave his whip another good crack on the horse's neck. The trees rushed by in green slashes. The horse cried out, but not loudly enough.

\#

Obadiah Newcomb Broke had been a gentle boy, in contrast to his father, Lampress Broke, who had been a hardworking, fiery-haired man with a booming voice. Perhaps in compensation to his father's roaring manner of speech, or the chattiness of his sister Wandabella, who even as a little girl was notoriously talkative, Obadiah had grown steadily quieter through his childhood.

The Brokes ran the town's only general store. At the age of twelve, Obadiah lost his mother Wilamina to an accident. The heavy wooden sign over the store entrance, with the black letters spelling out *Broke General Store,* was knocked down by a gust of wind at a moment Wilamina was standing underneath it.

Little Obadiah was there at the time, cleaning out
the grain room, and his mother had gone out the front
door. One of the things Obadiah never spoke of was the
vivid recollection of hearing the groan of timber from
above, watching his mother walk onto the porch, and
witnessing the sign break her skull to pieces.

While the loss of a mother seemed to implant a
troubling stridency in the heart of his sister Wandabella,
Obadiah withstood the tragedy without any apparent
damage. His father did as well as any man could to raise
the two children by himself. He continued managing the
General Store into extreme old age. Lampress
relinquished his duties only when he could pass them on
to his son-in-law James Shrenker, and he even worked
the counter occasionally up until the day a toxic spider in
his bug collection bit him on the cheek and filled his
veins with poison.

As a young man, Obadiah was known as the calm
one in the family. Touchingly devoted to Blossom, his
pretty wife, and to their little son George, he was not one
to fly into wild rages or to indulge in gossip. Obadiah
was known to possess a keen intelligence, and to weigh
every decision he made carefully before acting. Before
George was five years old, Obadiah left the running of
the store to his sister and purchased a modest apple farm.

The farm was close enough to the southern
swamps that Obadiah could supplement his family's
table with fish, mussels, oysters, and other wonders of
the bogs. He took young George with him sometimes to
gather treats.

Living at the southern fringes meant living near
the trappers and skinners who worked the forest. These
men—they were mostly male—were a clannish group
that lived beyond the borders of society. Whenever they
appeared in town to sell the skins they'd sliced from
their trapped raccoons, beavers, rabbits, and foxes, they

sent shock waves through the artisans and the farmers and fishers who were their customers. It was hard not to be frightened by the wild men, with their long hair crazed, their beards flecked with the remains of old meals, their ragged clothes splotched with dried blood. Yet, for the warm coats, hats, moccasins, boots and gloves that granted life in the winter, the town needed skinners.

Obadiah Broke became accustomed to the wild men of the woods. The odors of decay they exuded no longer bothered him. One autumn, a mysterious contagion struck Obadiah's apple orchards. Overnight, the fruits withered on their stems. By that time, Obadiah was making most of his money from the sales of his apples. He despaired as he watched helplessly while the source of winter sustenance for his family dropped dead to the earth.

As luck had it, that very day, some passing furriers asked for a drink of water and suggested that Broke could do some tanning on his farm. The forest-men were transient, with no fixed homes, so they couldn't set up the equipment needed for large-scale tanning. The furriers could sell their skins at a higher price if they were already tanned when taken to market, and Obadiah, if he helped them, could split their profits.

Ordinarily, farmers would not sink to working directly with skinners, but Obadiah's wife and child needed to eat.

The furriers taught him the basic tanning procedure, the stretching, washing and scraping. They showed him how to mash the brains of pigs in a vat and to simmer them over a slow fire until the consistency was right.

It turned out that the former apple farmer was a natural. Soon he was like a veteran tanner, slathering brain-mush on furs, working them with his hands until they were soft, smoking them. The tanning turned out to be much more lucrative than the orchards had ever been. People needed warm clothing more than apples. The business quickly became so good that Obadiah faced a shortage of brains.

He solved the problem by establishing special breeding pens for his pigs, so they produced litters at the fastest possible rate. Only a month after starting his tanning business, he was harvesting twenty pig brains a week and tanning a hundred skins.

All was looking rosy for him in his new business, except for one problem: the brain and water solution he used impregnated the skins with a sour odor which couldn't be washed out. People didn't want to wear clothes that constantly stank of death.

He conjectured the problem was the water. He drew it from a well whose source was the nearby froggy-smelling swamps. One day he decided to try mixing the brains with apple juice.

It was a momentous decision that would change his life forever. He'd only begun stirring the thick, brown brew in an iron cauldron. Flecks of apple skin and orangish chunks of brain floated on top. The mush exhaled a sweet-smelling yellow smoke. He leaned forward and sniffed. His nostrils filled with pain and he was slammed by a terrible sensation of falling, falling straight into a liquid fire of vibrating yellow ants.

Blossom found him on his stomach, rigid as ironwood. With the help of little George and an apple cart, she managed to get her husband into the house and onto their bed.

She sent George to fetch the doctor. The boy, scared that his daddy might be dying, raced on his horse through the black of night all the way past town. Tears poured from his eyes, slashed by the wind across the sides of his face.

Obadiah remained on his back in a petrified stupor, his eyes wide open. Apart from the almost invisible rise and fall of his chest, he was exactly like a corpse. Candles illuminated the room. The only sound was Blossom's quiet weeping. She kept her tiny hands wrapped around Obadiah's fingers, her head bowed. Obadiah was her life.

Doc returned with the boy in the middle of the night. He examined Obadiah by candlelight. Already the man's skin was transforming into a wormy canvas of the five colors of mold and clumps of hair were falling from his head.

The old physician could find nothing wrong with him. Ashamed, he told Blossom he had no idea what to do. He confessed the limits of his medical ability in a single sentence, not realizing how well it would define the remainder of Obadiah Broke's life:

"From now on, he has all the power."

#

Broke let his horse slow down. The beast was wide-eyed and snorting, his head tossing side to side in spasms. Obadiah was still furious. The noises of the animal irritated him more.

He snapped the reins to the left, and the horse turned onto a smaller trail branching toward the south. This was Broke Ranch Trail, where Obadiah had started to build his empire. He'd accomplished much in the seven years since he rose from his deathbed a new, better man. Yes, he had lost his hair, and his skin, and his lips, but his ranch had grown ten times over.

He was freed from the shackles of conscience. In their place, Eternity had given him *the dreams*. These visions first came to him while he was still in a coma and they followed him upon wakening, transcendental peeks of a world filled with gleaming towers and fantastic wagons capable of immense speeds, of delicious, limitless power. It was the dreams that first inspired him to change his tanning business to a cattle ranch and it was the dreams that made him add to that experimentation with metallurgy. The arrival of the Goddess nearly seven years later with the magic box confirmed the dreams were not, as he sometimes secretly feared, the delusions of an injured mind, but instead gifts from God.

The Goddess. Light of his Soul. Dagger in his Heart. When he had told her, his voice quivering in the presence of her ethereal greatness, of his plan to drive Adam Green from his farm so he could steal the magic black water, she'd sneered. "That's the stupidest fucking idea I've ever heard."

Even though he had her safely contained behind iron bars, the Goddess was the only one who could wither his manhood. "Why?" he demanded, his anger faltering under his fear.

"You think this guy's just going to pack up and walk off because he sees something strange in the woods?"

"But...but it's *really* strange."

"Idiot."

"He'll think his place is haunted and he'll want to move out."

"Moron. Let me out of here and I'll take care of everything."

His stomach was twisted into knots after that exchange, and they were twisting into knots again now that it turned out the Goddess was right. A half-baked plan. It had seemed so right at the time it came to him, but he didn't think it through. Obadiah's rebirth after the accident had galvanized his thinking, had endowed him with startling degrees of crystalline perception, but it had also, he realized with a twinge, made him in some ways a moron.

He had managed to bring off parts of his master plan with great success. Under the concealment of night, following the imagery of his dreams and the sketchy instructions of the Goddess, he'd constructed the bones of his vision. The huge cauldrons. The forges and molds. Broke and his most trusted men had sunk holes into sides of the mountains and were bringing up raw ore at twenty wagon-loads per day. But, Obadiah thought with a shudder of fury, I can't get anywhere without the black water!

His horse was limping badly. Broke was about to leap from the wagon and attack the animal with rocks, when he saw his son.

George was about thirty yards away, relaxing under a tree by the side of the trail. His horse was lazing in a small pasture a dozen yards down. George's neck was bent back, so the top of his head was leaning against the bark. A cap was tossed carelessly over his eyes. He had one leg crossed over the other. His head and foot bobbed as he whistled a tune.

Obadiah Broke leapt from the wagon. The boy had just lifted his cap to look when Obadiah grabbed him by his overalls and yanked him into the air.

"What are you doing?"

"Father!"

"You lazy pig!" Obadiah was a half-foot taller and twice as strong as his son. "I told you to plow up that north field today, but here you are under this tree."

"But, Mama told me to go to town to get some bread."

"But Mama told me to get some bread." Obadiah mimicked him in a whining, feminine voice. He roared, "I told you to plow the field." He lifted George higher. "Boy, you're turning into a bigger priss than your damn mother. You're even worse than your bugger boy Adam Green."

His father dropped him. "Get your arse home and plow that field. Or I'll beat you so bad you won't stand for a week."

As George scrambled to his feet, Obadiah pushed him down again. "Before that, you go into town and pick up a bag of pig feed from your Aunt Wandabella. And *don't* buy any bread. You hear?" George managed to nod.

Obadiah Broke started to walk away but suddenly turned around. With a thrust of his powerful arms, he shoved George against the trunk of the tree. The boy grunted as he struck the oak. As he started to collapse, Obadiah punched him, a quick hard jab in the left eye. George dropped to the ground.

Obadiah Broke leaped into the wagon, kicked at the horse's flank. The wagon disappeared around the bend.

A few minutes later, a squirrel peeked its head out of the bushes. It inched up to George. The small animal saw the tears spreading tracks through the dirt on his trembling face and moved closer. It sniffed at George's ear.

George knocked the squirrel into the air with the back of his hand. He stood up, slapped the dirt from his pants and shirt. With his shirtsleeve, he wiped away the tears, rubbing hard until his face burned so bad it seemed ablaze.

Chapter Sixteen
Get Away From Me, You Old Dyke

Joss Hankers shoved the wooden pedal-board up and down with her foot to pump ale from the big barrel. The lukewarm, orange fluid exuded a rich odor of hops as it spurted from the pipe and quickly filled the tankard under it. Joss kept pumping, turning the tray with one hand, her big arm muscles flexing, so that when one tankard was filled, the empty one next to it moved under the flow. She could fill eight large tankards this way in less than a minute, without spilling a drop. When all were filled, she hoisted the heavy tray on her shoulder, kicked open the door, and went outside.

Along with the blacksmithing and barrel-making it provided, Hanker's Barrel was also the town's only pub, and only one of two in all of Arcadia. And Hanker's Barrel was synonymous with the person who owned and ran it all by herself, Joss Hankers.

The Saturday crowd was as big and loud as ever, and Joss was kept busy moving from table to table with tankards and throwing comments into the conversations going on among each of the groups of customers. The atmosphere at Hankers was inevitably raucous and noisy and joyful as was Joss herself, and she did as much as the ale to whip up the spirits of the men. Joss was a large woman, more than six feet tall, and broad and stout and, while possessed of a boisterous charm, a kind heart, and a quick, irreverent mind, was completely intolerant of bullshit. If a customer had too much to drink and got out of line, she required no help catapulting the man from the premises, regardless of his size. Such measures were rarely necessary, because Joss had known most of her customers since they were children; she was as much a beloved fixture of the community as Reverend Branch,

Doc Midland, and Mayor Gladford, and in a way
respected as an authority figure more than any of them.

She slid tankards in front of a clutch of Grange
farmers. She slapped the arm of the one closest to her
and said, "Hey Sonny James, how's that wife of yours?
Didn't she hurt her arm getting winter logs?" The farmer
was pudgy, pink-faced, happy on ale. "Joss, yep, she
sure did. Doc wrapped her arm and said to keep it still
for a couple of weeks, so she's having to do everything
with that one arm."

Joss scowled down at him. "Then what in the
goddamned hell are you doing here drinking? You
should be at home, helping your wife."

The man nodded. "Joss, I knew you'd say that,
and that's why I got up early this morning and cooked up
both lunch and dinner for her before I came out. And I'm
going to work through this Sunday fetching that wood,
so she don't have to do it."

Joss slapped him on the back. "In that case, this
round is on the house."

The men drank a toast to Joss, and another toast
to Sonny James. "Hey," said Sonny James. He pointed at
a table on the other side of the yard. "Ain't that Obadiah
Broke's boy, George? Don't see him here much."

George had just sat down on a log, tore the gloves
from his hands, and threw them on the barrel.

"Not sure I've ever seen him here before, come to
think of it," said Joss.

"That boy has it tough," said one of the farmers.

Sonny James nodded. "His pa is strict with him."

Joss frowned. "Obadiah's a mean old bastard." At
the looks of surprise on the farmers' faces, she added,
"and I don't care how many nice things he's done with
his money, or how sorry people feel for him because of
his accident. The one we should really feel sorry for is

George over there. When they were handing out fathers in heaven, he got a bad draw."

The farmers took a long pull of their ales, looking around here and there nervously, as though they hadn't heard Joss's comment and didn't have to state an opinion about it one way or the other. Few men in Arcadia weren't somewhat fearful of Obadiah Broke.

Sonny James said, "Maybe you ought to go over there and cheer him up, Joss."

"What I'm figuring on doing."

Joss filled a tankard and brought it to George's table. "Howdy, George, and good day to you. Don't think I've seen you here before." She put the tankard in front of his downturned face. "You look like you could use this, so it's on the house."

George glared up at her. She let out a low whistle when she saw the bruise on his cheek. It was a gruesome blue-black wound that had swollen his left eye nearly shut.

"Goddamn, boy, what happened to you?" She smiled conspiratorially. "You try to give Miss Virginia a kiss and get punched?"

George lifted the tankard and drank all of its contents in one breath.

Joss sat down on the log next to George. "Boy, George, you're having a tough one today, ain't you? Want to talk about it?"

When he spoke, George's voice was tight with anger. "Leave me alone."

Over George's shoulder, Joss caught sight of Adam Green on the road, riding by in his wagon. She smiled and waved at him and he waved back. George glanced over too. As he watched Adam pass by, the intensity of his glare increased.

"George, let me get something cold to put on your eye."

"Leave me alone, I said."

Joss put a hand on his shoulder. "Come on, Honey. Everyone has a bad day sometimes. If you got something to get off your chest…"

George slapped her arm away. He stood. "I said, get away from me, you old dyke."

Before Joss could get over her shock enough to speak, George had already stomped out of the yard and was heading down the road the direction Adam had gone.

Chapter Seventeen
The Gaggle

When Adam departed from Doc's and set off toward town, the day was looking more promising.

Rosenlee clopped along at a donkey's pace, lazing in the late-morning warmth. The sun was high above the Grey Mountains. Adam could see the rocky faces of those distant hills warming in the yellow light. The trees luxuriated in the embracing sky, leaning back in the breeze, trilling their leaves. A squirrel shot up the trunk of an oak, froze in mid-sprint. It bent its head back at Adam and chittered. The animal looked so funny talking to him over its shoulder that Adam burst out laughing.

He rode into town. Saturday in Arcadia, at midday in early autumn, most folks were home finishing up their harvests, but there was still an ample crowd at Hankers Barrel. Among the thirty or so men drinking at the barrels, Adam caught sight of Little Victor seated at a table with some farmhands from Broke Ranch and some workers from the Grange. Joss Hankers was seated at a table with one of the men. He couldn't see who it was because his head was tilted downward. Probably drunk and Joss was counseling him to go home and sleep it off. She raised her eyes toward the road, saw Adam, and waved, the arc of her arm broad and her smile big and bright. Adam waved back. A few of the men looked at him too and immediately turned away.

When Adam was almost completely past the pub, he glanced back and caught sight of the man Joss was talking to. It looked a lot like his old friend George Broke. For a second, he considered going back to talking to George. But the two had grown distant over the years. He hadn't talked to George at all since the harvest festival last month, and then it was just a curt greeting. When Adam's parents died, and George was still in shock over his father's accident, the two travelled to see each other often. As the thickening of adolescence widened the gap between their childhood and their present, so too did it increase the gap between them.

A short way down, Adam could see Shrenkers General Store. A building right beyond Shrenkers, but towering over it because it was so much taller, was the Broke Bakery. Adam thought with a sudden trill in his heart that Virginia Baker would probably be there today, making her magic bread. And he needed to buy bread.

The road in front of Shrenkers was crowded with horses and wagons. Between Hankers and Shrenkers was an empty field, claimed by no one, big enough to fit another few buildings in. Adam pulled Rosenlee up into the field and walked the remaining fifty feet to Shrenkers. As he climbed down from the riding board, a crow cawed loudly from somewhere nearby. A chill shot through him. He'd always hated the crow's call. It brought back memories of a terrifying story he'd heard in childhood of a crow who settled on the cradles of babies, a crow whose call was a harbinger of death.

#

The front counter inside Shrenkers General Store was ringed by a dozen women. All were enthusiasts of

Wandabella's sartorial inventions. They all wore gowns
with shoulders puffing up like the inflated pig bladders
children like to play with, and skirts that flounced
dramatically from pinched waists, like inverted tulips.
The dresses were as ugly as they were impractical, with
spectacular splashes of yellow, green, orange and red.
On their heads, the women wore enormous hats that
sprouted the feathers of birds or the petals of flowers, or
displayed simulations of fruits and vegetables.

These wealthy farmwives constituted a notorious
Arcadian subculture, one that had appeared mysteriously
seven years ago. No one could recall a previous time in
history when wives had, like the Shrenker ladies, enough
free time to gather for the sole purpose of idle gossip.
The ordinary Arcadian wife spent her time tending to
daily needs of the farm and the family. Leisure time,
what little of it the Lord saw fit to provide, was likewise
spent with the family, telling stories or making music or
engaging in benign small talk, or at traditional
community gatherings, like harvest festivals or barn
dances or hayrides. It was not an Arcadian tradition for
people to spend time doing *nothing*.

The members of the gossip group at Shrenkers
were all female, but the group had a male counterpart,
whose members gathered along the banks of Silver
Spring, and did their gossiping while gripping fishing
poles. Or while drinking tankards at Hankers, although
Joss was known to hammer down such talk when she
heard it.

These ladies and gentlemen had time to gossip
because they didn't need to work. Their farms or
businesses had accumulated so much money that
quotidian labors were no longer necessary. These
nouveau riche could hire others to do the work for them.

The idle gossip, like oil seeping through sandstone,
found its way into the mouths of farmers from one end

of the land to the other. Hard-working family folk thought of these busybodies as loafers and oddballs, not worth the time of day, yet still, without even thinking about it, made a space for their gossip at the dinner table.

The dozen women at the counter at Shrenkers, listening to the shop owner, looked like animals circled around a carcass. Wandabella stood on the other side leading them on. The women were frothing over the most exciting object of gossip ever to hit Arcadia: Adam Green.

"Is Reverend Branch going to even allow him in the church?" said a lady wearing a yellow plumed hat.

"Reckon he needs to. The reverend's niece is related to that bunch out there. She's married to Adam's cousin," put in another lady with a round, pudgy face set off with a conical, orangish piece of headwear whose point was wilting, like a dying cornstalk.

"His *great* niece," corrected the yellow hat lady.

The conical lady wrinkled her nose. "What's the difference?"

Wandabella interrupted. "That reminds me, the reverend has another problem with this young man, doesn't he? Because his own female kin lives so close by."

Wandabella's tactic, as conductor of these gossip sessions, was to observe the ladies for any sign of the blaze dying down, then to cast on more tinder.

"What do you mean, Wandabella? Are you saying Adam isn't trustworthy around women?"

"Oh, no, no! I wouldn't want to say anything like that. Still, none of us can really know what's going on in the head of someone who says he sees spectrals in the forest."

"You are speaking my mind exactly, Wandabella Shrenker," said an ostrich-like woman in a purple dress splattered with sunflowers. "*Exactly.*"

"Yes! If he's crazy enough to see monsters in the forest, then what else might he be crazy about?"

"Could be anything!"

"Just think of how his parents were."

"My husband was saying just last night that we should have nipped this in the bud seven years ago."

"My husband said the same thing."

The ostrich woman pressed her palm against her bosom. "I wonder if I should keep my daughter at home from school."

At that moment, the lanky figure of Hildegard Shrenker appeared at the back door. She glanced at the women with her moony eyes, then started to cross the room.

"Where are you going, young lady?" Wandabella demanded. Hildegard stopped.

"Out to play," she said softly.

"With whom?"

"Daisy."

"Daisy Green?" Wandabella Shrenker folded her stringy arms.

"Yes'um." Hildegard looked up at her mother, then down again.

"I will not have you going all the way to the northlands at this time of day."

"I'm not going there. We're only going to the stream."

"Don't you dare come home after dark."

"Yes'um."

"Yes, *ma'am*."

"Yes, ma'am."

"Do not speak like a skinner."

"Yes, ma'am."

The dozen gossip women were all staring at the girl. They were imitating Wandabella's disapproving scowl perfectly, amplifying its effect. Hildegard looked like she was about to cry.

"And I'm not sure," Wandabella added, "I like you playing with that Daisy Green."

Hildegard continued watching her feet.

"She's blood with that Adam Green. It's only common sense for me to wonder about the quality of her family. You think about that, you hear?"

"Yes, ma'am."

"That's all."

Hildegard was reaching for the handle when the door opened and Adam Green walked in.

Chapter Eighteen
Small Trembling Fingers

Adam pushed open the door of Shrenkers and was surprised to see a girl standing on the other side of it. He stepped around her and found women in strange clothes gaping at him. Those friends of Mrs. Shrenker seemed to always be there on his monthly visits for provisions, each time dressed more strangely than the last. Adam removed his hat and nodded to them. "Afternoon, ladies."

When they didn't respond, Adam turned from their stares and walked down the first row of shelves. He forced himself to browse through the awls, adzes, mallets and hatchets laid out there, although he didn't need any. He sneaked a look at the counter. The women were still gawking at him.

He continued pretending to pore over the shelves. The silence in the store was oppressive. The sound of his feet shuffling on the floor was like thunder. All at once, the truth punched him: before he walked in, they were talking about him.

They all knew about what he'd seen in the forest, and now they were *gossiping about him.*

He wanted to tear up the floorboards and hide underneath. Forcing himself not to look at the women, he moved down the aisles, his bucket in his hand, gathering items. A spool of thread, a sack of tea, some leather string for his moccasins. The main thing he needed to buy was grain, and for that he needed to ask Wandabella directly. Adam took a deep breath and walked to the counter.

As he approached, the women hopped away like crows from a garbage heap. They began moving for the door. Wandabella glowered across the counter. To Adam, she was an imposing figure, so confident, so popular, so proud, so wealthy. Her hair was like some electrified mass of filaments ready to spring from her head and crawl down his throat. The condemning gaze she held him under as he approached made him want to dissolve into the floor. She possessed something like power in Arcadian society, power that emanated from the store and the old building from which it operated, and from her family relationship with Obadiah Broke, who had more power than anyone.

"Hello, Mrs. Shrenker." The words came out in a squeak. "Can I get some sacks of wheat and barley?"

"How many?" she snapped.

"Um, seven wheat, six barley." Adam pointed to the corner on her right, by the back door, where the grain bags were stacked.

Wandabella shook her head. "We're sold out."

"But you got all those bags there," Adam protested before he could stop himself.

"Those bags are spoken for. Old Miles Dunnett already paid for them. He'll be by later to pick them up."

"That's not true, mother."

Wandabella and Adam swung their heads around. The young girl who had been by the door when Adam entered had not moved. She had held the door open for the ladies as they left. Adam looked at her closer and realized she was Hildegard Shrenker, Wandabella's daughter.

"Mr. Dunnett picked up all his sacks yesterday, remember?"

Wandabella's eyes narrowed.

"And Papa said this morning for us to sell these bags here quick as possible, before they get moldy. Don't you remember?"

Wandabella was running the tip of her tongue over her fat front teeth. Back and forth, staring at her daughter. The strings under the skin of her rhubarb neck were quivering. "Reckon," she said, so low and airy she might have been leaking the word from her nose. She suddenly snapped at Adam. "You got money?"

"Yes, ma'am."

"Yes, ma'am what?"

"Yes, ma'am, I got money."

"Hildegard!" Wandabella rapped her bony fist on the counter. "Since you are so interested in what we have for sale, you will come here and finish this…person's…purchase. Then you will carry all of his grain bags to his wagon."

Wandabella stomped out from behind the counter. At the foot of the stairs, she halted, whirled around, and marched back. She hissed something in her daughter's ear. Hildegard's eyes widened. Wandabella stomped past Adam again and climbed the stairs noisily.

Adam's shirt was damp with sweat. He stared at Hildegard.

She had sprouted up since he's last seen her. Hildegard was friends with his sister Daisy, and visited the cabin next door sometimes, but Adam didn't really pay attention and the Hildegard of his recollection was only a child, six inches shorter than this Hildegard. Now she came nearly to his shoulders.

Hildegard had her mother's long, thin face and scraggly hair, but the green of her eyes had none of Wandabella's crazed energy. Instead, they were filled with a kind of wonderment, like a kitten staring at a piece of string.

She was taking him in now with those wide eyes. She stepped past Adam to the wall. The piles of grain bags towered over her. She said, in a voice that shook slightly, "How many?"

It dawned on Adam the girl was terrified. She was twisting her legs, the balls of her feet swiveling on the beams of the floor.

Adam wanted to just walk out. He wasn't sure why the girl was scared of him, but whatever the reason, it was mean-spirited of Wandabella to force her to serve him. Reluctantly, Adam pointed his finger at the sacks in front.

"Seven sacks of wheat, and six of barley."

A pause, then she hoisted a bag as big as herself over one shoulder. She said, her voice more controlled now, "Where's your wagon?"

"In front of the lot next door."

Adam lifted one of the sacks and followed Hildegard as she pushed her way through the door with her hip, one hand balancing a sack on her shoulder, the other shielding her eyes from the sun.

The two went to his wagon and tossed the sacks into the cradle in back. Rosenlee stood placidly facing across the street.

The two silently piled up the rest of the grain bags and went back inside. Hildegard retreated behind the counter. In a voice squeaking with tension, she said, "That's forty shillings. Or six clean skins."

"What?" Adam said loudly, causing her to flinch. He looked at the floor. He forced himself to lower his voice. "That's double the price I paid last month."

Hildegard stared up at him without answering and her eyes were filling with tears. The look filled Adam with horror. *Wandabella told her daughter to charge me double.*

Adam took a deep breath. "I only got thirty shillings today. And no skins. But...don't worry about it, Hildegard. Ain't your fault. I'll bring the bags back inside."

Adam started for the door, Hildegard called after him. "Wait!"

The girl glanced fearfully at the ceiling. "I'll...I'll sell them to you for half that."

"Are you sure?"

She nodded sharply.

"Thank you kindly, Hildegard. You're a good girl."

Hildegard caught his eye, and for a split-second Adam saw the mask drop. Behind it was not the little girl his sister played hoopball with in the back fields but instead a young woman. She dropped her gaze to the counter, blushing.

She didn't look at Adam as he paid. As he placed the coins in her hand, her fingers were trembling.

Chapter Nineteen
Magic Bread

Adam tied up the back of his wagon. Standing beside his horse, in the still of the main road, he closed his eyes. He tilted his head back and took a deep breath. On a breeze from the south the luscious scent of freshly baked bread reached out to him.

Broke Bakery was familiar to everyone in part because it was owned by Obadiah Broke, a man at once honored for his generous acts of charity, feared for his volcanic temper, respected for his wealth and, pitied for his heartbreaking injuries of the skin. It was even more famous for its magical bread and the beautiful woman who baked it.

Every morning Virginia Baker could be seen behind the front window in the opening procedures of creating her wonderful bread. For many men, it was a morning show. Farmers found all sorts of reasons to go out of their way in their daily travails so they would be passing by that window at the exact time the lovely girl was bent over the wooden slab, her peach-colored smock hoisted up to her knees to obtain freedom of movement and her long, plaited brown hair tied back, to watch her kneading and rolling and pounding the dough with her flour-covered hands.

She was standing at the window when she saw Adam approaching from Shrenkers. She dropped the ball of dough she was working on into the dough box and rushed to the back room. She slapped the flour from her hands. She untied her hair and fluffed it out and straightened the hem of her smock. The front door creaked open. She took a deep breath and entered.

"Adam!" she said in a surprised voice.

"Hi, Ginnie."

"How are you?"

"Okay."

Virginia peered through the window over Adam's shoulder. After surveying the street and finding no one, she touched his arm.

"I've been so worried about you."

"Why?"

"Well, about the…thing you saw."

Adam broke into a nervous laugh. "You heard about it too?"

"It's okay. Tell me what happened."

Adam gripped a piece of his shirt between two fingers and tugged at it. "Honestly, Ginnie, I can't make no sense of it." He told her the story of the talking head in the box, the forest demon.

She reached across the counter and rubbed his arm. "Oh, Adam, that's awful. Somebody must have played a joke on you."

"I'll bet that's not what they're saying over there at Shrenkers."

"Oh, don't pay them any mind. They're just a bunch of noisy fools."

"I went to see Doc this morning. He says I saw that thing because I hit my head with a shovel last week and it filled me with biles or something." Adam looked at his boots. "Everybody's talking about it, ain't they?"

Virginia rolled her eyes. "Only the stupid ones."

"Doc says I should stay home a few weeks, get over my biles."

"You look fine to me. I bet those good-for-nothing Fodder boys are behind this."

"But Ginnie, this thing was so real. Not like any prank. You sure look pretty." Adam gasped and threw his hand over his mouth.

Virginia burst out laughing. She put her hand on his shoulder and rubbed it, leaving a flour handprint. She looked into his eyes. Her eyes were large and brown, and the lids were delicately curved, like the eyes of a lamb. Adam felt delicious sparks shoot through his body.

A noise made them jump. In the back room, a door slamming.

"Papa." Virginia dropped her hand from Adam's shoulder and Hugh Baker entered the room.

"Ginnie, did you…" Hugh started to say before he saw Adam.

"Papa, you okay? You look like you saw a ghost."

"Good afternoon, Mr. Baker," said Adam.

Hugh wiped his blonde hair away from his eyes. He spoke stiffly. "Adam Green. I'm surprised to see you here."

"Why, Papa? Adam comes here every month to buy bread."

"Because I thought...he'd be working at the Grange today." Hugh tapped his hat and began to walk out.

"Papa?"

"Yes?"

"What did you want?"

"Hm?"

"You were going to ask me something."

"Oh. Yes. I wanted to know if…you ground that barley this morning."

"Yes, Papa. I put it in the sack by the door."

Hugh left. A few seconds later, they heard the back door open and close.

Virginia faced Adam. "Don't you think he was acting strange?"

Adam nodded sadly. "He was."

"I wonder why," asked Virginia.

Chapter Twenty
Crazy Boy

Virginia listened until she was sure her father had gone. She tilted her head playfully to one side. "What do you want from me today, Adam?"

"What do I…?"

"What kind of bread can I get you?"

"Oh." Adam considered. "Can you give me three loaves of that bread with honey mixed in? That's the most delicious thing I ever ate, I reckon." He asked for two more loaves, one oat, one flax and walnut. He requested a basket of brown butter buns too, for his aunt. And some sugar sticks for Daisy.

She took out baskets from a pile in the corner and put them on the counter. Strands of wheat-colored hair fell across her forehead. She brushed them aside with the back of her hand.

"My aunt gave up baking bread," said Adam, watching Virginia stoop under the counter to pull out the loaves from underneath. "Cause she says no one does it better than you, Ginnie."

She looked up at Adam. "Do you really think I'm pretty?"

Adam managed to hold her gaze. He nodded.

She placed the bread in front of him. Adam started to take out money for the purchase, but she shook her head.

"Adam Green, I can tell just by looking that you didn't bring enough money to pay for this. How could you do such a thing?"

"Why, Ginnie, I think I *do* have enough…"

"I don't think so." She peered into his eyes, an unwavering look that ignited sparks in his chest. "So happens that tomorrow is my delivery day. I need to come north, after church. It's a lot of trouble, but I'll come by your farm on my way out." She leaned forward across the counter. She brought her lips close to Adam's ear. "You can pay me then."

Adam backed out of the bakery, a basket in each hand. He bumped into the door, knocking it open, a dopey grin on his face.

He stumbled out onto the porch and nearly toppled down the three steps. He turned back to the bakery window and saw Virginia smiling at him. Out of the corner of his right eye, something was moving. He turned and found George Broke's face inches from his.

"Well, if it ain't the crazy boy."

"George."

Broke's smile was malignant.

"Crazy boy says he sees *fairies* in the woods."

Virginia came out of the bakery.

Broke saw her and shot his fist into Adam's face.

Virginia screamed. Adam dropped to the ground, his hands wrapped over his nose. Virginia fell to her knees next to Adam. "Oh, Lord, are you okay?" Adam only groaned in response. Blood gushed between his fingers.

Big Joss Hankers bounded up, her boot buckles jangling. "What's going on?"

"George Broke hit Adam!"

"The hell you say." Joss looked down the road.

George was ambling casually toward Cobble's shoe shop, where he'd tied his horse. Joss bent the fingers of one of her big hands into a fist. "Maybe someone ought to hit *him.*"

"Joss, don't. It'll just make things worse. Can you stay here and take care of Adam, so I can go talk to George? Please?"

Joss gave a reluctant nod and knelt beside Adam.

Virginia ran after George Broke and called out to him.

George glanced nonchalantly at her.

"Oh, hello, Miss Virginia," he said with exaggerated surprise. "Been a long time."

"Why did hit Adam?" she demanded.

He smirked. "Seemed like a good thing to do."

"It was a mean, stupid thing to do. What's wrong with you?"

Broke's face tightened. "Are you defending him? *Him*?"

Virginia folded her arms. "Adam is a friend of mine. I thought he was a friend of yours too."

"*Was.* I didn't realize what he was before."

"And now you do? What do you know?"

George Broke's face took on a look of pity. "You didn't hear, did you?"

He bent his head toward her and whispered, "he's a *sodomite.* Virginia."

He climbed onto his horse and said, "Careful about who you call a friend." He pointed at the young farmer moaning in the dust. "Kiss a pig, kiss an axe."

Chapter Twenty-one
Ripping at the Edges

When George punched him, time stopped for Adam. His life was reduced to a thumb-sized ball of molten iron that seethed in the center of his face and spread hot bits of itself through his humiliated body.

He opened his eyes. People had gathered, seven, fifteen, twenty of them, and they were all staring down at him. The first face he could make out clearly was Wandabella Shrenker's. She turned to a person beside her and scoffed, "Guess he isn't dead."

Adam looked frantically around, but could see neither Virginia nor Joss.

A voice he didn't recognize said, "He'd probably be better off dead."

A third said, "Too bad George didn't use a stick. Or a rock."

"You all leave him alone," said a familiar voice. Joss Hankers. But he couldn't see her.

"Maybe we ought to kill him now," he thought he heard someone say. Heart pounding, he jumped up and shoved his way through the crowd. An outcry of voices flared up behind him. He turned around and saw a distorted mass of faces, mouths chewing and stretching, eyes enraged.

He made to run. The world tilted on one side and he nearly fell down. He pivoted awkwardly, regained his footing, and sprinted down the road until he spotted his wagon. He leapt so quickly onto the riding board that he almost tumbled off the other side. He screamed at his horse to go.

Soon Rosenlee was in a gallop. The wheels flung up a tail of dust. They passed by Doc's in a shot and were swallowed up by the dark trail through the Merlin Grove. Adam touched his nose and winced at the pain that flared there. He looked down and saw blood.

It wasn't until he was back at his farm and securely inside his cabin that he realized he should have stopped at Doc's to get his injuries treated. By then it was too late. He was immured in his little home and he wasn't coming out.

Chapter Twenty-two
Better to Be a Hog

When George Broke returned home to the Broke ranch, the enormous black iron gate was open. He rode his horse through and followed the winding road toward the back of the property where latticework racks hundreds of feet long were set up beside trenches filled with green-white, oleaginous liquid lumpy with smashed pig brains. Along the latticework were dozens of men working on tanning the skins of rabbits and foxes and deer and elk and draping them on the racks to dry. When they saw him, they waved and hollered out greetings. He ignored them. He was in no mood for contact with others.

He wound around past a couple of red arched buildings that he could see through the large open doors had men astride benches next to forges from whose flaming maws they were using tongs to pull lumps of white-hot iron ingots onto anvils and then hitting them with enormous hammers. He swung around back of the towering white house that was now the Broke family home and passed the mysterious plain grey building his father forbade anyone, on pain of death, from entering, even though entry was impossible because the structure had no doors.

George's eyes were the same ash shade as his hair. The gossip went that their original color was leeched out by the tanning chemicals his father Obadiah forced him to use at the ranch. People said the young man looked like a grey panther. His body was slim and wiry, and his soot-colored hair was chopped in a disorderly bang across his eyes. Few people had seen him smile. He had an edgy way about him, always looking around with suspicious jerks of his head, like prey on the lookout for predators, or maybe a predator on the lookout for prey.

The young women of Arcadia found him unbearably handsome.

He parked the wagon, stepped silently up the back stairs and entered their house. At the rear vestibule, he could see through the doorway his mother cooking in the adjacent kitchen.

She turned and peered at him with her barren eyes. His mother always seemed to be asking a question with those eyes, but she never put it into words. They looked silently at each other for a time, then George turned down the hallway and went to his room. He fell onto the bed. He flipped onto his back and threw his arm over his eyes.

I hit Adam! Why?

Because he's a weakling, thought George with a surge of bitterness. And a bugger boy! Damned bugger boys deserved worse than a punch. They deserved *death!* It was in the Good Book. But, no matter how many times Father had told him Adam Green was a bugger boy, George knew it wasn't really true.

Still! He deserved to be hit! Hurt! Because of that crazy story he told about the head in the box! Because his witchy family had a devilish seed in its bloodline! Father had told him and his mother about all that. He was right to hit Adam. Even if he was a friend.

A *friend?* George rolled on his side and punched the wall. Damned Adam Green! A friend?

Father was right. The way he was playing around with Virginia in the bakery, trying to act so cute. At the thought of Virginia, George felt a starburst in his heart. He touched his hand to his chest and felt pain from where his father shoved him.

You're turning into a bigger priss than your damn mother. Worse than your bugger boy Adam Green.

The front door slammed. The walls trembled.

Father.

The noises of the old man's return brought to George the full enormity of his mistake. The previous summer, his father had come across George rooting through his private cellar, a place that was forbidden to everyone except Obadiah. That day, he'd beaten George with an iron chain. For two weeks, the divots in his back prevented him from getting out of bed. His father refused to send for Doc Midland, and he punched his mother bloody when she tried to slip out and secretly fetch him.

George had ridden into the night seven years before to fetch Doc Midland when his father was on the edge of death from the tanning solution accident.

Mama, why don't papa wake up!?
Quick, child, take the fastest horse and ride to Doc Midland's and tell him to come quick!

George had loved his papa so much he was stricken with dread at the idea he would lose him. And although Obadiah kept breathing, even as his hair fell out and his skin turned to mold, in many ways it seemed like George did lose him, because the man-thing who finally rose from the bed bore little resemblance, in appearance or character, to the father he'd so loved. But George still continued hoping all these seven long years that that kind, funny man, the one who took him fishing and gently taught him to stand and walk and run was alive somewhere inside that fish-body, and the man who beat him almost daily would hug him again.

Muffled conversation from the kitchen, a gruff male voice and a mousy female one. Bootsteps down the hall, like punches on the wood. George was really scared now. When Papa heard of the act of public violence he'd committed, which would certainly bring shame upon the Broke family, he would probably beat him to death.

The door opened. George closed his eyes and waited for the blows.

Nothing happened. When George opened his eyes, he saw something he hadn't seen in so long, he'd forgotten it was possible. His father was smiling at him.

"I'm so proud of you," his father said.

Obadiah Broke sat on the bed, draped his arms around his son and hugged him.

At first, George was rigid. He felt, from bone marrow to skin, like a thing carved of cold stone. A slow heat simmered deep in his organs, turning his insides into a warm broth that gathered itself in the muscles of his back and pulled him downward until he collapsed, sobbing, into his father's chest.

The two remained that way for a long time. Obadiah leaned to his son's ear and whispered, "I want to show you some things."

They ignored his mother's offer of dinner.

What proceeded was the most remarkable night of George's life.

Throughout those stunning twelve hours, his father had the giddy look of a man whose every cherished dream had finally come true. "Ha! Ha! Punched that little shit right on the nose!" he crowed again and again. He slapped George affectionately on the shoulder. "Until today, I thought you'd never become a Broke. But I was wrong!"

George was shown all the buildings in which he previously was not allowed. The mines lining the mountainside. The hidden recesses of the large ironworking building, where the secret machines were being built. Finally, the most amazing thing of all, his father showed him the way into the forbidden building behind the house, the one with no doors. It was there George learned the most shocking things, about his father, about Arcadia, about the world.

Come sunrise, George sat with his father inside the doorless building. He was suddenly gripped by an awful spell. None of this could be true! He collapsed from his chair, vomit boiling up his throat. Obadiah, as though anticipating this, produced a flask. George tried to push it away, but his father forced him to drink the liquid. In an instant, George's anxiety vanished. He'd never felt so tranquil, so perfect with the world. All at once, everything made sense.

He asked his father what the miraculous tonic was.

"Fermented pig brains in apple juice," said Obadiah.

In another state of mind, George would have thrown it up, but Obadiah had refined the fluid so it neutralized the very disgust it caused. All George could think was how impressed he was with this wonderful drink. How blessed he was also to understand the glorious secrets of the black water. What a miracle it was to have met the Goddess.

PART TWO

Chapter Twenty-three
Branch

Reverend Calvin Branch sat on the tree stump outside his cabin, running over the sermon he was about to deliver. He needed to announce a Day of Fasting and Humiliation and it was important that the wording be sufficiently fearsome. The congregants would start arriving soon. As he went over the words he planned to say, he etched a line in the dust with the toe of his boot, the same line again and again, deepening. Sunlight slanting from the eastern mountains brought a shadow out on the far side and splashed it on the ground, making the line seem deeper. The line seemed to be yet another in a series of portentous imagery God was sending him, this one reflecting the deepening, blackening line between himself and all that was on the other side.

Last night the preacher had seen a falling star descending to Earth, a white speck with a fiery snake's tail.

The demon in the forest, the falling star, the violence in the public road—to Reverend Calvin Branch, these were but three faces of the selfsame Animal.

He attacked the dirt with his boot, scraping back and forth in a fury, sinking the line deeper, fortifying a boundary between himself and the other side.

Their fault. Sinners!

Over the decades, Calvin had watched the community of Arcadia move further and further from God. It tore at him that the people so willingly forsook salvation, and it seared him with guilt, because he, their shepherd, had failed in his mission.

Beyond the line in the dirt was the Meeting House. The building could hold a congregation of 250, nearly half the Arcadian population, but the reverend hadn't seen a full house since his childhood, when it was his father's church.

The immortal Titus Branch! Every time Calvin thought of his father, instead of love, he felt burning inadequacy and bitterness.

Titus Josephus Branch had been a muscular, large-necked, ferocious-eyed, boulder-headed fist of Jesus. His ambition had been unshakable: to teach God's rules and force His people to follow them by any means necessary. Calvin could picture the man now, in place at the head of the meetinghouse, his eyes blazing straight at the transfixed congregants, his gaze burning into their souls as he shouted out quotations from the Good Book while punching the air like he was punching Satan himself. His voice was so loud the windows rattled in their frames.

Those were the good old days. When the Sabbatical Laws were still in place and Arcadia had a troop of church constables to enforce them. The meetinghouse was full every Sunday, standing room only, because everyone needed to come. No one dared disobey the law because no one wanted the array of sacred punishments the constables would use if they did.

The Mary Lena affair changed all of that. The law was tested by an extreme case and lost. Titus had asserted that Mary Lena's hearing mice in her garden trying to converse with her was a sign of witchcraft and devilry, the punishment for which was as brutally effective as it was unambiguous in the Sabbatical Laws: public burning at the stake, preferably after a series of torments and humiliations, shaving of the head, tarring and feathering, removal of certain appendages and eyeballs with a flaming blade, &cetera. Mary Lena was brought before the reverend in chains and a kind of trial was arranged in the meetinghouse. It was progressing as planned, with the punishment on the verge of beginning, when Mayor Increase Gladford, William Gladford's father, stood and gave a stirring speech that called into doubt the whole idea of witchcraft and the worthiness of the Sabbatical Laws and the brutal men who enforced them. The speech brought howls of protest in about half of the congregation, while the others were clearly moved by what the mayor was saying. Demands were shouted from the audience to drag Mary Lena out into the yard and burn her alive straightaway. Increase managed to quiet the audience enough to reveal irrefutable evidence that the Fodder Boys, out of resentment over excessive homework and just general cruelty, had played a funny prank on the poor school teacher, laying hidden behind some rose bushes and making "mouse noises" mingled with words (*Mary, we are mice and we are going to eat you,* &cetera). It was impossible to refute the mayor's testimony because it was provided by a dramatic, tearful confession by the two young Fodder Boys who had committed the act.

It horrified the community that their superstition had gotten the best of them, and they had come a hair's breadth from torturing and killing someone for no reason. The widespread humiliation spelled the end of the constable force, many of whom quit that very day, and cast a pall of doubt on all the religious laws too.

No longer compelled by threat of violence, fewer people came to church on Sundays. The drop in attendance provoked a crisis in Titus, who felt like his life's work was being destroyed. Calvin recalled his parents seated around the dinner table, back when his parents were still alive, fervently discussing plans to increase the congregation again. An idea Titus fixed upon especially was to enlarge the Meeting House and he tried to promote it during many long evenings to his wife, who was opposed. If the building were bigger, he would argue, a desperate look in his eyes, more people would surely come to his sermons. His mother pointed out repeatedly that the problem wasn't the size of the place but the motivations of the citizenry, but Titus kept returning to the idea because he knew of no other way to motivate the citizenry outside of brute force. Church attendance dropped off even further after the incident with Adam's parents. Titus perceived witchcraft again, this time infecting a whole family, and he saw it as an opportunity to bring back the Sabbatical Laws. He gave a string of blazing sermons denouncing the Green family and arguing that it was God's commandment that all direct blood-line relatives be burned alive in order to squelch forever the stain of witchcraft on the community. He was so confident this time that he even had men erect a post, fitted with chains, and stack firewood around it, in anticipation of the punishment he would certainly be able to inflict soon on Adam and Daisy Green. But the effort turned out doomed to failure once again as history repeated itself and the senior Mayor Gladford gave another impassioned, powerful speech in front of the congregation that ended up swaying enough of them to stop any punishment of Adam and Daisy. This time, the community was chastened by the idea they were on the verge of torturing and killing children for the possible crimes of their parents when children were obviously innocent. Although the Good Book was clear on the punishment for witches extending from fathers and mothers to sons and daughters, it was hazy on the point of whether God was okay with killing children. Also, many in the community who knew Adam and Daisy's parents thought the idea they were witches was nonsense. Adam's father was certainly something of an iconoclast, but a witch?

Now, as Calvin dug the line in the dirt with his boot, he hankered more than ever for a return of the Sabbatical Laws and the church police. He was only a small child in those days, and didn't remember them outside of the stories his father told him. But he did discover, seven years before, a binder of threadbare papers, tied in a leather cover, that Titus had buried under the floorboards. The papers were a long letter from father to son. It contained no words of love, warm recollections, or wise guidance one might associate with such a letter, but then again, Titus had never been very demonstrative. Instead, the papers described in great detail the Sabbatical Laws and how they had been enforced. The letter also contained instructions on how to implement the laws again, at a time when the community finally came to its senses and became amenable to the ways of God again. The two basic facets of such a re-implementation were, first, creating conditions that would nudge the community's thinking in the right direction and, second, forming an intimidating police force to instill terror in those who needed an extra push.

Calvin obsessed over how wonderful the community would become if he could bring back the old laws. He had read the old document, the instructions, scores of times, poring over all the details, considering their implications, committing them to memory. He had only shared the letter with one other person in Arcadia: Obadiah Broke.

Despite his reading the letter so many times, Calvin was still haunted by a single mystery. Why had his father hidden the instructions? They outlined the very style of community he aspired to bring back, yea, comprised a blueprint for it, yet he had squirreled them away underground. Even after having his commands and spiritual counsel rejected by the majority of the community, Titus Branch was not the kind of man to back down or to repudiate himself. So why hide them? It made no sense. If Calvin hadn't accidently broken a floorboard one day and noticed the box underground, he never would have found them and the papers would have eventually turned to dust unread.

Considering this mystery, the reverend started scratching hatchmarks with the toe of his boot to the small trench he'd dug, giving it a cage-like pattern. A sudden pain bit him in the groin. In the small, tight area above his thighs, he felt a hot nail pierce him. He gritted his teeth, waiting for the familiar pain to subside.

Calvin was born with unbalanced testicles. One large, one small. The larger hung considerably lower than its partner. The condition had been the origin of regular spasms of pain all his life. He'd never seen a physician about it, because not even Jesus Himself could compel the preacher to have physick practiced by Doc Midland, his nemesis, on so delicate a region of his anatomy.

The pain finally subsided. The reverend opened his eyes and renewed his thinking. This thing with the Green boy. At recalling the complexity of his relationship with Adam, Calvin winced again. That boy was becoming the locus of all his worst fears about Arcadia.

Calvin looked up at the Meeting House. Even now, just seeing the simple, inverted V of the roof, the modest porch, and the quiet strength of the gold-brown boards and beams brought a smile to his face. For the building's plain beauty and durability, Abraham Green, the designer, had chosen the wood of the oak tree. It was the finest building ever constructed in Arcadia, a priceless gift from a direct paternal ancestor of Adam Green. For days after Adam's parents entered the Forbidden Forest, Calvin couldn't bring himself to enter the Meeting House, for fear of contact with the wood hewn by the blood ancestor of the devilish couple.

Now, things didn't seem so clear.

Adam's father Jedediah had always been an odd duck. There was that strange piece of advice Jed used to give whenever someone was troubled. *Look up!* he'd say. Calvin had originally thought it was a religious reference, an entreaty to seek guidance from heaven, but when he congratulated Adam's father for advising people to rely on Jesus in their times of need, the man had smiled mysteriously, as though enjoying a private joke, and said, "Jesus has nothing to do with it." Calvin's worries about Adam's family became galvanized when Hattie Green answered a midnight siren's call and, half-naked, entered the Forbidden Forest, with Jedediah following right after her.

Why would anyone do something like that?

It was during this period that Clarissa, his cherished great niece, had approached him with the news of her love for Richard Auberon, son of the sister of Hattie Green and cousin to Adam. Clarissa desired his approval of their marriage. In a catastrophic lapse of judgment, Calvin gave into Clarissa's entreaties as she described her adoration for the big Auberon boy. He gave the union his blessing.

It wasn't until later that he realized he'd sealed himself into a familial relationship with Adam which would confound any attempts at distancing himself from what was apparently a polluted genealogical strain. Behold the twisted and convoluted vehicles by which Satan doth produce his handiwork, he mused sadly.

Obadiah Broke had visited again. He laid out the details of his plan and asked for the reverend's help. What he was proposing was extraordinary. To take on a wealthy man like Obadiah Broke as a partner, and use all the resources he was offering, was a thing of revolution. A thing that would cause massive shock and turmoil in the community. Many would be deeply disturbed. Many would need to be made examples of, and some lives would almost certainly be lost. A horrible price. Still, what Obadiah was proposing, if successful, would result in changing Arcadia back to its purity, of fulfilling his father's dream. Together, Obadiah and Calvin could make Arcadia great again.

Calvin could hear the grind of cartwheels, as the first congregants came up the hill. He slapped at the dust on his breeches. Tentatively, he took a step across the border he'd made, then another, then crossed the clearing. He went in through the back entrance of the Meeting House, moved through the rear storage room and entered the main area of the church. He walked out onto the raised dais from which he always gave his sermons.

A few people were already seated in the rows of benches below and more were coming in through the front door. Folks were greeting each other, and some were nodding up in greeting to him.

He caught sight of Henrietta Auberon, moving down the central aisle, holding her niece's hand. Daisy Green was bobbing this way and that, and moving Henrietta's arm with her, like a puppy on a leash. Clarissa, Calvin's great niece, was behind them, clutching her baby, followed by Richard Auberon. The reverend wondered if the Auberons knew about the fight between George Broke and Adam Green. Or how much they were aware that Adam's vision in the forest had become the talk of the land. None of the Auberons showed no sign of noticing all the stares they were receiving from the other congregants.

The Auberons sat together about halfway down the rows of benches. Clarissa, with her simple blue smock and bonnet and her upturned, dignified face, was a charm to the reverend, despite her poor choice of husband. She was the granddaughter of his departed brother Nathaniel, distant in lineage, but if Calvin had a daughter of his own, he couldn't have asked for a purer one than Clarissa.

As he waited for the starting time, he continued to scan the room. There was Wandabella Shrenker and her daughter, that tall, scrawny girl with the goggling eyes whose name Calvin could never remember. He noted that her husband James was absent, as usual, as was Walter Green. It seemed, he reflected grimly, that the sex into which the Lord had planted the most power and intelligence was also the one with the most problems keeping regular church attendance.

From a drawer in the simple wooden pulpit, Calvin removed his Good Book and held it in both hands. He cleared his throat. "Good morning, everyone. I am pleased to see our meetinghouse full this morning. Events have transpired that give today's sermon special significance."

The preacher let his gaze linger for a moment on the Auberons. "There have been peculiar happenings of late which pour more dread into my old heart than it has will to bear. Indeed,"—Calvin raised his outstretched finger toward the ceiling in a display of drama—"I feel my very faith challenged. It is reminding of the story of that good man described in the book of Corinthians, called by the name of Job, who lived in the Land of Ur in a state of comfort. And it came to pass that the Lord…"

"Preacher Branch?"

The heads of two hundred startled congregants turned toward the voice.

He ignored it. "…the Lord, who was much pleased by Job, was scoffed at by Satan. The devil said, 'of course, he's upright and God-fearing, for it troubleth him not to be so.'"

"Preacher Branch!" the voice called again. Calvin experienced a shiver of dread when he realized that the voice came from none other than Daisy Green. Adam's sister. She was waving past the arms of her aunt, who was trying to subdue her.

"I'm so sorry, Reverend," Henrietta said. "The girl's high spirited."

"Auntie, I want to ask a question!"

The reverend scowled. "Yes? What is it, child?"

"Where is the Land of Ur?" Laughter rippled through the room.

"Where is the…?"

"The Land of Ur. Is it near the Plains of Gladford?"

The laughter swelled, and the look of confusion deepened on the old preacher's face.

"Where is the Land of Ur? Erm, the…the Good Book, when describing geographical locations, takes liberties in description in favor of trueness of message."

Daisy frowned. "But where is it?"

"Where is what?"

"The Land of Ur."

"There is no *actual* Land of Ur. The Good Book is using the Land of Ur as a metaphor, to relate an important lesson about life."

"But Reverend Branch," Daisy persisted, "This story's about that man Job. Wasn't he a real person?"

"Of course."

"He must've lived somewhere. Why didn't the Good Book just say where he really lived?"

"It is not ours to question the ways of the Lord, or the wisdom of the authors of the Good Book," he answered firmly. Calvin was relieved to see the girl flop back against her mother, lips clamped together in dismay.

He continued. "On the topic of Job, the noble preacher, John Owen, once noted, 'the peace some enjoy is mere stupidity.'"

"Reverend Branch!"

The reverend rubbed his temples. "Yes?"

"Where does John Owen live?"

"The Lord took our beloved John Owen home long ago."

"Where is he buried?"

"In the graveyard, of course."

"But his name ain't on any of the gravestones in the cemetery."

Calvin ran a hand over his throat, which felt tight.

"How do you know that?"

"I memorized all the names on the gravestones."

There was a collective gasp among the congregants.

Daisy said, "it weren't hard. There's not even forty gravestones back there."

Calvin felt dizzy. He'd lost all sense of the sermon.

"Never heard of no John Owen," continued Daisy. "Ain't no one anywhere even *named* Owen."

"John Owen is…passed, and we lost him before the Great Migration…"

"But you said he was buried here."

"I said he was buried in the graveyard…"

Daisy heaved an annoyed sigh. She rolled her eyes. "Maybe he's buried in the Land of Ur."

This provoked loud laughter throughout the room. Calvin had forgotten what he was talking about, didn't know how to start his sermon again. He yelled, "I am announcing a Day of Fasting and Humiliation. Commencing immediately."

A moan spread through the congregation.

"Does someone have a problem with that?" he roared. "I do not apprehend what is transpiring in the land. The signs of peril are everywhere! And now this!" He pointed his finger at Daisy Green. "Being interrupted during my sermon! A day of fasting! A day of humiliation. For all of you! Starting now!" The preacher turned and rushed off the stage. As he descended the stairs to the door, his boots caught on something and he stumbled and almost fell.

Chapter Twenty-four
Ginger and Peppermint

For Adam, his day of humiliation had started a day early. Nose drooling blood, he had snuck back into his cabin without his family knowing and feigned sleep when Henrietta came by that night with some food for dinner. When the Auberons left for church the next morning, they had not yet learned of the fight between George and Adam.

At the moment Daisy was pestering Reverend Branch, Adam was still curled up on his bed, unwilling to face the day. He gripped the edge of his blanket over his eyes, pressing out the light.

The world outside of his farm was a foul, dangerous place. He had decided to never leave again. He had a good well to provide his water and a good cow to give him milk. He had chickens for eggs. He had enough acreage to grow whatever other food he needed. He could sneak to Silverton Stream at night and catch fish. He didn't need other people.

He might be willing to have contact with his family next door, but only a very limited way, perhaps conveyed with written notes hoisted across the barrier between the two farmhouses in baskets with ropes and pullies.

Sometime around noon, Adam heard wagon wheels on the hill. His family, returning from church. Aunt Henrietta's voice boomed out. A door slammed.

Adam crept to the door. Through a crack, he spied Uncle Walter bobbling across the land between their homesteads. He was holding a food basket. Daisy was skipping along behind him.

A rap at the door. Walter called out. "Adam, my life's in danger and you need to help. If you don't take this food, your aunt'll kill me."

Adam opened the door an inch and peeked out. Walter's mouth dropped open. "What happened to your face?"

"I fell off my horse."

"Liar," muttered Daisy.

"Daisy, hush. Adam, you should put a cold fish on that nose."

"It's okay."

"You going to make me stand out here with this basket?"

Adam opened the door. Walter took a closer look at Adam's swollen face. "Your nose's as big as an apple."

Adam nodded.

"You ain't never fell off your horse before."

"He didn't fall off his horse, Uncle Walter," put in Daisy."

"Daisy, be quiet."

"She's right, Uncle. I didn't fall off my horse."

"What happened then?"

"I got hit."

"By George Broke," piped in Daisy, excited. She bounded up to Adam's side. "I heard folks talking in church. George punched him, right in the nose. But Adam didn't punch back."

"Daisy, I said be quiet. You're in enough trouble already. Adam, that nose looks broke. You should go to Doc's."

"I went to Doc's," Adam mumbled. It wasn't a lie, exactly.

"Good. What did he say?"

"He gave me medicine." Adam picked up the pouch Doc gave him, still unopened.

Walter's face soured. "If I was you, I'd throw that stuff away."

"Why?"

"It tastes real bad."

"You know this medicine?" Adam eyed the bag.

"Think so. Let me smell."

Adam opened the pouch. His uncle sniffed it and grimaced.

"Yep, that's the stuff. Doc gave me some way back, about seven years ago."

Daisy leapt up and down. "Let me smell!"

"Shut your mouth, Daisy. You are in more trouble than ten bad children together after the stunt you pulled."

"What'd she do?"

"She was interrupting the reverend in church today, asking all sorts of fool questions. You know how she gets." Walter wiggled the sack. "It was that time I broke my finger. I only tasted a dab, but it was enough to make the hair come out my head. I threw it out."

Adam sniffed the medicine. He yanked the bag high above his head when Daisy sprang up in a surprise bid to grab it.

"Do like I done," said Walter, stepping for the door. "I threw mine behind the garden fence, by my apple tree, so's the cows wouldn't eat it. Adam, this here food your Aunt made you will heal you better." Walter wiggled the basket. Daisy reached up and snatched the basket from her uncle and thrust it out to Adam.

"Eat," she ordered. "And if that stupid George Broke ever hits you again, *hit him back!*"

Adam accepted the food, but still vowed privately he would seal his life away from others from that day forward.

He broke his vow only two hours later when Virginia knocked on his door. She came with soft cloth bandages and herbal remedies and a burlap sack filled with fresh bread.

He let her in and she crossed the room and knelt and lit a fire in the fireplace and heated some water in a pan. She dipped a piece of cloth in the water. With Adam leaning back in his grandmother's rocking chair, Virginia, with the gentleness of a ladybug, swabbed the dry blood from his nostrils.

"Does that hurt?" she asked.

"No."

It hurt like the devil, but he wanted her to continue. A piece of his hair fell across his face. She pushed it back behind his head, running the tips of her fingers along the side of his face.

"That George Broke is a snake. Don't move." Virginia left him there with his nose tilted toward the ceiling. She sprinkled some of the herbs in the water and let them steep.

"Adam?"

"Mm?" Adam nasalized.

"Why did he hit you?"

Adam shook his head. "I don't know."

"Keep your head up. Look at the ceiling, not at me."

"It's got to be because of that thing I saw in the woods."

The warm smells of ginger and peppermint spread through the room. Virginia dipped a second compress in the water and spread it carefully over Adam's face. She whispered, close to his ear, "everything's going to be okay."

They hovered in midair, taking in every delicacy of each other's young faces, each fleck of color in their excited eyes, then dove headlong into a kiss.

It was long and deep. Virginia put her hands on Adam's back, the strength of his shoulders surprising to her fingertips, and pulled herself closer to him. For the first time in his life, Adam felt the soft, warm slopes of a woman's breasts pushing against him, and a second later, Virginia felt, farther below, the mystery of a form that had not been there before. Heart hammering in her chest, barely able to breath, she grasped Adam's shoulders and pushed herself away.

She was giggling, stumbling backwards, her face pink. She blew him a kiss. She got the door open and backed out of the cabin.

For a minute after she left, Adam was too stunned to move. He listened to the sounds of her mounting the wagon and bringing her horse around with growing torment. He leapt up and tripped over one of the runners on the rocking chair and fell on his face. His nose erupted with the pain of a new injury.

Chapter Twenty-five
Fuel

Over the following seven days, the atmosphere in town sizzled with the tension of a small fire struggling to explode into a conflagration. Customers at Shrenkers gabbled endlessly about the fight between Adam and George. However, what people knew about what actually happened was excruciatingly sparse. George and Adam argued in the street. George had punched Adam. Adam fell down bleeding in the dust. George walked away. Virginia Baker pursued him, demanding to know why he did it. George didn't tell her. Adam rose from the dirt, still bleeding copiously from the nose, and fled town. Beyond that, no new information had come to fill out the massive black holes in the story. The combatants themselves were cloistered in their separate farms, to the north and to the south, and weren't saying anything. Virginia Baker refused to talk about it.

It was believed that the fight was connected somehow with Reverend Branch's declaration of a Day of Fasting and Humiliation. People had of course obeyed his directive to eat nothing for 24 hours and keep completely silent, and reflect upon their original condition of depravity, and to generally wallow in self-hatred for a day and night for all the sins they had committed, and all the sins they had contemplated committing, and all the sins they would commit or would even contemplate committing in the future. A tedious way to spend a Friday. Wandabella found it impossible to keep to the fast. She snuck nibbles of her own mouse-biscuits when her daughter and husband were not looking.

Had his last sermon not been interrupted by that strange Daisy Green, Calvin Branch would have been able to more fully express his thoughts on why he was calling for the fast. Daisy Green's pelting him with foolish questions in the middle of a sermon was an incident so shocking it had nearly no historical precedent, because no one was ever to interrupt the reverend during a sermon. It just wasn't done. That the only other person in history who had interrupted the reverend was Adam and Daisy's father, that bear-witch Jedidiah Green, was a disturbing fact not lost on most Arcadians. Nor was the fact that the person George had punched was none other than Adam, another Green, the same one who had seen a monster in the Forbidden Forest.

There was obviously something wrong with the Green family. And the Auberon family.

The following Sunday, the Meeting House was filled past capacity because everyone wanted to hear from Reverend Calvin why he had called a Day of Fasting and Humiliation, or, more precisely, what he knew about the fight between George and Adam. Reverend Branch disappointed everyone when he didn't mention the fight at all. It was a rather dull sermon, focused on the spiritual value of, after harvest, drying one's beans.

After a week, and the uneventful sermon, the gossipers at Shrenkers were finding it difficult to gossip about the fight, and the incident for most was fading into history. By Monday, people were turning their attention to more routine mechanisms of life, especially the beginning of school.

The community Meeting House served as a church on Sundays and as a school during the week. The children sat on the church benches with scratchboards and lunchbuckets and Miss Dorothy taught them how to add and subtract, and to read and write. These skills were of little use to farming, and the high attendance at the school was a mark of the importance of formal education to Arcadians.

Dorothy Rivers had taken over the job of schoolteacher after the tragedy of Mary Lena and the talking mice. The former teacher, who was reduced to a gibbering wreck by the incident, was eventually forced to move to a lonely cabin high up the southeastern slopes, where the elevation was inhospitable to mice. She survived on food provided by the citizenry and delivered each week by Little Victor, who reported the crazy lady must still be alive because the food he left at the front door of her ramshackle cabin always disappeared.

Walter and Richard stopped in front of the meetinghouse. Daisy leapt from the back of the wagon. "Don't forget your lunch, Sprout," Walter said. He handed her down a pail, covered with a piece of cloth. She ran back and snatched the pail from him.

Daisy found Hildegard in the crowd of children scampering around the front of the meetinghouse. They joined a group of girls they hadn't seen since before summer. On the ground, they crouched around a book one of the girls had made between whose pages she'd dried the petals of pretty flowers.

Some boys came bounding around the building. A big farmboy, his head shaved to burn off ticks, spotted Daisy Green. He elbowed a lanky boy in overalls and said something in his ear. Grinning, they approached the girls. The one with the shaved head called out, "Hey! Ain't that Daisy Green? Hey, Daisy, how's your crazy brother?"

The bald one was Fred Fodder, one of Gus Fodder's sons, and the one in overalls was Bobby Dunkel. Bobby's father, Bile Dunkel, and Fred's father were now workers at the Broke ranch. Seven years before, they had been trappers and skinners. The boys could remember helping their fathers slice open and gut captured animals, and at their encampments helping their mothers wash and hang the pelts on tree branches.

In the nastiest tone possible, Fodder said, "Your brother talking to any more heads lately?" He made a fist and moved his thumb and forefinger so they looked like a mouth. "Adaaaam! Where are my legs? Woooooo!"

Daisy looked up from the book. Other boys were gathering.

Fodder said, "George Broke beat up your girl brother with one punch. Adam was crying before he even hit the ground. Like a *bugger boy*."

He made a fist and pretended to punch himself. He fanned the air ineffectually and fell to the ground.

Laughter erupted from the boys.

Fodder said, "you get one crazy bugger boy in a family, then's time to get out rat poison, 'cause you got a whole crazy family. That shit's in the blood."

Daisy continued to look up at the boys, her expression unreadable.

"Maybe we should call you crazy Daisy from now on." This produced an uproar of laughter from the boys. Some of them toppled over, whooping and slapping their knees.

"How 'bout some poison for you and your faggot brother, crazy Daisy?"

Daisy leaped on him so fast that Fodder fell shrieking before anyone could register what was happening. The children encircled the fighters in a writhing, squealing mass. Miss Rivers soon appeared, hollering at them to stop.

After she pulled the other children away, she found Daisy sitting on Fodder's chest, pounding his face with both fists. Tears streaked his cheeks. Blood was flowing from his nose.

Miss Rivers lifted the girl into the air, spun her around and plopped her on the ground. Daisy leapt past her and jumped on Fodder again. She opened her mouth wide and chomped on his hand. He brayed in pain and terror. It took almost a minute to disengage Daisy's mouth from his arm and another to get her to stop trying to attack him.

After determining that Freddy wasn't going to bleed to death, Dorothy got the class settled into the meetinghouse and ordered Freddy and Daisy to sit on opposite sides of the room.

After school, Dorothy called the two combatants to her desk. "Daisy, are you ready to apologize to Freddy?"

Daisy shook her head. Dorothy ordered her to stay after school. She made the girl write, "It is a sin to strike or bite people" a hundred times on the blackboard.

"Now, are you sorry for what you did?"

"No, ma'am."

"Child, why not?"

"Ain't nobody gets away with saying like he done about my family. He talks like that again, he'll get it again, like this." Daisy chomped the air.

"Daisy, you need to start acting like a lady. Women need to be gentle."

Daisy considered this. "Why?"

"Because God has bestowed upon women the qualities of gentleness and nurturing. It is unseemly for a girl to fight."

"If fighting's unseemly for a girl, what's seemly?"

Dorothy smiled. "Why, to serve men, of course. To use our gentleness to nurture men. To feed them and clothe them and maintain a healthful home for the raising of children. To make men feel strong when they serve their natural role of fighting against challenges nature offers."

Daisy frowned, pondering the words Miss Dorothy had spoken. At length, she said, "Reckon I'll act like a gentle woman," she said, "when that Fodder fuck acts like a gentle man."

Without asking permission, Daisy stomped to the door of the meetinghouse, where she collided with her mother. Tired of waiting for her daughter to come home, Henrietta had come to fetch her.

Chapter Twenty-six
Into the Hole

Joss Hanker had stewed on the matter for a time and came to the firm decision that someone needed to kick the shit out of George and Obadiah Broke. And that someone should be her.

She rose before sunrise, threw some provisions in a saddlebag, and brought out her horse. Miranda was a big-boned mare, as no-nonsense in temperament as her owner. She scraped at the ground with her hooves, eager to get going.

Joss knew in her marrow that Obadiah Broke was up to no good. That somehow he was manipulating events in Arcadia such that people he didn't like would get hurt, and money he didn't have would end up in his pocket. She didn't say this outright at the meeting for fear of embarrassing the mayor, a decent man who trusted everyone, and because she knew it would make no difference. In Joss's younger days, she'd had run-ins with people in the community, those friendly to the reverend's cobwebbed ways of thinking, and she always conducted herself following the lessons of her wise mother, Sadie Hanker. Joss could still picture her by the fireplace in her rocking chair, big-shouldered and smiling, pronouncing, "Jossie, if there's a bad apple in the barrel, don't spend a week negotiating with the other apples about whether to throw it out."

The last straw for Joss had come the previous night, when Charlie Fincher told her he couldn't do business with her anymore. Charlie was one of her oldest customers.

He'd waited till after sunset to sneak up and tap on her door. Head bent in shame, he told her he could get his nails and spurs and hoes and rakes and pitchforks and barrels from the Brokes for less than the price she sold them for, and he needed to watch his money carefully. Why, she asked him more in amazement than anger, did he need to save so much money? He shook his head miserably. "It's not to save money," he said. "I'm in debt."

"Debt?" she asked. "Who the hell you in debt to?"

"Obadiah Broke."

There'd been a fire the previous season, and Charlie'd lost his crop and his wagon. Broke had loaned him the money to get a new wagon and even sold him—on credit—the new wagon.

Damned fool! Joss slammed the saddlebags shut and tied them tight. *He shoulda come to me and I'd a built him a new wagon for free.*

All the rumors going around about Adam about the thing he'd seen in the forest, that he'd seen a ghost, that he was playing with witchcraft, that he was lying, seemed like a load of horseshit to Joss. She'd heard rumors of Obadiah's repeated failed attempts to buy Adam's farm atop Green Hill. She felt in her bones that there was a connection between the thing Adam found in the forest and Obadiah's wanting to get his land. Broke seemed to want to own everything and be willing to do anything to get it.

Joss attached the harness to her horse, snapping the metal ring shut with a chop of her fist. Had Obadiah somehow created this talking head in a box thing to scare Adam and his family off Green Hill? If so, it'd be about the stupidest goddamned plan in the world. But Obadiah Broke was so shattered and strange, who knew what was really going on in that man's head? It was plain the accident had changed him in ways deeper than turning his face into a moldy, fishy mess. Maybe his brain was moldy too.

Joss steered Miranda southwards. The road was empty and the land quiet. Sunday morning, most folks were sleeping at this hour. Maybe a hundred up for church. Joss followed Mill's Trail out of town to Phagus Fork and headed southeast.

She was happy to be confronting Obadiah, but worried about Mrs. Broke. She had no interest in making that poor woman's life more difficult.

Joss's plan was simple. Obadiah Broke was a big man, but Joss was big too, with arms made strong by decades of blacksmithing pig iron. She would grab him by the coat and slam him against the nearest wall. She would push her face close to his and tell him she knew he was behind the ghost in the woods, so if he wanted to breathe another breath, he would swear to stop trying to steal Adam's land and cease any other of the dirty tricks Joss suspected he was playing to get people in debt to him. If George was home, she would also give him a spanking for being rude to her and for punching Adam.

It took her an hour to reach the Broke Ranch. The dirt road was pitted from the early Autumn rains, and Joss kept Miranda to an easy amble to avoid injury. Nobody was out at this time of day. The only person she saw was Mr. Cobble, the kindly old shoemaker. Joss hollered a greeting as she clopped past, but the man, stooped and half deaf and blind, only squinted up at her from under his straw hat and seemed befuddled as to who she was.

Joss brought Miranda to a halt at the entrance to the ranch. A massive front gate had been added since she'd been here last, with thick bars topped with snaking iron vines. At the juncture of the gates' halves, each set of twisting metal foliage sent out black tongues to grope the air for its mate. In spite of herself, Joss had to marvel at the craftsmanship. Joss had been the town's only metalworker for many years, had learned the skill from her mother. Broke had taken it up only in the past seven years and already he could make things well out of reach of Joss's abilities.

How?

One half of the gate stood ajar.

The wide courtyard was an expanse of flat, dry earth. Fifty yards away, many buildings stood around the perimeter. As Joss's gaze fell on the largest building of all, her mouth fell open.

The Broke family house, gleaming white, had grown beyond recognition. As Joss brought her horse closer, she saw Obadiah had added four more floors and attached enormous wings on both ends with sweeping staircases that spread wing-like around the ends of the house. Each of the five floors had railings running the length of their great balconies.

Joss was filled with a surge of disgust at this big building. She rode across the clearing in the other direction. At the northern end, a cluster of clapboard sheds stood around a larger structure with a wide swinging door open on the side. Inside, lurking half-visible in the darkness, was a contraption of some kind. Joss dismounted and entered the building.

For a moment she could only make out the vague contours of the device. She blinked a few times and the thing gradually came into focus. It was the strangest contraption she'd ever seen. Propped up on a long metal frame was the skeleton of what might have been a buggy. A raised platform of sorts, covered by a metal hood with panels cut away to form rectangular apertures, was somewhat like the enclosed buggies young men courted the girls in during the spring. The resemblance ended there. This was twice as big as any buggy. Also, much odder, sticking six feet out of the place where the horses ordinarily would be harnessed, was a square, waist-high box, covered with a metal lid.

She stared at the thing, baffled. She turned back. No one in sight. Behind the family house was a narrow space. There was a small grey building back there, crouching low to the ground. Joss rode over and climbed off Miranda.

The windows of the big white house were curtained and dark. Anyone inside should have heard her ride in, but there was no sign anyone knew she was there. She continued to the grey building. It was constructed of ash-colored bricks. The sharp-cut stones were sealed with burnt lime. Joss walked around the building. After coming all the way to the front again, Joss squinted, perplexed. She walked around again. No doubt about it. There was no door.

She wiped the sweat from her forehead. The day wasn't turning out like she'd expected. She had planned to find Obadiah Broke, beat the shit out of him, and be on her way back to her pub by now, but instead here she was standing puzzled by this strange building.

So quiet. Joss glanced around uneasily. The stillness lay upon the day like scum on a bog. The wall of the forest seemed to hang over her. Not even an insect could be heard.

A sudden sound, close, made Joss jump. She looked this way and that until her gaze rested on the source of the noise. A pig had appeared from somewhere and was snuffing along the base of the building. She laughed and placed her hand on her chest. "Damn, little feller. You gave me a start. Where'd you come from?"

The pig was sniffing urgently in one spot. It looked up at Joss, then pushed its nose deep into the dirt. The pig turned to her again, pieces of muddy soil dropping from its snout. Joss was astonished to see the animal trot up to her. Something dangled from its mouth.

Joss reached down, took the thing and held it before her eyes. In her hand was a metal ring with a key attached to it. "How...?" Joss started to ask.

The pig moved off toward the trees. It looked back at Joss. She followed. The pig entered a gap. Joss took a few steps into the gloom and almost tripped over the pig. She could make out the animal standing on something half-buried in the loam. She reached down and gripped something straight and rigid and rectangular. She pulled and brought up a large object.

A ladder.

She dragged the ladder from the forest and propped it against the side of the building. Like a puppy, the pig pranced excitedly around Joss's legs. Joss climbed up to the roof and peeked over the edge. In the center of the roof was a door. Joss moved onto the surface and walked over to it. It looked like an ordinary door, set flush with the bricks, except that it was horizontal.

A latch was sunk into the edge and attached straight to the brick with bolts. The latch was held tight by the thickest lock Joss had ever seen.

She stared down at the door, thinking. This building was invisible from the front gate, in the shadows, this crazy door hidden on the roof. Why?

To keep people from seeing what's inside.

Joss inserted the key in the lock. The curved metal rod snapped open.

The door was heavy. She needed to hold the handle with both fists and strain to lift it. After she managed to flip it open, she found herself peering into a black hole. A cool exhalation of dust rose from within.

Joss went to the edge of the building, yanked the ladder up and put it into the doorway and propped it up to one side. She awkwardly got herself on the ladder and started to climb down. The ladder creaked under her weight. When she got to the floor, she peered around, squinting into the room. After a few seconds, her eyes became accustomed enough to the dimness for her to see that, except for some crates heaped in the corner half covered by a sheet, the room was empty.

Just a storage room. So why make it so hard to get in?

Something was peculiar. Behind the pile of crates, an object was inserted next to the wall, covered by a second piece of fabric.

Joss removed the front sheet. There were about fifteen empty crates piled up. She took them down, one by one, until she made it to the thing next to the wall.

She lifted up the sheet, tossed it aside.

The thing was shaped like a box. But this was like no box Joss had ever seen. The front surface possessed a sheen so fine that it caught the shaft of light from the ceiling doorway and spread it into small white splashes. Cautiously, Joss reached out and put her fingers on it. Slippery smooth, like lake ice that melts during the day then freezes in a midnight shock of cold.

Not ice. Glass. A window? Why would a window be on a box?

Joss ran her fingertips along the perimeter. The pane was set in a kind of wood that didn't feel like wood at all; it was as extraordinarily smooth as the glass, but this stuff wasn't glass. At the base, she encountered a row of pebble-sized nubs. Some of the nubs were bigger than the others. She found they could, for reasons she couldn't fathom, be pushed into the small holes from which they protruded.

What in the goddamned hell is this?

It must be the phantom box Adam encountered in the woods. But what is it? And why is it locked away in this strange building? She ran her fingers over the nubs. She pushed in the biggest one of all.

A crackle erupted from the box. She screamed and fell backwards. The glass came alive with a shower of black and white dots. Joss slapped at her sleeves, glancing wide-eyed at herself. No bees. The storm of dots fizzled away and there appeared a man's head. It grinned, eyes glinting behind grotesque black spectacles.

It spoke to her.

The man vanished. Another image came into view. A landscape, filled with hundreds of wondrous bugs, shooting over rolling hills at incredible speeds. The bugs were enormous, their smooth bodies glinting under the bright sun of a cloudless sky. Again, the image changed to show—a wagon?—in motion, with people inside, a man and a woman and two children, smiling, all dressed in similar bizarre clothing as the first grinning man—Joss was jolted to understand this queer wagon, with the green shining surface of a moss beetle, was in fact one of those insects she first saw whizzing over the landscape, but shown much closer. Another image flashed on the screen—this time it was written words.

She at first couldn't read them because they were presented in such a distorted form, flaring with colors and rimmed with fat black borders, but after a second she could read:

DRIVE YOUR DREAMS

The words vanished, and then it was rolling hills, sprouting fantastic orange-silver trees that moved up and down, making screeching sounds, like panicked pigs.

Joss jerked her head away from the box. Outside, the pig was squealing. She sprinted to the ladder. Her head burst into the sunlight and her heart froze at the sight of George Broke standing over the hole. He grinned down at her.

He was gripping an axe.

A shadow dropped. Joss's skull roared in her ears as she plummeted back into the hole.

Chapter Twenty-seven
The Vacant Chair

Hildegard Shrenker was the first to notice Joss Hankers was missing. In the afternoon, the girl went to Hankers under orders from her mother to purchase a dough barrel. She found a handful of early customers in the courtyard waiting for Joss to come out from her house to serve them, grumbling that she'd overslept. Hildegard knocked on the door, then gained entry through an open window in the back.

By afternoon, the word spread from town into the farmlands that Joss Hankers had disappeared. Search parties were formed. By twilight, nearly every able-bodied man, woman and child was criss-crossing the land. On foot and on horseback, the searchers turned the world into a hullabaloo of whoops and counter-whoops. Even Adam Green emerged from seclusion to participate.

The searchers moved on the streams and lakes first, because it was common knowledge that on Sunday mornings Joss preferred solitary fishing trips to attending church.

Hankers Barrel, normally boisterous with afternoon customers, was deserted. Mr. Cobble, the ancient shoemaker, who'd been out on one of his long walks and was ignorant of Joss's disappearance, came by to have a rum. He opened the gate and sat down at his usual table.

He waited ten minutes. He looked to the right, then to the left, squinted hard, and perceived all the tables to be empty. While he was puzzling over this, the door of Joss's house opened. Little Victor, his back turned, emerged, lugging out a big satchel. He turned around and was so startled at seeing the shoemaker that he screamed. "What are you doing here?" he demanded, his voice squeaking.

"Getting my Sunday rum."

"Hankers is closed, old man!"

"What?" The old man cupped his withered hand against his big, flabby ear.

"Didn't you hear what happened?"

"What?"

"Miss Joss got lost."

"Jocelyn? Lost?" The old man frowned.

"She went fishing somewhere and no one can find her."

The man furrowed his brow. "Lost, you say? I've known Jocelyn Hankers since she was a little girl. She'd never get lost."

Victor made himself smile. "Don't worry your-...."

The old man cried out. "Wait! I saw her today!"

"What?"

"This morning, out south. I saw Joss on her horse, heading for Broke Ranch. She even waved at me."

Victor cleared his throat. "Now, old man, you really sure you saw her?" Victor brought an imaginary bottle to his mouth. "Jug can play tricks on your eyes."

"Nothing tricks these eyes, young man. I know who I saw and it was Joss Hankers." Mr. Cobble stared at Victor, making him squirm.

"Well, Mr. Cobble, sir, you can get something to drink at the Brandywine. Phagus's serving all day, I reckon."

Victor hobbled to his cart. After heaving the satchel into the back, he swatted Ewell awake and began a slow amble up the southwards.

Perplexed, Mr. Cobble watched Little Victor disappear up the trail. He raised his gaze toward the southern mountains, where sulfur-yellow clouds were thickening around the peaks.

Chapter Twenty-eight
An Unexpected Visit

Adam was finally motivated to come out of his cabin when he heard that Joss Hankers had gone missing and everyone was out searching for her. Searching by himself, he by accident came across a small search party of Grange farmers, people he didn't know and who lived far enough from town to seemingly not have heard of him. Together, Adam and the men searched a strip of land running along Silver Stream, starting from the grangelands and finishing at the edge of the central plains. They found no sign of Joss. Night set in. Hoisting lanterns that barely illuminated the brambles scratching their faces, they continued to call out Joss's name in hoarse voices and to slap the brush growing copiously on the stream banks with their sticks. Although night in the forested areas was the time when the monster bears came out, and they fretted they might be eaten, the men still continued five more hours.

When they at last gave in, the moon was high, and the land awash in soft, cold light that seemed to Adam, in his fatigue and sadness, to be a poisonous fog. After he put the horse in the barn, he moved up the footpath to the pigpen. His only pig came snorting up. Adam scooped enough feed into the trough to satisfy her until morning. In the cabin, he splashed water on his face from the kitchen barrel.

Only one pig left to his name. When he was a child, his father kept more than twenty. That was the time when life seemed to be an unending festival of good fortune. His father's crops provided enough extra that his mother could have chosen any fabric she wanted for the clothing she sewed for them all, and any other luxury, to the extent that luxuries even existed back then. But, following Arcadian tradition, his father and mother always donated the extra they had to the community Grange and added their surplus food to the community storehouses. Those were the best years of Adam's life.

Disaster struck with the deaths of both his parents in a
single night, in a way so inexplicable that even now, seven years
on, not a day went by without Adam getting stung by the desire
to know why. Why, he thought now, poking the fire with the
iron rod and kicking up a shower of angry red stars, did she
wander off into the trees of the Forbidden Forest? Did she want
to die? He could understand why his father would jump into the
trees after her, although rescue was almost certainly impossible
in the bear-infested woods at night.

Adam had himself run down the hill from their cabin to
the trees that night after his uncle's cries awakened him, and
even had the insane thought of dashing into the forest after his
parents, but the idea paralyzed him with terror. He recalled
shivering in a shaft of viscous moonlight, his aunt bounding up
yelling, *what happened?! what happened?!* Adam stood
petrified to the spot, gaping at the black diamond in the forest
wall that swallowed his ma and pa.

It was Daisy who brought Adam back. Only three years
old, troubled at being left alone, she stood at the summit of
Green Hill, screaming at the top of her lungs, a nub of
vulnerable humanity atop what must have been to her the tallest
mountain in the world.

They ran up the hill and hugged her and tucked her into
bed. Too young to understand, she fell asleep immediately, slept
soundly through the vigil of the family, and they would find her
the next morning asleep in the crawl space under the frame of
her bed.

Over and over his uncle and aunt told Adam everything
was going to be okay, even though everyone knew nothing
would ever be okay again. Richard, then a gruff, man-sized
adolescent, stood in a corner and stared straight ahead,
uncomfortable with the tears of his father and the glazed eyes of
his mother.

Sometime in the night Adam felt his legs move underneath
him past his dozing family and his arm reach out to the rack with
the slaughter knives. With someone else's hands, he lifted the

biggest knife, twisted the blade around and pressed the point against his own chest. The room erupted into howls and his aunt and uncle stopped him.

Someone sat with him while another rode off to fetch Doc Midland, but Doc Midland couldn't come that night because he had already been fetched by young George Broke, whose father was on the edge of death thanks to an accident that day with tanning chemicals.

The deaths of their parents left Adam and Daisy with their aunt and uncle as caretakers. Henrietta and Walter prepared a room for the siblings, but Adam refused to move.

After an afternoon of argument, Walter grew exasperated and lifted the boy over his shoulder and carried him the hundred yards to the Auberon cabin. The boy lay limp over his uncle's shoulder. The moment he was put down, he sprinted back home. No matter how many times they tried to carry him, he would flee back to the cabin. They tried every tactic: temptations of food, threats of punishment, pleas to family allegiance, admonishments to stay under the same roof as his sister.

Nothing worked.

Adam rubbed his hands and held them open in front of the dwindling fire. He turned on his haunches.

This cabin. Home.

Seven years ago, he couldn't bring himself to leave Home, and he wouldn't let his uncle and aunt help him tend the Home farm either. Henrietta and Walter at last let him live by himself despite his young age, and because of that, he let them remain his family. He nonetheless, for a long time, could barely force himself to leave his cabin. He sometimes tended to farm chores late at night, after Walter and Henrietta were asleep, so as to avoid human contact. Over the years, he gradually came out of his shell, went to work at the grange, so that, before he found the head in the box, he behaved almost like a normal person.

Now he could barely bring himself to leave the cabin again. Were it not for his respect and love for Joss Hankers, he never would have joined the search for her today.

Adam added another log to the fire. He could feel it. It was in the air, a slightly dangerous sensation, a bite. The first big snow was coming soon. Within a week, he'd need to keep the fire going day and night.

A loud rap at the door made him jump. He crept over and said, "who's there?"

He felt a chill scuttle through him when he heard a familiar voice. "It's George."

"What do you want?"

"Adam, please. Let me in."

Adam yanked the door open, ready to start yelling, but was struck dumb by the condition of his old friend.

Something was wrong with George Broke. His face was slick with sweat. His red-rimmed eyes were frightened. The knobs of his cheekbones stood out against skin that was so pale it was going blue.

"I need to talk to you."

Adam reluctantly stood aside. George stepped in and moved to the center of the room.

"What do you want, George?"

"You need to listen to me."

"Reckon it's what I'm doing."

"Big things, Adam."

"Big things?"

"Big things are going to happen. Big changes." George spread the fingers of his right hand, stared at his palm, wiped it across his moist cheek.

"Why did you hit me?" Adam's voice was quaking.

George blinked. "Hit you?"

"You hit me, remember? In town. George, are you okay?"

"Why?"

"You don't look right."

"What do you mean?"

"You're all sweaty. And your skin looks…not right."

George touched his cheek again and gawked at the moisture on his palm.

George's skin, Adam now noticed, was not only a deathly shade of blue, but was etched with a faint maze of worming blue-green lines.

"You don't remember hitting me?"

George said, "oh, that." He waved his hand as though waving away a fly.

"Forget about that, Adam. We got more important things to deal with."

"Like what?"

"I came to warn you. You've got to sell your farm."

"What?"

"Sell your farm, now. You don't need to sell it to my father. You can sell it to me. But do it. Before it's too late."

Adam yanked the door open. "Leave," he said.

George held out his hand, pleading. "I'll pay you double what my father was offering, out of my own pocket."

"George, what the hell is going on?"

"I can't tell you."

"Then leave."

"You won't sell?"

"Of course not. This is my home. Get out!"

George pulled a flask from the loop in his belt, removed the cork. He took a long snort.

Before Adam's eyes, George changed. The color returned to his face. His skin became less gaunt. Adam thought he saw the sunken eyes actually surge forward in their sockets with renewed life. The haunted desperation in them vanished and was replaced by the cruel, panther gaze he'd seen the day George attacked him.

"What is that stuff?"

"Want a snort? Puts hair on your chest." George jiggled the bottle in Adam's direction.

A foul odor filled the air, and Adam realized it was the liquid George was drinking. "Jesus, what is that?"

"You really like her ass, don't you?"

"What?"

"Virginia's ass, I mean." George ran his tongue noisily over his lips.

"Get out, *now*."

George replaced the flask in his belt and walked to the door. He faced Adam. He lifted his hand and Adam flinched. George pressed his palm against the door and leaned against it, staring deep into Adam's eyes. He smirked. "I gave you a chance and you turned it down. You fool. You earned what's coming."

George Broke turned and disappeared into the night.

Chapter Twenty-nine
Over the Hills

Two weeks later, the children were playing in the meetinghouse yard. Miss Rivers called a stop to the recess games of hoops and leap-frog and "Top the Barrel" and corralled her pupils into the schoolroom. She cast a worried glance at the black clouds swelling on the northern horizon.

Each child had a wooden tablet and a piece of chalk on his or her desk and an assignment to finish for the day. The teacher sat at her desk in front of a blackboard and waited for questions.

It wasn't long before the study-time dampened Daisy Green's spirit and her attention wandered from the too-easy spelling assignment. She gazed around the room, aching for a distraction.

Her eyes alighted on a boy a few rows in front. She took a sheet of parchment from her satchel, spread it quietly beside her tablet, and picked up her stick of charcoal. She sketched a figure, a semblance of the boy with splotches of dark matter on its shaved head that corresponded to the spattering of moles on the real boy's skin. Underneath her drawing, she wrote, *Freddy Fodder is a shit-head.*

Daisy placed the note on the desk next to her.

Hildegard read it and gasped. She threw her palm over her mouth and began making muffled, choking sounds as she fought to keep from exploding into laughter.

"What is the problem, Hildegard Shrenker?"

Hildegard snapped upright. "Nothing, Miss Rivers."

"Daisy Green?"

Daisy smiled innocently. "Nothing, Miss Rivers."

"Please study quietly."

"Yes, ma'am," the girls said in unison.

They sank once again into the wasteland of studies. Daisy felt she would go mad with boredom. She gazed out the side window. Across the big clearing, she could see Reverend Branch's cabin. To the left of the small building, on the edge of the cemetery, were three men. They were dressed in formal black suits. The tall, bony one facing the Meeting House was obviously Reverend Branch, but Daisy couldn't make out who the other two were. One was crouching, propping up a new gravestone.

"Daisy Green," intruded the angry voice of Miss Rivers. "What are you looking at?"

"Miss Rivers, what are they doing out there?"

"Who?"

"Those men." Daisy pointed out the window.

The teacher walked to the window. The children stopped their studies.

Upon seeing the new gravestone, Miss Rivers went pale. She said, "It doesn't matter. Attend to your studies."

"It's Joss Hankers, ain't it?" said Daisy.

"I told you…" Miss Rivers's voice trailed off. She walked over to Daisy's desk and crouched so she could look level into the girl's face.

"Yes," she said in much softer voice. "They're having the funeral this afternoon."

"They didn't tell me!"

"I know, Daisy."

Daisy looked at the other students for any sign they had known. "They didn't tell any of us!"

"I know. It was thought best to have only the adults attend the funeral." Miss Rivers seemed embarrassed.

"Damnit, that ain't fair!" There was a collective gasp from the students.

"You're right, dear. It's not fair."

The entire school gazed at Miss Rivers in wonderment. Never had a student cursed in her presence before without punishment.

Tears glimmered in Daisy's eyes. "We loved her too."

Miss Rivers patted Daisy gently on the shoulder. "Nonetheless, we must mind our elders. It is important that…"

"It's not fair!" Daisy shouted. She pushed aside the teacher's hand, snatched up her lunch bucket, ran to the big oak door, flung it open, and ran out.

For several seconds, the electrified students couldn't breathe. Then, over the shouts of Miss Rivers, they ran to the door, but Daisy was already gone.

It took a full five minutes for Miss Rivers to calm the students and get them back in their seats. In the end, she herself was so shaken by the incident she let the students go home early.

They threw open the door and burst into the sunny day. The horizon was growing heavy with black-bellied clouds but the children only noticed the rest of the sky was huge and blue and the air came alive with the sound of their laughter and their footsteps galloping across the grass. Hildegard lingered behind the rest, straggling as she moved down the hill until the others were far enough ahead not to see.

When she was sure she wasn't observed, she ducked off the road and climbed down the lumpy slope. She came to an alcove, a chink in the hill, where she found Daisy waiting for her.

"That was fast."

"She let us out early. You okay, Daze?"

Daisy tossed a pebble. "Sure."

"I can't believe you walked out like that."

Daisy stood up, brushed off her pant legs. With a whoop, she sprinted off down the hill. After an instant's hesitation, Hildegard shot after her.

Daisy and Hildegard flew down the slope, tripping and plummeting to the bottom in a hilarious, rolling confusion of shrieking somersaults. They collapsed at the bottom in a tangle. Their breath came deep and fast, choked with laughter. Straw and grass stuck in their hair.

Their gasps slowed and their laughter tapered away. Daisy stretched out and placed her lips next to Hildegard's ear and screamed, "Beat you up the next hill!"

In a flash they were up again, sprinting up the next slope. Hildegard, a foot taller, began to move ahead, but slowed herself and let Daisy win.

They paused for only a few seconds and then they were racing off again down the hill and up the next one. Facing up and moving fast to each hilltop, the girls felt they might burst clean into the beckoning vastness of the sky.

They came to the top of a hill overlooking Daisy's home. The slope eased into a flatland, the top of Green Hill, with her house surrounded in the back by a wooden fence with the giant apple tree close to it, and the forty acres of farmland behind it.

"You want to go to my house?" Daisy asked. "Auntie'll give us oat cookies."

"Can we stop up here a while?" Hildegard answered.

The two lay on the grass, pointing out patterns in the clouds.

"Ain't you scared, Daisy?"

"Of what?"

"Your aunt and uncle. You're going to be in so much trouble."

"Probably, but I ain't scared."

"Why not?"

"Because I didn't do anything wrong."

They watched the clouds in silence for a minute.

"Where do people come from?" asked Daisy.

"What do you mean?"

"I mean, where do people come from?"

"They come from their mothers."

"No, I mean, okay, for example, Uncle Walt told me my great granddaddy built our house down there and before that, there were no people here at all. So what I want to know is where did my great granddaddy come from?"

"From somewhere else, I guess."

"But *where*?"

"Why don't you ask your aunt and uncle?"

"I did ask them."

"What did they say?"

"They said from somewhere else. But they didn't know where, exactly." Daisy offered Hildegard a look of profound exasperation. "That's the trouble with grown-ups. You never get good information."

Hildegard nodded. "I know. With *my* mother, you get crazy information. But at least with your aunt and uncle, you get some truth. I mean, your great grandparents *must've* come from somewhere else. That's only common sense."

Daisy groaned. "You're missing my point, Hildie."

"What's your point?"

"I want to know where *everyone* came from."

Hildegard peered off into the distance, where the northern valleys shouldered down into an infinite haze.

"I thought about this too."

"And why did they come here?"

"Uh huh. And they tell us no one can go in the Forbidden Forest, 'cause no people can live in it. It's too dangerous."

Daisy jumped up and shook her fist. "*Yes*, that's right. And if people came from somewhere else, they had to *go* through those woods. And there has to be some other place past those woods where people lived..." Daisy gestured to the south. "Maybe up in those mountains somewhere..."

"Grown-ups tell us lies."

Daisy kicked at a stone. "They *sure* do. Hey! I have an idea!"

"What?"

"Let's go to the cave."

"Daisy."

"Please!"

"I told you before, I don't want to go there. It's dangerous."

"It's not! C'mon!"

"It's scary!"

"It's not!"

"It is."

"I'll do your homework two times this week!"

Hildegard wavered. "Two times?"

"I'll even do it three, but you gotta give me a shell."

"A small one."

"Okay, but I get to choose."

The girls moved down the slope toward the northeast, where the secret trail only they knew about led in a rambling semi-circle around the back of Adam Green's house, through the grove of poplars behind his pig-pen, and down the shattered face of the mountain.

Chapter Thirty
The Cave

The mouth of the cave was a black gash in the slope, so concealed by boulders and bushes that you could stand two feet from it and not know it was there. Daisy pointed to the hole excitedly and nudged Hildegard with her elbow.

"Let's go inside."

"It's too dark," protested Hildegard. "It'll be completely black in there."

Daisy held up a finger. "Wait."

Her red hair bobbing up and down behind her, the girl stepped down a narrow space behind a huge boulder whose side had been torn away by some cataclysm. On its injured aspect, its egg-like smoothness turned jagged, with four or five huge blades that hooked toward the face of the mountain. Daisy vanished behind the lowest of the blades, nearly as large as she was. She emerged holding an oil lantern in each hand.

"I stole them from Uncle Walt's shed," she said proudly.

She put one of the lanterns on a rock. "Look what else," she said and lifted her shirt. On a thin rope around her waist was a spool of string and a leather pouch. Daisy patted the pouch. "Tinderbox and other stuff. I brought a buncha candles too."

"You *planned* all this?" When Hildegard put her hands on her bony hips, she looked a lot like her mother. "Even after I told you a hundred times I didn't even want to go into this cave?"

"Yep." Daisy stepped past Hildegard. "Lucky for *you* I talked you into it."

Daisy tied the end of the string to an elderberry bush. "See? It's safe. We hang onto the string and we can't get lost."

"Right," nodded Hildegard. "Unless a bear comes along, eats them berries, and breaks the string. Or follows the string into the cave and eats *us*."

Daisy leapt down the descending slabs of stone. She stopped outside the entrance and gestured at her friend to come down too.

Hildegard stepped gingerly over the rocks until she reached Daisy's level. The entrance was as ominous as a spider hole. "I'm not sure about this, Daisy."

"Come on. You're *such* a scared little mouse."

Daisy jumped up the outcropping on the right of the hole. She inserted her foot into the blackness, held it there for a second as though testing the temperature of water.

Then she hopped in.

She was gone.

"Daisy!" Hildegard cried.

Daisy's head popped up from the hole. She grinned diabolically.

"Hildegard Shrenker. You've been a very bad girl. The devil sent me from hell to eat you."

Hildegard snatched the lantern and jumped down the stones, screaming. As quick as a rabbit, Daisy vanished again. Hildegard climbed down into the hole. She found herself standing next to Daisy on a flat surface. They were just below the opening. The light was not strong enough to reach even a few feet from where they stood.

They lit the lanterns with the tinderbox. Daisy gave Hildegard the end of the string. Moving forward with great care, the two walked into the darkness.

They felt the cold at once. It moved over and through them like a will o' the wisp.

Daisy rubbed her arms and stamped her feet.

"Listen to that."

"We're echoing."

"Echo."

"Echo."

They called out louder, listening to their voice reverberate into the darkness. They laughed, and the laughter came back to them in ghostly shadows of itself. Hearing their own laughter caroming back made them laugh even harder and the reverberations of their words ringing from the gloom became frightening and they stopped.

Lanterns held high, the girls crept along. Red-brown shadows pranced and weaved all around them. Their feet shuffled against stone in the closed space. The way was strangely regular, not like the cave at Mill's Wash that everyone went to. This floor and these walls seemed to have been fashioned by tools instead of nature.

Daisy's foot collided with something and she cried out. Something bulged from the right side of the tunnel.

Daisy reached out her free hand and touched the thing. A layer of old grime crumbled and fell away, and she felt canvas. She pulled it aside and looked back at Hildegard. "A barrel," she said.

The barrel was about three feet tall and a foot wide. Daisy handed the lantern to her friend. With a piece of loose stone from the floor, she knocked on the top. Nothing happened. She struck it harder, and the cover split in two. She pulled the dry, splintered pieces out and squinted inside.

"Can't see."

Hildegard held both lanterns closer. The barrel was filled with black powder. Daisy took some out, sniffed at it and coughed. "Bitter." She picked up a handful and held it close to the lanterns.

"What is it?" asked Hildegard.

"Don't know," Daisy said, tossing aside the powder. "Give me my light back. I want to look in there."

Both girls leaned with the fires into the hole from which the powder-barrel was protruding. The space was filled with stacks of similar containers.

"Moses. Must be fifty barrels in there," Daisy said.

"They old seeds?"

"Nah. Hey, what are those?"

Along the right wall was a row of long sticks.

Daisy pulled one out and squinted at it.

It wasn't a normal stick. One end was made of metal, very rusty, and had an end that flared outward. The other end was wooden, a thin, irregular board.

Recognition lighted on Daisy's face. "I know what this is. It's a musket."

"A what?"

"A musket. A…a gun. Long time ago, round my great grandfather's time, I think folks used to use these for killing things."

"You mean, like an axe?"

"No, it's a kind of…" Daisy struggled for the words. "Don't know how it works, but it's something like you put fire in one part, then the fire burns and makes rocks come out the other part."

"I don't understand."

Daisy gestured at the barrels of power and the stack of muskets. "And I don't understand any of this. All I know is someone else was down in this cave before, a long time ago."

"Think they're still down here?" Hildegard whispered.

"By this old dust, they haven't been here for years."

The girls continued down the tunnel.

"Shsh!"

"What is it?" said Hildegard.

"Listen."

From someplace far off came a whispery sound, the distant notes of human voices.

Before Hildegard could flee, Daisy grabbed her arm and pulled her forward. The girls tip-toed along the path. The voices became louder.

Daisy tapped on Hildegard's arm. She moved her mouth to her ear. She pointed upwards. "It's coming from up there."

"I told you not to leave these apples next to the door!"

A burst of laughter, quickly muffled by her own hand, came from Daisy. "It's Auntie!"

"But Henrietta, I need to peel them. And that's the best place."

"And my uncle," Daisy whispered. "We're right under my house."

"Well, get those damned apples, those damned buckets, and your damn self out to the back yard and out of my way!"

"Honey, ain't no need to swear like that. It ain't polite."

"Polite! How can I be polite with all that's happening? And now we got to go to this funeral? The world's falling down around our heads, and you want me to be polite?"

"Well, I know things ain't so good now. But you'll see. They'll get better."

"Things'll get better? Is that all you can think to say? What the hell kind of goddamn mouse of a man did I marry, anyway?"

Something big and hard slammed against something else.

"Now, get on out to the back yard. Or I'll start breaking them apples over your dumb head!"

A door slammed. The echo of shoes stomping on wood clattered down to the girls.

Daisy reached up. There was a hole there. When they held the lanterns up, the girls couldn't see any more than some shattered edges of rock reaching across.

Henrietta said, "Your aunt is scary when she gets mad."

Daisy yawned. "I'm used to it." The girls continued farther into the cave. "I'm so sad about Joss," said Hildegard.

"Me too. She used to give me pieces of pie."

"She and Mama didn't get on. Mama said no one would marry that woman in a million years."

Daisy laughed. "Bet she never said that to Joss's face. Uncle Walt said she was the toughest worker in the world."

She heard Joss Hankers would get up at four every morning, ride off to her wood pits to make charcoal, go another couple miles to the hills to dig up ore, haul the charcoal and the rocks back and use her ovens to burn off the iron, then finish hammering it out by sunup. Then she'd get ready to open her pub.

"I wonder why she worked so hard."

"Pa says it wasn't work to her, it was life."

"It's sad we can't go to the funeral."

Daisy scraped her nails against the tunnel wall. "Who wants to be with all those stupid grown-ups anyway? Hey, what's this?"

On the left side, the wall was interrupted by a jagged hole. It was a vertical crack whose separated halves protruded several feet into the tunnel. Daisy held up the lantern and put her face in the crack.

"Hildie, you feel that?"

"What?"

"A breeze. Hey, let's go inside."

Hildegard backed away. "I need to get back."

"Or your mommy will be mad?"

"Yes. It's probably getting dark."

"Dark? It's middle afternoon. C'mon, Hildie, please? We'll go in, look around a little, then come out. I promise."

Hildegard wavered. "Promise?"

Holding the lantern aloft with one hand and propping herself up with the other, Daisy crawled into the hole. An orange glow filled the orifice, overflowing into the tunnel. She called out to Hildegard, "It's okay. But watch your head."

They were in a chamber with close-set walls that melted into blackness a few feet ahead. Their lanterns cast a swarm of flittering, seesawing shadows.

Daisy took a few steps forward. "Hear that?"

"What?"

"Water."

"Where?"

Daisy slapped at the ground. "Coming from the rocks here. It's *warm*."

Hildegard managed to crawl up beside her friend. From an invisible gap in the floor, warm water was trickling into the darkness.

"Feels good," said Hildegard. "My hands are so cold." She tapped the floor with her foot. "I can feel it through my boot. Slippery."

Hildegard lurched forward. Her lantern flew up and the girl started to slip away. Daisy leapt out to reach her and slipped too.

A yard further and the floor dropped and the girls with it. All at once they were plunging into the Earth, twisting and turning on the wet, smooth tube of stone, their lanterns clanking amidst their screams, and then the shaft broke away and they dropped even faster, tumbling, airborne. With two horrible, whacking thuds, they hit ground.

For a long time, they lay in a stupor, gasping.

Daisy was the first to find her voice.

"You okay?"

"My lantern!" screamed Hildegard.

Daisy's lantern, miraculously, had survived. She'd hugged it to her chest. She was still clinging to it.

Its light illuminated almost nothing. They were in a hole of absolute black, the world before Creation. Their breaths reverberated on invisible walls, and under their aching bodies was sand or soil whose softness prevented them from being seriously injured when they landed.

Daisy crawled over to her friend, bringing light. "You okay?"

Hildegard started to cry. Daisy patted her on the shoulder. Painfully, they rose to their feet.

Daisy picked up some dirt and threw it. It made a vague hissing as it disintegrated in midair without hitting anything. She tried it again in different directions, with the same result.

"Hello!" Daisy yelled. Hildegard screeched at the cataclysm of echoes that rained down on them from every direction. She hit Daisy with both of her hands.

"Don't *do* that!"

The girls took a few hesitant steps together. On the third step, they squealed and leapt back.

"Water!"

"*Cold* water!"

Daisy bent low with the lantern. At their feet was black liquid.

"Stinks."

She picked up a rock and tossed it several feet into the gloom. A splash came back. It sounded deep. Hildegard squinted. "I think it's moving."

"A stream, maybe. Ain't moving fast. Could even be a lake." Daisy found a second rock. She threw it hard. A good distance away, a splash echoed. "Pretty far across."

The friends stood silent in the dark.

"Oh, Daisy, we got to get out of here."

"We will."

Hildegard's voice was cracking. "It's been an hour. Ma's going to be so mad at me."

The smaller girl trotted off with the lantern, toward the wall. "Bet we could climb up."

Hildegard scurried after the light. "Daisy, I'm scared."

"Don't worry so much."

The wall stood nearly perpendicular to the ground. At the point where they'd fallen in, a feeble stream of water, steady and warm, was trickling down. Daisy rubbed her hand against the slick, muddy face. "Can't climb here." She groped along to the left. Although the water stopped flowing there, everywhere she touched, the moist surface crumbled apart.

Daisy took a deep breath. "Maybe the other side." Hildegard trailing her, Daisy moved past the place they fell. Their feet sloshed through a puddle. About fifteen feet on the other side, the wall surface became dry.

"Solid stone here." She stretched her fingers above and felt as high as she could.

"There's chinks in the rocks. I think we can climb it, Hildie."

"It's too steep."

"I don't think so."

"And even if you get up the wall, you still got to go all the way back up that tunnel we fell down. We *slid* down that."

"Hildie, we got to try."

"There's no way!"

"Want to swim in that river instead?"

"I can't!"

Daisy grabbed Hildegard's arm. She hissed, "stop saying you can't. Don't think. Just climb."

Daisy went to the wall, found a low foothold and a crack in the rock to slip her hand into, and pulled herself up. She groped along the space above with her other hand, found another chink, much wider this time, and put her left hand in it and held tight. She tapped the toe of her left foot experimentally in the darkness, and found a bump jutting from the surface. It was irregular, but it could hold her weight. She pulled herself up a bit more. She repeated the operation a few times. "You okay?" Hildegard squeaked.

"Hildie, it's not so hard. Really."

Hildegard hesitated. "What about the lantern?"

"We need to leave it."

"But we won't be able to see," she responded, her voice quaking. "Your aunt and uncle will be upset to lose it."

Daisy suddenly screamed, "They'll be a damn sight more upset if we die down here."

Hildegard opened her mouth to say something but stopped. She put the lantern on the ground. She rubbed both hands against her face and held them, palm to palm, in front of her. The girl moved to the wall and began to climb.

Daisy continued to inch up. Her foot slipped out of the precarious notch she'd placed it in. She cried out. "What's wrong?" Hildegard called from below.

Daisy tapped frantically with her toe for another spot, her balance teetering. Her foot found another hole. She pressed herself flat against the hard, cool surface, the dry, earthy smell of dust and cold stone in her nostrils. Hildegard called up, panicky.

"Daisy?"

Daisy cleared her throat. "I'm okay."

Moving sideways was not hard. There were plenty of gaps in the rocks to carry her along, but Daisy stopped abruptly when her fingers touched liquid. It was seeping from someplace above and it made the wall slippery.

"Hildie, careful, there's water here."

Inching along with great care, Daisy moved onto a stretch of moist rocks. Her face was pressed against the stone and the liquid was trickling across her face. It smelled terrible.

Daisy stretched out with her left foot and found only one stone protruding far enough. She took a deep breath and pulled herself to it, then quickly found another handhold and stabilized herself. The water was flowing strongly enough now that it could be heard, small dribbling splashes against the ancient stone. She tapped some more, with her hand, then her foot.

Then she was stuck.

Ahead, the wall turned steep, too steep to pass. She found herself squat against the moist, cold surface with nowhere to go. She slapped out with one hand in the dark. Nothing.

She tried again, as far as she could reach. Her fingertips grazed something big and hard. Again. A rock, definitely, sticking out far. She couldn't get to it from here, but if she could move only a few inches more to the left, maybe she could grab onto it. Panting with fright, she crept along the wall, her body flattened like a tree-frog's, until she could get her hand to touch the top of the rock. It was cold and smooth but not wet. If she could use it to swing over to the other side, she had to be right at the hole where they'd fallen into the cavern.

Daisy counted silently to ten. With all her might, she slapped her left hand against the rock, braced her fingers against the top of it and pulled herself sideways, slashing the air then with her right hand and slapping it too on top of the rock. For a second she was there, in mid-air, both hands secure on the thick dry stone, her feet dangling.

The rock sagged. A belch of water exploded from behind, blowing the rock clean into the air and tossing Daisy with it. The water blasted out from the cave wall in a horizontal geyser.

Hildegard was instantly covered with water that loosened her grip and she was falling too, back to the muddy floor.

Daisy crawled painfully to her friend. She found her slick and muddy body by touch. "Hildie, are you hurt?" Hildegard found enough of her voice to say, "Don't think so."

The wall was now soaked, muddy, slippery. Impossible to climb. The truth started to creep up on the girls in waves of awful and increasing clarity. Reality descended on them with all its weight: they were stuck deep in the cave, far from any other people, and they had no way out.

Daisy didn't try to stop Hildegard's screams. She was screaming too.

Chapter Thirty-one
Cold Clots in the Sky

Joss Hankers was dead.

It was the only conclusion the weary search parties could come to. They had pressed on, checking the same places—the lake and riversides, the dry cornfields and leafless apple orchards—more times than was needed to understand Joss Hankers wasn't in them.

If she wasn't in them, she wasn't anywhere, at least anywhere visible. The conclusion that she was the victim of a terrible accident was impossible to avoid.

They were saying a bear got her. Two of the five fishing lakes had shores flush with the Brown Forest, and bears were known to criss-cross the Silver Stream during this season, hungry before winter set in. The weather was becoming colder. In the afternoons, the dull silver of the sky darkened with clots of clouds that were the seasonal harbingers of blizzards. It was the time of year when the risk of contact with the Monster Bears was the highest.

On the second Wednesday, after the children were let out of school, a somber crowd gathered at the meetinghouse. Hundreds of farmers, merchants, artisans and even some skinners, traveled from every corner of the land for the funeral of Joss Hankers.

The ceremony didn't begin until the children were out of sight. Reverend Branch had announced that it would be indelicate for children to attend the service. Parents were advised to make arrangements for their kids to be elsewhere. Mothers with small children were encouraged to stay at home and care for them.

Funerals were rare in Arcadia, and each pulled from the community a tremendous outpouring of grief. People were especially stricken by the death of Joss. Even those put off by her outspoken opinions and her unconventional version of female-hood knew her to be as fine a human being as God ever put on Earth. Few had not at some time enjoyed a glass of comfort at her pub and been soothed by her hearty laugh.

Skilled masons had donated a simple stone, her name painted on it with the juice of pomegranates. Reverend Branch stood next to the stone now, a copy of the Good Book in his hand, glancing uncertainly at the dark grey sky, which was surging at the edges with dangerous-looking clouds. Every minute or so, a freezing wind would lash the mourners. A few snowflakes flailed in the agitated air.

In the front, Virginia stood beside her father Hugh Baker and the three members of the Broke family. People snuck looks at the frail, sallow Mrs. Broke, who almost never was seen in public. Next to them was an uneven row of old farmers, Joss's regulars from the Barrel.

At the end of the row, his head bent toward the ground, was Adam Green. He stood next to his aunt, uncle and cousin. He seemed entirely wrapped up in the gravestone and the few yards separating him from it.

Reverend Branch beseeched the Lord to forgive Joss her neglect of churchly obligations while she lived, and to forgive all of them gathered their many sins, and the original depravity that infected their souls like mold growing on rotted vegetation, for which the Lord was now punishing them.

A bone-biting gust slashed the group. With one hand, Virginia gripped the side of her smock. With the other, she held her father close, as though to keep him from blowing away.

The reverend began expounding on the foulness of each of a litany of their wrongdoings, but was interrupted by another blast of frigid wind, which a moment later exploded in a biblical onslaught of snow that chased everyone away.

The first blizzard of winter had come.

Chapter Thirty-two
Obadiah the Matchmaker

Virginia and Hugh fled the funeral storm with the rest, leaping into their wagon and riding as fast as they could back to town. As they were going inside the bakery, Virginia was startled to see Obadiah and George Broke ride up behind them in their wagon. Snow whizzing around him, Obadiah climbed down and approached.

Hugh grinned. "Mr. Broke, I was hoping you'd still come. You'll be off home then, George? You'd better hurry, before it gets dangerous."

Virginia stared as Obadiah followed her father through the front door of the bakery. George sat on the wagon seat. He was gazing intensely at her, a hungry look in his eyes. He smirked, tipped his hat, and rode off.

When she got inside, she found her father stoking the fire and getting a kettle hot for tea. Obadiah was sitting on her chair.

"Papa, is Mr. Broke staying for the night?"

"I didn't tell you, daughter? I'm sorry, love, but yes. We'll prepare a tick near the fire for him." Outside, the wind picked up, bringing a groan from the timbers. Virginia grit her teeth and tried to feel relief at the warmth of the fire. She forced herself to smile. "Happy you could visit us, Mr. Broke."

Obadiah nodded. She removed her gloves, slapped them on her breeches to get the snow off, and peeled off her coat.

Hugh called over his shoulder. "Darling, we'll have dinner here."

"Yes, Papa. I'll go down to get something ready."

Hugh tossed his blonde hair off his eyes with a jerk of his head and smiled, showing his gleaming white teeth. The most handsome man in Arcadia, and the most foolish. "No need, Virginia. I already cooked. I did it in the bread oven this morning when you were out. Surprised?"

What on Earth was going on? It wasn't at all in character for her father to cook dinner, but if he did it, it would be just like him to do something as foolish as make dinner in the bakery oven. Now she'd need to clean it thoroughly, to keep the smell out of her bread.

"Why…why did you cook, Father?"

"No special reason." Her father giggled into his hand in that way he always did when he was trying to conceal a surprise.

"Can we get on with this, Baker?" Obadiah said gruffly. The rancher's sickly flesh was made all the more slippery-looking by the melted snow. He looked like some huge fish propped up in the chair, its lipless blue-green head poking out of a black coat.

"Oh, yes, of course, Mr. Broke. Virginia, before we have dinner, why don't we sit and chat a bit?" Since Obadiah was using her chair, Hugh removed the ashtray from the squat table and patted the hard surface. "Please sit."

Virginia remained standing.

"I've got good news for you, daughter."

"What?"

"Mr. Broke and I have come to an agreement about his son George."

"An agreement?"

"A family agreement, regarding George," said Obadiah. "And you."

"George and…" Virginia's eyes grew wide. She laughed. "Oh! Ho ho!" She brought her fingers to her lips.

Hugh was beaming. "I told you she'd like the idea, Mr. Broke."

Virginia shoved her giggles away. "You mean you intend for me to…marry him?"

"Yes, daughter! George Broke is to be your husband! Isn't that wonderful?"

"No, nooooo! Ho ho ho, are you serious? Noooooo way!" Virginia cackled and stuttered. When she saw the confusion on their faces, she clarified, "I don't want to marry him, Father."

Her father's eyes filled with terror. "Virginia, be serious now. This isn't a time for one of your jokes. Why would you say such a silly thing?"

"Virginia," said Broke. His breath whistled through his damaged nostrils. "My son told me he thinks you're a fine filly."

"It's true, daughter. He's smitten beyond repair." Virginia forced her incredulous smile to disappear. "Excuse me, Mr. Broke, but I *can't* marry your son."

Obadiah Broke threw a fearsome look at Hugh, who seemed ready to keel over.

"Why?" he demanded.

"I'm very sorry, Mr. Broke, but I feel more comfortable discussing this matter alone with my father."

Broke grumbled, "I see." He stood and marched to the door and snatched his hat from the rack. Hugh pranced after him. "Mr. Broke, don't go. I'll speak to her."

Broke threw open the door. The snow was coming down steady now, diagonal white slicing the air. A blast of freezing wind raked the fringes of the rancher's coat.

Virginia jumped up. "Mr. Broke, I didn't mean for you to go out in this storm. I meant I would talk to my father tomorrow. There's no need…"

"There *is* a need, Miss Baker." He glared at Hugh.

"Mr. Broke," pleaded Hugh.

"This better be a misunderstanding, Baker. For your sake." He slammed the door and was gone.

When Hugh turned around, he was trembling.

"Why did you act that way, young lady?"

"Why did I act that way? I should ask you the same question. What on Earth do you think you are doing, arranging my marriage without saying anything to me?"

"Everyone does it that way."

"Well, I don't."

Hugh sighed. "Okay, Virginia. I understand. You're just as stubborn as your mother was. You don't like to be *told* to do something. I'm sorry I didn't consult with you before. Now.

Would you be so kind as to consider a proposal of marriage with George Broke?"

"No."

"Why?"

"I'm marrying someone else."

Hugh started coughing horribly, gripping his throat and fighting for breath, without moving his wild gaze from his daughter.

"Who?" he finally managed to ask.

Virginia folded her arms across her chest. "Adam Green."

Hugh gagged again. He collapsed into his chair, flailing dramatically.

Virginia told him about everything, his secret visits to the bakery, her secret visits to Green Hill. She kept out those details that would provoke eternal damnation in the eyes of Reverend Branch. Each word was like another punch, slap or kick to her father's body, but Virginia was unleashing a torrent under the same forces of nature that govern volcanoes.

She ended by saying, "I love him, Papa."

"Virginia, if you don't marry George, we will lose everything."

"What are you talking about?"

"You see," he said, trying pathetically to embolden himself by raising his voice, "I made an agreement with Mr. Broke that you would marry his son if he would clear the bakery of debt."

"You did *what?*"

Hugh fingered his collar. "So, it would behoove us to accept this offer and…"

"No," Virginia said. "No, no, and no!"

"But…"

"I will never marry him! I'm marrying Adam! And you can't stop me!"

She ran weeping from the room. Seated on her bed, she ignored her father's pleas to unlock the door.

She fell onto the bed and yanked the covers over her body. She listened to the roar of the wind, the attack of the snow, the shudder of the beams holding up the building, and felt the world agitated in sympathy with her abused heart.

She didn't sleep that night, kept awake as much by her troubled thoughts as by the noise of the storm. Just after sunup, she at last fell asleep, only to be jolted awake by the screams of Henrietta Auberon.

Chapter Thirty-three
Feinting

Magically, the blizzard stopped. Expecting to be imprisoned by the onslaught of grinding white powder, Arcadia instead awakened to a winter paradise. Usually the Arcadian blizzards lasted a minimum of three days. No one in memory had seen a blizzard start and stop in so few hours, but no one pondered much about what celestial forces might have brought on the meteorological miracle, so happy were they to find the snow only ankle deep, and the hills and valleys, like something out of a children's fairy story, a twinkling wonderland.

The Auberons were initially alarmed that Daisy had not yet returned home from school when the blizzard hit, but upon reflection, they thought she must have taken shelter at the home of her friend Hildegard Shrenker, who lived above the general store. While the rift between the Auberons and Shrenkers was deep, Wandabella nonetheless, however begrudgingly, had permitted Daisy to stay overnight sometimes, and had allowed Hildegard to stay overnight at the Auberons too. So they assumed that Daisy was playing with Hildegard and had gotten stuck in town by the storm and forced to spend the night at the Shrenkers. At first light, after the storm broke, Walter and Henrietta set out to town immediately to fetch their daughter.

They rolled up in front of Shrenkers, their horse huffing white vapor, their wagon wheels setting winding ruts in the fresh snow. James Shrenker stepped out on the porch. James was a meatless, forgettable man, skinny and unusually short, with barely any hair. The fearful look in his eyes never left. He was a man who spent almost all of his waking hours fishing in order to escape contact with his firebreathing wife.

"Howdy, Mr. Shrenker," called Walter.

"Howdy, Walter." James was squinting at the covered section of the wagon. "So, you brought her?"

"What?"

Wandabella stepped onto the porch. She was clutching a woolen sweater over her morning smock. She said begrudgingly, "Thank you for coming all this way."

Henrietta said, "No problem. Is she here?"

James and Wandabella exchanged looks.

"Who?" asked James.

"Why, our Daisy. She spent the night here. Didn't she?"

The stringy muscles on Wandabella's neck tightened. She looked at her husband, anxiety growing on her face.

James said, "Daisy wasn't here last night. We thought Hildegard was with you."

It was then that Henrietta Auberon started to scream.

Within minutes, the road was filled with townspeople. Before noon, word of the girls' disappearance was spreading across the land. Believing Hildegard and Daisy might have taken refuge from the storm on someone's farm, riders volunteered to visit all the farms from north to south. By afternoon, searchers were fanning out. The fresh snow was driven into mud by the hundreds of passing wagon wheels and horse's hooves.

As the sun descended, there appeared on the northern horizon the disturbing sight of more black clouds. Searchers who had been heartened that morning by the blue skies and taken the boards from their windows needed to rush home to re-secure their farms. The winds were kicking up even harder and the clouds seemed, by their inky, roiling substance and the jagged spears of lightning crawling through them, to foretell an attack far worse than the first storm.

Thirty or so of the searchers converged at Shrenkers. No trace of the girls had been found. Dorothy Rivers accompanied them and she told everyone about Daisy's outburst at the school. It was likely her disappearance and her tantrum were somehow connected. Wandabella went pale at hearing how children had seen Hildegard dawdling in the schoolyard, probably waiting to meet Daisy.

While more search parties were being assembled, the storm struck in full fury. The timbers of the store groaned under the power of the wind, and stinging jets of frigid air whistled through the boards.

The searchers, mostly the youngest, strongest men, departed, vanishing into an atmosphere so turbid with blowing snow that neither the buildings across the street nor even the front porch could be seen. While the searchers were gone, the others waited with the two anxious mothers.

Henrietta was quiet, showing her fear only by her steadfast stare. Wandabella, on the other hand, couldn't stop sobbing. It was surprising to see someone so infamously gossipy and mean-spirited collapse into such a display of maternal love, especially when many in the room had seen how cruelly she treated her daughter. Dorothy Rivers and Virginia Baker stayed close to the frightened store owner, trying to comfort her.

At last from outside came the sounds of bootsteps. Wandabella and Henrietta both leapt to the door and flung it open. In blew a barrage of snow and powerful wind that nearly knocked the women down. The exhausted searchers piled into the room. Their fingers were almost frostbitten. Hildegard's father had a savage gleam in his eyes and he was actually smiling as he related how they'd tried to search the river but failed.

"We couldn't even find it," he laughed, tears starting in his eyes.

"The storm beat us. We spent most of our time trying to find our way back here," whispered Walter.

Powerless to do anything, they settled into a terrible silence. The storm clawed at the building like some forest monster trying to rip it down.

The air was too close, too stifling, for all the humanity crammed inside, and the fire so cozy that the warmth seemed obscene. Like a chunk of hot coal stuck to the skin, the image lingered in everyone's minds: two little girls, out there somewhere. Huddled together, freezing to death.

Wandabella rocked back and forth in her chair, clinging to her daughter's favorite sock-doll.

James Shrenker lit his pipe, tamped it out. He stood. "I'm going out again. It's better to die than sit here."

Wandabella shrieked. She grabbed him by the coat, shoved her face against his chest. She cried, "I can't lose you too!"

The couple's eyes met and held for a few seconds. James sat and put his arms around his wife.

For the next three days and nights, the storm did not stop.

Chapter Thirty-four
The Searchers

On the morning of the fourth day, they awakened to a breathtaking silence. James was startled from his fitful sleep by the cease of noise. He jumped to the window.

"It's over!"

His enthusiasm didn't extend to the others. The group remained seated, too exhausted and sad to move. Even Walter and Henrietta merely blinked back at the announcement.

James exploded. "What the hell are you all just setting there for?" He grabbed Walter by the shoulders. "These are our children!"

Walter's eyes opened wide. He nodded. He took off his hat and started slapping people on the heads with it. "Get up! We got to search."

At that moment, Mayor Gladford hammered on the front door. He'd made it out of his own home in the flatlands the moment the storm stopped, digging out his barn and extricating his old two-man sleigh. He'd set out for town before the sun rose.

They found more sleighs in storage. They brought out the horses. Searchers were assigned to sleighs, and the remaining men and women donned snowshoes. The search parties set out again. Other search parties were breaking out in different places, for no one had forgotten the plight of the girls when the storm struck, and many other vigils had been held throughout the land. No one dared mention that there was no way two little girls could have survived outside for three days in such a storm.

Little Victor appeared downtown to volunteer. He offered to help search the northlands, explaining that even if they didn't find the children there, the people in that region were certainly in the most difficult straits because of the storm, and he was well-placed to deliver provisions.

Walter joined James and other townspeople to search along the riverbed. Henrietta, with Mayor Gladford, led a team heading north. On the way, they encountered another group of about two dozen searchers. The groups joined and headed toward Green Hill. It was a good place to begin. There was even a small chance Daisy had found her way home.

After breaking through a snowdrift piled up on the side of the cabin, the searchers were saddened to find only Richard, Clarissa and their baby inside. They'd waited out the storm alone and heard no news from anyone. They had not gone to Adam's, nor had Adam come to them.

"You didn't even bother to check on him?" asked Walter. Richard looked embarrassed, but Clarissa set her jaw and stared back defiantly, as if to say, "no one can make me go near that witch." Walter ordered Richard to go with him to see about Adam and to get him out to join the search for Daisy and Hildegard. Adam answered the door in his coat. His hair was tangled and dirty, and his eyes blinked in surprise at the cloudless sky. He'd moved his bed close to the fireplace and stayed in it for most of the storm, tucked under several hay ticks and nourished by Virginia's bread, a family of mice for company.

Blood drained from his face when Richard told him about the missing girls. Tears shimmered in his eyes. He frantically threw on his clothes and boots.

The rest of the search party was waiting outside, beside the poplar grove lining one side of the farm. The tall, straight trees were half-buried in cracking membranes of snow. Suddenly, the silence of the frigid air was fractured by a voice squealing from the trees.

"Come quick! Oh, God, come quick!"

The voice was Little Victor's. A crowd gathered around him and Adam and Richard pressed through from behind.

The small man was kneeling, his face in his hands. People in front of Adam and Richard were letting out strangled gasps upon seeing what Victor had found.

The cousins saw it too. Adam nearly fell backwards. A moan came from his mouth. Richard's eyes grew wide, then narrowed with rage.

It was the most horrible of sights. It was the footprint of
the devil, right in front of their eyes.

Victor held the little pink smock aloft. "Look!" he
screamed. He was pointing at the jagged rip all across the lower
section of the dress, the gash up the side, the copious splashes of
livid, frozen blood.

"Lord God," whispered Walter. "It's Daisy's smock."

Next to the pink dress was a larger green one, which
someone recognized as belonging to Hildegard. It was sliced up
the side, a blood-splashed slit sloping sideways, so the entire
front of the dress was opened wide.

Someone collapsed into the snow and vomited. Grown
men fell to their knees and wept. Adam stumbled away from the
crowd. Without thinking, he weaved across the clearing toward
his cabin. He fell against the door and into his front room. He
kicked the door shut and dropped to the floor. He shrieked into
the crook of his arm, *Daisy!*

Outside, Henrietta appeared, demanding to know what
was going on.

When she saw the savaged pink clothing of her sister's
child, the girl she'd raised as her own, the sound that erupted
from her lips was not human. It was the primal discharge of a
violated beast.

"Another one!" People were pointing toward a farmer
who'd been searching beside Adam Green's cabin. In the narrow
space under Adam's side window the farmer spied a piece of
fabric sticking from the snow. It was actually coming from
beneath the frozen ground itself, because the snow there was
shallow. The man started shouting while he kicked at the frozen
soil until the garment came clean. It was a piece of clothing
everyone recognized, for no one but Joss Hankers wore overalls
with a barrel painted on it.

With the fresh discovery, the spell of grief crushing the
crowd began to dissipate and a new one to creep in. First one
face, then another, then dozens, turned to the farmhouse where
the owner of this patch of bloody land lived.

The people moved toward the cabin of Adam Green.

Chapter Thirty-five
Flailing

Some men pulled knives and hatchets and machetes from their belts. Others tore branches from trees and wielded them menacingly. They all started to move toward the front door of the cabin. Mayor Gladford charged up and cut them off. He waved his arms over his head.

"Wait!"

The men stopped.

"Think about what you're doing! This is not God's way!"

A bulky farmer in front with a long red beard lifted a long machete and shook it at the house. "That monster don't deserve to live!"

"But we don't even know all the facts," shouted Gladford.

Another farmer yelled. "What more facts you need, Mayor. More ripped dresses?"

"More blood?" shouted another.

The mayor's voice was quavering. "Let's talk about this."

"No more talk! Get out of the way, Mayor. We don't want to hurt you."

"The bodies might be in his cabin!" someone called out.

This set off a new roar, and the whole mass of them surged forward. Someone shouted, "Kill Adam Green!"

Through a chink in the wall, Adam, his heart beating wildly, watched the mob moving in. Out of nowhere, a crazy thought struck him, of Daisy in this room, looking at him, saying, "if George Broke ever hits you again, *hit him back!*"

He took a deep breath, placed his hand on the door handle and prepared to open it.

He froze. Through the chink he could see at least two dozen men, brandishing sticks and knives.

How could he fight them?

The crowd had now reached the mayor, their shouts drowning out his pleas. In another moment, they would have tossed him aside, broken down the door and torn Adam limb from limb but suddenly Henrietta leapt up and blocked their path.

"Don't you take another fucking step." She said it in the voice of an animal, crouched low, eyes blazing wildly, every muscle knotted to spring at an enemy threatening her young.

"No one's hurting that boy, not while I'm breathing."

A man in front said, "but Henrietta, look at those dresses. He killed those girls. Daisy's your family."

Henrietta's face twitched. Tears flashed in her eyes. Brutally, she drew her arm across her face to rub them away. "Adam would never hurt anybody."

All at once she was leaping at the crowd, striking out at them with her fists and feet. "Get out! Get out!" And the dozens of men were scattering, fleeing her slashing arms, moving to the other side of the clearing.

Henrietta slunk back, casting glances over her shoulder in case they tried to approach again, and paced in front of the door of Adam's cabin.

Mayor Gladford approached the mob. "Listen," he entreated, "we will have an emergency public meeting tomorrow morning to share our ideas. Then, you can say your piece and we can work together to decide what's going on here." The men, wide-eyed and goggling still at Henrietta as she strode cat-like back and forth in the front of the cabin, glaring at them, nodded. They backed away and mounted their steeds and wagons. As William watched them disappear down the hill, he felt his confidence return and thought he'd regained his authority as mayor of Arcadia.

He was wrong. It wasn't the mayor's authority that moved the mob to retreat. It was the savagery of Henrietta's face. With saliva frothing from her lips, and her eyes wide and red, Henrietta Auberon herself seemed possessed by the devil.

Chapter Thirty-six
Hiding in the Dead Corn

Henrietta kicked Adam's door open. Adam leaped out of the way barely in time to avoid getting his face smashed. "Where are you?" she screamed. Adam stumbled backwards, his hands held up defensively. Henrietta stomped up to Adam with her fists raised. She glanced to the right and the left. "Where are you, you bastard?" she shouted.

"I'm right here," squeaked Adam.

Henrietta ignored him. She ran from the house, shoving the mayor out of her way.

The mayor and Adam gave each other bewildered looks. From behind the cabin, they heard her shout,

"There you are!"

They ran after her, and found the wiry woman bounding toward the corn field, where, crouching among the broken corn stalks, was Richard.

Henrietta jumped on her son. "You son of a bitch!" she shrieked. She pummeled him with both fists.

"Don't you ever leave a member of your family in danger again!" She slapped her son one more time for good measure and wiped her hands on her smock.

She faced her nephew. "Adam, you need to go away."

"Go away...? But Aunt, you don't think I really killed..."

"Of course not." Henrietta's slammed the words down so hard, Adam cringed. "But *they* think you did. We're living in a time of fools. Get your things together."

"But, Auntie."

"Now."

"But where can I go?"

"The Grey Mountains. Get yourself into the valleys, where it ain't so cold. Make fires. Trap and fish for food. Don't you come back until I come out and tell you it's safe to. And if I don't, never come back."

She started to walk away.

"Aunt!" he protested.

She turned around. "Adam, it's time for you to become what your Uncle Walter, and this one"—she jabbed her finger disgustedly at Richard—"obviously never became." She rubbed her hands together. "A *man*."

Richard muttered something.

"What did you say to me?"

"Said *you* ain't no man, Ma."

"That's how's I see it better than you."

"He ain't going to be a man by running away."

"He ain't going to be a man by getting himself killed, Richard. He's going to become a man by taking care of himself, and counting on no one else to do it for him."

She stomped away to the Auberon cabin, deaf to the cries of her sister's son and those of her own.

Chapter Thirty-seven
The Smoking Gun

The news of the bloody dresses found on Adam Green's land soared through the land like a comet across the heavens. Sledders raced over perilous drifts to disseminate every grisly detail of the murders. Embedded in the news was the story of the madwoman Henrietta, who'd transformed herself before their very eyes into a feline demon.

Early the next morning, the roads filled with sleds and wagons and horses. No one wanted to be absent from the special public meeting the mayor called to discuss the matter.

Although the storm had passed, school continued to be cancelled. Adults ordered their children to stay indoors. Lest any adventurous child be emboldened to naughtiness, parents had at bedtime broken out the old artillery and recited some of the most frightening cautionary fairy tales they could dredge up from their own childhoods. The worst of the stories of course were the ones involving Merlin, the demon of the pecan grove, who inflicted all manner of torments upon wee children before charring them on an open fire and chewing them to death. The stories had not been told for a long time and were only half-remembered, but the point was still made. No child dared to venture outside that day, terrified by the assorted ghouls and goblins and witches, and worst of all, Merlin, who would snatch them away.

New parties of people continued to arrive at the church throughout the morning.

Wandabella and James Shrenker entered the Meeting House, feeble with shock, and found a bench. The people on either side of the aisle offered consolations as they passed.

Behind them came Hugh and Virginia Baker. Garish dark bags had accumulated under Hugh's eyes. Virginia was glancing around angrily.

Obadiah and George Broke came accompanied by a party of around twenty men who stood together in a row at the back of the church. The Brokes surprised everyone by bringing a barrel of apple cider, as well as a box of cups, as refreshments. Obadiah Broke nodded to the mayor, who was standing behind the reverend's scratched old podium on the raised platform in front. On the platform next to the mayor was Reverend Branch, seated on a chair to William's right.

The mayor seemed a decade older than a week before. He'd been sitting up all night with his wife. The news of the murders had traumatized Annie. When he'd left the house at sunrise to go to the meeting, she was unable to rise from the bed, where she was still sobbing into her pillow.

When Walter and Henrietta entered the church, all conversations stopped.

It had been a difficult evening at the Auberons. Walter had learned the news of the murders on the road, when his search party ran into others leaving from the scene. He'd galloped home, unable to believe what had happened until he heard it from his wife. Henrietta related the events, from the discovery of the dresses to her ordering Adam to escape to the Grey Mountains. Walter made for the door to go to Adam's and talk to him, but Henrietta cut him off.

"He's already gone."

Richard refused to speak to his parents about fleeing from the mob, refused dinner, refused to interact with anyone. It wasn't until they'd collapsed into bed that Walter and Henrietta allowed themselves to hold each other and cry for the loss of Daisy. In the abysmal quiet, they could hear Richard and Clarissa whispering sharply to each other in their bedroom but couldn't make out what they said.

No one slept.

In the morning, Walter and Henrietta broke out their sled and headed for the meeting. Clarissa and Richard stayed behind with their baby.

The iron woodstove was flaming bright and the stovepipe was pluming dark brown smoke into the mountain air, but in the Meeting House, the heat, as though suppressed by some unseen, antagonistic energy, didn't seem to permeate through the room, and the shivering congregants breathed out thick clouds of white mist. As Walter and Henrietta entered the church, the atmosphere turned even more frigid. The Auberons looked every bit as dazed and melancholy as the Shrenkers, but no one offered condolences.

When the mayor finally called the meeting to order, the church was overflowing. There were people outside, peering in through the frosty windows.

"Well, everyone, by now, you all heard about what happened. This is a very sad day for all of us, and I know there is a lot of emotional talk about Adam Green, but the most important thing is to not to jump to conclusions."

James Shrenker shouted, "Jump to conclusions? That monster killed our daughter!"

Henrietta began to shout back at James, but her words were swallowed up by a general uproar of voices. Mayor Gladford banged his hand on the podium and shouted for order. The crowd grew quiet.

William said. "Listen, I know that emotions are high right now, but we have to be rational. Shouting will do us no good. James and Wandabella, Henrietta and Walter, I'm sure your losses, the losses of *all* of you, are felt in the hearts of everyone here. We may not be perfect, but Arcadians are the Lord's people, decent, peaceful, clear-thinking people, but we're all right now as torn up as those dresses we saw yesterday. I thought long and dispassionately on this, and I think I have solved the mystery of what happened. Bears got them girls."

A roar of disbelief moved rose among the people.

"Bears?" sneered James.

The mayor waved his hands in the air to bring order. "Now, now, hear me out. Think about it. Think on how the dresses were ripped. Just the way a bear rips with its claws. I mean, let's take a look at them together. Where are those dresses, anyway?"

"I got'em, William," called Obadiah Broke. The fish-faced rancher stood amongst his men at the back of the church, next to his son George, a thumb inserted casually into his belt.

As if on cue, George Broke held out an open box, from which Obadiah removed a blood-covered gown. He held it aloft. Groans and cries erupted throughout the room. Wandabella collapsed sobbing into the arms of her husband.

Obadiah wiggled two fingers along the long, clean slice. "Mayor, you saying a bear done this?"

The mayor moved down the aisle to look at the gown. The dress was cut with precision, from the neckline to the hem. Obadiah chuckled. "Musta been a bear with shears!"

Gladford seemed at a loss for words. He coughed. "What's the matter, Mayor? Cat got your tongue? Boys, let's get some apple cider for Willie here."

"It's just that…" started the mayor. He started coughing harder. One of Broke's men came with a cup and handed it to the old man. The mayor drank. "Thank you. I think a bear might have indeed, *hack, hack,* sliced up a dress like that, maybe with one claw sticking out and using a long, quick blow?" Obadiah gave the mayor a look of pity.

"Come now, Obadiah. A bear attack is far more likely than the superstitious belief that Adam Green had anything to do with it."

Broke answered, "I got another way of looking at this. What do you say we put out both our solutions to this mystery before all these fine people and see which one they think is the most *rational?*"

"Obadiah, I don't think…"

"Everyone! It was my son George here who thought this out, so I want him to speak about it." Obadiah rubbed his son's hair. "Fine head on his shoulders, this one."

George cleared his throat. He removed a flask from a pouch on his belt and took a gulp of whatever liquid was inside. He gazed from one end of the room to the other, taking in all the people. He said, a little shyly, "I've known Adam Green all my life. And I think he killed those girls."

Walter and Henriettta Auberon leapt from their seats and tried to rush up the aisle to get at George. Several of Broke's large ranchhands stepped in front of them.

Walter Auberon turned around and entreated to the mayor, "William, can't you stop them?"

The mayor blinked and yawned and seemed confused about where he was. "Erm, Walter, reckon we ought to hear'em out. The most rational ideas always come out on top."

George smacked his lips. "Friends, the idea that Adam Green would do such a thing is so horrible that it's understandable that some of us here, our good mayor Gladford included, has a hard time believing it. I know how he feels. I stayed up all night, thinking, how could my old friend Adam do these things? If I can't think of a good explanation, I'm going to come here this morning and defend him! I'll stand right beside Mayor Gladford, and defend this man because he must be innocent! But then one of our workers brought me something. He was at Adam's farm, fixing his wagon. He went inside to have a drink of water and found this thing by accident. When I looked closely at this object, the truth hit me with the force of something falling from heaven and striking me down."

George moved through the audience and climbed up onto the stage. "Mayor, I hope you don't mind if I speak from here, because I think some folks in back can't hear me."

Before William could muster an answer, George called out to one of the Broke workers. A gargantuan man with moles splattered on his shaved head approached and handed George a box. George lifted the cover and pulled out a bound sheaf of parchment. It was a diary, the kind familiar to everyone, bound by Mrs. Thimble, the old tailoress. To everyone's surprise, George called on Henrietta.

"Henrietta Auberon, could you come up here?"

"Huh? Why?"

"Won't take but a moment."

Confusion battled with the flames in her eyes. She moved cautiously toward the stage.

"That's it, a little closer."

George shoved the book close to her face. "Do you recognize this?" he demanded.

She peered into the book, then up again at George. "That's Adam's diary!" She tried to snatch it but George jerked it away.

He opened the book wide and showed her the pages. "Whose handwriting is this?" She lunged for the book again, shouting, "Give it to me!"

George jumped back and read aloud from the book. "October 17. 'Today auntie come by with her rabbit stew. At first wouldn't take it but she got mad so I took it. Pretty tasty.' Sound familiar, Henrietta?"

Henrietta tried to climb onto the stage but was blocked by George's men.

"Goddamn you!"

George turned a couple of pages.

"'November 25. Come back from Doc's and mayor and Uncle Walt come over and talked about my Pa.'"

He turned the pages and read from a different page. "'Today I done it. I looked into the eyes of Lord Satan and turned my soul over to him.'"

A gasp rose from the audience.

"'And from those eyes, I got happy like I never done before. And Father Satan said to me that after thirteen nights you will sacrifice a child to me. To your father in Hell you shall drink from its open throat the blood of the virgin girl.'"

No one breathed. No one dared. For here was a confession of actual communion with Satan.

George flipped ahead a few pages. "'Today, I done it again. Thought I wouldn't have the nerve, but I didn't disappoint Master. I done more than I was asked cause it was my own sister this time. I took the girl out, threw her on the rocks, and with a knife I *opened her up!'*"

Pandemonium. People were slapping themselves, wailing at the ceiling in ear-splitting appeals to Jesus.

Henrietta was lunging wildly at the stage, her husband behind her, both being shoved back by Broke's men. Behind them, Virginia was screaming hysterically.

They ignored the mayor's feeble attempts to regain order. It was George Broke who at last controlled the crowd and got them to be quiet. He accomplished this feat simply by raising his hand.

"Ladies and gentlemen, it's plain. Adam Green did these crimes because he has embraced Satan. Like his mother and father before him, he is a witch!"

Henrietta broke free of the men restraining her and jumped onto the stage. Teeth bared, she landed fully on George Broke, who tumbled backwards. Instantly Broke's men were on her. They picked her up and threw her off the stage.

A dozen others shoved Walter back and he and Henrietta joined in the middle of the room. George stood, dusting off his breeches. Henrietta shook her fist at him. "As God as our judge, you'll be buried alive for this, George."

Henrietta pulled her husband toward the door, shoving people out of her way as she went. Virginia followed, slapping aside her father's hand when he tried to stop her. The three pushed their way out of the church.

George took a sip from the flask on his hip. He said, "Seems this kind of thing runs in the family."

Chapter Thirty-eight
Coup d'Etat

"Well, I suppose that's all." George started to climb from the stage.

"What?" someone shouted.

"All?"

"What do you mean?"

George blinked at them. "That's all, I said. What more do you want?"

"Adam Green needs to be punished!" shouted a farmer.

"Punished?"

"He did a horrible thing! He can't do that without anything happening to him!"

"But, we don't have any…system?…in place to deal with this kind of thing. So, I'm not sure what to tell you."

James Shrenker addressed the crowd in the room. "You all, come with me. Let's go to Adam's cabin and kill him!"

George smiled indulgently. "Wait, Mr. Shrenker, you can't just go off and kill a man like that."

"Why not?"

"Because it…it would make you just as bad he is. Wouldn't it?" George turned uncertainly to the mayor. "Can we do something like that, Mr. Mayor?"

William didn't answer. The old man seemed fascinated by the dancing light from the big torch on the wall. George gave him a sympathetic smile and turned to the reverend. Calvin had remained seated and silent throughout even the most chaotic parts of the meeting, as though awaiting a cue to play his part. "How about you, Reverend Branch? Are we permitted to kill Adam Green for what he has done?"

Calvin responded authoritatively. "No. This is explicitly disapproved of in the Good Book, for judgment is the Lord's, not ours."

"But isn't there a part that says something about an eye for an eye and a tooth for a tooth?"

"Yes, this is true. When we, God's People, first found our haven in this wilderness, we brought with a heritage of civil law, based on the Lord's teaching."

George raised his eyebrows in surprise. "Civil law? What is that?"

"It is a means by which our community can enforce moral rules and punish sinners."

"But we don't have any of these civil laws now, do why? Why not?"

Reverend Branch sat up in his chair. He thundered, "because we thought we didn't need them anymore! Even while our society has been riding happily straight into the hindquarters of Satan, we pretended we had no problem! What have I been saying to you all these years? Moral decay! Wild dancing! Unmarried boys and girls holding hands—in public! Imbibing of spirits on the Sabbath! Prancing about maypoles! Bowling on the green! SIN!"

Reverend Branch stood to his full, awesome height. He pointed at the audience. "I can see the wickedness in all of you!" Everyone in the room cowered, not one of them had not at some point sinned secretly in his or her thoughts and, like the preacher said, excused themselves, thinking it not really so bad.

The reverend looked at George. "We need to reestablish the Sabbatical Laws! We need to bring back the punishments of old! Adam Green is proof of our failure! We must use our reconstituted laws on him first!"

George said, "this is a most astounding thing I have ever heard. It seems that we're able to do something about Adam Green after all. First, we will need Mayor Gladford, as the highest authority in the land, to formally decree the reestablish of these laws. Can you so decree, Mayor Gladford?"

At the sound of his name, William turned his head slowly, taking in the audience. He appeared surprised to find them there. His eyes glazed over and the lids fell shut. From his throat came a confused grunt. Then he began to snore.

George turned to Calvin.

"Poor man. He's gotten so old, and he's been under so much stress lately. I think perhaps it's time he retired."

An approving murmur was heard throughout the room.

"Reverend," continued George. "We have to decide who will be the new mayor. In line with that, do you think, if you were to teach me and my father more about these Sabbatical Laws, *we* could help you implement and enforce them, with our workers?" He gestured toward the gang of dangerous-looking men standing along the wall.

#

In this way, a new government was installed in Arcadia. It was decided that the posting of the new laws, as well as the construction of a town jail, would begin the next day.

The citizens left the meeting feeling more secure than when they entered. They had faced a heretofore unimagined threat to their security and taken bold, decisive action to protect themselves. They looked upon Reverend Branch with new respect. Many were already vowing to attend church more diligently.

A vote was taken and George Broke was overwhelmingly chosen to be the new mayor of Arcadia.

As the people shuffled out, they tried to keep the noise down, to not disturb poor old William, still snoozing in his chair.

"

PART THREE

Chapter Thirty-nine
Snow

Two weeks later.

If you take Mill's Trail south past town and follow the Brown Forest until the road starts to climb into the mountains, you will come to a fork. Choose the left path and you are on Broke Trail, which runs along the jagged hem of the mountain range clear through to the Grey Mountains on the eastern horizon. Along the way, smaller paths splinter from the trail, leading to the scattered farms and ranches of the southlands, including the huge Broke Ranch, and the southern swamps.

Take the right branch of the fork, and you will find yourself on a narrow, overgrown path, which some call Phagus Trail, that climbs into the Forbidden Forest. Lone riders have vanished without a trace on this road. Some folks claim these unfortunates were murdered by the trees themselves, the low-hanging, stringy branches snatching them from their horses and tossing their bodies into some orifice concealed in the boughs.

It is a place civilized people avoid. This is the region of the skinners. These people had no use for settled living of any kind. The townspeople and civilized farmers mostly saw the male skinners, tough, wild men who lived off the land or from earnings made from the hides of animals they trapped and flayed. The only times they emerged from the wilderness was to carry their blood-spattered sacks filled with animal skins to Shrenkers General Store and to haggle over prices with James (Wandabella refused to come close to them).

The nasty trail circles to the right as it climbs higher, and the trees grow thicker as you go, until the light is snuffed out almost entirely. It's easy to miss the turn-off, a blotchy trail winding sharply to the southeast, even more careworn. Just when it seems you are buried fully in these terrible woods, and the monster bears are about to take you, you come to the Brandywine Inn.

The pub is inside a single, freakishly mammoth, hollowed-out pine tree. It is claimed the enormous tree was the largest, oldest one in the forest. The trunk was at least five times wider than a typical family cabin, such as that of the Auberons or William Gladford, and so tall the top was lost in the black canopy.

No one knows who decided to drill into the monstrous tree, and the present owner, Mr. Phagus, won't say.

A tall man with a long, slender, gloomy face, Phagus towers over his customers from his spot behind the bar. He is such a silent, watchful creature that there are men who have come to the pub regularly for years and never heard his voice. His eyes are so dark, keen and unblinking, and his face so long and narrow, there was a rumor afloat claiming his father had been an elk that had taken his human mother by surprise from behind, while she was bent hunting for bog-snails, and planted an unnatural seed.

Phagus permitted much unseemly behavior by the wild men who patronized the Brandywine, activities that would have been intolerable to Joss Hanker. But his customers knew that even in this unruly place there were some things they couldn't do. An old, cautionary tale still whispered to new customers is exemplary: one night long ago, a drunken skinner forgot himself, removed his pants and pissed upon the floor. Mr. Phagus showed no sign of noticing. That night, at closing time, everyone went off into the night as usual. The next morning, the man was found hanging from a tree beside Broke Trail, a chamber pot upon his head, his cock missing.

The interior of Brandywine was cavernous and dark. The countless nicks and pocks taken from the now-petrified wood resembled the scarred walls of a grotto. The splashes of firelight that provided illumination came from the hundreds of candles Mr. Phagus placed in them.

Since George Broke became mayor, the Brandywine was doing record business. This wasn't because Joss was dead and Phagus had inherited the customers from Hankers. Farmers who used to visit that happy town inn were too frightened to come to this untamed place. In fact, few townsfolk even wanted to drink at all after the publishing of the Sabbatical Laws. Parchment copies of the new rules were nailed to every surface of the buildings in town. The consumption of rum itself was not illegal, but the amount one could consume, and the days one could consume it, were severely restricted. A violation of the spirits law resulted in being locked into the public pillory for up to three days.

If any ordinary farmers were interested in challenging the laws—and none were, because George Broke was still considered a hero—they would have been stopped by the Constable Force. This large crew of men was enlisted by George and Obadiah from the most muscular and savage of their ranch-hands and from skinners to enforce the laws. These men, armed with machetes and other bladed weapons, were employed to patrol the trails and to ensure no one was breaking the laws.

The Brandywine Inn was untouched by the new laws. Instead of being patrolled by Broke's constables, it was *patronized* by them. Now that they were gainfully employed by the government, they had loads of money burning in their pockets. The Brandywine was the perfect place to spend it after a hard day's work enforcing the law.

One evening two weeks after the coup, the pub was clogged with drunken men. In one of the alcoves, little Victor sat behind a table. He had a small bottle of rum for himself, which he'd been sipping the whole evening.

At a table next to his, two of Broke's constables were swigging rum and talking loudly.

"So we finally got him?"

"Found him this morning. He was catched sneaking in his own corn field."

"Bugger shoulda run for the Greys."

"Some's say his aunt told him to do just that, but he'as too scared."

"Still, in his own corn field! Where's the sense in that? Ain't Master Obadiah's men digging back there?"

"That's how the damned fool'uz caught."

"How about his family?"

"Mr. Fodder—" the man gestured with his thumb at a table near the bar, where a giant, mole-ridden man sat, now the chief of Broke's constables. "—he's got'em locked up in their cabin."

Another of the men belched. "They can't be too happy."

"Word is, they tried to fight their way out. That Henrietta witch had a good go at the balls of one of the guards. No matter, Fodder and the rest beat'em right back."

"Did the witch tell what he done with the girls's bodies?"

"Not so far's I heard. Right likely he cooked'em up and ate'em."

"What they gonna do to him?"

"Have a trial, Mayor Broke says."

"A what?"

"A trial."

"What's that?"

"I got no idea. But it's going to be at the Meeting House tomorrow and everyone can come."

"Where they got him now?"

"Locked up at Shrenkers. Hey, look, there's that fucking Mr. Cobble. The old bastard who's been talking dirt about Master George."

On the opposite side of the room sat a very old man with a jug of wine. He was muttering to himself.

"Hey, shoemaker!" shouted the constable. His shout brought the attention of several other constables ranged about the room.

Mr. Cobble looked up. Three men at the bar, legs splayed drunkenly over the sides of their stools, were grinning at him. One of them raised a cup. "To Mr. Cobble, who talks to ghosts, his only friends left in the world."

The bar erupted into laughter.

The old man curled his lips like he'd tasted a mouthful of powdered snake. He grabbed his jug by the neck and took a long gulp.

He hollered, "You bastards can har har all you want. I know what I saw. Miss Joss Hankers, a woman who's always been good to me..."

"Only a horse-face like her wanter take off yer britches, old man!" someone yelled. The shoemaker continued, ignoring the laughter. "I saw her riding past on the road that day. She waved at me, she smiled at me, friendly as always, and I turned around, and she was going straight toward Obadiah Broke's ranch."

Flatulence bleated in the crowd, and a hundred men erupted into howls of laughter.

"God as my judge, she turned onto the road to the Broke Ranch. Only a minute later, I come across George Broke riding in the same direction. I thought nothing of it then, but when I heard later Miss Joss'd gone missing, then you can bet I thought about it."

The old man took another swig. "He was right behind her! And now they say her clothes was found way out near the Grange. And they's got that Green boy, and they's saying he killed Joss and them girls. Say they're having a special judgment trial tomorrow, and the whole town's invited to watch! And who is going to preside over this judgement trial? None of than that goddamned George Broke!"

Mr. Cobble punched the air. "The devil is at the prowl, and mark my words, he's wearing George Broke's face! George Broke's evil! George Broke's weak! Joss Hankers was a fine, good woman. Anyone who'd hurt her's weak!"

Only Victor did not laugh. He simply watched from the shadows as the man continued his drunken tirade.

Mr. Cobble stood unsteadily and made for the door. As he paid his bill, Mr. Phagus regarded him with his bottomless eyes and curled his fingers around the coins. A few minutes after the old man was gone, Phagus flashed a look at Gus Fodder and his three men. They stood and left the pub. Victor waited a couple of minutes, then paid and departed.

Gus and his constables followed the old man's footprints in the snow. They disappeared up the road. From the shadows at the side of the Brandywine, where he'd been listening at the window, stepped George Broke. He began up the road too, following the five new sets of footprints. As George Broke vanished around the bend, Victor stepped out into the snow and crept cautiously behind the rest.

#

"Old man!"

Mr. Cobble turned around and squinted at the four men approaching him. They moved quickly, their boots crunching through the snow, fanning out and circling him.

Gus Fodder said, "You got a big mouth, old man."

"Yeah," said another of the men menacingly. "Big mouth telling big lies."

Cobble looked at each of the men in turn. He was drunk and so old he had trouble walking but his eyes were awake and there was no fear in them.

"What do you want?"

"You're the one wanting something, old man."

"You don't scare me."

One of men shoved Mr. Cobble. At the same second, another punched him from behind. They likely expected he would fall to his knees. Instead, Mr. Cobble shoved himself clear of them. He faced them and put up his fists.

"So that's how it is, is it? Four young fuckers going to beat up an old man. I'll tell you something. You're all going to be crying in your mommy's teats tonight, you bastards. I ain't lived this long for no reason." The man's jaws were grinding away under his stubbly cheeks.

The sight was hilarious to the four skinners, who fell into each other, bawling with laughter.

"Begorrah! Rot your arse!" the man shrieked. He kicked snow at them.

Gus slapped the old man. Cobble's eyes went feral, and he leaped forward and bit Fodder's face. The four constables fell on him together and four sets of fists and boots slammed over and over at the writhing old man beneath.

George Broke stepped out of the darkness. He snapped his bullwhip. "Get off him."

The four men jumped away. George coiled his whip and reached out his hand to help the shoemaker to his feet. "Are you okay, sir?"

The old man checked himself over with tentative touches of his fingers. One of his eyes was swelling, and there was a smear of blood on one cheek. He looked at George Broke and didn't answer.

Broke attached his whip to his belt. Shaking with anger, he addressed his constables. "Don't you *ever* hurt an old man."

He removed one of his gloves and slapped it across their faces. "Get out of my sight." Heads hanging, the men slinked off toward the bar.

The shoemaker stood gawking at George Broke. "Thank you," he managed finally to say. George grunted and turned away. The two parted awkwardly on the road.

Mr. Cobble continued on his way, aching all over.

He was limping, his right leg dragging in the snow.

"Damn them all. This world has gone mad." he muttered.

The shoemaker stepped off the road, into a gap between the trees. Wincing at the darts of pain in his hand, he untied the rope holding up his pants. He pulled out his manhood and pointed it at a tree. He was about to start when a sound startled him from behind. He turned around and was jolted at the sight of George Broke standing only a foot away, a wild grin on his face. In his fist he gripped a long-bladed knife.

With a flip of his arm, he slashed open the old man's coat. He shoved him against the tree and brought the knife to his chest. Cobble could feel the metal point pressing against his skin. He tried to scream and George smacked his gloved hand over his mouth. He gazed into Cobble's wide eyes.

"Old man, do you promise to stop talking about me and Joss Hankers?" For a second, Cobble hesitated. George pressed the knife tip harder. The old man nodded.

"Good boy," said George and shoved the knife in.

Cobble's chest filled with fire. He tried to drop to the ground, but George jammed his arm under his chin and forced him to stay against the tree. He pulled the knife out and shoved it in again.

"Now who's weak?" George asked.

#

George pushed the body into the forest. Snow was falling again. Soon Mr. Cobble would vanish. The body would be buried there until Spring, and then the animals would take care of the rest.

He cleaned his knife in a drift. He replaced it in the scabbard under his coat and returned to the road. He came to the spot where his horse was concealed. A moment later, he was on his way home.

Victor emerged from his hiding place. He slipped into the gap where the old man and Broke had gone. He crouched and slapped away the snow from the body.

The shirt was slashed diagonally from the bottom, right to left, almost severed at the collar. Exactly like the bloody dresses that had been found on the farm of Adam Green.

White mist emanated from the oozing wounds in the poor man's chest. Before dissipating into the chill air, the mist hesitated, an inch above the skin, as though struggling to return.

Victor's eyes were burning. He picked up some snow and pressed it into his face.

The old man wasn't lying. George Broke killed Joss Hankers. And he killed them little girls too.

Joss's words came back to Victor, and sent tendrils of ice licking into every part of his body.

If a body can't do right when right is needed, a body's got no right to live.

Chapter Forty
On a Spit

As is so often the case in life, it was simple hunger that got him caught.

Instead of taking his aunt's advice and fleeing for the mountains, Adam stayed close to home. Half-sleeping on frigid boulders down the pitted cliff at the edge of his property, he spent two weeks in the wild, living off berries and old corn. In first days he managed to spy on his farm from a thicket and was horrified to see it populated by dozens of men with shovels who arrived early. As though they owned it, they entered his cabin freely and made it theirs. Most of the men left at sundown, but he was sure some remained inside his home to sleep and stand guard over whatever project they were conducting. One time, he swallowed his terror enough to slip onto his farm as the first glow of morning swelled on the horizon, praying the men inside were still asleep. Dying with worry about his animals, he'd snuck into the barn. He was relieved to find that someone was feeding his horse, cow, pig, and chickens. It was during this dangerous excursion that he'd seen the holes up close.

The men who were invading his land were doing it to dig holes. There were lots of them, all over the property. It was like they were searching for something, and when they couldn't find it digging in one place, they moved to another.

Another odd thing concerned the mysterious bulge that had grown from the ground on Adam's property, the one that leaked black, rancid water. The first thing the men had done was rip that mound away, and dig a hole beneath it. The black liquid that hole had leaked apparently had vanished. The hole the men had made in this spot was especially deep and wide, but it too evidently hadn't yielded whatever the men were looking for.

When they caught him, it happened so fast there wasn't time to be afraid. After looking at the holes, he started searching for corn that had been left over from the harvest. He was on his stomach, desperately chewing at a corncob, and someone had crept up silently and clubbed him on the head.

The next thing he knew, he was inside a moving cart, a mighty pain in his head. He was gagged and his hands and feet tied. The two men riding up front chuckled at his moans. After a long ride during which each bump and rift in the trail rattled the creaking cart and set off explosions of pain in his skull, they came to a stop.

"Get out, witch."

Rough hands grabbed him by the arms and legs and he felt himself lifted and carried. He heard a door kicked open and sensed they had entered a building. Then, he was suddenly airborne.

He landed with a painful collision on a hard floor. Someone ripped the mask away. He blinked at the light. The room came into focus and Adam saw hanging by spikes on a wall a huge, petrified claw of a bear.

Without a word, the men who had tossed him left the room and slammed the door.

Adam was on his side. His hands and feet were still tied. Light was flowing in through a window about three feet from the floor. He rolled himself to the wall and pushed himself against it. Inch by inch he wormed up to the window until he could see outside. The second he saw the ragtag sheds in back, he understood he was in the back room of Shrenkers General Store, next door to Broke Bakery.

He started screaming and pounding his head against the glass. The men burst in. He was again thrown on the floor.

The men tied a strip of cloth around his mouth so tightly it was forced between his lips. One of them, a burly giant with black spots splattered on his bald head, produced an axe, lifted it by the handle and made as to bring the blade down on Adam's skull. At the last moment he flipped the axe around, gripped it by the metal head, and shoved the handle into Adam's stomach.

They left him weeping with his face against the dusty floor.

That evening, he had a visitor. He felt a burst of relief at the sight of Wandabella Shrenker until she stepped up and kicked him in the groin.

The guards stopped her. "Don't worry," one said, patting her on the back as they led her away. "You don't need to wait long."

When he became conscious of his surroundings again, it was dark. A man entered the room. He carried a candle in one hand and a tray in the other.

"I brought you something to eat," the man said gently.

He placed the tray on the table and the candle next to it. From his belt, the man pulled a long, flashing knife and leaned over Adam. His heart seizing in his chest, Adam felt a tug at his wrists and another at his ankles. A third came a second later behind his head. Adam found he could move his arms and legs again, and his gag was gone.

The man smiled and gestured to the food.

"Please. Eat."

Adam was wobbly on his aching legs, and his knees crackled as he sat on the chair. He tentatively tasted the stew in front of him. Rabbit.

"Mrs. Shrenker made that. Oh, don't worry," the man laughed, when Adam spat the food out, "she doesn't know we're giving you some. She probably *would* try to put poison in if she knew." The man gestured toward the door. "This is from the guards' meal. We had plenty, and there's no reason to make the prisoner starve, even if he is a child-killing witch."

The man's words hung half-understood in Adam's brain. The incidents of the day had left him in a stupor. Why was this man treating him nicely? Witch? The guard was a skinner type, but with friendly blue eyes and a jolly face.

The man laughed. "They're really going to fry you."

"What do you mean?"

"Tomorrow. At your trial. They're going to cook you up like a pig on a spit."

"My what?"

"Your trial."

"What is a 'trial'?"

"It's a meeting. To decide if you did the bad thing you did."

"What?"

"To decide if you're guilty of the crime you're guilty of."

"I'm not guilty of anything."

"There's no point in denying it. They're all saying you're guilty."

"But I'm not. Who's saying it?"

"Everyone out there. The whole mob."

"Mob?" Only now did Adam Green realize that the hornet's drone in the distance was the sound of many people.

"You can't see them from here, because the guards ain't letting them come around back. They want to throw torches through that window, to burn you alive. Don't worry."

"How...how many of them are there?"

"Guards? Most went home, but, well, me, and one more."

"Not guards. The mob."

"Oh." The man considered. "About three hundred."

Adam dropped his spoon.

"They say you killed them girls, and you should burn right now. But Mayor Broke says a trial is necessary."

"I didn't kill—did you say *Mayor* Broke?"

"Yup. George Broke is the new mayor."

"What happened to Mayor Gladford?"

"He's locked up in his cabin. He's sick or something. Can't wake up. I'm guessing he won't be at your murder trial."

Adam took a couple of deep breaths, trying hard to clear his head. "I'm innocent. I didn't kill anyone."

The man chuckled. "George said that's what witches always say when you catch them."

"But I really didn't kill anyone!"

The man clapped his hands. "Spoken like a perfect witch!"

"I'm not a witch!"

The mob outside became louder, a sudden roar.

"Don't worry, son," said the man in a voice intended to be reassuring, "You're going to get it tonight or you're going to get it tomorrow, with fire, with rope, or both. With choices like that, you might as well just relax and enjoy it."

The man took his dish away and Adam collapsed to the floor in misery. Hours went past, and he drifted in and out of tormented sleep. The faces of two people kept nudging into his fevered consciousness. The first was his little sister. Daisy kept shaking her finger at him, saying *the next time he punches you, you punch him back!*

The other was his father, who, with a sly wink, offered his universal cure for every problem: *Look up!*

Adam, whose hands were again bound, and whose head lay on the floor under a table, couldn't punch anyone and couldn't look up. He laughed weakly at the irrelevance of these visitations, but they kept returning.

Chapter Forty-one
The Trial

The trial of Adam Green was held in the church.

People started to arrive before sunrise. There wasn't enough room to park all the wagons and horses in the clearing, so they crammed them among the tombstones in the cemetery.

Some would claim later a full thousand folks came to Adam's trial, nearly the entire population of Arcadia. A few notable absences were Claire and Doc Midland, the mayor and his wife, and the Auberon family. No one knew it, but they were all prevented from leaving their homes by Broke's constables.

Virginia, Dorothy and Hugh also did not attend.

The evening after the emergency meeting, Dorothy and Hugh found Virginia unconscious on the floor. They put her to bed, where she lay speechless, refusing to eat.

The most striking absence was Obadiah Broke, who, it was reported by George, had injured his leg in a horse accident and couldn't get out of bed.

A roar came from outside. They were bringing in Adam Green in a covered wagon. Folks rushed up and tried to pull away the canvas to get at the witch inside, but Broke's men shoved them away.

Inside, the audience needed to wait another ten minutes, simmering in anticipation. At last, Mayor George Broke entered the room. His appearance inspired a burst of applause.

"Ladies and gentlemen, thank you for coming. I'm pleased you're all here today. We are gathered for a new and an important civic procedure, called a *trial*.

"As some of you know, the original home of the People of God was in a different part of the forest. My own grandpa's grandpa, the Great Armada Broke, was one of the first settlers of this land. From my boyhood, I recall hearing of him telling stories of the old land, how it was ruled by wickedness, licentiousness, and disease. It is hard to imagine, but people in the old place stole from each other with abandon. Women were not safe on the roads at night.

"Back then, constables forced these bad men into cages called *jails*. And the citizens of the land, to ensure innocent people were not punished along with the guilty, had special meetings, to determine the guilt or innocence of the accused. These meetings were called *trials*.

"In Arcadia, we haven't needed trials. We haven't had real crime for as far back as anyone can remember." George's face contorted in pain. "But now all that's changed."

As if on cue, two of Broke's constables entered through the side door. Between them was Adam Green.

The crowd gasped.

Adam's hands were tied behind his back. His feet were connected with a short length of chain. He was gagged with a piece of black cloth that covered half his face. He had a large bruise on his right cheek and his right eye was swollen nearly shut. Adam looked around the room, a sliver of his wounded eye glinting within the bulging flesh.

The guards shoved Adam into a chair at the edge of the stage.

George explained, "when a man embraces the Evil One, he gains animal strength, and fights like a beast if captured. It took ten of my men just to restrain him."

Adam latched the gaze of his remaining good eye onto the new mayor's face.

George held his hand over his heart. "We are not animals. We are a civilized race. A fellow like Adam who has committed crimes should be given an unbiased trial to fairly determine that he is guilty."

Adam vaulted through the guards and hopped straight for George, slamming into him and knocking him off his feet.

The stage disintegrated into bedlam as Broke's men struggled to pull Adam back, while he, despite his chains, flung himself free from them and threw his body atop George again.

The prisoner was dragged from the room, wailing something from under the gag. No one could understand what he was saying.

Broke slapped dust from his pants and smoothed back his hair. He cleared his throat and said shakily, "There. With the devil-afflicted criminal gone, we can continue with some dignity."

He gestured to the side door. "We will now hear the evidence. I call the first witness, Reverend Calvin Branch."

The ancient preacher moved across the stage and sat on one of the iron chairs.

"Reverend Branch, did you recognize this man the constables just removed?"

"Of course. It was Adam Green. His family has come to my church for many years."

"His family, you say? But not him?"

"As a boy, he came. Since the tragic incident with his parents, I have rarely seen him."

"Was he a good boy?"

"He used to be. But seven years back, his family...his family came under a contagion of the spirit."

"What does this word mean, 'contagion'?"

"It's like...damage...to the spirit."

"What sort of contagion did his family have?"

"The sort of contagion that comes from intercourse with the Devil. Satan's hand descended on that family's home as surely as black clouds before a blizzard."

Calvin recited the story they all knew: Adam's mother, dressed in only her nightclothes, an enchanted smile on her face and a feral gleam in her eye, had strolled out under a full moon straight into the Forbidden Forest. Adam's father, perhaps guided by a similar spell, or perhaps concern for her safety, followed her into the trees. Credible reports followed, describing sightings of Jedediah and Hattie in friendly company with wild bears, known to religious experts as the Beast of Witches.

Seven years later, when the memories of those tragic events were fading, their son, Adam Green, suddenly reported an outlandish vision: a black box with a talking head inside it. The spot in the woods where he found this devilish box was exactly the same spot his parents vanished.

"Naturally, my father Titus detected the first spoor of the Evil One's presence with the behavior of his parents. At that time, he attempted to raise the alarm about it in his sermons. It was as though Adam's parents had heard a Satanic voice calling them from the woods, and they lacked the spiritual purity to resist the temptation. Of course, even prior to this, Jedediah Green was well-known to have suspicious inclinations."

"What sort of suspicious inclinations?" asked George.

"Well, for example, he and his wife had an unusual interest in music and dance. And Jedediah possessed an unnatural dislike for the weaponry of old—guns, as we used to call them—and campaigned strongly against their use."

"We don't use these weapons anymore, do we, Reverend?"

Obadiah frowned. "No, we stopped using them, largely because of Jedediah's campaign against them. We have domesticated our meat-animals. And we depend on trapping for fur. The old practice of using muskets acquired a dark reputation, largely due to the efforts of Adam's father, who found sympathy in many others in the community, including former Mayor Increase Gladford. He claimed they promoted weak morals and were a hazard to children. Rather ironic claims, given his own behavior. Even I was sympathetic to his efforts at the time, given the metal balls that were exuded from the barrels of these weapons were animated by charges of sulfur, which, as everyone knows, is the devil's powder. Guns have never been rehabilitated, although our ability to protect our loved ones from wild animals would improve if they were."

George cupped his chin. "Maybe in this time of social change, the issue of gun control is something we should reconsider."

"After Adam Green reported the phantom in the forest," continued Calvin, "I began to study his actions more closely. And I was filled with alarm by everything I saw. Naturally, with the killings of these girls, there was nothing left to doubt. I knew the Beast had returned."

"Reverend, your knowledge of godly things is unmatched by any other in this land. Consequently, your knowledge of the Dark One is also great. Please tell us, sir. Is Adam Green to blame for the acts he's committed under the influence of the Devil?"

The reverend stroked his jaw. "You ask an important question. If the Lord works in mysterious ways, even more so does the Wicked One. Adam invited the Devil into his life. However, once his soul was possessed, his heinous acts were committed in the manner of a puppet, where the puppeteer is Lucifer."

George Broke gestured dramatically. "So, Adam, the man, is not guilty of any wrongdoing except a lapse in judgment. If this is the case, shouldn't we let him go without punishment?"

"No. Because, in the manner of a rot of fungus infesting the roots of a tree, which cannot be gotten rid of without cutting the tree to the ground, yea and even burning it to ashes, Adam Green must also be disposed of, to chase away the spirits devouring his soul. Otherwise, he will continue to imperil our community."

"Couldn't the Devil be made to flee by other means?"

"That's not how it works," answered the reverend, bringing to bear all the knowledge he'd accumulated during his theological practice. "It's essential to destroy the body that carries the infested soul."

George removed a flask from his belt and took a swig. "This is terrible news. Adam is an old friend of mine."

The reverend nodded. "I understand. But remember that this creature is no longer the Adam you knew. He is, in fact, not human at all."

George Broke looked out upon the electrified crowd with moist eyes. "Reverend, what is the preferred means of executing an individual for witchcraft?"

"There are three ways. Two of these involve the use of extreme cold or heat, that is, by freezing or by burning. The third, hanging, ensures the constriction of the throat, and thereby prevents the vaporous escape of pestilential humors spawned by the Devilish presence in the body cavity."

"I see. Thank you for sharing your scientific expertise." George sighed heavily. "This is all so hard to believe, like something more from a children's ghost story than from real life."

"Scary children's stories are intended to trick children into experiencing fear, with an underlying moral lesson. Real witches are another matter entirely."

"Thank you, Reverend Branch."

The crowd cheered as Calvin stepped down from the platform.

George Broke continued the trial by calling a string of other witnesses.

Wandabella Shrenker testified about how her bread dough mysteriously split in two of its own accord, after she'd charged Adam Green more money than he had, and how the rolls then changed to stone. Upon reflection, she perceived the witchery of Adam behind it. James Shrenker told the crowd how his wagon had nearly struck a snake-shaped root the very day of Wandabella's dough mishap, but hadn't flipped over. "It was like a warning," he said.

When George called the next witness, a spark of excitement shot through the room. No one had noticed Clarissa Auberon standing in the shadows. She climbed onto the stage clutching her child to her breast.

Her distress was plain. Her bonnet and smock were filthy. Swollen half-moons hung under her red eyes. George introduced her as "the very cousin of Adam Green." She'd run away from her husband, George explained, two days before. She was now staying with her great uncle Calvin in his austere cabin out back, sleeping on the floor with her baby.

Mayor Broke faced Clarissa. "Good Lady Auberon, as someone who lives next to Adam Green, and who interacts with him regularly, could you share with us your impression of him?"

Mouth curling with distaste, Clarissa told them about Adam's behavior on the day he found the box, his refusal to eat nutritious food, his avoidance of gainful labor after the incident. "It humiliates me to say these things, but the truth is the truth. Adam Green, a member of my family, has embraced Satan."

She struggled to keep from crying. She held her baby tight to her chest, as though to protect it from the dangerous things she spoke of.

George spoke softly, "This is difficult, but I need to ask you about the rest of the family. Henrietta and Walter Auberon are Adam's aunt and uncle, right?" Clarissa nodded.

"And Richard Auberon, Adam's cousin, is your husband?"

Clarissa nodded, her chin trembling.

"And the father of your baby?"

Clarissa held a hand over her eyes and nodded again.

"You know these people intimately. Do you believe Henrietta, Walter, and Richard are free of the contagion that infected Adam's parents and Adam himself?"

Clarissa sobbed. George put his hand on her shoulder. "Maybe we should take a break. The poor girl's been through so much."

Clarissa pushed his hand away. "I can finish. I'll say this about my married family. They've not only got a spiritual contagion living next door to them, but they also have a contagion in their own house." Suddenly Clarissa was yelling, her tears conquered by outrage. "They've had a thousand chances to snuff out the evil that took root seven years ago. They've done nothing! Why aren't they here today? Those girls are dead!"

"What do you think should be done to, as you say, snuff out the evil growing on the farms of Adam Green and the Auberons?"

"It is as my great uncle Calvin has stated. Death is the only way to stop the contagion of evil when it has infested a human soul."

George lowered his voice almost to a whisper. "Even your husband?"

She reddened and bit her lower lip hard. Tears were dripping freely down her cheeks. She nodded, once.

Every soul in the crowd was deeply moved by the revelations of Clarissa and her courage, and by all the others who gave testimony. At the end of the day, the Arcadians felt crushed by shame because they had permitted such wickedness to flourish for so long under their very noses.

And it came to pass that Adam Green was sentenced to death.

Chapter Forty-two
The Pillory

The Brokes reasoned that a public execution might disturb the weak-hearted and inspire dissent against the new government. Therefore, a few trusted constables were sent to construct the pillory for Adam's execution in an unfrequented area. These men understood carpentry and metalwork. They were to construct the pillory well, so that it might be put to long and frequent use.

They chose a grassy clearing at the end of an overgrown patch branching to the east from Mill's Trail, about a mile before it forked at the mountains. At the edge of this clearing was a deserted, two-room shack. Concealed from sight by wild bushes and hunched under a massive oak tree, the building was in shambles.

Broke's carpenters labored through the day to set up the pillory, using the designs penned by George Broke, which were based on Calvin's old letter about the Sabbatical Laws penned by Titus Branch. By the time Adam was sentenced to death, the contraption was ready to receive him.

After George pronounced the sentence, he left the church without telling anyone the details of how Adam Green would be executed. Not knowing what was happening, Adam, still bound, found himself dragged away and tossed into a cart again. A roaring crowd encircled the wagon, some throwing stones at the prisoner. A driver leapt onto the board, snapped a whip, and they were off.

The temperature was plummeting. In the twilight sky, clouds with black underbellies were amassing for what promised to be another blizzard.

#

Adam felt himself lifted from the wagon bed. He was in front of a broken-down cabin he'd never seen before. Under a huge oak tree was a wooden contraption, a kind of frame with outstretched boards, that reminded Adam of a loom.

Someone slashed the ropes binding his hands and feet, and tore the gag from his mouth, and gripped him by the shoulders, knocked him to his knees and pushed him over the wooden frame. A man stood in front and another in back, and the two yanked him straight. The man behind gripped Adam's shirt and ripped it open, and used a blade to cut it free. Someone else pulled off his boots. Icy pins stung his back and feet.

Resistance didn't even occur to him. He was so exhausted he could barely move. The man in front grabbed him by the hair and pulled him down. Adam felt his neck meet a frigid surface. His hands were jerked forward and his wrists touched cold wood. Something hard slammed down on either side of him. In a daze, he saw he was trapped under a wooden bar. A man inserted a lock into a latch on the right and snapped it shut.

Sounds of a horse, shouted greetings, and there he was, George Broke.

"Adam!" he called. George's grinning face was at an angle. "How are we tonight?" George had a flask in his hand. He gulped from it. Whatever he was drinking stank so bad it bored through Adam's wracked senses and woke him a little.

"A bit nippy tonight, eh?" Broke laughed wildly.

"George?" Adam formed the word with difficulty.

"Yes, Adam?"

"Why?"

George cackled again. "Why?"

"Why?"

George put his face close to Adam's. He whispered, "You should have sold your house."

"My...?"

"Your house! I warned you!" Adam opened his mouth, closed it.

George tittered. "Oh, don't you worry, Adam. We fixed the problem. Work is already underway. Twenty of my best men are digging for the black water."

Insane, thought Adam. He felt a twinge of something like pity for his former friend, but in an instant it was gone, and all he wanted to do was kill him. He lifted to his arms to fight, but he was trapped beyond hope by the pillory.

"Forgive me, Adam, but we need to be off. There's another blizzard on the way, and it's not safe to be outdoors."

"George," Adam croaked. But George had already turned away. From all around, the crunch and creak of wagon wheels on snow resonated in his bones, then Adam was left in silence, alone.

Heavy snow began to fall.

#

Adam was home in his cabin. Snow was blowing in. He jumped up to shut the window and was yanked to the ground by an iron hand on his neck and wrists that snapped him painfully at the joints. He yelled and the yell awakened him enough to remember.

How many hours had he been here? Night had fallen, but he didn't know how long ago. It was very cold. Out of the black sky, a swirling blur of white. Across his back, he felt stabs of distress, frozen flames cooking his skin. Heavy snowflakes were roiling up sideways and slashing his eyes. He tilted his head down to avoid the torrent.

The smell of fresh-cut cedar stung his nose. It was so strong, Adam at first thought it was somehow blowing at him in the snow. Then he realized. The apparatus in which he was trapped was new. The men probably cut the wood that day.

He was struck by a spasm of shivers, which set loose a swarm of agonies in his muscles. The cold was so bad it seemed to drill into his flesh and burrow clear through him and inject ice into his bones.

He screamed. He cried out like a madman the names of his aunt, his uncle, his cousin, the name of God.

He was surprised he could still move his fingers. The tips were burning, but the rest of his hands were numb. He must not have been locked in very long then. Not even past midnight yet. Still time to live, if he could get out.

This can't be happening. He thought the words so hard they came out of his mouth in a gravely, alien voice. He strained against the wood, but couldn't move. He pressed his teeth together, so tight he thought they would crack, and pushed up his shoulders as hard as he could. The only reward was a slight creak of the wood, and the sound of metal parts clinking.

He sagged. Ice crystals rang against his teeth and sent chills through the nerves.

He was going to die.

Adam struggled not to cry. He closed his eyes. He wiggled his fingers, offended by the little stabs of pain in them. In the field of his vision, colors congealed, assumed shape. A face emerged. It was his father. He was right there in front of him, saying in his amused voice, *Adam, look up.*

Adam, irritated by his rambling thoughts, forced his eyes open. Why on earth was he thinking about his father now? Useless. *Look up, Adam. Look up. When you can't find the answer to your problem, always look up.*

Adam looked up. It was hard. He could bend his neck backwards and raise his head a little, then bring his eyes up in their sockets and see, more or less, directly above.

All he could see was snow, slashing across a black universe. Nothing else. Thanks, Pa.

Now look to the left.

Adam could have sworn he heard a real voice say it.

On his left he could make out his hand, sticking through the hole between the two slabs of wood. The hand seemed somehow alien, like it didn't belong to him. Nothing else. Thanks again, Father.

Now look to the right.

This time the voice was so loud it boomed in his ear. What the hell? Was this what it was like when you die? You hear the voices of the dead?

On the right was another hand that didn't belong to him. Snow piled up on the fingers, a neat row of white nubs. Adam tried to force a connection between his brain and his fingers, and miraculously, there they went, wiggling creakily, like snow-blown beetles.

What was that? With all the power he could muster he turned his hand. At first, when he touched the blue-black blob, he didn't realize it. When the sensation finally registered, it was only of touching something heavy. It took a whole minute of fiddling with it to understand.

The lock.

Adam set to pushing the chunk of metal back and forth and up and down as best he could, but soon gave up. Locked tight. Adam gritted his teeth. Of course it was. That's why it's there.

Look up.

Alright, alright, I'll look up.

No, look down!

Just as Adam recoiled from the shout in his ear and looked down, a tremendous *crack!* sounded from above and something colossal came slamming all over him. When Adam opened his eyes and looked up again, he was surrounded by shattered wood. Under the weight of the snow or the punches of the wind, the oak tree had fallen on him. The main portion, splintered at the end into jagged teeth, was only an inch from his face.

Adam was amazed at his luck. If that branch had fallen slightly different, he'd be dead.

He realized a second later how ridiculous the thought was. His laughter had a dull, cavernous quality.

The broken tree was a chaotic latticework lit up in blue. Through the spiderweb of fractured wood, something glinted.

Adam stared up for a long time, thinking he'd imagined it. No. There it was again. Tiny and white. Glint. A star? Again. No. Directly above him, hanging among the branches, was something metal.

It took another five glints, while Adam looked up unblinking at the thing, to understand what it was, and the knowledge sent Adam into a panic of joy.

A key!

But, he thought, his hope dying again, this was all an evil joke. If his hand were free, he could just reach up and grab it, but then he wouldn't need the key anyway.

Yet his father had led him this far.

The moment he thought this, he knew. The leaves were still dangling from the branch, slapping at his face. Adam snapped off a mouthful and chewed. He kept his eye on the glint, working the leaf into a ball. The bitter taste was awful, but it made him feel alive again. He took careful aim and spat, hard. The ball flew up only an inch, off course.

Adam snatched another bite of leaves and chewed again. He spat. This time, his shot was closer to the direction of the key, but still not high enough. He shot his face forward to chomp another bunch of leaves.

He twisted his neck until it hurt, forced his eyes up as far as they would go, and with all his might shot his head forward like a striking snake. The wad was hurled high and straight. It hit the edge of the key, sending it into the air.

No thought. Only the twisting and turning of flashing metal in air, hovering, then plunging downward, where that strange, frozen, foreign hand caught it.

"Ah ha!" screamed Adam.

Meant to be. Meant to be. He whispered the words over and over, while he ever-so-gently twisted his wrist toward the lock.

The lock was a grey lump in the dark. Adam couldn't see where the hole was. He contorted his freezing wrist to the limit. The best he could get his numb fingers to do was grip the key by its base and jab blindly.

He flipped the lock up and down and knocked it side to side. At last he perceived the tip of the key catching on something. He focused, squeezing the last fragments of strength from his fingers, and sure enough, it was slipping into a keyhole.

Just as Adam got the key in halfway, he twitched. The key flounced out of the hole and out of his hand, and plummeted to the snowy earth, an eternity away.

His head wilted in the trap. His eyes were squeezed shut. He listened to the howl of the storm, imagined it carrying him away. Save some stinging here and there, he could no longer feel his body.

He would never have opened his eyes again, if it hadn't been for the odd sound that invaded his death trance. When he looked, he knew he'd gone mad. For seated right there, on his shoulder, so close he could have chomped it as easily as he had the leaves, was a mouse.

A mouse.

The hallucination didn't end there. The tiny animal held the goddamned *key* in its mouth!

The world was the roar of the wind, the burn of the snow, and the phantom mouse with a key in its teeth making its way now along Adam's arm to his hand. It was nudging Adam's fingers.

Somehow Adam managed to move them around the key. When he couldn't move his hand well enough to push the lock in his direction, the mouse climbed over the lock and used its nose to tap it into a better position. In the last moment of the insane dream, Adam felt the latch slip.

The lock popped open. A slight flip of his wrist, and the chunk of metal fell to the ground.

Adam closed his eyes and waited for Jesus to come. He leaned backwards, spreading his arms to heaven to embrace the Lord, and, his arms and head lifted the unlocked wooden bar. He fell backwards into the snow.

Adam still thought he was dead. The mouse needed to climb onto his chest and bite his nose to arouse him.

When Adam climbed to his feet, his legs nearly buckled. He looked around. The ghostly shape of the demolished tree. The abandoned cabin. Adam stumbled toward the building, his frozen, naked feet barely feeling the pressure of the ankle-deep snow. He tripped on the wooden step and fell face-forward. He grabbed onto the door handle and pulled himself up. He shook the handle. Stuck.

He scraped along the wall and found what seemed like a window. He lifted his hands and banged on the glass.

#

Gus Fodder, the only guard left to watch Adam Green, awakened to the sound of a hand banging on glass. He was lying on the floor of the only room in the cabin, under some blankets. When he sat up, the empty rum jug toppled from his chest and clattered to the floor. He saw in the moonlight the shadow of a man outside, hitting the window.

He grabbed his gut knife from the counter and went to the door. He threw it open and was astounded to see Adam Green, somehow free from the pillory.

With a shout, Gus lifted his knife and brought it down. Adam ducked, fell to the side, off the porch. He dropped into the snow and was up in an instant, fleeing across the open space toward the trees.

Gus pursued Adam to the edge of the forest, where he saw the witch run straight into the trees. The guard stopped where he had entered. The snow was slowing. He watched along the edge of the woods, right and left. Adam didn't come out. He heard the snap of branches deep inside the forest.

Gus shook his head in amazement. No one was crazy enough to go deep in the Forbidden Forest, because the bears would rip you up in seconds. The guard realized that Adam had just done the same as his parents. Run into the woods to die a witch's death.

He felt chill fingers on his skin. He looked down at himself and saw why. In his haste to catch Adam, he'd run out without dressing. He was naked.

Chapter Forty-three
The River

Three weeks before.

Daisy brought herself slowly and painfully to her feet from where she had fallen when the water had exploded from the wall. Miraculously, her tinderbox was intact and the twigs inside were dry.

Sniffling, Hildegard pushed herself up onto one elbow. Daisy took out a handful of twigs and put it on a spot on the ground that felt dry. She placed some tinder in the striking chamber and scratched the striker until sparks shot. A tiny green flame flared up, grew. Daisy dropped it on the pile.

Orange blossomed in front of them. The girls saw each other russet and ghostly, rimmed under the eyes with black crescents.

A short distance from where they landed, they caught the glints of a shattered lantern. When the water burst from the wall, it had hurled rocks into the water too, and one had hit the lantern.

"Damn," said Daisy.

"Look," said Hildegard. In the place where she was pointing, the fire didn't reflect like it did on the rock face, but appeared as a wobbling duplication of itself.

"The water."

The girls started to search along the edge of the body of liquid. They moved down one way and back the other, reaching the fringes of the weak light. Hildegard cried out.

"What is it?" said Daisy.

"I hit my foot on something."

They felt around and discovered a hard, cool surface rising from the mud. It was curved and rough, knee-height. It was a wooden structure, half floating in the water, with a rim that gave way to a deep hollow

"A boat?"

"Must be."

"How can it be?"

The boat seemed intact. Groping more, they found two oars mounted on the sides with iron fittings. The cuffs were so rusted the oars could barely move.

"No one's used this for a long time."

"Maybe it got washed down here by rain."

"Didn't come down the way we got here, that's for sure. Would've busted to bits."

"Whose do you think it is?"

"Could be skinners."

Hildegard glanced around. "Really?"

"Could be."

"Skinners." Hildegard said with disgust. "They're like animals."

Daisy mused, "strange. They look like animals, but they skin animals too, for money."

"I'm scared of them."

"I'm not. I'm not scared of anyone. Oh, the fire's going out."

The fire had waned to a bluish, pine-cone sized flame. With heavy hearts, they watched it dwindle to nothing. They were again swallowed up by darkness.

"Can we break up the boat and use it for firewood," asked Hildegard.

"All that will do is keep us lit up and warm for a few hours until the wood is gone, and then we'll be right back where we started. You know what I'm thinking?"

"What?"

"We ought to take that boat on the water, see where it takes us."

"It'd be safer to just walk up the shore, see where the water goes. If this is a a river, then we should be able to follow along the bank out to the end, which should be outside, right?"

"The water goes flush against the wall of the cave, Hildie. When I was trying to find a place to climb up before, I felt all along there. There's no way to walk next to it. Here's an idea.

Why don't we try to row the boat to the other side? It can't be that far. Maybe there's a way out over there."

What if the boat sinks?"

"Don't think it will."

"But what if it does?"

"Guess it'll sink then. We can swim to shore."

An uncomfortable silence. Hildegard said, "I can't swim."

"What?"

"I can't swim."

"How can you not know how to swim?"

"Just can't."

"All anyone does in summer is swim. You can't swim?"

"I'm scared of the water."

"You're scared of *everything*. Don't worry. If we sink, I'll carry you back on my shoulders. Now let's go."

The girls slid the boat until it was almost floating freely. Only the tip of the bow rubbed against the shoreline.

"Okay. Let's get in." Daisy climbed in first, then helped Hildegard in after her.

When they sat down, the boat rocked and wobbled. "Strange," said Daisy, "how it moves. Like the water's...thick."

Daisy leaned over and cupped her hand into the liquid and brought some to her lips. She gagged and spit it out violently.

"Jesus in a henhouse, this ain't water!"

"What is it?"

"I don't know, but it sure ain't water. It's like mud-shit-water."

They each took an oar and tried to row. The heavy rods of wood groaned, and the circles of iron that connected them to the rim of the boat creaked horribly. After managing to row three or four times, they had hardly moved at all and were huffing and puffing from the exertion.

"This is hard," said Hildie.

"Can't quit now."

Painfully, they continued to row. They felt the boat moving inch by inch. It also seemed to be turning as it progressed. In the pitch blackness, it was hard to tell how far they'd gone or which way they were facing.

After they'd rowed a few more minutes, they were finding a stride, and the rust on the moorings had ground away. The girls could feel the boat moving faster.

"Stop a second, Hildie."

"What?"

"Listen."

Apart from drops splashing from the oars into the water, and their heaving breaths, the world was enormously black and silent.

"I don't hear anything. What is it?"

"Don't know exactly. Thought I heard something. Hold on. I'm going to throw a rock." Daisy took out one of the pebbles she'd put in her pocket at the shore and threw it. A second later came a splash, maybe ten feet away. She took out another pebble and threw it as hard as she could. A few seconds, and another splash came, deep and distant. She repeated the operation in the opposite direction, with the same result.

"I don't know which way we're facing anymore."

"I think it was that way, but I'm not sure," answered Hildegard.

"I can't see where you're pointing, if you're pointing."

"Think like a line between me and you, then keep going straight behind my head. Think that's where we were."

"You sure? I thought it was the opposite way."

"I can't believe this."

"Well, let's not think on it too much, 'cause you'll start to get panicky again. We don't need that."

Hildegard was surly in the dark. "Don't worry about me."

"Hildie, look up!"

"What?" Then she saw it too. It was glittering off in the distance, like a star midway up the sky. A light.

It was like seeing heaven.

"Lord, that's the sun. Let's row. Row! Row!" And they both were shouting *Row! Row! Row!* and doing it with all the power in their small bodies. The light grew brighter. Around its edges, rocky contours became visible, orange and brown, floating in miniature, in the black universe.

They kept shouting and rowing for another five minutes, got the boat going to a good speed. They were shouting so loud, their eyes fixed on that distant prize above them, they didn't notice the other noise until it was too late.

"Sssh!" said Daisy.

"What?"

"Listen. The water."

Not far in front, there was a breathy swoosh of fluid in motion. "We're moving faster." They stop rowing, but they were still moving. Faster.

Within seconds, they were going so fast they felt air moving across their faces like a strong breeze.

"Oh, Daisy, I'm..."

"Hold me."

The girls hugged and the Earth collapsed. A shiver, then a feeling like a giant hand had reached out and jerked them, and then they were plummeting, falling free in the awful black, icy water slashing them, the bow of the boat tipping forward in mid-air like a diving arrow, their screams swallowed by the roar.

From the right, a rock punched them and instantly, another, smaller one cut in from the left, and they slammed into water again, the boat grinding against the bottom of the river that continued to throw them cascading downward into the gullet of the mountain, plunging faster and faster on a surface as smooth as glass, inky water slicing into their eyes.

Overhead, the light they had seen flew past.

A jolt from the side again, and something stung Daisy. The boat was diving once more, and the girls were lying in the bottom, clinging to each other, shrieking through their teeth, the boat snapped up, tossing them in the air. They landed again in the descending boat, and just as quickly were flipped into the air again when the boat struck something even bigger, which broke open the air with the sound of splintering wood.

In the water, they floated in a drifting dream where bodies were no longer needed.

Chapter Forty-four
Vaults

Bit by bit the girls regained consciousness. They found they were half buried in the mud of the riverbank.

In this new place, the swallowing darkness was much worse because they ached so badly and a gummy liquid saturated their bodies. This place was clogged with a heavy briny stink that settled in their lungs.

They fell against each other in the dark.

Before her sobbing had ebbed entirely, Hildegard pulled back and peered at an invisible Daisy. "Boat?"

"Gone." Daisy croaked.

"Tinderbox?"

Daisy's bag was still tied to her. Everything inside was mud-soaked but intact: the tinderbox, the coil of rope, and about seven candles. She detected two carrots she'd packed for a snack. She groped for Hildegard's hand and slipped a carrot in her fingers. They took bites and spit them out, hacking.

"Oh, that's bad."

"What's wrong with this?"

"It's whatever shit that river is made of."

"Shit smells better than this."

"Daisy, what're we going to do?"

Daisy's voice broke a little. "I'm so sorry. I never shoulda brought us down here."

Hildegard patted her friend on the arm. Daisy let out a screech of pain that knocked Hildegard backwards.

She found Daisy, crumpled and trembling. "My arm. Oh, God, it hurts so bad. Hildie, I can't move it."

"Lord, we need to get you to Doc Midland."

Daisy sat up and tentatively touched her shoulder.

"Now it's getting better. Can't feel anything in it now.But I sure ain't going to move it again."

"We need to find a way to get out of here."

"Let's light a candle."

Daisy tried to use the tinderbox, but it was impossible with one hand. She held her bad arm crooked against her ribs. "Hildie, can you do it?"

It took only one strike to get the tinder to spark.

Soon, Hildie had a candle burning in her hand. "Daisy! You're all black!"

"You too, even your hair. And your eyes are bugging right out of your head."

"Yours too."

"Hey, what's that?"

"What?"

"Eek!" Hildegard jumped up and took several jittery steps back. She was pointing at a spot behind Daisy.

Daisy looked over her shoulder and smiled. "Ain't nothing but a mouse."

The rodent was on a stone, regarding the girls with its whiskers twitching. Daisy reached out slowly and stroked the mouse's head with one black finger. "Wonder how it got down here."

A blinding bolt of light blasted through the cavern, sending jagged fingers of reddish-orange crackling all around them.

The girls shrieked. They looked around frantically, but there was nothing.

"What was *that?*"

"Dunno. Whatever it was, it sure chased that mouse off. We better do like it done, the faster, the better."

The ceiling of the cavern was low enough to be visible in the candlelight. The surface was hung with thousands of icicle-shaped formations that twinkled in a galaxy of sparks and flashes. Some of them were as long as a tree, and others mere infants, glittering polyps nestling next to their parents. The cones seemed to draw the candlelight to them and multiply it. The girls could make out the opposite bank of the river nudged up against the wall.

Behind them, the cave was rocky and looked dry. A roof was visible there too, with more glinting stalactites emerging from pools of darkness.

"You should stay here, 'cause of your arm. I'll go up and look around."

"What if you get lost?"

"I'll use the rope. You hold one end, and I'll hold the other."

"Come back, okay?"

Hildegard tied the rope around her wrist. She lit another candle, and moved over to the nearest pile of rocks.

Soon Hildegard had walked up the rock-shelves and disappeared into the darkness above. The rope was not all gone before Hildegard came running back, her hand cupped around the candle flame. "Daisy! There's a light up there!"

Daisy gathered her things in a second. Holding her arm bent close to her, with her right hand touching her right cheek, she followed Hildegard back up.

Hildegard had found a path, walls close together, an arrangement of boulders a foot overhead leaning against each other like bald men with their heads pressed together. The path moved through the walls in a twisting tunnel that rose quickly.

They emerged from the spiral into a vault with a dry, flat floor that weaved through a garden of jagged rocks that were the reverse of those hanging in the chamber below and much smaller. The walls were studded with golden egg-shaped stones, interspersed by countless smaller gems. In the candlelight, they trilled with rainbow colors.

Daisy was mesmerized. "I don't think I ever seen anything more beautiful."

"Even better, look up."

The chamber didn't seem to have a ceiling, but appeared to open directly into a much wider chamber filled with black. And somewhere up there was a speck of light.

"God, Hildie, that's got to be a way out. We got to get up there."

"It looks so far."

"We got to try."

Daisy ran the fingers of her good hand over the wall. The surface was rough with the pretty little rocks but didn't have any footholds. The cluster of stalagmites prevented her from getting close to the farthest stretch, but she could see it. It was all the same. Impossible to climb.

Hildegard whined, "So we're back where we started."

"Can we stand on these pointed things?"

"On *those*? They're not tall enough."

"How about the rope?"

"Yeah, the *rope*."

"Maybe we can pitch it up there and catch it on something."

Daisy uncoiled the rope. She made a loop and pulled it tight. She tossed the rope over her shoulder, leaned back, and threw. It caught the wall at the lip and tumbled back down. She tried again. This time the loop went straight into the darkness, over the edge of the wall. She pulled it slowly toward her, but it soon came down again. She tried three more times at different points, and couldn't get it to catch on anything.

"It's no use. It ain't gonna work," said Hildegard.

"Will you shut up?"

Daisy tried again. This time, the invisible surface the rope was grazing felt rougher than before, as though ridged with something, but still the rope wouldn't catch. Nothing stuck out far enough. She tried the same spot several more times with no luck. Her throws were awkward because she could only use her left arm.

"You could at least try to help me, Hildegard. You got two arms."

"It ain't going to work, Daisy. I think we need to go back where we came from."

Daisy whipped around. "Are you crazy? We don't even have enough candles to go all the way back. I don't care what you do. I'm finding a way up there."

Hildegard leaned against the wall. "I'll just stand here and watch while you figure out how to do something that can't be done."

Daisy gripped a stalagmite with her free hand and pulled. It didn't budge. She bent low and peered at something. "Hildegard, can you at least bring the candle here?" Hildegard obliged, sighing dramatically.

"What is it?"

"There's a crack here." She gave the rock a good kick and it broke off intact.

Daisy couldn't lift it with one hand. "Here, I'll do it." said Hildegard in a persecuted voice. She put the candle on the floor and picked up the cone.

"Tie it to the end of the rope and throw it up there."

"You're joking."

Daisy hissed through clenched teeth. "Just *try*."

Hildegard secured the rope around the wide end of the cone and hoisted the rock onto her shoulder. Daisy put her foot on the other end of the rope.

"Aim good."

"It's too heavy."

"Quit being a baby."

Without aiming, Hildegard hurled the stone at a shallow angle, slamming it low into the wall. A shower of twinkling rocks clattered on the ground. A fist-sized crater was chopped into the surface.

"Hildie, why are you acting like this? Do you *want* to die down here?"

Hildegard was gaping at the wall. "Daisy?" She pointed to the hole a few feet above her head. She picked up the still-intact stalagmite and drove the point into the wall. When the dust cleared, there was another hole, about a foot beneath the first one.

Daisy smiled.

Hildegard attacked the wall with the rock. Within moments, there was an evenly spaced series of holes leading to the top. Hildegard pushed her hand into a hole. The material was strong enough to hold her weight.

"It's perfect! I made a ladder."

Daisy tried to unbend her injured arm, and was stabbed by a deep pain. "Well," she said when she could finally get the words out, "Not so perfect for me."

Hildegard fell to her hands and knees. "Climb on," she said.

A moment later, Hildegard was climbing her first steps up the wall. Daisy was on her back, the good arm across Hildegard's chest, clutching the burning candle next to her shoulder. Daisy was heavy and it was hard for Hildegard to stay balanced. By herself, the crusty material of the wall could hold easily, but it was on the verge of breaking apart with Daisy's added weight.

They managed to reach the top. Hildegard flung first one arm, then the other, over the edge. The lip of the wall was curved and swept outward, like the petal of a flower. Hildegard flopped over the top, and Daisy, holding the candle aloft, slid down the easy incline. The girls came to a surface only a few feet below.

They stood and stared at each, then burst out laughing. With the hand of her good arm, Daisy high-fived Hildegard.

"Wow. We did it," marveled Hildegard.

"*Told* you we could."

The new chamber was larger. The candlelight didn't reach any walls. Pebbles were scattered on the cave floor. The spot of light above seemed reddish, but it was hard to be sure.

"Let's get up there, Hildie. Be careful not to fall down. Stay close."

Daisy lit a new candle. The floor at first sloped down so steeply they could only slink down on their bellies. Afterwards, they had to creep around a couple of big pits that disappeared into places too dark and deep to see. They wended their way around obstacles and were forced to backtrack once when they found no way to continue without plunging into an abyss.

Gradually they climbed higher and higher, and the red light grew brighter.

"That's gotta be a fire, Daisy. Maybe someone's up there. Should we yell out?"

"Wait."

The path veered left, dipped into a maze of stalagmites, and started to climb into a zigzagging tunnel. They lost sight of the fire. They were in a tunnel similar to the one that first brought them into the cave. Smooth floor, regular walls, slanting upward. Like something manmade. All of a sudden, a hundred feet away, they saw the fire.

It burned in a tunnel branching from the one they were in. They tip-toed toward it. Along the left wall were several black, forbidding, man-sized openings.

The torch blazed in an iron basket bolted to the stone wall. Aside from the snap of the fire licking at the air, the tunnel was silent.

The girls crept past the fire. The path continued until it was far enough from the torch to be swallowed again in gloom. They moved past two of the openings in the wall and stopped in front of a third.

"Should we call for help?" Henrietta whispered.

"Who's there?"

The girls jumped. The voice was loud and angry and very close. It came from the black opening next to them.

Daisy and Hildegard bolted screaming down the tunnel. But Daisy stopped in mid-flight and turned around.

Someone was calling her name.

She snatched the candle from Hildegard and ran toward the voice. She reached the hole and shoved the candle forward.

Inside was Joss Hankers.

Chapter Forty-five
Wrenched

Daisy reached out for Joss but was stopped from hugging her by a wall of metal bars separating them.

"What..?"

Joss was looking frantically to the left, where the unexplored tunnel continued. "They with you?"

"Who?"

"The men."

"I don't understand."

"Quick! Find help. BringMayor Gladford."

Daisy realized that Joss was not alone in the cage. Another woman was lying on the floor.

"Get us out of here!" hissed Joss.

From the unlit section of tunnel to Daisy's right, a big hand suddenly shot out and grabbed her wrist. Daisy screamed. With awful strength, the hand wrenched her arm behind her back. A man's voice growled, "So who's this, I wonder."

Chapter Forty-six
The Goddess

I grew up in a small town in Texas. My father was the manager of a convenience store. My mother was a secretary in a plumbing company. My parents were honest hardworking folks. Over the front door of our trailer were two flags: one for America and one designed by Pastor Ted Harold for the Gainesville Church of God. It was a field of blue with a crown, a cross and a star.

I was raised among jack rabbits and ranchers. As a teenager I grew embarrassed at my parents' ways and was disgusted by our windblown little town: the big, dumb men in the pickups roaring dusty through the desert void, the dull concrete buildings, the oil rigs pumping in dull perpetuity at the edge of town. How many boys tried to get me out to the flatlands to chug Falstaff beer and lay in the dust with my jeans pulled down in front of those horrible rigs to imitate their joyless pumping movements?

By the age of eighteen, I had laid the groundwork for my escape. I was accepted at a university on the other side of the world, Boston, Massachusetts, where I could go a lifetime without finding another armadillo or oil derrick.

Since I'd always loved to read and write (a trait which marked me as leprous in my hometown), I studied creative writing. My choice of major had the expected effect on my parents, who nearly cut off my tuition (they thought I was going to become a nurse). After a year, I met Dale, the handsome Forest Ranger and, to the doubled shock of my parents, I dropped out.

Dale worked for the U.S. Forest Service in Vermont's Green Mountain National Park, at Five Fingers, giving directions to campers, and protecting people from fires and bears. I'd stay with him in his government-subsidized cabin, a forbidden but tolerated thing. I'd remain a week, drive back to Boston and crash on the couches of my still-student friends there, then drive back again. Homeless, jobless, I needed to figure out what to do, but the decision didn't seem urgent.

I got the battery-operated combination TV and VCR from an electrical engineering major friend who'd cobbled it together. For people who couldn't stand camping without carrying a TV with them, he said. Dale had electricity in the park housing, but had none in the more remote cabin where he spent half his nights. I thought the gadget would be a good gift.

When I loaded the player into the car to take to Vermont, I didn't even know about the old videotape inside, a throwaway corporate promotion of a car company, or an oil company maybe, my friend probably used to test the machine.

Entering the Green Mountains, a storm struck. I hit a slick and was flung off the road. The car rolled and came to rest, upside down. When I came to, it was the next morning. I saw in the cracked car mirror a wide, purple blotch swelling across the right side of my head. At first I thought my handgun, the one my father forced me to take to Boston and which never left the glove compartment, had gone off in the crash and shot me. I remember taking it out and checking it, but not putting it in my pocket. I don't remember climbing out of the car. I can sort of recall vomiting in a streambed. Terrorized by fleeting realizations I was in the forest when for eerie patches of time I actually believed I was at my boyfriend's house.

By the time I started thinking more clearly, I'd wandered deep into the woods, left my jacket and my boots in the car, but was, incredibly, carrying the stupid TV set. I couldn't find the car again, I didn't know where I was. I went crazy, and kept on hauling the fucking TV set with me. It was a source of comfort, an anchor to civilization. I figured it must have gotten broken in the crash, because I couldn't get any TV stations on it. All I could watch was that stupid car company promotion tape, called Drive Your Dreams. A title which seemed, with my burning head and bursts of vertigo, especially goddamned fucking ironic given I'd driven my car right into this weird forest dream-world.

I wandered for a week.

I used the gun only once, to fire into the air, hoping the sound would attract rescuers. After that, the gun jammed or something and wouldn't work.

I lived off berries. And fish I caught by sweeping them out of the water of the stream that was the closest thing I had to a static landmark. I ate the fish raw.

On the eighth or ninth day, I was sitting under a tree on the stream bank, beyond tears, freezing. I had about given up hope. Suddenly this giant, hairless, deformed madman lunged out from the bushes and grabbed me. I passed out.

When I woke up, I was in an underground jail cell, a barred chamber in a cave, a prisoner of this strange man called Obadiah Broke. This psychopath. He spoke English with the most bizarre accent I'd ever heard. He sounded kind of like a Swedish immigrant, with those hard Rs and rolling, elongated vowels, but the intonations were different. He was dressed in what appeared to be an American colonial period costume. Or maybe the kind of clothes you'd associate with the New England Puritans.

My impression at first was that I'd been kidnapped by a demented mountain man sex pervert whose face was burned off by fire, escaped from prison and living in the wilds and kidnapping hikers and keeping them as slaves to do whatever sick thing he wanted.

But he never touched me.

He seemed as scared as I was, actually. He soon revealed his crazy belief that I'd been sent from heaven to deliver him some sort of special message. He called me "Goddess."

Now, here's where things get really weird. I mean, things I've described so far are pretty fucking weird, I know, but what follows is outer space level bizarre. *The fucking TV was to blame.* This freaky forest dude had *never seen a television before!* It provoked the kind of goggling wonder in him you'd feel if you suddenly came across a machine that could transport you to another time in history. But his reaction to the TV was nothing compared to when he watched that videotape inside. That stupid

Drive Your Dreams oil company promotion fucking video was literally like something sent straight to him from heaven.

Obadiah introduced me to his son George, a handsome young man with normal skin and ash-grey hair, who seemed even more scared of me than his father. Father and son dressed and talked in the same strange way. Their lack of basic knowledge about modern life was shocking. They didn't understand what a phone was. Not only was there no electricity, but they had never *heard* of electricity.

They had never heard of Boston.

For the first weeks of my captivity, I fought Obadiah Broke constantly. I spat at him through the bars of my cell.

While Obadiah never tried to physical harm me or touch me inappropriately, but he also only provided me with only the barest of bare minimum to survive in that jail cell. Three times a day, I was fed a bowl of foul-tasting gruel. For a bed, I had only a filthy blanket. A toilet was an antique wooden bucket.

In time I grew cleverer, encouraging Obadiah to talk with me. What he desired was nuttier than anything I could have imagined. He was completely mesmerized by the cars in the video. He wanted to build one and drive it. He figured since I brought the video, I must have known how to make a car. Our talks on that topic gradually convinced him that he needed a substance he had never heard of (!), called gasoline, which was refined from a black, watery liquid he also had never heard of, called oil, to run a car, and it wasn't enough just to piece together a "wagon" that had the shape of a car (which at one point he informed me he had actually done).

I certainly didn't know how to build a car, but once I figured out how important it was to him, I sure wasn't going to tell him that. I started to give him tiny bits of precious "knowledge" about car-building in exchange for privileges. For teasing him with glimpses into the nature of the cars and oil derricks in the video, I was able to purchase a straw mat and a warmer blanket. For suggesting ways he could dig for oil to make fuel, I was rewarded with fresh vegetables. I became adept at playing a psychological chess game with the men, using fragments of memory from my upbringing to pretend I knew how to extract and refine this "black water" the Brokes wanted so much.

The day they brought Joss to stay with me, I first thought she was like me—a hiker who got lost in the woods. But she also wore those strange colonial clothes and spoke the antiquated English the men did.

It would take a book in itself to describe the complicated maneuvering Joss and I needed to go through to move from being creatures from different planets to being friends. There were so many things she related that I didn't understand and couldn't believe, and she had the same complex of confusion about me.

In time, we needed to accept that we'd stumbled across a universe-shaking contradiction to the way we'd always thought reality was.

She had to take me at my word when I said I was from a place where giant machines flew in the air. I needed to accept the impossibility that she, although living somewhere in the tourist-heavy Five Finger Lake area of Vermont, spoke a dialect of English that hadn't been heard in hundreds of years, lived like the original Puritan settlers of New England, and believed she was residing in an Edenic splash of farmland tucked inside a geographical region called Arcadia comprised of thousands of miles of forest too dangerous to enter because of monstrous, man-eating bears.

Joss and I learned to ignore or laugh about these conditions and the fantastic differences between us that went with them. We were aided much in forging a bond by our mutual desire to escape our prison cell and destroy the Brokes. We could ignore our differences also because of one marrow-deep thing we shared: we were both women who refused to take shit from anyone.

Despite our toughness, and despite the strategies we formulated to get privileges from them, things were starting to fall apart between us and the Brokes. It felt like something very bad could happen. Obadiah, by far the more polite of the two, reduced his visits to us and George came more often. George had a dangerous air about him. He was a frightening, erratic man who compulsively drank a mysterious liquid from a flask. At first, I thought it was alcohol, but the nasty odor of the stuff was nothing like alcohol and it had effects on him that reminded me of serious drugs I'd heard about—the kinds that drove people to insane, violent behavior. Joss told me that George had once been a nice young man, but he had changed radically under the influence of his crazy father.

With each visit, George grew angrier at my gambits for more privileges and at not giving him all of the information he and his father wanted about building cars and making gasoline. It seemed to me that the only thing that was stopping him from starving the information out of us was his father holding him back.

George assigned guards on our cage. They called themselves constables and were the scariest men I'd ever met. Sometimes after they finished feeding us, the huge one with the bald, mole-covered head who was called Gus would stand in the tunnel and gaze silently into our cage, a creepy smile on his face.

The men never opened the cage door. I think Obadiah and George forbade them to. They slipped our food and toilet bucket through a hole under the door. Even if they had opened it, overpowering them was out of the question. There were more of them and they were bigger than me or even Joss, who was pretty big herself.

I suggested to Joss one night, during our whispered sessions of brainstorming how to get the fuck out of that cage, faking an illness to force them to bring a doctor, Joss blew me away by saying she didn't understand the word "illness". I tried to explain, but she seemed to not have any clue what I was talking about. It seemed she had no understanding of being sick. When I reached a point where I was too frustrated to argue, I suggested faking an injury instead. This she understood and immediately took a shine to. There was a good chance they'd really bring "Doc," she said, because they'd worry I, the Goddess, would die. We'd just started to work out our plan when the little girl came and showed us how wrong we were.

Chapter Forty-seven
A Competency

Reverend Branch was pacing furiously back and forth inside his tiny cabin. He was furious at George and Obadiah Broke. Since Obadiah was bedridden thanks to an accident with his horse, George had acted in his place and sealed the deal between Calvin and the Brokes to make Arcadia great again. In exchange for his support of their coup over his cherished but misguided old friend William Gladford, Calvin would receive their backing on his re-establishment and enforcement of the sabbatical laws.

But things were not going the way George had promised. And now Calvin couldn't even gain access to the new mayor to complain. He had not seen the young man even once in the weeks since Adam had killed himself. The three times he tried to visit George at his ranch, he was turned away by a cordon of menacing guards.

It amazed him that he could not freely visit the mayor. Calvin could see good reasons for forcing those in league with Satan, such as the Auberons, or their defenders, such as that reprobate Doc Midland or even former mayor Gladford, into segregation by house arrest, but he couldn't understand at all why he, the spiritual leader of the community, should be prevented from entering the Broke Ranch. Especially by those low-class, unclean ruffians the Brokes hired as constables. Yet that was exactly what happened, no less than three times that week.

Calvin was trying to think of a way around this problem when out of the blue George Broke himself dropped by to see him.

"Howdy, Reverend," George said after Calvin stopped his furious pacing to open the door.

"George! I've been trying to talk to you for a…"

George cut the reverend off with a chop of his hand. "No time for that. I came by because I have a few things I want you to say at this week's sermon."

George stepped past the preacher and into the little cabin. He went to the pantrybox, lifted the lid, and started to root for a snack. Talking over his shoulder, he continued. "Our fishermen have been unproductive lately. The snows are melting off and it's trout season. The fish are jumping. I figure there are about sixty fisherman working the rivers, but they only bring in the bare minimum to sell to the community." George frowned. "Don't you have any rabbit jerky in here?"

"Look behind that sack of corn."

George reached into the box and took out a hunk of dried meat. He ripped off some with his teeth and chewed as he talked. "They could be bringing in three times that much. As part of the community development program I'm starting, I want them to double the number of hours they work every day. From what my constables say, the fishermen now have no set work times. Real dawdlers. And for some reason they only catch what they need." George ripped another mouthful of meat. "Starting today, I'm establishing a workweek of a minimum of five days, eight hours per day. I want you to start preaching about the importance of fish in people's diets, so people will buy more fish, and I want you to preach about how important it is to work hard to catch fish for Jesus."

Reverend Branch stared at George for several seconds as he continued to chew noisily. "George, on what Biblical basis to you expect me to justify that?"

"Do you need a Biblical basis?"

"It is a church."

"Didn't Jesus do something with fish?"

"The Lord was indeed a fisher of men, and several of his apostles were fishermen before they cast down their rods to follow Him. There was the story of the loaves and fishes, too. It was about Jesus feeding the hungry."

"That's exactly what I'm talking about. Feeding the hungry. We sell the fish, they buy the fish when they are hungry, and they eat it."

"We? Who is 'we'? I thought you were talking about the fishermen."

"Yes, but the fishermen, Rev, are part of the community, of *my* community, and of *yours*. That's why I say *we*. And that's why I'm also going to apply a tax to all fish sold."

"A what?"

"A tax."

"I don't know this word. What is a tax?"

"It's money collected by the government—by the mayor—that is used for the public weal. And to pay the mayor his salary."

"Salary?" The reverend couldn't even minimally hide his shock. "Mayor Gladford never had a salary."

"I beg to differ, Reverend. Ex-Mayor Gladford was paid food every week."

"That was because he was…is old, not because he was the mayor. Like me. I get food from the community too. That's what the grange is for. To produce community food stocks. You know that. Farmers produce part of the food they eat by themselves, and this amount is supplemented by the community food stores, to the extent of their need, especially in winter. Speaking of that, I'm expecting little Victor to arrive any moment with my week's provisions."

"Old people get food because old people used to work, right? Or they still work…"

"I'm not sure. Everyone works."

"Charlie Glump doesn't work."

"He's a drunk."

"But he doesn't work."

Calvin blinked in confusion. "He's not old, either. I'm not sure what your point is, George. Charlie gets all his food from people who sneak it to him under the table at the bar. Some folks gossip horribly about him, but those same folks are the ones who slip him food. He gets fed by the community in a different way."

Broke tore off a chunk a rabbit jerky, jammed it in his face, and chewed.

"Why quibble?" he said.

"I'm not quibbling. I'm just pointing out that William did his job as mayor for no reward other than the honor of doing so."

"But what sort of job did he do, Reverend? Oh, my! Kissing brides on the cheek at harvest festival! Saying a few words to start the barn dances! Ouch! Must have been rough."

George jabbed a finger at his own chest. "I have big plans! Things that will change the community for the better, and my duties as mayor are going to take up most of my valuable time." George belched and wiped flecks of rabbit from his mouth with his sleeve. "I love helping people. That of course is reward enough. But with all the money from the ranch going now to pay for my guards, I can barely find a scrap of food to eat, not even a fish. My father is still bedridden with his leg and my mother needs to be by his side all the time, and we're deprived, so deprived, all because of my sacrifices for Arcadia."

George had acquired dexterity at speaking rapidly, jumping from idea to idea so fast that opinions contrary to his were extinguished before they could be expressed or even formed.

Reverend Branch decided to forestall arguing against George's fishing plan. Instead, he brought up what was really bothering him.

"I've been trying to talk to you for weeks, George. I even came out to your ranch to see you but was turned away by your guards. Rather rudely, I must say. Three times."

George stroked his nose. "Awfully busy these days, Rev."

"When I helped to install you as the new mayor, I did it with the understanding that we both wanted to reestablish the Sabbatical Laws."

George nodded. "So?"

"Things are not working out as you promised."

"What are you talking about? You got to tack up your new laws, and you've got fifty new constables to enforce them. I built three pillories. I've been training my men to whip harder, and next month we'll be moving into branding."

Calvin winced. "George, listen. The soul of our original community was for every person, by honest work, to acquire a *competency*. The highest achievement in this world is to attain a competency."

"A what?"

"A competency."

"What's that?"

The reverend sighed. "I discussed this with you before. It means each man is provided by God with the ability to make exactly enough, no more and no less, to independently feed and clothe his family, and thereby reach a serene Earthly life while awaiting his greater reward in heaven."

George yawned. "Interesting."

"Young man." Calvin spoke with the tone of indulgence an adult uses when explaining something to a child. "A competency means acquiring a sufficiency only, not an abundance, which our faith forbids."

George smiled as indulgently as had the reverend toward him. "Old man, you've done your share to earn a reward in my organization. Think more about what sorts of hot words you can toss at the congregation to promote fishing. Maybe you could point out how fish make people healthy."

Calvin rubbed his temples. "The people are already healthy, George."

The sound of an approaching wagon came through the window.

"Little Victor," said Calvin.

"Good. I want to talk to him."

They went outside. Victor came up the road in his small wagon, his dour donkey slogging in front. He was startled at the sight of George Broke.

Broke called out to him. "Hey there, Victor. Been looking for you. You haven't been out to my ranch to pick up any deliveries, and your stack has grown mighty tall. I asked about you at the Brandywine, but no one's seen you for a while. I was worried about you, Victor."

Victor watched George with his big moony eyes. "Sorry, sir," he squeaked. "My wheels got caught in a bog. I had to break'em and make new ones. Been tied up with that."

"You need you to clear up your deliveries, by tomorrow. Is that clear?"

Victor nodded.

George smiled. "Good. Then I'll be on my way. I got to see now to the arrangements for my wedding. Oh, don't congratulate me yet!" he said, gesturing to halt their congratulations, although they didn't offer any. "Rev, give some thought to what I said about fishing."

George climbed into his wagon, snapped at his team and headed down the road.

By himself, George lost his chummy smile. He glowered at the sunny day and the trailside blossoms poking up through the dwindling patches of snow. He yanked out his flask and gulped down some brain-juice.

So many goddamned troubles.

So far, the black water had been a failure. When Victor had first reported that he had seen the black water coming from the ground at Adam's farm, Father had been so excited. And had set in motion events to acquire the farm so he could dig freely for the magic substance. But the bulging mound had turned into a dud, yielding nothing. The few jugs his men managed to collect, after digging a score more holes in Adam's land, were worthless, because the Goddess refused to tell them how to use it.

Goddamn to hell that Goddess! She was still conspiring with that sweaty bitch Joss Hankers, her cellmate, holding out for more privileges, demanding their freedom, playing George for a fool. He should have killed her when he found her snooping around in the secret room, but he was weak and chose to let her live. He thought the Goddess would be more cooperative if she had another person in her cell to talk to. Now George wanted to yank the Goddess out of that cage, lock her in a pillory, and whip her until she revealed all the magic liquid's secrets, but his father forbade him.

There was also the problem with Virginia. Today, he was going to make his first direct effort with her to persuade her to marry him. Papa was griping daily that he hadn't approached her sooner, calling him a coward. With Papa, it was starting to feel like the old days again, and George required more and more brain juice to subdue the eruptions of turbulence in his mind.

George glared back toward the church. Victor was acting oddly. That little freak should have shown him more respect. He was paid a small fortune, so why did he stare up like he was looking at a monster?

And the reverend! How did the old bastard expect him to respond to all this nonsense about competencies?

Chapter Forty-eight
You Are Free

"I can't, Papa," whispered Virginia. She receded farther into her chair, refusing to touch the food on the tray her father had brought.

"But daughter, you must eat. You have to gather your strength, so that you can bake the bread. We have customers waiting."

"I don't have the will. Can you bake the bread this week?"

"Virginia, my hand at baking bread is not as skilled as yours. My bread is…"

"What, father?"

Hugh bowed his head. "Unpopular."

"It is truly horrible, Virginia," said Dorothy, who stood at his side. "Your father's bread is profoundly unbread-like, more geological than culinary, and it lets off a disturbing odor. It is almost as bad as that catastrophic substance Wandabella bakes and calls bread. I wonder if they are using the same recipe."

The three were in the living room. They had taken to sitting together several hours a day after Hugh begged the schoolteacher to come over and help coax Virginia out of her melancholy.

Hugh was especially agitated on this day, because George Broke was scheduled to arrive at any moment, to ask Virginia directly for her hand in marriage. He had not yet mustered the courage to tell her about his visit.

He looked over at Dorothy. They'd been secretly seeing each other for more than a year. Although their actions were explicitly against the Sabbatical Laws regarding behavior between unmarried persons, how on earth could he ever tell Virginia he would marry anyone other than her mother?

Dorothy was a dream come true. Against Hugh's expectations, she understood the practical needs for Virginia to marry George and promised to support him in his efforts to convince her.

Weeks had passed since the death of Adam Green. The news of his execution had nearly killed Virginia. It had damaged her spirit even more than the death of her mother in the fire. She had collapsed in her bed and scarcely eaten for six long days.

At first, Hugh closed the bakery so he could spend all his time caring for his daughter. Dorothy all but moved in to nurse the ailing girl.

Soon after Adam's death, Obadiah Broke sent a message, informing Virginia's father that while he understood why Virginia might be wearied from recent unpleasant events with the Green boy, Hugh still owed the Broke family a debt, and the Broke family still owned a goodly portion of the bakery, and business needed to proceed in times of good weather and bad.

It was Dorothy who managed to talk Virginia out of her bed, although she could do nothing more than sit in her chair in the living room, wearing her night smock all day. Cobwebs seem to sprout on her, and her body began to emanate the odors of a very old woman. Buzzards were appearing at the window, flapping their ebony wings, staring through the glass with greedy eyes.

"I hate those things," said Hugh, opening the window and shooing away the beasts with a broom.

"Virginia, please. Just a little soup," said Dorothy.

"I can't," responded Virginia.

Hugh was in a tempest about how to get his daughter to agree to marry George. It was an impossible subject to bring up, but he was coming soon and he could no longer avoid it.

He cleared his throat. "Daughter?"

"Yes, Papa?"

"Um."

Dorothy cut in. "Virginia, I know this is the worst time, but your father has a pressing concern to discuss. Involving your marriage."

Virginia's eyes opened wide for the first time in weeks. "My what?"

Hugh said, his voice cracking. "Yes, darling. Your marriage to…to…George Broke."

Virginia narrowed her eyes. She said, her voice cracking, "George Broke killed Adam. Do you seriously believe I would *marry* him?"

"Virginia, that wasn't George's fault," said Dorothy.

"What?!"

"What else could he have done? There was so much evidence. Mayor Gladford, bless him, was doing nothing."

"Have you both gone mad?" Virginia was staring wildly at them.

"Virginia, there was the diary. In Adam's own handwriting. Confessing his crimes."

"No! Not you too, Miss Dorothy!"

"Please listen," Dorothy said gently.

"It's a lie!" Virginia clasped her hands over her ears.

"Daughter, I know it's very hard for you to hear, but you were there yourself. His own aunt said he wrote it. The evidence was overwhelming."

"They found the dresses buried next to his house."

"George had no choice. I talked to him myself, at length." The look Dorothy was giving her was filled with deepest sympathy. "I am absolutely convinced of George's goodness in this affair. He's a fine young man, and you are misjudging him. People all across the land are calling him a hero."

"Then there is no God, nor heaven neither!" Virginia screamed. She sobbed into her folded arms.

Dorothy touched her shoulder.

Hugh said, "Daughter, I'm sorry, but I don't know what to do except say this directly. If you do not marry George Broke, we will lose everything. If you do marry him, we will be almost out of debt."

Virginia looked up, sniffling. "What do you mean, 'almost'?"

"Er, Obadiah Broke said he would pay in bridal money an amount that almost covered what I owe him for the bakery."

"But before, it was for the entire amount."

"Yes, but some time has passed, and there is interest on the debt."

"What is 'interest'?"

"Mr. Broke taught me the concept. It is an extra amount of money added to the original amount owed, a kind of payment for the time it takes to pay. This extra money is called 'interest'"

"Why," asked Virginia, her tears stoppered by rising anger, "would they call it 'interest'? Wouldn't 'robbery' be a better word?"

"But daughter, this is a normal business practice."

"Since when? Only last year, you loaned Mr. Cobble three sacks of flour, which he paid you back six months later. Yet you didn't demand he give you four sacks, did you?"

"No. I was a more naïve businessman then."

"A more…? Who told you this is the normal way of running a business?"

"Obadiah Broke."

"You stupid man."

"But…"

"But what?"

"Daughter, the fact remains. We owe money to the Brokes. They can put us out in the snow."

"Maybe that's where we deserve to be."

"Virginia." Dorothy said. "I understand how you feel. But I think you have not thought through this situation enough. You trust me, don't you? George Broke is *not* the bad man you make him out to be. I've talked with him at length and am convinced he has the interests of the people at heart."

A knock at the door interrupted them. Hugh jumped from his chair. "I wonder who that could be?" He hurried to the door.

Outside stood George Broke. He held a bouquet of flowers.

"What a surprise!" cried Hugh. He whirled around and chirruped at Virginia and Dorothy, "Look, everyone! It's George Broke!"

"I'm going upstairs," said Virginia and she started for the hallway door.

"Miss Virginia, please wait!" cried George. "I must speak with you. Please hear me out. Only one minute! If, after I finish, you wish to turn your back on me, then you may, and I swear I'll never trouble you again."

Virginia hovered in her tracks.

"I beg of you, my lady."

"God, another one!" interrupted Hugh. He was staring through the window at a huge black buzzard. It was bobbing up and down in midair, flapping its shiny wings, its glinting eyes hungry, the crooked blades of its beak parted. "How do they know what's going on *inside?*" He slammed the shutters closed.

Virginia turned on George. "What do you want?"

George held out the flowers. "I came to express my affection for you."

Virginia heaved an iron pot at him. With the sound of a hatchet chopping into the neck of a chicken, it caught him on his left cheek. George toppled backwards, flowers flying. He emitted a pitiful cry.

Hugh bounded over and bent over George.

"Daughter, you killed him!"

Virginia bolted from the room and returned with a wet rag. She fell to her knees and dabbed the cloth on George's face. His skin was a fishy color and his eyes were shut. Blood dribbled from a gash on his cheek.

The lids on Broke's eyes flickered. He looked around wide-eyed. He climbed to his feet, pushing the others aside.

Virginia stared up at him. The rage on her face was now tempered by concern and guilt. "George, I'm...I'm sorry. I shouldn't have done that."

"No, Miss Virginia. You had every right to throw that very heavy and dangerous iron pot at me. If I were you, I would hold a man like me responsible for every evil and more." Tears of remorse were starting in George's eyes.

"The only reason I am here is to beg your forgiveness. I know you will never accept a small man like me as your husband. I only ask that you try to accept my apology." George dropped to his knees. "The guilt is tearing me apart!" He took Virginia's hand and held it to his chest.

Virginia felt like giggling. She said, "this is not what I expected."

"I swear that my plan was to help Adam, but nothing went the way I wanted it to. When that diary appeared, it was all I could do to keep the lynch mob from killing Adam on the spot. Although I became mayor, there are some things that even I am powerless to stop."

"I guess that's so."

"Virginia, please forgive me. I can't sleep at night. I can't eat."

"Um, okay, okay."

Broke burst into sobs. Clutching both her hands now, he bawled, "I never wanted to hurt you!"

"Okay, okay. It's okay, George. I forgive you."

Virginia was whispering now, touched in spite of herself by the force of his emotion. She glanced at her father and Dorothy. They were both nodding.

He continued to hold her hands while he wept. For a split-second, she permitted her hand to stroke his face.

"I forgive you, George."

They all sat down and a long discussion began. Virginia raised objections to George Broke's continued house-arrests of the Auberons, the Mayor, and Doc. To her surprise, he agreed without argument to remove the guards as of that moment. His worry had been solely the safety of the community, and the safety of the people he had quarantined, because there were still roving mobs that believed that all three parties were conspiring with the devil.

They discussed anew the verdict that led Adam to be executed and George spoke once more, from the bottom of his heart, begging her to understand that he would rather have found himself guilty if he could have, to spare his old friend, but the evidence was overwhelming and no one would have believed

Adam innocent after seeing it for themselves. Although she could not explain the diary or other evidence against Adam, Virginia still bristled at the idea that Adam had been guilty of anything. Nonetheless, she saw that George was not the monster she'd thought he was, and that he was driven by circumstances to make decisions that were acutely painful. It was hard for her to know what kinds of heavy responsibilities the mayor of the land was forced to shoulder during tumultuous times like these, and so she gradually accepted that it was indecent of her to pass judgement on him.

Her father at last turned the conversation to business. George willingly agreed he would not charge interest on the loan to her father, thereby enabling him to become completely free of debt at the moment of their marriage. In fact, he said, if it were up to him, he would never allow his marriage to play any role in the size or timing of the debt, and he would happily cancel the debt even if Virginia refused him. But his father insisted upon it and he was the one in charge.

While it didn't happen that night, or the next, the regular, warm visits by George over the following weeks gradually wore Virginia's resistance down. He came with flowers and sweet words. He was funny and self-effacing and kind.

In the end, it took only a month for Virginia Baker to agree to marry George Broke.

That evening of George's first visit, when she was readying for bed, Virginia looked at her hands and found spots of blood on her smock. For a moment, she didn't know if it was George's blood or hers.

Chapter Forty-nine
Jitters

The announcement of George and Virginia's nuptials was the best thing to happen to the community in a long time. For the first time since the murders, people felt stirrings of hope. The wedding bans were published according to tradition, the sheets of parchment tacked up on trees and hitching posts and shop walls alongside the ubiquitous copies of Sabbatical Laws.

George Broke took control of the wedding arrangements. He insisted on inviting at least two hundred guests. One hundred would be the constables, field hands, tanners and metalworkers who comprised the corps of the Broke Empire. The other hundred would be handpicked for having been supportive of the Broke coup. George envisioned rousing music, a forest of flowers, his bride bedecked in garlands and a crown.

Virginia was embarrassed at the idea of such a spectacle for a wedding. Her own parents were married without a ceremony, in the middle of the road, by Increase Gladford. He glimpsed them together, in public, scandalously walking hand in hand. He halted them. He asked each if the other was desired for a spouse. They nodded, and he said, "you're married."

Still, she was touched by George's enthusiasm and in the end went along with everything. She decided to trust the strange, uncontrollable forces sweeping her life along.

The day of the wedding, guests were gathering an hour early. A room in the back of the Meeting House was designated for the bride to make her preparations. Wandabella Shrenker made her a white dress and a crown of red blossoms, and Dorothy volunteered to help her put it on. For once, Wandabella had done it right; the dress was magnificent. The blooms were adorable: deep red, small, teardrop-shaped. Virginia's gold-brown hair fell in gentle curls over her shoulders. Her beauty was breathtaking.

Dorothy finished the crown and crouched behind Virginia to pin up something on the back of her dress. Virginia was trying to follow her orders to stay still.

"How do you feel, my dear?" she said, speaking through the pins she was holding between her lips.

"I'm okay."

"Not nervous?"

"A little."

"That's normal. Just put your faith in God, and everything will be fine. George was telling me an hour ago how happy he is."

"He's turned out to be so nice."

"Things aren't always as they seem, dear. Could be that meanness you saw in the past was really the pressure of loneliness. All these years, George has been around mostly men. His mother's so quiet, it's like she isn't there, and then there's only been his father and all those workers."

"I admit that I misjudged him. George has turned into the nicest—almost—man I've ever met."

"Life has a way of springing surprises on you, and sometimes it's best just to go along with it. Oops!"

"What's wrong?"

"Lost a button back here." She waved a hand dismissively at Virginia's look of alarm. "Not a problem. Let me run to the wagon and get a replacement."

Dorothy dashed out of the room.

Virginia went to the back window. At the far end of the empty clearing, at the end of the grove of trees at the perimeter, she could see the reverend's austere cabin. To one side, peeking through the scrub and poplars, a couple of gravestones. The southern fringe of the Acadia cemetery. With a twinge, she thought of Joss Hankers, Daisy Green, and Hildegard Shrenker. While no bodies had been found, all three had gravestones there now.

She thought of another—who had no stone erected in his memory, and felt tears come to her eyes.

A large, dark bird swooped down to the window. It flew right up to the glass and hovered there. The flap of its wings rattled the pane. The tiny, colorless beads of its eyes stared right into hers.

She moved away from the window and opened the back door. She stepped outside. The bird shot across the clearing, climbing sharply upwards.

The sun was shining. A handful of tranquil white clouds relaxed in the field of blue. Only a few patches of snow remained.

The bird swooped down close to the ground, its blue-black wings grazing the grass, then up again and came directly at Virginia. It flew toward her as it climbed and passed so close she felt the wind of it flush against her face. The bird rocketed straight up again, turned in a slow graceful circle, and made for the edge of the grove. It landed on a branch and sat, head tilted to the side, eyeing her.

Virginia stepped into the yard and crossed to the border, where the bird was sitting.

The grove was mostly poplars, with pines standing above them. The poplars were pushed close together, naked and bony, and seemed to be guarded by the bigger, greener pines.

Virginia shivered. A chill wind was picking up, lifting the fringe of her white dress. She was about to go back inside when she heard voices. Close by. Coming, strangely, not from the church, but from somewhere in the trees. Two men talking.

"So she don't suspect nothing?"

"Bitch swallowed every word."

"Good work, Mr. Broke."

"It was easy. Flowers here, sweet talk there, all humble-like...You could learn the same trick, Gus."

"Me? Nah, Mr. Broke. I had me a woman once, and got me some chillun from her 'fore she died in the swamps. She damn near drove me out of my head. Women's too much damned trouble."

"It's good to have you working for me, Gus. My father is happy with you too."

"You really want to let that Hugh Baker keep the bakery? You could snap it up in a second, put the fool in jail. Or just kill him."

"No, that's one promise I will keep to the girl. She marries me, I let that weakling father of hers live, under a roof. She doesn't marry me, her father dies in the snow. Bear food. Like Adam Green."

"Why'd she like that nancy-boy, Mr. Broke?"

"I don't rightly know, Gus. She must have seen him as her best girlfriend or something."

Gus hawked up something. "If he didn't run away to die in the woods that night, he'd a had my knife in his guts anyways. Either way, he'as done fer, Mr. Broke."

"I know, Gus. It wasn't your fault he got out."

"Reckon it'll be babies for yer next, Mr. Broke."

"That's the whole point, isn't it? The Broke line must continue unbroken. I aim to start filling her with babies tonight."

George made a grunting noise and Gus laughed. A burly slap on a shoulder.

The blood was gone from Virginia's legs. Stock still in the clearing, sunlight burnishing her hair, hand on her chest.

She turned and ran back to the Meeting House. She made it inside just as George and Gus emerged from the trees.

#

A second after Virginia came in, Dorothy entered the room from the other side with a handful of buttons.

"Now, Virginia, let's see if these…oh, what's wrong, Dear?"

"No-nothing." Her heart was beating so hard she could feel her ribs pulsing against her skin. Dorothy drew closer. "Are you sure? You look like you're going to faint."

I can't. I can't marry that monster.

"Are you hurt?" Dorothy touched Virginia's hand.

But if I don't marry the monster, he'll throw my father in the snow to die.

"Child, you're cold as ice!"

Like he did to Adam.

"Tell me what's happening."

Virginia squeezed her eyes shut. She pressed her lips together.

No choice.

"Virginia?"

Pulling together more strength than she thought she had, Virginia forced her lips into a smile. "Just…wedding night jitters."

"Oh, *that!*" answered Dorothy with a laugh. "Trust me, honey, it's *nothing*. My husband, God rest his soul, well, I was scared to death of him on our wedding night. I thought the Lord's final damnation were going to smash me to bits the second I got near that wedding bed. But honey, let me tell you, I was making a mountain out of a molehill." She considered as she crouched down behind Virginia. "Or, more accurately, an anthill."

Dorothy continued with the wedding dress, prattling on about her marital memories, while Virginia smiled and nodded like someone who knew she no longer had anything to lose.

Chapter Fifty
This Dog

Inside the church, the air was alive with excitement. The altar was decorated with beautiful flowers. The forest of spring colors, the most delicate pinks, newborn blues, and lively yellows, seemed to reflect all the enduring romance of a treasured fairy tale.

It was an article of Puritan faith to forbid the use of reverends at weddings. Believing the formalization of marriage to be a civil rather than religious matter, the Puritans used civil authorities to preside over matrimonial ceremonies, so the wedding ceremony of George Broke and Virginia Baker could not be conducted by the Reverend Calvin Branch, but instead needed to be superintended by the highest civil authority in the land. However, that authority, the mayor, was the bridegroom, George Broke. George could not officiate over the vows and recite them also. The second highest authority, the Vice-Mayor, was the groom's father Obadiah, who was unable to attend the wedding because of a leg injury from his fall from a horse.

To avoid using Calvin, George decided to promote one Arcadian into civil office for only that day to perform the wedding. Given his comfort with addressing large crowds and his familiarity with the community Meeting House, the most appropriate person to promote, George decided, was Calvin.

So, in a ceremony early that morning, using words contrived off-the-cuff by Mayor Broke, Reverend Calvin Branch was changed into Special Assistant Mayor Calvin Branch.

Special Assistant Mayor Branch had slept poorly. His long, withered fingers were shaking. During the days leading up to the wedding, his heart had been filling with grave doubts. He didn't know how to do a wedding, and his trust in George was diminishing rapidly.

The only person who understood the proper way to do the ceremony was William Gladford, so Reverend Branch decided to ask the former mayor for advice on how to do it, but as he traveled on foot on the eastern trail toward William's cabin,

Calvin was confronted by a gang of Broke's constables. There were three of them. They arranged themselves in a line across the trail to block his passage. One was rather short and scrawny, with a mangy straw hat that had lost half its straw. The other two men towered above the scrawny one. They looked like brutes, gigantic and muscular.

The small one held out his hand to stop Calvin.

"What do you want, old man?" The little guard had huge, protruding front teeth, like those of a horse, and his voice was so high, it could have been a girl's.

"What do you mean, what do I want? This is a public road. Stand out of my way."

"No, this here's a *private* road, and no one can pass without permission. On the orders of Mayor Broke."

"Well, Mayor Broke would certainly approve of my coming here. I am visiting William Gladford."

"No one kin see Gladford," piped the little constable.

"What do you mean? Why on Earth not?"

"Orders of Mayor Broke. He's not allowed to see anyone. He's not permitted to leave his cabin."

"Why? He was supposed to have been released from quarantine weeks ago. He hasn't broken any laws."

"Any what?" The skinny man's nonstop grin was unnerving to Calvin.

"The laws! The Sabbatical Laws!"

The man tittered. "Oh, those."

"Yes, those. I was told that since he was not being held for violation of the law, he would be released."

One of the big men leaned over and shook a scolding finger down at the preacher. "Old man, you shouldn't listen to rumors."

"It wasn't a rumor. George Broke told me himself. It was a promise he made to his fiancé."

The other giant spoke, a bit of menace in his voice. "Mayor Broke didn't say nofin' to us, old man. So piss off."

Calvin was flabbergasted by their stupidity.

"Listen carefully. I can see him. I am officiating over George's wedding tomorrow, and I require counsel with the former mayor about the proper way to conduct the ceremony."

The scrawny man tittered again. Making a feminine gesture with his fingers, he deepened his voice and did a comical imitation of Calvin. "Oh, look at me! I am officiating over George's wedding!" The two giants laughed.

"Let me pass," commanded Calvin.

The scrawny man grinned. "You can't."

"I demand that you let me pass!"

"No."

"Step aside!"

"Tee hee!" said the scrawny man.

Calvin tried to push through the men, but all three shoved him back. With a flush of alarm, he felt knuckles digging painfully between his ribs.

"Come, holy man," said one of the giants. "We gots orders."

Reverend Branch was struggling not to cry. Never before had he been prevented from travelling anywhere and never before had he experienced such disrespect. "None of this makes sense! Why can't I see him?"

"Arcadian security," answered the scrawny constable.

"What does that mean?"

"I don't know."

They really didn't know, but they had orders, and in the end Reverend Branch was forced to turn back without seeing William.

In the days before the wedding, Calvin tried to speak with George about the incident but never could pin him down. He tried to concentrate on the problem of how to conduct the wedding. He sought advice from his great niece Clarissa, who had moved in with him after running away from her husband. But she was too tormented by her own marriage to offer help on how to start a new one.

Calvin had tried to make her comfortable in the tiny cabin. For privacy, he'd strung a rope across the single room and tossed a blanket over the top to create a wall. He'd brought in a wide-backed chair from the storage room of the church for her sit on while she nursed the baby, but it didn't rock, and the baby cried nearly all the time. Clarissa, who in truth missed her husband terribly, cried often too, so that at all hours of the day and night, the reverend was subjected to the wails of both infant and woman.

He felt like weeping too. When the noise wasn't keeping him awake, a recurring nightmare was: he was walking the hills, hearing William's voice crying for help. The voice seemed suffocated, pained, worming up from underground, where Calvin couldn't reach. As the preacher frantically scraped at the ground to save his friend's life, the voice grew fainter, weakening until it was gone. Suddenly, a head would burst up through the soil, and the ghastly face of an old woman would be looking up at him, a catastrophe of a face, wild eyes bulbous and yellowed, a spider-shaped web of burst capillaries spread over one cheek. The dream ended each time with the woman making a grab for his pants with her clawed fingers.

In the end Calvin cobbled together some words he imagined would be appropriate for cementing a lifelong union between George and Virginia. He was now pacing the stage, trying to remember his lines and think only about the task in front of him, instead of the ominous changes in his world.

His attempts to concentrate were complicated by Hugh Baker, who was also on the stage, practicing, incompetently, screechingly, the romantic barn dance tune *My Pretty Daughter Mabel How Sweet She Is* on his fiddle.

According to the ceremony plan, he was to begin playing the song for the audience at the start of the official ceremony, when the reverend gave him a signal. The audience, however, had more or less completely arrived, so Hugh was, in a sense, already playing for them, and they were already becoming irritated.

Gus Fodder appeared at the front door. He gestured to the reverend. Calvin in turn signaled to Hugh. Hugh stopped playing the fiddle and stared dumbly at the reverend.

"Start playing," said Calvin through gritted teeth.

"Oh." Hugh struck up the same tune again, exhibiting no improvement in his performance.

When Hugh was finished, Reverend Branch stepped up to his podium. "Greetings," he said in the cheeriest voice he could muster. The murmuring stopped. "We are here to bear witness to the start of one of life's most wonderful experiences, that of holy matrimony." There was a smattering of applause. "Without further ado, let the ceremony commence. I'd like to ask the groom to come forward."

George Broke appeared at the door. He was dressed in a new black suit with a gold-buttoned vest and gleaming ebony hat. This time, Hugh remembered his cue and went into a somewhat recognizable performance of a popular tune of the time, *The Finest Young Gentleman of the Grange*. George moved forward slowly and deliberately. His handsome face, his confident walk, and the fine cut of his clothing evoked shock and awe in the crowd. What wisps of doubt yet lingering over the unconventional ways George had ascended to the position of mayor, and the martial changes he had brought to the land in the name of decency, were flushed away at the sight of his big rolling shoulders and his beautiful suit. Basking in the dazzled silence of his admirers, Mayor George Broke came to a stop before the altar.

Calvin said, "And now, may we have the bride come forward too."

Dorothy had been listening through the door for the moment the reverend asked for the groom, for this was the signal for Virginia to go out the back door, come round the building, and enter through the front. Given the urgency of timing, she expected Virginia to bound along with her to the front. Instead, Virginia moved slowly, her head bowed.

"Virginia, we must hurry. Why are you moving like a snail?"

Virginia forced herself to smile. "Don't worry. I'm coming."

The front door was propped open by a wedge of wood. People were on the porch, straining their necks to get a look through the windows. Through the glass Virginia could see George Broke midway up his walk to the front.

She turned toward Dorothy, who was watching him too, a smile on her face.

"Dorothy?"

"Yes, dear?"

"Promise me something."

"What, my child?"

"That no matter what happens, you won't hate me. That you will try your best to understand."

"Virginia, what on Earth are you talking about? A fine time to start talking nonsense."

Virginia opened her mouth to speak, thought better of it. It was done. She was determined that in only a few hours, after the marriage was secure and her father safe from harm, she could do it with a clear conscience. What was the best way? A rope? A leap from the building? God would show her the way when it was time.

"It's time," said Dorothy, nudging her. She heard the reverend calling, "where's the bride?"

Virginia took one step, then another, and it was easy after that, walking in a dream, a sea of faces gawking at her. She cringed a little when she saw her future husband waiting at the altar, grinning.

From all directions disjointed sounds washed against her. Children giggled and a woman was issuing an eerie, staccato laugh. The reverend crooked his finger at her, a strained smile on his face. Someone was clapping, but the noise was deformed, harsh, iron on wood, like horse hooves.

She was really here. The slinking fabric chill of the wedding dress on her shoulders, the groom at her side, handsome, every bit the gentleman. Straight teeth. Grey eyes, sinking into her. The reverend was saying something.

"Virginia?"

"Hm?"

"Do you accept George Broke as your husband?"

She wiped her hand across her lips. "I don't think so."

Virginia was shocked. She hadn't spoken a word, but there her words were, in the open, the precise substance of her thoughts. It was like her mind had found a way to speak aloud when her lips refused to part.

"I don't think so at all." She spun around, because it wasn't her voice.

Virginia's body went numb.

A few feet away stood Adam Green.

"She'll never marry this dog."

For a ghost, Adam appeared healthy. He was dressed in a long leather coat. His hair was longer and wilder, and he'd grown a beard. The sun seemed to have tanned him a dark brown, and he possessed an animal confidence he'd lacked when alive.

He held a long, thick stick. He whacked it on one of the benches. "No, sir!" he shouted. "Don't think so."

Virginia was petrified to see the ghoul coming closer. For one dizzy moment she was sure this was the moment of death God had sent for her. A second later, she was looking into the face of her Adam, very much alive, the boy she'd loved since childhood. His gaze fell upon hers and remained, searching. Then he saw and smiled. "Do you take him for your husband, Ginnie?"

Virginia shook her head and Adam had her by the hand, pulling her to the door. George Broke, at first paralyzed like the others, found his voice. "Hey!" He began to run after the couple. "Stop!"

To which Adam whirled around and jabbed the stick into George's belly. He brought the stick up and whacked him under his chin, then lifted him in the air and tossed him with a cracking swipe to his ankles.

George lay on the ground moaning. Adam spit on him. "Another day, *Mayor* Broke."

By the time the bravest of the crowd peeked their heads outside, the couple was gone. The only thing remaining was the swelling cloud of dust kicked up by the horses they'd escaped on, obscuring the direction they'd gone.

PART FOUR

Chapter Fifty-one
The Oasis

Morning light was pouring through the entrance of the cave. From the ledge outside came the fragrance of early flowers and the chirps of birds. On one side of the opening, its leaves flickering in the tranquil sunlight, its broad branches leaning protectively, stood an oak tree.

Virginia opened her eyes, startled momentarily at her surroundings. Then she remembered, relaxed. Under the blankets, Adam's body was pressed close.

She'd awakened this way, with a jolt of confusion followed by the relief of memory, for five days.

When they'd galloped away from the wedding, she was so dazed with excitement and fear she questioned nothing. She didn't even protest when Adam said they needed to leave the horses and actually enter, on foot, the deadly Forbidden Forest.

She moved along with him through miles of dark woods. Snow remained only in patches, and they could see from the copious piles of scat that the monster bears had certainly risen. But Adam moved like there was no danger, strolling without haste, smiling, holding out his hand to her when she faltered.

They'd emerged from the trees and moved onto a grassy clearing. In front of Virginia was the widest, deepest chasm she'd ever seen. Gargantuan cliffs formed the far wall. Rising from the unseen floor was an unfurling breath of white mist. With a childish kind of thrill, Virginia realized it was a cloud. The rocks across the gorge were thick with trees. Through the mist, she glimpsed vibrant patches of wildflowers.

Adam had helped her to descend the wide plates of stone that jutted from the face of the canyon. Their cave was a cozy chamber several tiers down, with a floor warmed by a dozen blankets. A wide plate of rock stuck out from the top. This would keep them dry even in hard rain. On the plate of stone next to the entrance, Adam had built a fire-pit.

Over the course of five days, sitting together eating fish caught from a nearby stream, or curled up next to him listening to the soothing sound of his voice as they watched the stars, Adam told her the story of how he'd found this place, and the adventures he'd had since escaping from the pillory.

#

After escaping the pillory and from Gus Fodder, he'd run blindly through the forest, understanding even as he fled for his life that he was going to die.

The bears would get him. Everyone knew that's what always happened to anyone who went into the Forbidden Forest, except the transient skinners, who knew how to survive because they were half-animals themselves. He ran through knee-deep snow, slamming into black trees, face torn by branches. Pain clawed every part of his body.

All at once the trees were gone, and Adam stumbled into a piece of naked land. He pirouetted, fell to one knee, leapt up again at the lightning bolt searing his leg, tripped on a rock and fell into the canyon.

He dropped seven feet at least, plopping onto a thick drift of snow, rolling off the surface and dropping again into thin air, striking more snow, then rolling, rolling, downward, falling five feet here, five feet there, banging himself against bushes, trees and rocks.

He came to a stop, arms flopping to his sides, head turned, waiting for death. Of the many pains in his skin and bones, one stood out. The side of his tongue felt like it was on fire. He realized his mouth was wide open. His tongue was dangling out, like a dog's, and was lying in the snow.

In the canyon wall was a cave. He crawled through the opening and passed out on the stone floor.

When he came to, it was still dark. His groans rang off the sides of the chamber and trickled back at him. A movement sent a blast of agony through his right arm. He lost consciousness again. He awakened later to the sound of insects chittering and a blade of night sky, tingling with stars.

A great weariness fell upon him and he slept a long time.

Day. He tried to sit up and shuddered at the spike of pain in his skull. He lowered his head carefully until it touched the cool stone floor.

He was startled to find a mound of something next to his face. The purplish blob came into focus. It was a small pile of berries. He was pretty sure it hadn't been there before. Ignoring the pain, Adam jerked his head up and gazed around the room. No one.

He painfully nudged the berries closer with his stiff fingers, and ate them in one gulp. He slept.

Sunlight was flooding into the cave. Was it the same day? He was aware of feeling soggy all over. His head again surged with pain when he tried to move. When the blaze receded, Adam was struck by a hallucination. The purple blob of berries had returned. He ate them again, marveling at how real they tasted.

Each time he fell asleep, he woke to another pile of food. It was mostly berries, but there were other forest edibles, nuts, mushrooms, alfalfa. He found grubs too, mixed in with wild strawberries, and earthworms sometimes crawled amidst mustard leaves. Adam at first resisted eating them, but he was so hungry that at last he forced them down.

Determined to catch his benefactor, Adam feigned sleep. His ears peeled for the sound of approach, he waited. Finally, he heard a scraping at the entrance. He kept his eyes closed and counted to ten.

He opened them and was stunned to see not the human hand he'd expected, but an animal nose. Two black eyes and a fluffy tail that pointed upward, twitching, behind the creature's head. Clutched between its paws were a couple of blueberries. In its mouth was a walnut.

Adam shouted. The squirrel dropped its load and scurried out. Adam started after it, but collapsed under legs flooded with agony.

Adam worried his shouting had scared the squirrel away for good. For a whole day, he was on tenterhooks over whether it would return. At last, he dropped to sleep and woke to a pile of grass and chestnuts, topped with a grub.

In time, Adam discovered it was not one squirrel bringing him food but several, along a couple of rabbits, and at least one badger. He once opened his eyes to find three sparrows prancing close to his head. To his amazement, he saw the birds disappear through the opening and fly back several times, dropping off more berries and nuts for him.

Adam was thirsty. The moisture he received from the berries helped, but it wasn't enough. The very day he became alarmed at his growing thirst, Adam witnessed the most astonishing thing of all. Five mice appeared at the cave entrance. Each gripped in its mouth the border of a large leaf, so that as they transported it, it took the shape of a bowl. Inside was water. Adam by then was able to lift his hands enough to support the edges of the leaf. He lapped up the water, trembling with gratitude.

Adam could only conclude that the animals bringing him food and water was a miracle. Either that, or he had died and really was in heaven. The latter impression was strengthened when he at last found the strength to crawl to the cave opening and across the stone porch.

Paradise. At both sides of Adam's ledge was lush growth. Trees, and bushes sprouted from numberless gaps between rocks and in patches of soil. Flowers of every color were bursting out all around him, and the air was rich with their perfume. Birds chased each other in play. The opposite side of the gorge was a lovely patchwork of greens and browns climbing halfway up the sky. Adam had never seen anything more beautiful.

Gradually Adam regained the ability to walk. As he came able to forage for food himself, he was disappointed to see the animals stop visiting him.

Once the pain receded, it was easy to climb to the top of the gorge. A short distance away was a narrow stream, running so fast the water splashed and foamed silver under the sun. In the stream he found fish he could catch by sweeping his hand through the water as they raced by.

Along the forest, he found an endless supply of dry brush for building fires, which he could easily start using the friction method his father had taught him. By weaving the thin branches and grasses together, he made a rough basket to carry food and supplies in.

One day, he was fishing in the stream, preparing to brush out with his hand a speckled trout pausing in an eddy. He perceived something cross the sun's rays. He went rigid. A short distance away was a bear.

The beast was a dozen feet tall and had a great fanged mouth and searching brown eyes that regarded him passively, as though he were no different than a tree or boulder. The animal sniffed in Adam's direction, clubbed out a fish from the water and caught it in midair. It chomped it down, regarding Adam from the corner of its eyes. Adam held his breath. The bear went on its way, disappearing over a ridge.

In the next few days, he encountered two more bears, and they treated him the same. They regarded him curiously but left him alone.

To the human world and its treacheries, Adam gave as little thought as possible. He grew determined to live out the rest of his life in this heavenly land, where food was abundant, the animals were his friends, and no one wanted to kill him.

Nights, he was haunted by images of a beautiful young woman with plaited brown hair. She appeared in a multitude of dangers, lost in a blizzard, beset by evil men, crying out his name.

Several nights passed, and the dreams troubled him so much that he couldn't stand it. After one especially bad night, without fully understanding why, Adam decided to sneak back into town, to get an idea of what was happening.

Within minutes of setting out, he was cursing himself for his stupidity. Why take the risk of getting caught? What could he gain? Yet even as he had these doubts, he pushed stubbornly onward.

He crossed the field and reentered the forest and followed roughly the same path he'd used during his escape. Within an hour, he came to a place where the trees thinned considerably. Through gaps in the foliage, he could see a cluster of buildings.

Dread grew inside him. There it was again. The town of the people who decided to murder him.

He could see Mr. Cobble's shop, completely dark, and across the road from it, Shrenker's General Store. To the right, he could see the third floor of Broke Bakery surmounting the shoemaker's building, and the glint of Virginia's window on the left face. Farther down, Joss's pub sat, gated and abandoned. Except for a couple of wagons parked outside Shrenkers, the road was empty.

The sun was low, almost touching the Grey Mountains. Four men galloped up to Hankers and tied up their horses. One fiddled with the lock and got it open. The man walked inside Joss's home and emerged a moment later carrying a bottle. He came back to the other men, displaying the bottle, smiling big. They uncorked it and passed it around. The four left Hankers and galloped down the road going south.

Adam twitched with impatience. Lanterns appeared in the windows of Shrenkers and in the bakery. When night was well on, and it was very dark, he ventured from the trees.

He slipped across the road to the bakery and tiptoed up the side stairs.

The door to the second floor was on a small landing on the side of the building. A gate led onto a wide balcony that overlooked the road below. The sign with the words *Broke Bakery* was nailed to the railing, the top sticking up three feet higher than the balcony. Adam dropped to his knees, crawled across, and crouched in the shadow of the sign. He suffered a seizure of panic when he found himself looking straight into the second-floor window, the room lit up with lantern light. Virginia, her father, and Miss Dorothy Rivers were right there in front of him.

Hugh Baker walked to the window and looked out. Adam held his breath. Virginia's father surveyed the night sky, his gaze moving slowly from the left toward Adam. When Adam was about to bolt away, Hugh looked straight at him and past, to the right. He hadn't seen him. Adam realized that clouds were blocking the moonlight and he was invisible.

"Wasn't his fault?" he heard Virginia say.

Her father answered, "Virginia. I know this isn't easy, but what else could he do? There was so much evidence."

"What are you saying?" Virginia was flashing troubled looks at the schoolteacher and her father.

"Even if all the other evidence were washed away, Virginia, there was the diary. In Adam's own handwriting. He confessed. What was George supposed to do?"

"It's a lie!" Virginia screamed, voicing precisely the same words in his mind.

When Hugh and Dorothy praised George and told Virginia why she needed to *marry* him, Adam could barely restrain himself from leaping through the window and confronting them. If Virginia didn't marry George, he heard with plummeting spirits, she and her father would lose everything. Adam's horror was soothed slightly by each of Virginia's protestations and set aflame again with every new kind word he heard about George.

Bootsteps on the stairs. Then none other than the demon, George Broke himself, appeared at the door, a bouquet of flowers in his fist.

Adam looked around for something—a rock, a stick, anything—to kill George with. There was nothing. He could run up from behind and grab him by the coat and throw him from the roof, but the door opened and George stepped inside.

The moment the door closed, out of the dark sky came a huge black bird. The vulture shot straight for the window, pulled up and hovered there.

"How do they know what's going on *inside?*" Adam heard Hugh say before he slammed the window shut and pulled the curtains.

On the road below, some horses clopped by. From the Shrenker building next-door, Adam heard a woman laughing.

The moon moved from behind the clouds and poured blue light onto the roof. Adam sneaked down the stairs. At the first floor, he looked up. If he could find something to fight with, he could burst in and...what? Kill George? Mr. Baker and Miss Rivers already both thought he was guilty of murder. Actually committing murder would only support their unjust belief. They certainly wouldn't help him. If he were caught, he would face the same punishment as before. Maybe worse.

Wracked with grief, feeling pathetic and powerless, Adam made his way back to the forest.

In the following weeks, he returned to the land of people several times. To his despair, he couldn't get close enough again to Virginia's windows to eavesdrop.

Broke's men took to patrolling the roads all night.

Adam could only manage to listen at the windows of outlying farms. From the conversations he heard, he learned that the belief that he was a Satan-worshipping murderer was widespread. During these nocturnal visits, Adam at last became a real criminal, though not the murdering kind, by making away with blankets and warm clothes farmers had hung out to dry.

Adam also learned that everyone thought he was dead. He didn't know how to feel about this. Should he be troubled that his fellows were celebrating his death? Should he be happy, because it meant he was not being hunted?

One evening about a month later, crouched under the window of a farmhouse, he heard a family talking about something even more troubling. There was to be a big wedding in only two weeks, at the church, uniting George Broke and Virginia Baker.

Adam returned to his cave in a fever of rage. From the oak tree next to his cave, he tore off a branch. He used it to attack the boulders scattered on the ledge outside his cave. He beat them until he was exhausted. When he stopped, the branch was still whole in his hands. His thoughts began to clear. He went to the edge of the stone plate. Gripping the stick upright between his legs, he balanced on his haunches.

The canyon, a thousand-foot drop only an arms length in front of him, was invisible in the dark. Adam could have walked straight into the abyss without realizing it was there.

He started to make a plan.

#

Virginia gazed at Adam. He was half buried in the blankets, smiling in his sleep. A shiver passed through her. This was all a wonderful dream, something right out of a children's tale. She knew she couldn't permit it to continue.

Chapter Fifty-two
Paradise Lost

"Adam?"

Adam rubbed his eyes. "Yes, my love?"

"Are you happy?"

Adam leaned back and smiled. "Happier than I've ever been."

"Me too."

"Good."

She touched his hand. "That's why it hurts so much for me to say we can't stay here."

"Huh?" Adam sat up. "Why not?"

"This isn't our home."

"It sure is *my* home. Now it is, yes, ma'am." Adam folded his arms and looked out the entrance. A pleasant breeze was catching the mouth of their cave.

"We're without our people."

"Our people? Our people tried to *kill* me."

"They were tricked, Adam."

Adam scoffed. "Tricked? It was easy to see I wasn't guilty, Virginia! They had it in for me ever since Ma and Pa walked into the woods. They're crazy."

Virginia touched his arm. "Don't."

He shook her hand away. "Those people treated me like shit since I was a kid. And you're telling me we can't stay here because we left them behind?"

Adam stood and walked to the entrance. He tapped the roof of the cavern with his fists.

"Adam, it's better to forgive…"

"Do you know what they did to me?" He gripped a piece of his ragged coat and shook it at her. "They ripped this in half, tore my pants off, too. Then they chained me into that contraption, bent over so I couldn't stand *and* I couldn't sit! In the snow!" Adam punched the air. "Left me there to die, Ginnie! To *freeze to death*."

"But, Adam…"

"You can't tell me you don't understand! Mayor Gladford left me there! My own *aunt and uncle* left me there!"

"Adam, that's not true!"

"What do you mean?"

"George's constables had them trapped in their cabin. They couldn't leave. Didn't you know?" Adam shook his head.

"Mayor Gladford, and Annie too, and Doc and his wife. George and Obadiah had their houses surrounded by those horrid constables. Now that I ran away, Lord knows what George will do to them." Virginia pressed her face into her hands. "He said he would throw my father into the snow to die if I didn't marry him."

Adam sat on the blankets and put his arm around her. She buried her head against his chest. He ran his fingers through her hair. On the opposite face of the canyon, visible through the protective branches of his solitary oak tree, splashes of brightly colored flowers rested under the deep blue sky.

He said, "We need to make a plan."

Chapter Fifty-three
Hibernation

When the big man in the cave grabbed Daisy, Hildegard quickly ducked into one of the holes branching from the tunnel. "So who's this, I wonder?" she heard the man say to Daisy.

Joss shouted, "She's Daisy Green. I know her. Let her go."

"Why the hell's she down here?"

"I don't know! Let her go!"

"Why are you down here, little girl? Who sent you?"

"No one sent me. I was playing in the cave and got lost."

"The hell you did!"

"It's true! Let me go!"

Gus squeezed her injured arm and Daisy shrieked with pain.

"Gus, her arm's hurt. Let me look at her."

"Shit, I'll do more than let you look at her." Gus stepped up the cage door. One arm holding Daisy, he flipped out a key hooked to his belt, unlocked the door, opened it, and threw Daisy in. He slammed the door closed. "You can have her."

Other men came, their boots thundering through the tunnel.

Both Joss and other woman bent over Daisy and examined her arm.

"Oh, God, Gus, her arm is swelled up bad. And it's turning green." At hearing this from her hiding place, Hildegard bit her lip in anguish. "Gus, we got to get her to Doc Midland."

Hildie could hear Daisy sobbing quietly.

Gus sneered. "See Doc? She'll be lucky she sees food."

"You bastard."

"Don't think we got enough to feed one more."

"You're gonna burn in hell."

"Don't reckon I'll be the one burning. I know what pigs look like when they got barbecue in their future. And I can see three little roast piggies sitting right here."

"You come near us, I'll kill you with my own hands."

"Don't think so, Miss Jocelyn. Only reason I feed you at all's 'cause of the goddess here. Mayor Broke says, keep feeding'em, don't mess with'em, on account of the goddess." Gus did a whiny imitation of George's voice. "We need the goddess to tell us how to use the magic water. We need the goddess to show us how to make the magic wagons." Hildegard heard Gus hock up something and spit.

"Mr. Broke, he pays me a lot better'n I got cutting skins, so I does like he says me. But to me it's clear this'un here ain't no proper goddess at all, and don't know balls about making no magic wagons. Can't say I get her story, but I know she's stringing Mayor Broke along to save her own hide. Broke ain't caught on, but he's close. When he does, any day now, he'll be giving the orders. On that day, me and my men are going to have us a good time. There's a thing or two we been missing."

Hildegard heard a scratching sound, fingernails against fabric.

"You sick bastard!"

"I'm going to tell Mayor Broke everything you said." This came from a different female voice, steadier than Joss's. One Hildegard had never heard before.

"And I'll say you're lying," responded Gus. "Who's he going to believe? He already caught you in a lie about that injeen nonsense."

"Engine. Not injeen, you fucking hillbilly!" the woman shouted. "And I wasn't lying."

"Ain't how I see it."

Hildegard heard his bootsteps recede as he departed, whistling.

Hildegard was about to step out into the tunnel when the bootsteps suddenly returned. A metallic rattling and banging.

Gus's sneering voice rang out. "Here's your dog bowl." A clatter and scrape of something on the floor.

The footsteps clopped away again.

"I should've thrown the bowl in his face," snarled Joss.

"Then we'd go hungry for a day, like last time."

Hildegard tiptoed to the cage door. The two women were huddled around a big wooden container that really seemed like a dog bowl. In it was a nasty-looking gruel, slimy grease shimmering in the torchlight. Joss had some of the gruel in her palm, and was holding it to Daisy's mouth.

Hildegard's stomach heaved when she saw her friend. Daisy seemed wadded up in her own world of pain. She was crumpled on her side, eyes closed tight. Whatever Gus had done to her arm had made it worse. Her bad arm was now unfolded, and indeed did look like it was turning green, tilted outside on the ground at an odd angle.

The women saw Hildegard at the same time. The unknown woman, the one Gus called goddess, looked at Joss, confused. Joss put a finger over her lips. She stood up and came to the cage door. Joss whispered into the girl's ear, "Hildie, is it just you?"

Hildegard nodded.

"Then you got to get us out of here."

Hildegard, hands trembling, fished around on the ground and found a big rock. She lifted it over her head. Joss gestured at her to stop. She whispered again. "Won't work. Lock's too strong. And they'll hear the noise."

Heavy footsteps again. Hildegard tip-toed fast back to her hole. From there, she heard boots tromp up to the cage and stop. This time the voice was familiar.

"Well, I'll be a pig in shit."

"George , it's…" said Joss.

"You will address me as Mayor Broke," he snapped.

"…It's Daisy Green," said Joss.

"I can see that. So, Daisy Green. You're alive after all. Where is that other girl you were with?"

"Daisy was alone. George, I think she's…"

"Call me Mayor Broke. Why is she on the ground like that?"

"Your man hurt her, George."

"I wasn't talking to you." George snapped his fingers. "Little girl! You were with someone else. What was her name? That tall, skinny one. The daughter of my aunt…"

"Your cousin?" asked the goddess.

"Yeah, that one. My cousin."

"Daisy's in shock. She's too hurt to talk, George."

"Mayor Broke."

Hildegard heard a small moan come from the cage and the sound of a leg scraping feebly on the sandy floor.

"You see, George? She can barely move. What is it, honey?" Daisy made a pained sound, a half-formed word.

"What did she say? Little girl, where is your friend? I know she was with you. What was that?" demanded George. "She hide? Your friend…hides…is hiding?" George's voice took on predatory intonations. "Maybe hiding somewhere near here?"

From her hole, Hildegard, heart jumping through her ribs, heard him take a couple of steps down the hall in her direction.

"She didn't say hide, George." Joss's voice was breaking. "She said died."

"Died?"

"George, I think her friend, your *niece*…her name is Hildegard, by the way, *died*. Somewhere in the cave."

Daisy was crying loudly now into the crook of her arm..

"What happened, honey?" asked Joss. "Did she fall down?"

Daisy cried louder and couldn't answer.

George was silent a long time before he spoke. "She really died?" he said finally.

"You don't seem too broke up about it, George."

"Call me mayor."

"What is wrong with you? Your own flesh-and-blood, a child, died somewhere in this cave, and you don't seem to care at all."

"Man's got to get used to things like this. Getting weepy is for women."

The goddess said, "When you speak so rudely, it makes me believe you don't want to hear anything more about the magic water."

"Goddess." George's voice was suddenly faltering. "We still can't find any."

"I told you it's hit and miss."

"More like miss and miss."

"I also told you I should be there. I can't survey the land without seeing it. Let me out of here and maybe I can help you."

"But you are supposed to be a goddess!" George shrieked. "I need to find and collect the black water. My men have been trying to fill the barrels using pipes, following your directions, but nothing comes out!"

"Did you build a pump like I told you?"

"We tried," George whined, "but we couldn't figure it out." In an explosion of frustration, he shouted, "You don't tell us enough! Why don't you tell me everything!"

"Why don't you set us free?"

"We've already explained all that. You can't be seen by others. The people wouldn't understand. They'd…" He made a gagging noise as George's voice suddenly caught in his throat. Hildegard heard a cork pop from a bottle, and rapid swallowing of liquid.

"Mayor Broke," said the stranger. "Your father has kept me locked up here for months. Despite that, I've played along with you. But today, with the way that guard of yours treated this little girl, everything's changed."

She suddenly began shouting. "He *hurt* her! *Look!* Get a doctor, you fucking moron!"

"I can't."

"You bring a doctor now, or you'll never hear another word from me about the magic water."

"Please!"

"That's all!"

"Goddess!"

"Get out of my sight."

Hildegard could hear George huffing with frustration. He shouted, "Okay! I'll ask Papa!"

When she was sure George was gone, Hildegard tiptoed back to the cage.

Joss was next to the stranger, rubbing her back. The other woman's head was tilted downward, the tight coils of her frizzy hair dangling over her face.

Joss said to her, "you did great."

The stranger was close to tears. "But I gave him an ultimatum. We agreed…"

"You were right. Daisy changes everything. She needs a doctor."

When Joss noticed Hildegard, she jumped to the cage door. Hildegard could see Daisy on her side, sweaty cheek pressed into the straw, upper teeth biting her lower lip.

Joss whispered again to the terrified girl. "Get us out of here."

Chapter Fifty-four
Night and Day

Hildegard thought it was ten days since Daisy was captured, but it was hard to tell for sure. Life in this echoing, rocky prison did not separate night and day, or rather did not have day at all. The only rhythms of ordinary life were the visits from Broke's men to draw gruel from the barrel in the adjacent cavern, plop it in the dog bowl, put some water in another dog bowl, and give them to the prisoners. And replace their toilet bucket.

Fortunately, the food and water barrels were unguarded, and Hildegard could steal freely without the missing gruel being noticed. It was foul and thin, and the water brackish, but at least they fended off hunger and thirst.

For sleep, she crept far back down the path and hid herself in a tiny cavern. Sleeping on the cold stone was fitful, but at least she could curl up in her hole without being discovered.

Hildegard spent much time exploring the surrounding tunnels for a way out, and eavesdropping on the men when they came to feed the women.

There were four guards. Sometimes as many as three came together, but usually it was just one or two. Hildegard knew them by their voices, and Joss and the goddess, whose real name was Laurel, described what they looked like.

Gus was the huge, bald one with the mole-covered head and cruel voice. The thin, stupid one with the big front teeth, who was always tittering even when nothing was funny, was called Gnarl. The other two guards were twin brothers. Orlando and Oliver were almost as huge as Gus. Both had ragged black hair. If not for Oliver's eye patch, they would have looked identical. Oliver spoke nearly as cruelly as Gus, baiting the women with suggestions of nasty things the guards planned to do when George gave them permission. Orlando spoke much less than his brother, and when he did, his voice was gentle.

Hildegard's first idea for escape was to trick the guards into opening the cage door, then leap past or fight them, but hope of that faded when it became clear the women weren't strong enough to defeat even one of the big men. Gnarl, the only guard small enough that they might be able to successfully overcome him, never came alone.

Joss and Laurel could give her only one idea: follow the guards. Then she could at least discover how they came and went from the cave.

The mere thought of following those men, with the risk they might turn around and catch her, filled Hildegard with so much dread she knew she could never do it.

Since her capture, Daisy had stayed coiled up in a kind of hibernation, her condition getting neither better nor worse. She stopped talking. To their many questions, she responded as though she didn't hear them. In spirit, she seemed to have transcended the cave to exist in some place far from here, while leaving her body behind as a placeholder in case she decided to return. When they held a rag to her mouth sopped in gruel or water, she would suck at it without opening her eyes.

Because she could think of nothing to help them escape, and was too cowardly to follow the men to the cave exit, Hildegard sank into the deepest melancholy. She started avoiding the cage. The sight of Daisy was too much to bear.

She took slight comfort in the hope that maybe some people in town were searching for Daisy and her. She nurtured a fantasy that Adam Green would be the leader of the rescue party. Again and again, seated in the dark of her hole, Hildegard felt the roil of her anxiety reduced by the fantasy of Adam, like an heroic figure in a fairy tale, bursting into the cave, battling the guards, and carrying her away into the light. She made a vow that if she ever got out of this cave and saw him again, she would tell him how she felt about him.

Hildegard crawled back to her sleeping hole and curled up. She simmered in a pool of her own sweat. She sank into feverish dreams where the cave darkness was a living animal, an eel-like beast comprised of lightless space, coiled into an immensity of inky folds, twists, and knots. A face appeared on the creature, pushed itself toward her. The face of her mother. The face, and the creature, struck at her, slipped into and through her, consumed her bit by bit, became her.

After uncountable hours, she awakened and the fever was gone.

She left her hole. Joss and Laurel were overjoyed to see her. Dull with fatigue and hunger, she told them about her cowardice, about her fever.

Joss said, "Hildie, you don't need to…"

"Yes, I do," she said. "Because I am not her."

Without explaining, she moved down the tunnel and concealed herself in the nearby chamber where she had hidden the day Daisy had been captured.

She waited until the men came to feed the prisoners. The guards finished and disappeared up the tunnel. Hildegard took a deep breath and came out of her hiding place. As she passed the cage, Joss and Laurel made gestures to encourage her.

Hildegard was plunged into darkness. She nearly panicked and turned back. The men could be two feet in front of her and she wouldn't know it. Then she heard their voices some distance away. She was distressed by the explosive scrapes of her feet on the cave floor, but she pressed on, touching the walls to guide her. A turn to the right and all at once she saw the glow of a lantern. She could make out the four guards clearly. Gus, body bent to avoid hitting his head, was holding the lantern near his face. The other three were following close behind.

They proceeded through a labrynth of tunnels. Hildegard worked frantically to remember landmarks, a path opening to the right, a rough patch on the floor, a cluster of stalactites she almost collided with.

The men took a turn and the tunnel went dark. Hildegard groped for the break in the wall where they must have changed direction. She turned into the new tunnel that twisted sharply into yet another, and she nearly fell headlong into a fire-lit chamber.

A few feet away, the four guards were sitting on the floor. Hildegard threw herself against the wall, and flattened herself into the shadows of a slight indent in the stone.

A shrieking male voice stopped her heart. "Oliver, got any more yat coon meat?"

"Sack," said another voice gruffly. "But you can't have none, Gnarl."

"It isn't there," said a third, much gentler voice. "I moved it under my water bag."

"Why the hell you do that?" Oliver demanded.

"Because Gnarl was getting at it, brother."

Gnarl broke into a torrent of high-pitched cackles. It was a terrible noise that echoed all through the cave walls.

"It weren't yer meat, but mine!" protested Oliver.

"If I hadn't moved it, you'd have none at all. You should be thanking me."

"Orlando, I told you to keep yer hands off'n my things."

Orlando answered calmly. "You had best put that knife down, brother, unless you want your other eye cut out too."

"He's right," came a growling voice that Hildegard recognized as Gus's. Gnarl released another fusillade of nerve-shredding cackles, and Gus roared, "Shut it, Gnarl." Gnarl's voice chopped off in mid-cackle.

"*All* of you, shut up!" yelled Gus. "I got to get some sleep. The sun's already coming up, and George'll be here soon."

After some time, Hildegard heard the men's breathing turn heavy. She inched her head out of the niche until she could see into the chamber. The room was a few feet below her. The remnants of a fire glowed in a rough cooking pit. The men were sprawled around it. The floor was littered with gnawed bones and empty rum bottles. Next to the opening, close to where Hildegard stood, was a foul-smelling heap of rags and animal skins. Leaning against the opposite wall were some poles with nasty-looking hooks at the ends, nets, traps, and a couple of long-handled knives.

To the right, Hildegard saw something that sent her heart flipping with joy. The chamber floor inclined slightly upwards where there was a round hole. Through the hole flowed glorious morning sunshine.

One of the men stirred. He turned his face in her direction. It was Gus. He yawned and rubbed his eyes. Hildegard crept even farther back into the alcove and waited. No one came. Heart beating so heart her whole body was throbbing, she turn and slipped back down the tunnel toward the prisoners.

Chapter Fifty-five
Gots Ter Piss

At first, when Hildegard told Joss and Laurel about the exit from the cave, they became excited. Their excitement faded instantly, because the knowledge didn't get them any closer to actually getting out of the prison they were in.

Down the tunnel came the tromp of boots. Hildegard fled into her hiding place. The bootsteps halted outside the cage, and the clipped voice of George Broke spoke. "Goddess. I talked with my father about the newest development and your demand."

"About goddamned time," said Joss.

"When is the doctor coming, George?" said Laurel.

"There won't be any doctor until you tell us everything about the black water and the magic wagons."

"But..."

"My father decided this has gone on long enough. You will tell us everything. About how to find the black water, and how to take it from the ground. About how to...how did you say it?...*refine* it so we can push the wagons."

"Goddamnit, George," Joss said.

"You have," George suddenly yelled, "exactly one day to obey. If you don't, not only will you get no doctor, but you will also get no *food.*"

"Come on, George!" said Laurel, half scolding, half pleading.

"I will come back tomorrow. The rest is up to you."

"Wait, George, come back," called Laurel as the mayor made to leave.

"What?"

"You have to tell me. Why is this so important to you and your father?"

"You mean the black water?"

"I mean everything. Why do you want to make cars— magic wagons? What's the point?"

"I already told you."

"Not in any way I understand."

"What is not to understand?"

"Come on. 'My father had a vision of a world filled with magic wagons. And everyone was buying them from him'"? That's your reason?

"Yes."

"It doesn't make sense. What is the real reason? Is it just to make lots of money? There are other ways to make lots of money."

George blinked in confusion. He removed a flask from his coat pocket. His fingers trembled as he removed the cork and took a long drink.

"And what the hell is that smelly stuff you keep drinking?"

George grinned and licked his lips. "You want to know the real reason we want to make cars?" He brought his face close to the bars. His eyes sparkled in the firelight. "It's because we're gods."

In horrified silence, Joss and Laurel sank back in the cage.

"We're gods! But no one knows it yet. We need your magic, *Goddess,* to prove it to everyone. But if you were a real goddess, you wouldn't need to ask about that, would you?" George wagged a scolding finger at her. "Naughty, naughty lady, pretending to be a goddess to save your hide. Tomorrow is the deadline. You'll tell us everything we need to know or we'll leave you all here, including that little girl, to starve to death. And don't try to trick me again. You will lead us quickly to a functioning magic wagon or…or…" He gulped down some more liquid from his flask. "Or…I'll bend you over and lock you in a pillory and line up all hundred of my guards, yes! And order each and every one of them to forcibly bugger you!"

George marched away.

The two women in the cell remained paralyzed for a long time. Hildegard also remained frozen with terror in her hiding place. Finally, Hildegard heard Joss's voice.

She sounded like she'd been crying. "I've known him since he was a little boy, but I don't understand him at all. He's completely evil."

Laurel said, "He's completely bat-shit crazy."

A few hours later, after Broke's constables came back and fed the women, Hildegard followed them again to their lair. From her chink in the wall, she eavesdropped.

Gnarl giggled.

"Why are you laughing this time, Gnarl?" Gus growled.

"I gots ter piss. Tee hee."

"Don't do it in here like you done last week."

Gnarl tittered. The sound of his boots scrambling out of the hole made Hildegard want to scream with envy.

"Good, he's gone. I need to talk to you two."

"About what?" said Oliver.

"Mayor Broke told me last night, he needs them girls finished off."

"But he told them today they had one last chance," said Orlando.

"It's a last try to get information, but no matter what he finds out, it's all decided. Tomorrow morning, first light, we kill 'em."

Hildegard put her hand over her mouth. She felt her legs go wobbly.

"All of them?"

"All of them. The kid too. In town, people think Joss and that kid are dead already, so it ain't no loss. Don't neither of you tell Gnarl. That fool might tell the prisoners, and then we got problems."

"Hey, Gus, we gonna get paid extra for this?"

Gus laughed. "Big silver, gentlemen! No more fighting alligators in our future."

Gnarl dropped into the chamber screaming. He toppled onto Gus, who shoved him away. He started rolling on the floor, slapping at himself.

"What the hell's wrong with you, Gnarl?" said Gus, rubbing his stomach.

"Ants!" he wailed.

Oliver laughed. "Ants can't do noffin' to you. Here, we'll get'em off you, Gnarley." Hildegard heard hands slapping at fabric, then Oliver cried, "Stupid! These ain't ants! They's bees!"

The slapping became more frantic, and the men were cursing through an angry insect buzz. One by one, yelling in pain, the men fled the chamber for the open air. Hildegard heard their shouts growing distant.

Muscles tense to bolt, she climbed down into the room.

It reeked. Amidst empty rum bottles, she could see brown splotches where the men had spat up tobacco chaw. She looked closely at the row of tools against the far wall. She touched one of the poles, looked up at the hook on the end. Is this what they would use to kill her best friend?

Hildegard stared at the sunlight streaming in. Could she run out and get help in time? She was about to leap through the hole, when she heard the men approaching. She jumped back and fled down the tunnel. On the way back, she took a side tunnel that allowed her to avoid passing the cage. She went around, navigating by touch the path all the way to her safe hole. She curled up on the floor.

Morning. It was probably already getting dark outside. At most, she had twelve hours.

She wrapped her hands around her legs and pressed her chin between her knees. What can I do? she whispered. The darkness offered no answer.

Chapter Fifty-six
A Herd of Fools

Hildegard prayed.

She prayed to Adam Green. She begged him for strength. She whispered in a chant, on her knees, fingers twisted into a trembling ball, give me strength, give me a plan.

But there was no Adam, had never been one. It was only the bottomless black, staring back at her, and in the void she saw not a little girl but a new young woman. It was from her that Hildegard's plan came.

She slapped her own face. Hard. *Don't think. Move!*

She ran to the cell and woke the prisoners. Without giving details, she told them what needed to be done. Joss tried to argue.

Hildegard cut her off. "Remember! *Don't* let George leave! Start now!"

"Now?" Joss asked. "But first we need to…"

"*Now!*" barked Hildegard.

The women only hesitated for a second. Then they started screaming.

Hildegard darted up the passageway and ducked into the first side passage she could find. It was just in the nick of time, because Gus came thundering around the bend ahead, Oliver and Orlando behind him.

Hildegard heard Joss and Laurel screaming, "Help! Help!"

"What the fuck are screaming about?" demanded Gus.

"It's a ghost!" both women shouted back.

All three men were shouting back at the women as they continued shrieking, "Help! Ghost!"

In the chaos, Hildegard slipped into the tunnel and sprinted for the men's chamber. She walked straight into the room. A fire burned in the center of the floor. Seated next to it with his head pressed against his knees was Gnarl.

When Hildegard appeared, he goggled up at her in astonishment.

Hildegard lifted her arms over her head and wagged them slowly, simulating cobwebby things in a breeze.

"Booooo," she said.

Gnarl squealed and ducked under the pile of skins. Hildegard jumped to the tools against the wall. She grabbed a pole and snatched a sack from a pile. She tossed the things out the entranceway, pitching the pole out like a spear. She climbed out of the cave.

For a second, she was overwhelmed by the feeling of open air. It was so delicious, the sensation of the breeze against her skin, the freedom of having the whole sky open above her, all the stars in heaven twinkling overhead. She stood transfixed, her mouth open wide, looking up.

She remembered herself. Enough moonlight shone to make out the shape of the land. She didn't recognize this place. She hid in a nearby cluster of trees and listened carefully.

It took only a moment to hear what she wanted. Behind the whisper of the breeze, she caught the steady, busy hum.

She moved farther through the trees toward the sound. She continued until it was close, overhead. She couldn't see the hive, but she'd be able to at first light.

She listened for any sign of pursuit, but no one came after her. No one wants to pursue a ghost.

Soon a slender line of purple spread on the horizon, swelling and brightening to pink. Little by little a pure blue sky, dabbed with small clouds, opened up. Hildegard stared at the glorious sight and all she wanted was to keep staring for the rest of her life.

The bees snapped her out of it. The hive was close, only seven feet above the ground in the next tree. Cold fear flushed through her at the sight of it. The whining, gnawing sound filled her with the urge to run away. One look at the huge grey, bulbous mass cemented to a large branch and she knew these were the monstrous southern species, bees as long as a grown man's finger, with bright orange stripes and fearsome barbed stingers that couldn't be removed because they would break off at the ends. She gritted her teeth. One step forward, then another and another, don't think, move.

She lifted the hook, closed her eyes and slashed the air. It struck the branch a couple of inches above the hive. She could see them now, bubbling out from a hole in the grey, stomach-like mass. She swung again, this time with her eyes open.

A perfect hit. The hive came free from its cementing and tumbled, whole, to the ground. Hildegard rushed up with the sack. She grabbed the hive with her bare hand and shoved it in. As she closed off the sack and spun it around, choking off the opening, she was aware of her skin alighting with small blazes. She left the pole and sack behind the trunk of a pine and sprinted down the grove, swiping at the bees that tried to follow her. She had just stopped behind a tree when George Broke rode up. She watched him tie his horse to a tree and disappear into the cave.

She slipped out and sprinted to the hill. The outside gave no hint of the maze of caverns underneath. The entrance could be taken for a shadowed spot amidst the outcropping of rocks that surmounted it. She crept along the face of the hill until she was only a couple of feet from the entrance.

Male voices were shouting underground. George Broke was raging, "Idiots! Those bitches played a joke on you and you fell for it!"

"But they saw the ghost of that dead girl." It was Gus, sounding shaken. "Then Gnarl saw it with his own eyes."

In a jittery voice, Gnarl said, "I s-seen her. She come up'n say boooo."

George Broke sneered. "A herd of fools, I've got here. This nut sees all sorts of imaginary shit every day of his pathetic life. You all know that, but this one time you decide he's seeing something real, 'cause you're scared of ghosts. Are you men or are you mice? You're lucky I don't tell my father about this. Let's get busy. Gus, Oliver, Orlando, take these." Hildegard heard the sound of metal scraping on stone.

"Gnarl," George ordered, "stay here and guard the cave. You three, come with me."

Hildegard ran to the grove and grabbed the sack and rod. She dashed back and dumped the beehive on the ground. Bees were boiling up furiously.

She stomped on the hive and kicked it into the cave. In an instant, Gnarl was screaming. Hildegard leapt down into the cavern. Gnarl was writhing on the floor. She dashed past him and sped through the tunnels. As she came close to the passage leading to the cage, she heard the guards running in her direction to investigate Gnarl's screams. She ducked into a side passage. A second later, Oliver and Orlando flew by, nearly touching her as they passed.

Hildegard got behind them and ran along, her footsteps drowned by Gnarl's screams. She followed the men to the chamber opening. When Oliver and Orlando entered, they immediately set to slapping at the swarm of bees covering Gnarl.

Hildegard twitched with frustration. Why didn't they run away? She glanced up the tunnel then back to the chamber. In the fire, fat sparks were flaring up and crackling as bees flew in and combusted. The men were still grappling with Gnarl and showed no signs of fleeing even as they cursed that the bees were now attacking them too.

No time!

The girl leapt into the men's chamber. She raised her hands like claws and snarled at them.

"Ghost!" Gnarl shrieked. As the men turned around, Hildegard used the hook to yank a chunk of blazing wood from the fire and tossed it on the pile of furs. As she stumbled backwards into the tunnel, she caught a glimpse of the men, their astounded faces illuminated with a burst of seething red.

Hildegard raced back toward the cage. She dived into a side-hole in time to avoid colliding with Gus Fodder, now running to the front to investigate the noise. His voice joined the tempest of howls. A few seconds later, the screaming became more distant, then stopped entirely, as the men finally ran out of the blazing, bee-infested cave.

From the other direction, not far away, she heard Joss saying, "George, wait!"

Hildegard crept up and peeked around the bend.

George was facing the cage, a nasty grin on his face.

"I'll tell you everything you want to know," pleaded Laurel.

George sneered. "A little late for that, *Goddess.*"

Laurel sounded exhausted. "Please don't hurt us."

"You aren't a goddess. I don't know what you are, or where you got that magic box, but you sure as hell don't know anything about making the magic wagons."

"I do, George, I swear. I will tell you everything, right now, and I'll leave nothing out, I swear. Just please don't hurt the girl," she begged.

George folded his arms. "Okay, tell me."

Hildegard lifted the hook above her head and bounded up behind George. He turned around as she struck him as hard as she could on the head. With a groan, he fell sideways, bumped against the bars of the cage and collapsed.

Hildegard dived to the floor and shoved George against the bars. At the same time, she was groping frantically through his coat, screaming "Get the key!" Joss and Laurel put their hands through the bars and dug into Broke's pockets. Joss fished out the key and threw it to Hildegard. Hildegard let George fall to the ground. He flopped down heavily, like something dead. The right side of his head was spilling blood, a black-red pool spreading past his ears. She rammed the key into the slot and turned it.

The door swung open.

Joss gathered Daisy in her arms. The hostages moved out of the cell.

"Where?" demanded Joss.

"Follow me. Put your hand on my shoulder."

They moved as quickly as possible through the lightless tunnels. Hildegard led them, panic propelling her every step, guided only by her memory and her fingertips brushing along the wall.

They were almost the outer chamber when Hildegard heard the sound that told her they were going to die.

The men had returned. They were pouring back into the cavern, their outraged voices booming up through the tunnel.

"Go back!" Hildegard screamed. They groped their way back to the cage tunnel again. She waved them on, past the cage, over the bloody body of George Broke. Hildegard snatched up the hooked pole and jabbed it toward her old hiding place. "Get in there." They crowded into the hole.

"Don't come out till I call you."

She had no plan at all, just raw instinct. She rushed back to the cell, leapt over George's body. She shoved the door wide open. The frame pushed George over onto his side.

Hildegard moved around the door and bent over him. She couldn't hear breathing. She braced herself, then stuck her finger into the growing blood puddle. She dabbed some on her forehead. She smeared more on her face, in streaks.

She slipped into the cage and sprawled on the floor against the back wall. The sound of boots on rock approached and halted. The sight of Broke and the open cage brought a fresh chorus of howls.

Before the men could collect themselves, Hildegard moaned.

"Look!" said Gus. He approached Hildegard and looked close. "Bloody hell, here's your ghost, boys. I never heard of a ghost that bleeds."

He jabbed her stomach with his boot. "Where are they? Tell me now and I might not burn you alive."

In jerks, Hildegard lifted her hand. Her half-extended finger pointed at the wall. She gurgled, "That...way."

"What?" Gus looked at his comrades. "What the hell is she saying?"

"A krraaaku. Wall. Oopens."

Oliver came up and tilted his face closer to her.

"Oop-p-pen it. Quick!" Hildegard's eyes rolled in their sockets.

"Think she's saying there's some kinda crack here in the wall, Gus," Oliver said.

Gus bent closer. "Don't see nothing."

Hildegard coughed and spat blood. "There," she rasped.

Orlando entered. The three men stooped. Gus ran his finger along the rock. "This…"

Hildegard was on her feet. She darted to the door so fast she was already in the hallway before the men turned around. She slammed the door behind her, whipped out the key, which slipped from her fingers and dropped in the dirt.

The men rushed to the bars. Hildegard was grappling frantically in the dust, screeching, "help!" Joss and Laurel came rushing from the hole. They struck the door just as the men rammed it from the other side.

A pushing match started. The women were straining as hard as they could, but they had no chance against the combined power of the men. The door inched open.

Without warning, Joss let go of the door, jumped backwards over George's body, leaped against the cave wall, jettisoned her bulky body forward, and threw herself against the bars. The door slammed shut so hard that all three men were knocked over backwards. By the time they stood up again, Hildegard had shoved in the key and turned it. The door was locked.

The women whooped in celebration, dancing and embracing each other, Tears fell down their cheeks.

"I'm glad you're crying," said George.

He was standing in the tunnel, between the cage and Hildegard's hiding place. Blood was slathered across his forehead and leaking steadily in a ribbon down his cheek. He held something in his hand and was pointing it at them. "Starting the tears now is good practice." He snapped his head sideways. The movement flung a splash of blood in the air.

George jiggled the thing in his hand. "Have you ever seen a gun? When our ancestors first settled Arcadia, they all had them." The blood on Broke's face was gathering on his chin and dripping steadily onto his coat, leaving a black line down his front. "My great grandfather kept some for posterity under our pantry. They were completely rusted out when I found them, and I couldn't make them work. But the goddess here, she had a new shiny one when my father caught her. Pa took it apart and figured out how to make new ones."

George pointed the gun at the wall. A flame flashed from its snout and a sharp *crack!* battered the tunnel. The women screamed. The surface across from the cell blasted out in a geyser of dirt. A fist-sized crater opened up on the rock.

He pointed the gun at the group. "Who's first? Oh, I know. The one who caused all of this." He pointed the gun at Hildegard.

"Cousin George…"

He aimed. "You're a nuisance, just like your mother."

George suddenly toppled forward. He landed flat on his face and dropped the gun. Daisy had crawled from the hiding place and, using her good arm, yanked his legs out from under him. Laurel kicked the gun away as Joss and Hildegard jumped on George together. He rolled, flailing his arms and legs wildly and managed to slip out of the tangle. In an instant, he was on his feet, rushing down the tunnel. He disappeared around the corner.

By the time they got to the men's chamber, there was no trace of him or the other men. Only the smoldering remains of the big fire, the buzz of the few remaining bees and the clop of George Broke's horse receding into the distance.

Chapter Fifty-seven
The Big Brown Head

Virginia and Adam needed a plan. They decided that the best first step was to go to Doc and Claire Midland's farm to ask for their advice. If there was anyone in the world who would know the best way to fight back against the Brokes and Reverend Calvin's Sabbatical Laws, it was Doc Midland.

It was hard for Virginia to accept traveling in the forest as safe. It took Adam an entire day to convince her they should keep to the trees while journeying to the Midland farm.

The idea ran afoul of everything she'd been taught. Her head was filled with tales from her childhood, of the endless dangers of the woods, especially the monstrous bears. She had felt safe in the cave with Adam next to the Edenic gorge, but being in the trees again terrified her.

Spring had arrived and the forest was bursting with life. Shafts of sunlight pushed through the canopy. Adam and Virginia headed north, he holding her hand and trying to comfort her and she constantly glancing around for bears. After a time, they reached a break in the trees and could see Mill's Trail.

"If we keep just inside the trees, we can probably follow the trail straight north from here to get to Doc's." said Adam.

They stepped cautiously out of the woods to get a look around.

Virginia screamed. Adam turned to where she was pointing and his mouth dropped open.

There was someone rounding the bend on the trail. Adam's blood froze at the sight of her. If he didn't know she was already dead, he would swear the girl approaching them was Hildegard Shrenker.

Chapter Fifty-eight
Her Tea and His Powder

Hildegard ran up to Adam and stopped, peering up in confusion at him while he peered down in confusion at her. Adam could see the girl's hair was ratty and her skin was splotched with black, and he could smell the very unghost-like smell of fear on her. All at once, she threw her arms around him and sobbed into his chest.

Virginia came forth and embraced the girl too. They didn't have time to start asking her questions before another specter appeared, this one looking a lot like Joss Hankers.

Shouts of joy and astonishment rose from both groups as the members of both realized that everyone, most of whom had been thought dead, were actually yet among the quick. The road became a disorder of hugs and tears. Adam experienced another shot of euphoria when he discovered the bundle of blankets Joss was carrying contained his slumbering sister, but Adam's joy was crushed when he saw Daisy's condition.

Her broken arm was bound tightly to her side. After knocking George down in the cave, Daisy had returned to her state of hibernation. One eyelid was parted slightly, but no consciousness registered in the sliver of eye underneath.

"We're going to Doc's, *now,*" said Adam.

It was also tough convincing Joss and Hildegard that it was safer to travel in the woods than on the road. Adam almost had to push them into the trees. After they passed through the tree barrier and walked for a time without being eaten, and Virginia explained all that had happened, Joss and Hildegard's fears lessened slightly.

Hildegard described the adventures in the cave, and everyone praised her for her courage in helping with the rescue. The former prisoners learned about the coup by the Brokes and the failed execution for witchcraft of Adam. Joss cheered when she heard of Adam's rescue of Virginia at the wedding. "*Now,* you are your father's son!" she said.

Joss related how she was captured by George and did her best to describe Laurel, her mysterious cellmate, made all the more enigmatic because the moment they were free from the cave, she had vanished while Joss and Hildegard were gathering food.

Joss could only repeat the fantastic claims the woman had made of herself. The story was so incredible that Virginia and Adam would have doubted the cooper's sanity if Hildegard didn't confirm the existence of the foreigner. Laurel's tales of flying machines and buildings with a hundred floors and lightning-fast wagons and boats visiting the stars were so outlandish that it was impossible to believe any could be true. However, one thing gave credence to the fairy tales: the black box. Both Joss and Adam had seen the thing with their own eyes.

At length, they couldn't make any sense of the mystery of Laurel. The only thing clear in relation to her existence was that George and Obadiah Broke were insane and evil.

"*They're* the witches," said Adam.

They were moving through a meadow between two banks of trees.

"Excuse me," he said. Adam moved away from the group and made to climb over a dead log.

"Where are you going?" Virginia asked.

Adam muttered, "Privy."

Adam walked a short distance, moved behind a tree and untied his breeches. Aside from a chirp here and there from birds high in the canopy, not a sound interrupted the magnificence of the forest. Snow lay in patches, clinging to the layer of pine needles that covered everything. Spring plants were poking up shoots everywhere. Flowers were appearing in the rises of the tree trunks and even from the bark itself.

Screams broke from the clearing. Adam leaped over the log and saw Virginia on the ground. Joss and Hildegard were standing nearby, shouting. Like a cast-off bundle, Daisy lay in the grass some distance away.

Standing over Virginia was a bear. Forelegs up, yellow claws extended, maw open wide, the brown fur of the hump on end.

Adam leapt out from behind the tree. He roared.

The bear swung its head around and fixed its black eyes on Adam, who charged and threw himself between the bear and Virginia. Shaking his fists up at the animal's head, he bellowed again. The noise from his throat was raw, primitive, wordless.

The bear's eyes met Adam's. From deep in its chest, the bear groaned. It made a slow movement of its head, lowering its long nose. It dropped to all fours, the weight shaking the ground. The muscular furrows along its spine rippled as it turned away.

Without looking back, the bear loped to a space in the trees and disappeared through it.

Adam jumped to Virginia and hugged her. Hildegard collapsed in a dead faint and Joss remained standing, still uselessly brandishing a stick she'd found.

"How…how did you make it go away?" Virginia said, gazing at him in wonder.

"Yeah. How'd you pull that off?" Joss asked.

Adam frowned. "I surprised it?"

They set out again. Adam and Daisy led the way, Virginia following close behind, and Joss and Hildegard bringing up the rear. They tore strips of fabric from Adam's coat to tie his hibernating sister to his back. When they finished, the siblings seemed to combine into a kind of magical creature, like the one in the children's tale about the animal with two heads, one for contemplation, the other for action.

At last the trees gave way to a rough wagon path leading to Doc and Claire's homestead. On the left, huddled in the fringe of the woods, was their cottage. Between the buildings was the lush forest of Claire's cultivated flowers.

Adam stepped from the trees. Joss leaped forward and yanked him back.

"What?"

"Not so fast. Don't forget. They were held prisoner by George's constables."

He frowned. "But…they wanted to kill me because they thought I killed you and Daisy, right? But here you both are, alive. So they can see I'm innocent. So they have no reason anymore to want to hurt me."

"Should be that way, Adam. But I think them accusations against you were just a trick. To cover up what was really going on."

"What do you mean?"

Joss struggled for words. "It was a distraction, but I don't know what the real reason was. Something about that black water on your farm and making these stupid, fast wagons we both saw in the crazy box."

A dozen robins chased each other overhead, pattered onto the branches of a tree in front of them, stared at the group for several seconds, then, in unison, took off and headed north.

Adam peered through the trees. "Alright then. We'll be careful. Let's move up real quiet. And get ready to run."

"Or fight," said Joss.

As silently as possible, they walked around the flower grove. They crouched and hid in the growth and surveilled the cottage. The front door of the cottage was open. A pig was snuffing at the ground, moving around the opposite end of the building. The pig looked over at them, then trotted to the house, climbed up the stairs to the porch and entered.

"Will you look at that?" whispered Adam.

Claire Midland appeared at the front door, looked right at the place where they were concealed and called out to them, "You can come out now."

Before they could get over their surprise, the old woman walked quickly up to them, her vast bosom heaving to and fro. A second later, she was hugging them in turn, squealing their names. She pulled back the blanket covering Daisy's head and looked at the girl with concern. "Let's get her inside."

"Broke's constables aren't here?" asked Virginia.

"Oh, yes, dear. They're still here. Don't worry!" she laughed at Virginia's look of terror. "The most important thing is our having a look at little Daisy here." Doc's wife unpeeled the layers of blanket. Daisy was like a slumbering squirrel. "Doc said she'd be in a bad condition, but this is worse than I thought, poor dear. Let's get her inside."

"Doc said...?" asked Adam.

"Inside," said Claire and she walked back to the cottage. The bewildered fugitives followed her. In the living room, they were even more surprised at what they saw.

In a cushioned chair next to a tea-table sat Doc Midland. William and Anne Gladford were seated on an adjacent sofa. On a long wooden bench were two of Broke's constables. These latter two were slumped against the wall with their heads pressed together, their arms wrapped around each other drunkenly. One was snoring.

"They can't hurt a fly. They've been slumbering this way for three days."

Doc said proudly, "I slipped'em a medicinal powder."

On a work bench along the left wall were dozens of small wooden bowls. A galaxy of colorful powders was in the containers. There was a pitcher of water and a box filled with leather pouches. Mingled with the bowls were two iron pots with burned remains of something inside.

Claire said to Doc, "Francis, we must help the little one."

Doc stood. "Serious break, wasn't it? Right here?" He bent his arm backwards a bit, so the forearm was pointing slightly in the wrong direction.

Hildegard's mouth dropped open. "How did you know?"

"I know how he knows," said Joss. "These two constables here talked to the ones in the cave, and they told you, right?"

"Nope," said William, smiling deviously.

"Adam," said Doc. "I need your help. The rest of you, stay out here." Doc took Adam and Daisy to a back room of the house. Hildegard tried to follow, but Doc waved her back.

Claire said, "Hildegard, honey, don't you worry about your friend. She'll be good as new."

"How did Doc know about her arm?" said Joss.

"Oh, my!" Claire cried. "You have nowhere to sit. Help me bring in some chairs."

Hildegard, Virginia and Joss carried in stools from the barn while Claire made more tea. When they were all seated, Virginia said to Anne and William, "I heard you were held at your house by constables too. How did you get out here?"

"We're old," Anne answered, "but we aren't stupid."

William smiled at his wife. "She made them some powerful sleep tea."

"They're probably still asleep," said Anne.

Claire laughed. "Doc's envious, because her tea's stronger than his powder."

"Aren't you worried George and Obadiah will come here looking for you?" asked Joss.

William's face darkened. "We are indeed. So far, they've been too busy to bother with us."

"Busy?"

"A lot of things have happened. Bad things. George's constables are running wild. They're using those Sabbatical Laws to punish people for just about everything. Folks are scared to even leave their houses."

"Punish people?"

"You know that pillory Adam was in? Well, George built five more of those damned things, and they're full up, all the time. They had Miss Thatcher, Ole Jud's girl, locked up there for six hours, just for holding her boyfriend Thomas's hand. And they *whipped* her."

"Lord have mercy," said Joss.

"You remember Pearl's mother?"

"Hester, the one out north, past the orchards?"

"Yes. You know how she does her seamstressing for free, for those Brooks Farm people?"

"Uh huh."

"Those damned constables arrested her. Gave her a trial, found her guilty of refusing to make Arcadia great or some such nonsense, and punished her by, you won't believe it, *branding* her."

"No!" Virginia cried.

"I swear. They held her down and branded a big 'C' on her face."

"God," Virginia whispered.

"'C'?" asked Joss.

"For 'Charity'. But even that's not the worst. We've heard awful stories. The constables have been catching women on the roads and…" William glanced at Hildegard. He said, "It's just beyond belief, the things we've heard."

Doc and Adam emerged from the back room. Adam looked drained. Doc winked at Hildegard. "She's going to be alright. It was a bad break, plus she was dislocated." Doc tapped his own upper arm, then his shoulder. "She's the toughest person I ever have seen. Adult or child."

"Can I talk to her?" asked Hildegard.

"She's sleeping. I gave her a powder, and there's no telling when she'll wake up. But she's fine, honey," answered Doc.

"I was telling them about what George's men have been up to," said William grimly.

"Why don't people fight back?" said Virginia.

"They're too scared. And some still hold to the idea the Brokes are protecting us all from something even worse, that a little rough stuff from the constables is a small price to pay for that protection."

"What could he protect us from that'd be worth *that?*" said Adam.

Anne smiled sadly. She reached over and patted Adam on the hand. "From you, dear."

Adam stood and walked to the window. Fresh green leaves were spreading over the trees. Flowers were blooming everywhere. There was nothing out there to suggest the world was ending.

"Are you ever going to tell us how you knew about Daisy's arm?" asked Joss. "And all this other stuff? You said you've been hearing about all these things, but you haven't left here for days."

Doc said, "It's true. We haven't gone anywhere. We haven't had any visitors either." He had a mischievous look on his face. "Least not any human ones."

"What do you mean?" said Joss.

"You wouldn't believe us if we told you," said Claire.

"I don't think anything you tell me could be more unbelievable than things I've seen recently."

"Hildegard?" said Doc. "Do you remember when your boat was smashed apart in that stinky river?" Hildegard mouth dropped open. "How...?"

"Do you remember meeting anyone?"

Hildegard fidgeted. "No, sir. We didn't see anyone."

"You did meet someone, young lady." The old man moved to the set of shelves on the wall. He took down a wooden box, removed the lid, and reached inside. When he took out his hand, there was something brown and furry in it, with scrambling little feet.

Doc laid the mouse in his palm and smoothed its fur. He brought it to Hildegard. The creature peered up at the girl, whiskers twitching.

Hildegard touched the creature. "Is it the same one?" she whispered. The old man nodded.

Joss was exasperated. "Alright, can someone please tell me what in the blazes is going on? That *mouse* travelled all the way from under the ground to this cottage and told you about her."

"Technically, that's not precisely correct. Although the mouse did eventually get here on its own."

"The one who traveled here to tell us was a bird," explained Anne.

"A robin, to be exact," put in Claire.

"What?"

"The robin heard the news from the rabbit, and the rabbit heard it from the squirrel, and the squirrel heard it from this brave little mouse." Doc stooped and gave the mouse a kiss.

Joss gaped at the old couple. "You're both crazy."

"We are many things," said Claire. "But we are not crazy."

Doc said, "I know how this all sounds, but it is nonetheless true. I have spent the last decade refining this particular powder. The ingredients are numerous and the refinement of the herbs and roots to create them is complicated. But after much experimentation, I have succeeded in getting it to work perfectly. I mix the medicine in a cup of tea, drink it, and for twenty minutes or so, I can go out and have an intelligent and lively discussion with my lovely pigs out there. Or most any other animal I choose. I can speak their languages and I can understand them too."

"This is a joke."

"Joss, how else can you explain that pig at the Brokes, giving you the key to the building?"

Joss's mouth fell open.

"Yes, we know about that too. We heard about it from one of our pigs to whom a passing fox conveyed the news; the fox got the news from a ferret who learned about it from a dove who got the word from a turtle who was eavesdropping on some minnows who heard it from a cat who gossiped about a pig who witnessed George Broke climbing up after you. Unfortunately, we misunderstood the news. Instead of hearing that George Broke hit you on the head and was holding you hostage, we heard that George accidentally hit himself on the head when he was jostling a horse stage."

"Huh?"

"The point is that because the message was garbled, we didn't help you while you were prisoners of the Brokes. I've very sorry about that, but we simply didn't know." Doc sighed. He gestured at the powders on the table. "I've come far toward developing a potion which breaks down the barriers, but interspecies communication is dicey even in the best of circumstances."

Virginia was listening to Doc with her mouth hanging open. Adam seemed lost in thought. Henrietta was taking in Doc's words with keen interest.

Virginia spoke nervously. "You heard about all these things through this...animal...talk. Did you hear anything about my father?"

"Or my family?" asked Adam.

"I'm sorry," said William. "None of us have heard anything about them for a long time."

Adam took Virginia's hand, and Virginia laid her head on his shoulder.

Joss spoke in a voice drenched with incredulity. "Thought you knew *everything*, thanks to your chit-chat with critters."

"I do not *chit-chat* with them, Joss," sniffed Doc. "I *communicate*. And I don't have contact with every living thing out there, far from it. That would be ridiculous."

"Of course."

"There are problems with the linkages. Some species refuse to talk with other species."

"I see."

"Try to get a mouse to talk with a fox. One predates the other. It's not a good basis for friendly exchange."

"Right."

"Also, snakes might have a lot to tell you, seeing how they get around. But they're tight-lipped about everything."

"Snakes are tight-lipped?"

"Secretive."

"Adam? Virginia?" Joss pointed at the front door. "Time for us to get out of la-la land."

"You can laugh all you want, Jocelyn Hankers. But regardless of how we learned of the horrible things happening out there, they're still really happening. Just as your imprisonment with that strange woman really happened. She's a real mystery to us, by the way. What happened to her?"

"She ran away. I think she panicked."

"Too bad. I was hoping she could explain why George and Obadiah are doing all this to begin with. Can you, Joss?"

"I don't think she understood it any better than me. George and Obadiah want to get their hands on some kind of black water. They think they can somehow use it to build wagons that can travel ten times faster than any horses. They also want to make wagons that can fly like birds."

A strained silence took hold of the room.

"Why?" Adam finally asked.

"Dunno. Money? Power? I'm not sure they even know. They said Arcadia would change into a paradise if we'd have all these magic wagons. Strange, but I thought Arcadia was paradise already."

Mayor Gladford cleared his throat. "If we want to save Arcadia, we have our work cut out for us. To add to our troubles, most of Broke's men have guns now."

"Guns?" said Adam.

"George has been making new ones with his forge," said Doc. "These guns are the worst thing of all. They are more dangerous than you can imagine. They give a single man the power to kill many people, from a great distance. It wasn't for nothing that your father worked so hard to rid the land of those damned things."

Adam gave Doc a sharp look. "My father?"

"Your father. Jedediah was obsessed with removing every gun from Arcadia. He went around campaigning for people to voluntarily destroy them. Got into a big fight with Calvin's father about it. He used to say, 'Jesus would never have a gun.'"

"I don't remember this."

"It was before you were born. He didn't have much luck at first, because guns made life a lot easier back then. You could shoot yourself some dinner a lot easier than catching game some other way. And of course people wanted protection from dangerous animals."

"So why did he want to get rid of guns?"

"He said he wasn't really worried about guns in the present but guns in the future."

"The future?"

"Your father had these dreams that he said let him see with the future. He'd tell people that something would happen, and it would. He did this successfully enough times that when he said he'd had an awful vision about guns, many folks listened to him."

"What was his vision?"

"That one day, if we didn't get rid of every gun in the land, an evil man would rise up in Arcadia and take over by using guns to kill anyone who got in his way."

After a thoughtful pause, Adam said, "but he didn't succeed."

"Not completely. Some insisted on keeping them, saying that they needed them for self-protection. What if bears came into someone's cabin? How could you fight a bear without a gun? Of course, a bear has never done that, but still a few believed it. But most believed in your father and destroyed their own guns. Some people didn't have them to begin with. But mysteriously many of the guns just vanished."

"Vanished?"

"Your pa felt very strongly about this issue. One night, he got so agitated, it was impossible to calm him down. He was pacing back and forth in his cabin, talking his head off about how Arcadia was in danger if we didn't throw away every single gun. Finally, he couldn't take it anymore. He went out into the night and started taking people's guns away while they were asleep. He did it so quietly and quickly that no one ever knew he did it. Within a few days, he managed to reduce the number of guns in Arcadia to almost zero. Must have collected five hundred of them."

Adam stared at Doc. "How is that possible? It takes a whole day just to cross Arcadia."

Doc smiled at Adam. "It was possible because I helped him do it."

William and Annie said in unison, "we did too. And a lot of our friends."

"Your papa wasn't alone by any means," said Doc.

"What happened to all the guns?"

"That's a secret that only your father knew the answer to," said William. "We left them all heaped up in your chicken coop, hidden under blankets. Jed then put them somewhere else, but he never told us where."

Doc said, "One thing's for sure. Obadiah Broke managed to hold on to some, and he's somehow used them to create new, more powerful models."

"And your father's vision is coming true," said William.

"But Mayor Gladford," said Adam. "This whole thing started 'cause they thought I was a witch. They said I killed Joss here, and my sister and Hildegard. Now that they're found alive, everyone will know I wasn't a witch, right? There's no witchcraft going on, so there's no need for guns or any of this. We can go back to the way things were."

"This was never about you being a witch. It was never about whether you killed anyone. There was something else going on, something to do with that woman."

"But if we convince the constables…"

"The constables won't care. They're skinners. They've lost their humanity living the way they do. All they've got left to care about is the money and the extra trash it can get them. Wandabella Shrenker and her gaggle of gossipers are similar. They've also lost sight of what's important and become obsessed with money and possessions. And they're fanatically loyal to George and Obadiah. They'll do anything they're told."

"So what can we do?"

William, Anne, Doc, and Claire peered up from their seats at the worried faces of the young people awaiting their counsel.

"We have no idea," said William.

Chapter Fifty-nine
Over the Line

"The question is, how can we, a group made up mostly of old folks and children, take control of Arcadia from a much larger gang of well-armed men?" said Doc.

"We can't," said Adam.

Joss cracked her knuckles. "I can do it by myself. I only need to get my hands around the neck of that George Broke. And his father. Cut off the heads of the snake."

One of the Broke guards snorted in his sleep. He rolled onto his side, flinging an arm over the chest of his comrade. They were big, hairy men whose foul odor was made worse by days of constant slumber.

Claire said, "Darling, I think we need to give them more powder."

Doc filled a teacup from the pot and added a spoonful of purple-green powder from one of the bowls scattered on the table. The couple approached the constables. Doc placed his fingers on one of the men's lips and pulled his mouth open. The teeth were green-black and peppered with rot-holes. Claire spooned the liquid into his throat. They repeated the operation with the second man.

Doc said, "that should keep them under for at least another day."

Joss said, "Hey, Doc! Why don't we use that powder on the rest of Broke's men?"

"There's nowhere near enough powder to knock them all out."

"Can you make more?"

"It'd take me years to make that much. Even if I could do it faster, how could we possibly give it to them all? There's more than a hundred of them."

"Which leads us right back where we started," said Adam, "It's impossible."

"We have to try something," said Virginia.

"But there's too many of them," said Adam.

"We could organize other people."

"How?"

"Go around to each farm and talk to folks, get them to join us."

"The problem with that idea," said William, "is that you don't know who might be secretly supporting the Brokes. You could talk to someone who behaves like they support you, but the moment you leave, they'll send the constables after you."

"Also," said Anne, "traveling from farmhouse to farmhouse requires movement over the roads, which are crawling with constables."

"It's not possible," said Adam.

"Boy, are you all dumb."

Eight startled people turned to find Daisy Green standing at the bedroom doorway. Her arm was heavily bandaged and in a sling. Dark orbs were draped under her eyes, but otherwise she seemed as healthy as she had months before.

"Daisy!" cried Hildegard. She ran up and hugged her, careful not to touch her arm.

"You should not be out of bed, little girl," scolded Doc.

Daisy walked to the center of the room. "The answer is plain as can be."

"Baby," said Anne. "It's time for little girls to be in bed. These things are not for the ears of children."

"What the fuck are you talking about?" said Daisy.

"Daisy!" gasped Adam.

"Daisy Green!" said William. "You do not talk to your elders like that."

"I do when they talk horseshit."

"Young lady, go back to bed at once."

Daisy went over to Joss and tugged at her smock.

"Please, make them listen!"

"Everyone," said Joss. "She and Hildegard saved our lives. They helped us a lot better than we did ourselves. Maybe you should hear her out."

"If she promises," Adam growled, "to keep a polite tongue in her head. What's your idea?"

"There's one other person who has power," said Daisy, "besides George and his fish-face father. Reverend Branch."

Doc's countenance turned stormy. "That stubborn old scarecrow conspired with the Brokes in everything they've done. He's gotten his crazy old laws back. He's completely happy."

"Reverend Branch has a weak spot."

William smiled dubiously. "He does? I've known him for decades. He's the most stubborn man I've ever known. If he's got a weakness, I don't know what it could be."

"Her name is Clarissa."

"His niece?"

"His great niece," Daisy corrected. "And she's married to our cousin Richard, right, Adam?"

Adam nodded, the light of Daisy's idea dawning on him. "You're thinking of trying to convince Clarissa to influence the reverend to convince George and Obadiah that they should be kinder to people?"

Daisy looked at her brother like he was an idiot. "Of course not. I'm saying we should kidnap Clarissa. We tie her up and drag her into the Forbidden Forest. No one will dare follow us there. Then we send a message to Reverend Branch that we'll kill her if he doesn't make George and Obadiah give back control of Arcadia to us."

"Daisy," said Virginia.

"Don't you think 'kill' is too strong a word for a little girl to use?" said Anne.

"No, I don't think it's too strong for a little girl to use," Daisy responded, mimicking Mrs. Gladford's talk-to-children voice. "After what those fuckers done to my brother and my friends…"

"You cork up that toilet mouth of yours now, sister. And killing ain't no way to solve problems."

Daisy rolled her eyes. "I don't mean we'd *really* kill her. Just make it sound like we would. My plan would work, that's the important thing. 'Course the Brokes would try to trick us somehow, but we can think around that. Or at least I can."

Doc drummed his fingers on the arm of his chair.

"That bone-headed old man won't change for anyone."

"He will for Clarissa. I promise. He loves her more than life itself. If he thinks she's in danger, he'll do anything we say."

"Doc, she might have a point," said William. "I'm not sure I'm comfortable with kidnapping, but desperate circumstances call for desperate measures."

Adam said, "Clarissa lives with Aunt Henrietta and Uncle Walt, and I feel we need to check on them anyway. They were locked up too."

"I don't know anything about how they are, but if you get them freed, you'll free Clarissa too. Maybe you can encourage her to have some influence on that old Puritan fool."

"Not encourage her," said Daisy. "Tie her up. Throw her on a wagon and take her into the woods."

Adam nodded reluctantly. "Okay, then. Let's get on with it." He looked at Virginia and Joss. They also nodded, their faces grave.

Their plan was to travel through the Merlin Grove until nearly upon the Auberon farm. They would wait there until nightfall to sneak up the hill and carefully check to see if there were any constables guarding the house. Daisy offered the idea of creating a diversion that would lure away any guards, and knocking them out by throwing big rocks on their heads from the boughs of trees.

"Hildie and I can start moaning from the cornfields to lure them into the trap."

"You two ain't going," said Adam.

"Hell we ain't," said Daisy.

"Hell you are."

Daisy tromped up to Adam and stuck her chin up at him. "We're coming."

"This is too dangerous for children," said Anne.

"Too dangerous? Of all the godda—"

"No, no," said Mayor Gladford, waving his hand at his wife. "Annie, you're wrong. These girls are tough and brave. But even brave girls need to get some rest after what they've been through. Right, Doc?" William gave Doc a little wink.

"Oh, yes. Absolutely. Daisy, you still have an injury. You must spend some time resting in bed before we leave. And Hildie, you must go in the bedroom and keep your friend company. How about a day of rest? We'll all leave tomorrow."

"Okay," said Hildegard.

"But..."

"Daisy, let's go to the back room and let the grownups make their plans. I still got some marbles we can play with."

Before Daisy could respond, Hildegard grabbed her by the good arm and pulled her into the back room.

"I'll bring some warm milk and cookies later on, girls," called Claire.

"Thank you!" called Hildegard, closing the door behind them.

"Such nice little girls," said Claire.

A short time later, Adam, Joss, and Virginia emerged from the cottage, followed by the two old couples. They carried satchels filled with provisions.

Afternoon was getting on. The sun was setting behind the cottage. Shadowed dabs of silver-white rested in a sky fringed with lavender.

"I promise we'll come back for you," Adam said to William.

"We're going to keep these fellows asleep till you do."

As the fugitives walked around the pigpen. Doc's favorite sow Ursa raised her chin and sniffed at the strangers. Adam and Virginia looked down at the pig.

"You suppose it's really true? About talking to animals, I mean?" said Adam.

"Do you?"

Adam reached down. Ursa pushed herself up a couple inches and sniffed his hand. The pig snorted a few times, sloppy, cadenced noises.

Virginia whispered in Adam's ear. "Think she said she loves you."

He whispered back, "I'm already taken," and gave Virginia a kiss.

They moved into the forest. The sow continued to watch them until they were gone.

A short while later, the pig turned its head toward the cottage. She watched the peculiar event of two young human girls, one tall, one short, slipping quietly through a window on the side of the building. They tiptoed across the yard. The tall one tapped the shorter on the shoulder. "Sure you're okay?"

"I'm fine. That medicine Doc gave me was a miracle worker. No pain."

"You ain't sleepy?"

"Nope."

"There's that pig Doc was talking about."

Hildegard reached over the fence and patted Ursa on the head. "Good pig," she said. Ursa brushed her nose against the girl's fingers.

"We gotta get," said Daisy. "Before they figure out we run off."

The sow regarded them as they moved off into the trees.

Chapter Sixty
Special for You

Adam, Virginia, and Joss kept to Mill's Trail, ready to leap into the trees at any sign of riders. Feeble clumps of snow lingered on the edge of the trail. The only sound was the crack and hiss of snow falling from distant boughs.

As the edge of Merlin Grove came into view, they caught sight of someone ducking into some bushes.

They could see a filthy pant-leg sticking out. Recognition alighted on Joss's face.

"That you, Charlie Glump?"

"Don't hurt me!" the man wailed.

"We ain't going to hurt you," said Adam.

In the old days, the town drunk's uncouth appearance, his ragged clothes and filthy body, would have aroused disgust amongst the travelers, but they felt only pity for him. His toes, open to the cold air because he had no shoes, were showing signs of chilblains. Through the tatters of his shirt, his ribs were standing out. It seemed the coup had not only deprived the creature of drink but of food. He was shivering violently.

"Please, Mr. Ghost, let me be!" he whimpered.

Adam kneeled beside the man. "Charlie, I ain't no ghost. I'm alive."

Charlie Glump squinted. "Golly, is it really you, Mr. Adam? And Miss Joss! She ain't a ghost?"

"No, Charlie, none of us are ghosts."

"Howdy, there, Charlie," Joss said.

"Hello, Charlie." Virginia smiled warmly.

Charlie gazed up at the group, his waxy jaws chewing away in wonder. A new cloud of fear descended on him. He tapped his chest. "May-maybe...*I'm* the ghost."

"Charlie, you aren't a ghost either," said Virginia. "You didn't die."

Charlie thought it over. "So George Broke didn't shoot you all."

"What do you mean?"

"You ain't been to town?"

"No."

"His men are everywhere and they all got them guns." Charlie's grizzled chin was going up and down. "They're damned bad, them guns. Can blow a man's head right off his body from a hundred feet away."

"I haven't had a drink in weeks. Your pub's my regular, Miss Joss, and you ain't there no more, so I ain't neither. The Brandywine's full of constables. They're evil, them constables. Can't even be outside your house anymore after dark, or they'll whip you half-dead."

"They're really whipping people?" said Virginia.

"And shooting people. Just for the fun. Seen it myself. They go around downtown, beating on women special, if their dresses don't touch the ground. But whipping ain't half of it. At night, the really bad things happen. Don't even want to say, some of the things I seen and heard." The drunkard shivered.

In a strained voice, she asked, "Have you heard anything about my father?"

"Who?"

Virginia snapped, "My *father,* Charlie. Hugh Baker. He's the manager of the bakery. He gives you bread sometimes."

Comprehension seeped into Charlie's bloodshot eyes. "Yes'm. Now I remember. Broke's men, they threw him out. Couldn't believe it. Threw him right into the snow."

Virginia bit her lip.

"When?" asked Adam.

"After you took Miss Virginia here from the wedding." Charlie's face brightened at the recollection. "You really did that, Mr. Adam?"

Adam ignored his question. "Where's Hugh Baker now?"

Charlie leaned forward with a conspiratorial look. He whispered, "I hear rumors that old John Bede at the Grange, he put up Hugh. Hid him in one of them big community warehouses."

Adam put his hand on Virginia's shoulder. "It's probably true, Ginnie. Bede's the sort that would do that for a man."

Virginia was close to tears. "It's all my fault!"

Adam rubbed her back. "It's not. And he's going to be okay."

"How many constables does George have, Charlie?" asked Joss.

The drunk's face struggled. "Reckon about fifty of'em. Mr. Adam, be careful about them bastards. They's more dangerous than you can think," He grabbed the young farmer's hand and squeezed it hard. "And they's looking out special for you."

Chapter Sixty-one
Mr. Question Mark

Not a chirp could be heard and not a bird could be seen in Merlin Grove.

Moist leaves sloshed with alarming loudness under the feet of the fugitives. They halted often to listen for any sign of Broke's men.

A circle of sunlight appeared at the end of the path. They decided to hide among the pecan trees until nightfall, then slip up to the cabin under cover of darkness. They found a place where the trees were thin and they had enough space to lay down. At first, they were on edge, but soon fatigue overcame them and one by one they dropped off to sleep.

Adam awakened to a whisper in the trees. He blinked in the dark. The others were still sleeping. He moved toward the sound, tiptoeing. Within the brambles, something was standing out, a shadow within shadows.

The rock was pale yellow, as smoothly parabolic as a tombstone, as concealed as a crouching goblin. The crumbles of Adam's vision came together, and out of the vagueness came converging threads. Adam stood mesmerized as the stone began to pulse with orange light and to emit a soft hum. He took a step forward. The spidery threads gathered into straight rows of print, letters, words, whose message sent a shiver through him:

PUSH THE STONE

Adam looked over his shoulder. The other fugitives could not be seen. Something told him it was not a good idea to wake them, that this was something for him alone.

The stone was warm against his fingers. He applied pressure. Nothing happened. He applied more and all at once the stone toppled and Adam was falling straight down a hole that opened to swallow him.

A trap! was the only coherent thought he could form in the breathless freefall he found himself in. He flailed wildly but could find nothing solid; it was as though he'd plummeted from a cliff into thin air.

The blackness was thickening, congealing against his skin, turning the consistency of water, mud, yet he could breathe normally. He was swept sideways abruptly by a massive tongue of liquid. He felt the bump of a hot, slick membrane against his chest and stomach and he dropped again, faster this time, his heart leaping into his throat, and he landed on a hard, flat surface.

"Ow!" he cried.

For a moment all he could do was remain on his side, moaning. The pain ebbed. He opened his eyes. He tried blinking but the amazing sight was still there: a universe of fireflies hovering in front of his face.

Candles. Thousands of them. Stuck in chinks in the cave walls. Wincing at the pain in his neck, Adam turned to see they were everywhere, rising in the air on all sides as far as he could.

"Took you long enough."

The woman was sitting a dozen feet away, crosslegged on the floor. She was wearing only a ragged gown of sackcloth. Her tangled hair fell like brambles over malnourished cheekbones and a toothless mouth. In the prancing candlelight, Adam saw a pattern of broken blood vessels on her left cheek like an attached spider.

"I've been waiting here forever," she said.

"Who are you?"

"You know who I am."

Adam's voice dropped to a whisper. "Mary Lena?"

"Jackpot!" Mary Lena cackled.

"Jack...what?"

From somewhere behind her, a breeze flushed into the cavern. The candle flames trilled and sent spots of light racing about the woman's face like sparks in a whirlwind.

Adam's mouth fell open. The woman's face was swirling with the flames, the wrinkles twisting into spirals. Her cheeks were bulging and her chin widening as though being inflated from within. From the jaws sprouted tendrils of dark hair.

He wanted to look away, but couldn't, because the person sitting cross-legged in front of him was no longer an old woman but an old, bearded man.

Adam was petrified. "Who…who are you?"

"You know."

"I don't."

"You do. Your friends are now taking a nap in my woods."

Adam sat up straight. "Merlin?" he whispered.

"Bingo."

"What?"

"I said Bingo. It means correct, you're right. I'm Merlin. Merlinus Caledonensis, more precisely. Never mind what Geoffrey said about me with all that tripe about Arthur. It's the stories before that are the truth. Mostly."

"I don't understand anything you're saying."

"You have *heard* of me, haven't you?"

"I know the Merlin Grove, and heard stories of a crazy…an old man living there, but…"

Disappointment showed in every crease of the old man's face.

"What is this place?"

"My home."

"Where is it?"

"Here."

"Where is here?"

"Not there."

"Where is there?"

"Not here."

"Why don't you give me a straight answer?"

"You sure ask a lot of questions."

"Wouldn't you, if you were me?"

"See what I mean?"

"If you answer, maybe I won't ask so many."

"Why don't you ask me why you're here?"

"Will you answer?"

"Maybe."

"Why am I here?"

"Because your time has arrived."

Adam shuddered. "What does that mean?"

"It means, dear boy, that the time has come for you to fulfill your destiny and save Arcadia."

There was mirth behind the gleam in Merlin's eyes. "Why don't you ask me what you really want to ask?"

"What...what was that box?" He gulped. "with the head?"

"Not that question! Idiot!" roared Merlin. Adam cringed. "Ask me the question you've really wanted the answer to all your life."

Adam was jangling with alarm. He whispered. "Are there others?"

"Other what?"

"Other people."

Merlin grinned. "Yes," he answered. And Merlin told Adam an impossible tale, a fabulous children's story, about a land filled with humans beyond count who lived in shimmering buildings of not two or three stories but scores, edifices that rose to such heights they chiseled holes in the sky and he spoke of wheeled machines propelled not by horses but by fiery processes of internal dynamism that shot them forward at speeds faster than the fastest animals of the land, sea or sky, and he described winged machines that flew in the air like birds and tremendous iron boats that carried hundreds of people across shoreless bodies of water that made Peachtree Lake seem like a droplet on a leaf. Adam's head was bedazzled.

"I want to go there!" he said.

Merlin chuckled.

"I'm not joking," said Adam. His eyes were glazed with enchantment. But the demented old man only cackled harder.

"What is so funny?" Adam demanded.

Merlin pulled himself together. "Sorry, my boy," he said with genuine contrition. "It really isn't funny."

"What isn't?"

"You can't visit that place."

"Why not?"

"Because it's gone."

"What do you mean, gone?"

"Gone. As in finished, demolished, bye-bye, kaput. Blown to smithereens. Blasted to fuck-all."

"I'm having a hard time following you."

"It's all there in the prophesies, although Geoffrey must have been drunk when he wrote a few of those pages. *Histories*, chapter seven. That world has been destroyed."

"Destroyed?"

"Well, there are bits remaining here and there, charred ruins and the like. And even a few people are scavenging about, but they're not the kinds you'd want to meet, Adam. Probably eat you alive if they caught you."

"Destroyed." All at once Adam felt a terrible sense of loss at the devastation of this place he'd never seen. "Destroyed how?"

"Folks living there destroyed it. Or let it be destroyed."

"Why?"

"That, son," said Merlin, all humor gone from his face, "is past even my understanding. But I do know a thing or two about how things work on a grander scale, and I can tell you that when Arcadia was first set up…"

"Set up?"

"Set up. Established."

"Established by who?"

"By…you sure are Mr. Question Mark, aren't you?"

"Yes, sir."

"Why don't you shut up a minute and let a person speak?"

"Yes, sir."

"There'll be a question and answer period later."

"Yes, sir."

"When Arcadia was established, it was intended as a kind of repository for…what is it now, Adam?"

"Repository, sir?"

"Don't you have a dictionary?"

"A what?"

"Never *mind*. A repository. A place to put things."

"Okay"

"Arcadia was set up as repository for…"

"For what?"

Merlin sighed. "Innocence."

From an iron pot suspended over a small fire, which had appeared seemingly out of nowhere, Merlin conjured up two cups of tea. Adam sipped the warm, sweet liquid gratefully.

"As I was saying, Arcadia was started to harbor— to keep and protect—qualities, virtues, values—that were vanishing from the world, as a kind of big boat to keep everything safe until the flood passed."

"What qualities, sir?"

"Old, old qualities, Adam, that would make little sense to you because you don't know much about their absence."

"I guess it's like honesty, or not stealing, or not being greedy, like the Brokes are doing now."

Merlin slapped Adam.

"Ow!" Adam shrank back, touching his cheek. "Why did you hit me?"

"Idiot!" shouted Merlin.

Adam threw his arm over his head and cowered. The old man lifted his head and yelled at the ceiling. "'Honesty,' he says. 'Greed,' he says. How did such a simpleton get to be in his position?" He fixed Adam in a gaze that could melt iron. "It has nothing to do with those things. Are you a child? It has to do with *balance*."

Merlin held his fists in front of him. He moved the right fist up and the left down, then reversed the movement. "You see?"

Adam was terrified to say no.

"Imagine my left fist is this fancy-pants world you're so keen on visiting, even though it's now just a ball of ashes. Imagine my right fist is Arcadia." Merlin held his fists at the same level, so a horizonal line could be drawn between them. "See? Balance."

Hazy comprehension flickered on Adam's face.

"The trouble is that for this balance to remain, you need separation. Now think if I do this." Merlin extended the thumb of his left hand and inserted it into the aperture formed by the crooked index finger of his right. "I make a connection between the two worlds. Certain qualities of one world can come over to the other." Merlin dropped his left fist an inch, and raised his right. "And we got imbalance." Adam nodded.

"Seven years ago, just such a connection was made."

"How?"

"One Mr. Obadiah Broke stumbled across a chemical formula that incorporated—that used— primordial—very old—ingredients, in just the right amounts at exactly the correct temperature."

"His tanning solution?"

"That accident cost a lot more than his pretty skin. It opened a Pandora's Box—it started lots of troubles, a cycle of events that culminated in an actual person coming to Arcadia from the other side. A side effect of this disruption was that Broke was filled up with lots of nutty dreams, which he mistook as divine providence. In a way, he's as big a victim as anyone in this. When Miss Laurel…"

"The goddess?"

"Yeah, only she's not a goddess, she's just a run-of-the-mill university dropout. A good kid, a little smarter than average. Bookish. Sweet smile, nice ass. She comes to Arcadia, and goes, naturally, right to Obadiah, because without knowing it, she's drawn to the one who opened the way for her."

"Oh."

"So…as we in the magic business say, the rest is history, except for the ending."

"The ending?"

"And that, Adam, is where you come in."

"Me?"

"See, when Arcadia was first set up…"

"During the Great Migration?"

"Stupid!" Merlin shouted. Adam ducked as the old man raised his hand to slap him again. "Were you born in a barn?"

"Yes."

"Oh," said Merlin. "That's right." The old man mused. "You really were born in a barn, weren't you?" Adam nodded.

Merlin laughed. "*That's* rich. Our savior was actually born in a barn."

"Savior?"

Merlin sighed. "Yes, Listen carefully before you offer any more interruptions, Mr. Know-It-All. Arcadia was set up a good 900 years before your silly little migration from New England. I should know, 'cause I was put in charge of setting it up."

"Who put you in charge?" Adam asked without thinking.

"Stop with the questions already!"

Adam nodded.

"This Great Migration you keep harping on was not the first time people came to Arcadia. There were others before you, and there were other…" Merlin rocked his fists up and down. "…imbalances. However, all the other times, the direction was opposite. Arcadians were sucked out, as it were, from their land, by some fool on the other side. They love to mess around with chemicals over there, which is a big part of the problem and an example of poor planning on the part of the Creator, if you want my opinion…oh, stop looking so *confused*, Adam!"

"Sorry, sir."

"How do you expect to save the world with a look like that on your face?"

"S-save the world?"

"That's why you're down here, isn't it? To save the fucking world? Or, rather, world*s?*"

"I don't know."

"Listen, Adam, and listen good. I won't waste my breath explaining the metaphysical dynamics to a born-in-a-barn bumpkin with a vapid look like that on his face." Adam nodded.

"But this much you need to get: you have been designated as the person in charge of fixing this imbalance."

"Why me?"

"It's complicated. You inherited the obligation, and you were raised in a situation that prepared you for it."

"Huh?"

"You inherited generations of concentrated magic from your mother, heightening your sensitivities, your hand-eye coordination, your field independence, and your ability to delay gratification. All the raw stuff of a hero."

Adam simpered.

"Your father's contribution is simpler. All his male lineage going way, way back set down roots in Arcadia using the original materials that have imbedded in them the power that I personally implanted in them all that time ago. Specifically, I'm referring to wood."

"Wood?"

"Oak, in particular. You were raised surrounded by wood from a very special tree, carried through the generations, from my own homeland in Carmarthen, down through France for a while, back up, then to the new land, then Arcadia."

"Wood?"

"Wood! Wood! Are you a dunce? It's like talking to a log, conversing with you."

"What wood?"

"Your distant ancestor, who was the first of this present crew to set down roots in Arcadia, used this special wood to build his pigpen." Merlin stared at Adam meaningfully. Adam face showed only the hum of absolute confusion. "And a certain…chair?" Further waiting by Merlin produced no evidence of comprehension in the young man.

The magician sighed. "Oh, Christ, okay, let's keep it simple. You need to stop the Brokes. It's your destiny."

"My what?"

"Your destiny, goddamnit! Your…unavoidable future activity."

"But how?"

"You got to be tough."

"I'm not tough. Ask anyone. Richard's the tough one in the family. Maybe you got the names mixed up and it's his destiny."

"No, Adam. It's you. It's always been you." Merlin paused as though trying to decide whether to reveal any more. "You...and your sister."

"But how?"

"I already told you how."

"You told me what, not how."

"Use your brains. Use your balls too. Go with that raw thing in your gut that's always been struggling to get out, but you were too frightened of what people would think if you let it."

Merlin rose.

"But..."

"But nothing. I need to go. I got errands."

"You can't just leave me."

"Sure I can."

"What if I ask Laurel, the goddess woman, to leave Arcadia? Wouldn't that make the balance happen again?"

"She's not the problem. The problem is that Obadiah Broke opened up the connection with that brain wine of his, and George Broke is now feeding the same stuff to himself and his whole army."

"How about if I stop the brain wine?"

"That isn't the solution. The solution is taking away the power from a couple of nutjobs and returning it to everyone."

Merlin started away.

"Sir?"

"What now?"

"If I stop the Brokes, will the other world be fixed?"

Merlin considered. "Temporarily," he said. "Until they fuck it up again." The old man jabbed Adam's chest with a long finger. "It's okay, son. All you need is right here. Good luck."

The darkness that swallowed up Merlin reached out and snatched up Adam too, and when he shook it off, it was a blanket, and behind the blanket were Joss and Hildegard, asking him why he was screaming for them to come back.

Chapter Sixty-two
A Low Rumble

When Adam awoke, it was morning. The fugitives had given into their exhaustion and slept all the way through the night. Now the cover of darkness was lost, and they were stuck with approaching the Auberon cabin fully exposed.

Joss stepped out from the trees and up the path until she came to the place where the grove opened into the sunlight. Virginia and Adam watched as the cooper peered up the hill as far as she could, then took another couple of steps. She waved for them to come.

They crept up the hill together, on alert for any sign of the constables. Finally, they could see the Auberon farm, and Adam's cabin off in the distance. All around Adam's farm were dozens of brown spots, holes the constables had dug in his fields in their search for the black water.

The Auberon cabin appeared normal. Walter's garden was brimming with spring vegetables, and the apple tree was covered with new leaves. The brown logs of the cabin stood out in placid contrast to the clear blue sky.

They went to the front door. Virginia knocked softly. No sound came from within. She touched the handle and applied pressure. "Locked," she whispered.

The door snapped opened. Richard was standing there, wielding an axe. His eyes grew wide and the axe went to his side. "Ma!" Henrietta and Walter appeared at their bedroom doorway.

The room turned into a series of joyous woops as Henrietta, Walter and Richard discovered Adam and Joss were brought back to life. Henrietta was so elated to see Adam alive she threw herself at him so hard she knocked him down and almost killed him.

When Virginia told them that Daisy and Hildegard were also alive, Henrietta and Walter embraced her and wept with gratitude. It was some time before Virginia managed to ask, "Where's Clarissa?"

They learned that Richard's wife had moved out weeks before, to live with her great uncle, Reverend Branch. Richard hadn't been allowed to see her or their child.

"There goes Daisy's plan," said Adam.

"What plan?"

"Don't matter now. I want to go to my farm, to see my animals."

"Don't bother, Adam," said Walter. "They run off."

"What?"

"Just after the constables caught you."

"But, where did they go?"

"Don't know, but they sure seemed to know."

"How'd they get out?"

"Broke's men took the cow out and started throwing rocks at her."

"Rocks?"

"Adam, throwing rocks ain't nothing compared to worst those bastards can do," said Henrietta. She looked enormously tired. The keenness of her blue eyes was clouded by exhaustion. "Those constables are the Devil's own, and George Broke owns them."

At first, there were more than twenty guarding them, Walter told him. They stayed day and night. They wouldn't let the family leave the cabin. When they tried to leave through a door or window, the constables shoved them back inside and menaced them with axes. After a couple of weeks, the number of men decreased, and the family was permitted to come outside for short periods. A kind of truce was made between the remaining constables and the Auberons. Walter was even allowed to plant some new seeds in his garden and tend his apple tree.

The Auberons had no wish to fight. They'd lost all faith in the community and only wished to cultivate enough good will—if it could be called that—with the guards to be permitted to move away, into the wilderness of the Grey Mountains, and start a new life.

"They couldn't find much of that black water they were looking for. They stopped digging. A few days ago, there were only three men out there. Only yesterday, one of George's men came and ordered them back to the ranch. Like something urgent was happening, but he didn't say why. We were alone here for the first time in months, then you came. Say, you don't think their riding off had anything to do with your coming here?"

"You were saying before about my animals."

Walter said, "That was back when the guards wouldn't let us out. Early on, we tried to fight them. Richard here got beat so bad, he couldn't walk a few days. And Henrietta got herself hit in the eye when she tried for them with an axe. One day, they got it in their heads to throw rocks at Beth the cow. They started doing it, and Beth started bawling, and Rosenlee looked out the barn window at them and jumped over the barn door."

Adam gawked at his uncle. "*Rosenlee* jumped? She's the laziest horse in the world."

"She wasn't lazy that day. I saw it with my own eyes through a chink in that wall."

Richard said, "then he galloped to the pigpen and —I couldn't believe what I was seeing—he opened the gate and let your pig out."

"*What?*"

"As the Lord is my witness, he used his nose to flip open the latch, then his hoof to kick open the gate. And out comes Algie. But the chickens, they stayed in there. They wouldn't leave. Sorry, but I think Broke's guards took them."

Adam was still gaping at Richard. "Rosenlee opened the gate to the pigpen and let Algie out?"

Henrietta said, "it's true, Adam. It was like he knew that Broke's men were going to hurt that pig after they were done with your cow."

"That was nothing compared to what happened next." Walter's eyes glistened as he thought back. "Rosenlee rushed straight at Broke's men and attacked them. Ran circles around them, whinnying like she was on fire, wheeling around and kicking them with her hind legs and even butting them with her head."

When they realized a horse was rampaging against them, the constables were at first frozen with surprise. Then Rosenlee shot out a stupendous kick of her back legs and smacked one of the guards in the face. The man fell over backwards and didn't move. The others fled in every direction.

Walter described how the horse, pig, and cow then made a break for it through the corn fields. The last the Auberons saw of the animals, they were headed southeast, toward the Grey Mountains.

As Adam was absorbing this news, they heard a rumble of approaching horses from outside. Richard was closest to the window. When he looked out, he groaned. "They're coming."

Chapter Sixty-three
Ready to Pop

They saw through cracks in the walls dozens of George's constables on horseback topping Green Hill. More and more came, an awesome force that seemed to crush the hill with an attack of leather and dust. The power of their approach rattled the logs of the cabin. The men wielded an artillery of sticks, scythes, and axes. But there were no guns to be seen.

In front of the army was George Broke.

Adam crouched near the front door and observed George. His former friend seemed to have aged many years. His face was gaunt. His hair had thinned, and there were bald patches opening on his head. George's skin had become inscribed with the same coiling pattern of blue-green streaks as his father's.

George called, "Adam Green and Virginia Baker. You are under arrest. Come out now."

"Goddamn him." Joss made to open the door. Adam grabbed her hand to pull her back and the others crowded around to help.

Henrietta called out, "Don't know what you're talking about, George."

George held a hand aloft. Two of the constables came forward. Each gripped a child by the arm. Daisy was struggling hard to pull away. Hildegard was peering ahead, dazed.

The men brought the children to George. George pulled something metallic from the side of his belt and pointed it at Daisy's head. The rancher called out again. "Henrietta, you say Adam and Virginia aren't in there, but I know they are. If they don't come out in ten seconds, I'll kill these kids here."

Adam pushed everyone aside and pulled the door open and tumbled out and fell to the ground under the weight of the others in the cabin who'd been pressing against him to also get out. Joss, Richard, Walter, and Henrietta ran over Adam's back and toward George, and almost reached him, but several of

George's constables blocked their path. Cut off, the four adults stood screaming curses at George.

Virginia had tumbled out also from the cabin and fell beside Adam. The two pushed themselves through, Virginia slapping dust from her smock. The guards parted to let them pass and closed behind them.

Adam and Virginia stood face to face with George.

"Okay, we're here. Now let them go," said Virginia, pointing to the children.

"What the fuck do you want from us?" said Adam.

George pointed the gun at Adam's crotch. "Take off your pants."

"My...?"

"You embarrassed me, Adam. Now take those off. Pants. Off." said George. Snickers rippled among the constables. Adam looked at Virginia, who seemed not to have understood.

A voice squeaked from the crowd. "Wait!"

Something jostled the men behind George, and little Victor pushed his way through. He hobbled up and faced George.

George gave Victor a look of surprise, which gave way to a grin at how comical the little man looked. Victor was puffing with emotion, his chest moving up and down, his beard jiggling.

"Why, Victor. What is the matter, little fellow? You seem ready to pop."

"You got no right to do this." Flecks of spittle jumped from the man's agitated lips. "Not after what you done to that old man."

George's smile slipped a notch.

"I seen what you done. I'm talking about Mr. Cobble." Victor stood with his head level with Broke's waist. He jabbed a finger up at him. "You done him in with a knife. I seen you do it with my own eyes!" He turned to the guards. "After he done told you all off, and slapped your faces, his own constables, for abusing Mr. Cobble! Then he killed the old man hisself!"

Fear flashed in George's eyes. Victor pointed at Virginia and Adam. "These two aren't your enemy. It's this bastard! George Broke is a liar and a murderer."

Emboldened by the silence his words had brought to the crowd, Victor spoke louder, his voice cracking with emotion. "Turn away from George Broke before it's too late! He's just one man and you are many."

A moment of silence passed, wherein the men seemed to be considering deeply what Victor had said. Then one of Broke's men shouted, in a high-pitched, squeaky imitation of Victor, "He's just one man, and you are many." And all the constables erupted into laughter.

Victor's lips parted in dismay.

George was grinning again. He bent, bringing his face close to the dwarf. He patted him on the head with one hand while bringing up the gun with the other. He pointed the barrel at Victor's chin, pushing the muzzle through the hairs of his red beard. "Anything else you wanted to say, you little freak?"

Victor slapped George.

For an instant, the gun was knocked from under Victor's chin. The little man tottered backwards, bent his good leg all the way back and shot it forward, smashing the toe of his boot into George's ankle.

The amazed guards watched their leader drop to the ground. Victor picked up George's gun, whirled around, pointed the pistol and fired a bullet into the calf of the constable guarding Daisy.

Pandemonium. Fists and weapons slashing wildly and men shouting in rage and pain. Through the mad swirls of humanity crawled, rolled, and ran Daisy, Hildegard, Joss, Virginia, Adam, and Victor. Henrietta, Walter and Richard ran behind them. Joss kicked open the cabin door, and the whole crowd leaped into the front room. Richard was last, shoving Victor in front of him. He slammed the door. For a second, they lay sprawled on the floor, panting. Then they were on their feet, flying to look through chinks in the wall.

The constables were huddled around George, who was telling them something.

"We're really in it now," said Richard.

Joss rolled up her sleeves. "Then we're in it, so let's go all the way. If they try to get in, I'll knock their heads off their shoulders with my bare hands."

"There's got to be fifty of them out there," said Adam. "Broke's whole army."

"Maybe we should escape out back," said Walter. At that moment, George shouted an order and the constables fanned out to either side of the building and around back. The prisoners were surrounded.

"We could fight them if we all ran out together," said Joss.

"No. They outnumber us ten to one," said Adam.

"Pile the wood!" George shouted. The prisoners exchanged looks.

Several of Broke's men marched off to the back of the clearing. They returned whipping at horses that pulled carts filled with branches and boards.

Men began pulling down the wood and moving it around the cabin. From all sides, the prisoners heard a terrible pounding.

Virginia put her hands over her ears. "What are they doing?"

From a place at the north window, Richard yelled, "they're hammering boards over the windows."

Adam ran to the door, threw the latch and opened it, but there were already panels of wood covering the doorway, and the nails were being hammered in by many hands. He shouted through one of the rapidly disappearing gaps, "What the hell are you doing, George?"

George called back, "I'm enforcing the laws."

"What laws?"

"The laws that protect the land from witches."

"We aren't witches!"

"Exactly what a witch would say."

"Let us defend ourselves! Let us talk to the others in town!"

"You had your trial."

"You didn't let me defend myself. And the people you say I killed are alive!"

"You had your trial," George persisted, "and all the rest of you in there are guilty too. You're bad hombres."

"Fuck you!"

"See? Bad language."

"George! You and your men are the real witches!" screamed Henrietta.

The comment provoked a rumble of laughter in the army. The last thing Adam saw before they finished hammering the final board was a mass of brutal faces grinning back at him.

George shouted, "Okay, get ready!"

From the walls of the house came mysterious sounds: clanks, scrapes, and scratches. Adam was still crouched by the front door, struggling to understand what the constables were doing, when he heard his sister's voice calling his name.

Daisy's face was pressed against Henrietta's side, her good arm clutching her mother tightly. "Adam," she said again.

Adam came close and asked, "What is it, sprout?"

Her voice was clear and calm. "He's going to burn us." She lifted her good arm and jabbed Adam's shoulder. "*Do* something!"

"But…"

"Did you hear me? He's going to *burn* us. It's up to you!"

"I…" Adam began, but he was overwhelmed. Too many strange and frightening things were happening at the same time. Daisy pulled herself away from Henrietta and stomped up to Adam. She slapped at his stomach. "Think! We can't escape out the back or the front. We can't fight them."

"I…I could try to speak with him some more…talk sense to…"

"You're useless!" she screamed. She spun around toward Hildegard, who was standing nearby looking just as overwhelmed as Adam. "Hildie, it's up to us." They heard George ordering, "Start them!"

The room was murky, illuminated only by grey light pushing through the wood itself. Outside, scratches of flint against metal, pops, and hisses of kindling ablaze.

"God Almighty, they're really lighting it," said Richard.

"No," said Henrietta.

The first hint of smoke moved into the cabin.

Then they were rushing to the walls, pounding, crying. Richard kicked at the boards over a window, but they held firm. Henrietta tried to embrace Daisy, but the girl ducked under her arm and ran up to Hildegard. The two girls' heads touched. Daisy's eyes widened. "Hildie, remember?" Recognition blossomed on Hildegard's face. "Yes."

"But where?"

Daisy tugged at her mother's smock. "Ma, where were you and daddy talking a couple of weeks ago, when you were yelling at him about his apples?"

"What?"

"Oh! Never mind. Hildie! It had to be by the back door!" The two girls sprinted into the next room.

Daisy crouched on the floor, searching franticly. "Nothing!" she screamed.

"It's got to be there!"

"Under the floorboards. We need something to cut with."

The room was filling with dense black smoke and the air was getting hotter.

"Daisy, look!" Hildegard pointed to the corner. By the door was one of Walter's giant apples. Grey-black smoke was twisting around it. Hildegard dashed to the corner, lifted the fruit with both arms and returned, waddling under its weight. The two girls together lifted it over their heads and brought it down on the kitchen floor. A small hole appeared.

The rest of the prisoners were pouring into the room, gasping and coughing.

"Again!" screeched Daisy.

They brought the apple down three more times, opening a large hole in the floor.

"That's it! Everyone! Go down there!" Daisy shrieked.

Daisy and Hildegard shepherded the people into the hole. Then the girls climbed in themselves.

They were in a tunnel going straight down. The walls were shattered on all sides, with jagged rocks cutting across. People were climbing down the rocks as fast as they could, weeping, shouting. Raw, terrorized movement.

Hildegard looked up. A voice was coming from above. A woman. Screaming.

Daisy had already vanished into the labrynth underneath. Hildegard hesitated. The scream came again.

Hildegard forced herself back into the room. It was now so thick with smoke she could hardly see. The scream came again, much closer. It was the most desperate sound she'd had ever heard. Eyes stinging and dripping from the smoke, she made out ominous flashes of red and heard the snap of timber.

All at once, claws dug into her chest. She fell onto her side, gasping, her cheek pressed against the floor. Light was filling the room. Not firelight, but a silver luminescence that pressed through the boiling smoke. Hildegard felt hands on her and a sensation of floating.

Something punched her in the head. A blunt, shocking jab, next to her right eye. She was descending. From nearby, someone's dreadful gasp, a noise grinding at the throat, and she realized the sound was coming from her own mouth.

Then she was on her side again, but the floor was different, cold, dusty, a good smell, without smoke.

"Hildie? Hildie?"

"Huh?" She leaned on one hand, lifted her head and threw up.

She continued vomiting until she was emptied out, and then retched more. She was dimly aware of others shouting around her, but could think of nothing else but the sour, sick bog swallowing her up.

After a few minutes, she was feeling well enough to perceive Virginia gently rubbing her back.

"Are you okay?"

"What happened?"

"You came in and found me. I heard you fall, and it made me get up and get us both out. You saved my life."

"You saved mine."

Chapter Sixty-four
Boom

"Quiet!"

It was Adam who shouted it. Chaos had broken out in the lightless tunnel; people were tripping over each other in the dark, crying and cursing.

"Listen, don't be scared. We can find each other, but we need to stay calm."

They called out names until everyone was accounted for. As they finished the roll-call, they heard an odd sound, like the snuffling of a dog, nose pressed to the floor.

"Who's there?" said Adam. He explored the space where the sound was coming from and touched something rough, like a burlap bag. He jumped back at the unmistakable feel of hair. "Victor?"

The little man was weeping into his sleeve. "I'm sorry!" he wailed.

"What's wrong?"

"I done bad!"

"Victor, you saved our lives."

He screamed. "You don't understand!" He pounded the rocky floor with his fist.

"Victor, don't..."

"It was me! I helped the Brokes with everything!"

"You..."

"I sinned!" They could hear the man's fingernails tilling the slopes of his face, flesh ripping in self-mortification.

"Victor..." tried Virginia.

"I took Mr. Adam's diary!" he squealed, and he lunged forward on the floor. Adam jumped back at the touch of the man's fingers on his feet. Confessions started pouring out of him. Following George's instructions, he'd forged the new entries in the diary, claiming Adam's allegiance to Satan. He'd stolen the clothes of the girls and Joss Hankers, ripped and covered them with pig's blood and placed them near Adam's cabin.

In the end, the only wicked act of the Brokes to which he hadn't been an accomplice was the placing of the magic box in the forest for Adam to find. About that demonic apparatus, he knew nothing.

A long silence followed the completion of his confession. The only sound came from his sobs.

Of course, they would have forgiven him.

It was the kind of people they were.

But they were interrupted by a throb of red that swelled in the opening. For an instant, they could see each other, black and orange figures that blossomed in the blackness and vanished. The glow was followed by an acrid exhalation of smoke.

"We got to get out, now," said Daisy. She started tugging at them as she pushed through the line toward the front. "We can go this way. It's not far. We got to make a line." They groped in the dark, struggling to form a chain. They succeeded in moving forward as a group for a few seconds, but needed to stop when someone stumbled, knocking down the person behind, causing others to fall.

"Wish we had some light," Adam said.

Daisy let out a little cry. "I'm so stupid."

She dropped Walter's hand and groped at her waist. In a moment, she was holding her tinderbox. She had been holding it, and the remaining candle nubs, ever since they'd been in the cave. To the immense relief of all, she lit a few and passed them around.

A short way down the tunnel, they came across the hole filled with barrels and guns. Walter took out one of the antique muskets and ran his fingers around the trigger. He touched the barrel the girls had opened and ran his fingers through the black powder inside.

"So this is where Jed hid them."

"Adam, do you understand?" said Henrietta.

"I think so."

"Your father put these down here. He stole all the guns he could find, and all the gun powder, and this is where he hid them. I didn't realize he stuck them all right under your cabin. No!"

Walter yelped at Daisy, who was leaning forward with the candle. "You get one spark on this powder, and..."

There was a clamor down the tunnel. From the ceiling, another throb of firelight illuminated the cavern, much brighter, revealing the jagged contours of the tunnel.

"Oh, no," said Daisy.

A great *crack!* from above, followed by the ruckus of boards tumbling downward.

An avalanche of blazing debris exploded fifty feet down the tunnel. The passage roared into a blinding orange flash. A wave of heat sighed past.

"Run!" shouted Walter. The rocks above groaned. They were sprinting as fast as their legs could carry them, their way opened by a slab of radiation that was changing the tunnel bright red.

"There!" cried Daisy, pointing at the white star glinting in the distance. Running faster than they'd ever run before, they made for the exit. One by one, they shot from the hole and into the sunlight.

The last was Joss, who'd taken on the burden of carrying little Victor. She emerged with the small man cradled in her arms like a baby at the moment a ripping blast came from behind as the kegs of gunpowder exploded. A tongue of fire surged out of the mouth of the cave, missing them by inches.

All of the party collapsed here and there among the white boulders of the mountain slope. Some touched their backs gingerly; the heat had chased them so close they felt they'd caught fire.

They gradually took account of each other. They were scraped and exhausted, but no one was seriously injured.

"Thank God we're all safe," said Virginia.

When she said it, a noise louder than any thought possible, a boom beyond imagination, tore at their ears.

The mountainside lurched.

Those standing fell to the ground. They slapped their hands over their ears. They looked up. Climbing over the summit was a tower of fire.

"It's Satan!" cried Henrietta.

"Or maybe it's Jesus," said Walter.

"No," someone said. Everyone turned to find a stranger in their midst. She was a short woman with frizzy hair, staring up at the fireball.

"It's not Jesus," the stranger said. "And it's not Satan."

"What is it then?" asked Daisy.

"Oil."

Chapter Sixty-five
Barbecued

They moved with the timidity of mice, unable to tear their eyes from the fire.

The column of flame was at least fifty feet high. Uncoiling balls of red tumbled out of the top and broke into orange and black streamers that jettisoned crackling showers of sparks which congealed into clods of smoke and debris. The smoke lingered, spread, rose. The debris fell on the trees below, snapping the branches away and setting them ablaze.

Little was visible below the fire. Just thousands of swirling fists of smoke veined with surging sparks.

The eyes of the fugitives were streaming with tears, but they couldn't look away. The turmoil of the smoke was dispersing, whipped away by the internal wind of the fire. They caught momentary figments of something so shocking they knew it couldn't be real, but which kept returning, clearer and clearer with each culling of the smoke until there was no denying it.

The farms were gone.

All that was left of the cabins, barns, sheds and fields were black smears, footprints of a giant with oily boots. Walt's garden and his famous apple tree were incinerated. Everything was churning black, red splotches spread all over the ground.

As the survivors gradually worked out the disaster unfolding in front of theirs eyes, they became aware that the red splotches were the remains of Broke's constables.

The fountain of fire was shrinking. As it dwindled, it spat and snapped angrily, like blazing logs do when they've eaten their own insides and still crave more. The serpent at last slunk back into its hole.

Someone noticed a figure at the other side of the smoking perimeter, a queer, jerking dab of flesh color in the steaming expanse limping down the hill toward the trail.

It was George Broke.

Chapter Sixty-six
Surging

Henrietta started after George. But she suddenly screamed, jumped backward, and collapsed, gripping her feet. The ground between them and the other side of the hill was still hissing with chunks of near-blazing wood. Richard tried to go for George too, but something in his right leg was hurt in the explosion, and he collapsed with his face screwed up in pain.

"Adam!" Daisy was jabbing him with her finger. "You need to go after him."

Adam sighed heavily. He looked at where George had just been. He'd limped down to the trail and headed in the direction of Merlin Grove and disappeared into the trees. The man had looked charred from head to foot.

"There's nothing more we can do to him. All his men are dead. He's broken. The only thing I could do to him is to hurt him the way he was trying to hurt us." Adam looked down at Daisy. "And that ain't our way."

She started to argue, but he interrupted. "Sister, you need to learn that all the bad things George and Obadiah did ain't for us. We'll never have jails in Arcadia. We'll never have whips and pillories. We'll never have people so greedy they want to do like the Brokes did." As Adam spoke, he felt unaccustomed confidence surging in him. His voice became loud enough for everyone to hear. "From this day forward, I say the only Sabbatical Law Arcadia will ever have will say no man will ever own so much that it threatens another man with too little."

Adam was proud of his speech. The others were nodding. Daisy, however, was staring up at him like he was stupid.

"Yeah, yeah, yeah." she said. "You still need to go after him."

"But…"

"It's *you*, Adam. It's always been you. You need to bring back the balance." And Daisy gestured with two fists, raising one slightly above the other and then aligning them again, just as Merlin had done in Adam's dream.

"How could you…" he started to ask his sister. "Oh, never mind."

Beyond all reasoning, Adam found himself climbing back along the shattered, smoldering poplars, towards the still-intact footpath at the back of his property. It would lead him over the hills where he and Virginia had played together as children. It would take him into the central valley, where thousands of spring rabbits were timidly emerging from their holes. He would travel beyond the town, where he'd experienced his first violence and his first love. He would be drawn south, to the Broke Ranch, where something like destiny awaited him.

Chapter Sixty-seven
The Fall of Obadiah

"Papa, what should I do?"

George found his father again in the stone building, seated in front of the magic box. The old man had pored over that videotape (this is what the goddess called it) so many times, seeking the sacred truths he believed were concealed within.

All lost.

Weeks before, George's father had fallen. The old man limped and stumbled to their big house. Although his leg was seriously hurt, and the world was spinning from where he'd hurt his head, Obadiah still managed to drag himself up to the bedroom. When George found him in bed, the father stared up at the son and groaned, *my head hurts*.

Every day since then, his father poisoned the air with the same complaint, in the same saliva-rattled voice, George, *my head hurts goddamnit my head hurts*, with the same look of accusation.

Obadiah's hairless head was splashed in the back with dried blood. He'd refused his son's offers to clean it off and bandage the wound. *Don't you touch me*, he'd yell, no matter how gently George tried, *you'll just make it worse. Put the food over there. Go.*

Three days after his fall, Obadiah, despite his injuries, demanded to be helped to rise from his bed and watch the magic box again.

Getting the old man into the stone house was hard. With his bad leg, Obadiah couldn't walk, so George had to contrive a way to get him on the roof. Even preliminary steps, though, filled his father with nausea and dizziness, and triggered such rage in him that his insults at George spumed from his mouth with sloppy discharges of spit.

Finally, George gave up on the idea of getting his father onto the roof. George found a long iron bar from the factory. He'd jammed it into the foundation and pried off the bricks in the wall concealing a door hidden underneath. It was unlocked.

His father had designed the building in this crazy way, with one door on the roof and another concealed behind a barrier of bricks. He'd never explained why. And George wasn't about to ask him about it now.

As George hacked away at the bricks, Obadiah roared insults from his place on the ground. It didn't really bother George that much. Verbal abuse wasn't much compared to the beatings he had endured for the past seven years. He would be forever grateful to his father, crazy or not, for the gift of the brain-wine, which charged his life with pure joy and pure power, while sharpening his senses beyond those of any mortal.

There was no place by the magic box for his father to sit. George went to the big factory building and found a skeletal iron frame of a chair, a defective one, lumpy with rust.

His father had without a word plopped down in it, activated the ghost box, and set to watching the magic world inside. George could never get accustomed to the flickering, moving pictures within that tiny planet. Seeing small, real people grinning and waving at him was the most disturbing. They sat in gleaming wagons of silky colors not found in the real world, and jetted through a rolling landscape of gargantuan praying mantises. Then those mysterious words, flashed on the box-window:

DRIVE YOUR DREAMS

"Papa, help me. I don't know what to do."

After the underground river of oil exploded and massacred his men, George returned to the only place left that felt like home. He stumbled into this cold stone room, fell to the floor, weeping before his father.

"Something terrible happened, Papa." Broken by sobs, the story poured out, the escape of the Goddess from the cave, the second escape of the prisoners at Auberon farm, the explosion and deaths of his men.

Obadiah Broke sat rigid and frowning.

He grumbled, "I knew it'd come to this if I let you handle things."

"But it wasn't my fault. Those girls…"

"Those girls!" Obadiah's voice was sneering. The nose sticking up, lips pulled open, cackling. "Look at yourself! Bested by a couple of little girls!"

"Father, I wasn't there. My men were. I…"

"You chose the men, didn't you? You chose not to be there, didn't you? Now you choose to say it's their fault, not yours. Like always. A lazy irresponsible baby!" Obadiah spat the words out one at a time, like fist punches. "You make me sick!"

"How did you do it?"

George Broke turned his head only slightly to the new voice, enough to perceive Adam Green in the doorway.

"Did you use one of those fancy new guns of yours, George?"

George closed his eyes. "Spike hammer," he whispered.

"How long's he been in here?"

"Dunno."

"Smells like at least three days. Your head is bleeding."

"I don't care."

"We should get you to Doc."

Adam looked at his old friend on the floor, then at the corpse in the chair.

"Why'd you kill him?"

"Mama."

"What?"

"My mama."

Adam realized with a flush of embarrassment that in all his recent dealings with George and Obadiah Broke, he'd not thought even once about Blossom Broke. George's mother was so quiet, so ensconced in the shadow of her husband that she had simply disappeared from Adam's thoughts.

"What about her?"

George moaned. "She ran away, Adam."

On a moonlit night shortly before George made himself mayor, Blossom Broke had left her husband's bed and walked into the clearing outside. Wearing a nightgown as diaphanous as the wings of a new butterfly, and smiling for the first time in years, she'd walked straight to the border of the Forbidden Forest.

Without pausing, she'd vanished into the trees. Her husband did not try to save her.

"Lord God," said Adam.

"Just like your mama, Adam."

"Maybe for different reasons."

George pointed at his father's dead body. "When she done it, he said *good riddance*."

"Good riddance?"

"Called her a weak little pig."

"So you…" Adam made a hammering gesture.

"I had to do it," answered George confidently. Then, with less certainty, "didn't I?"

"I don't know. I still don't understand why you two did all the things you did. What was it all about, George?"

George's eyes widened. "Papa's dream."

"His dream?"

"A great dream, Adam. Shake up the world! Make it a new, magnificent place. Like it showed in the magic box there. That he got from the woman he caught in the woods."

"Laurel."

"Yeah. She had this magic box with her. It showed pictures of flying wagons, going over the land faster than the fastest horse." George's pointed at the TV. "You never saw the whole thing. Press the red button."

"I never want to see that goddamned thing again." George touched his head and let out a small whimper of pain.

"Papa put the woman, the Goddess, in the cage. I didn't know about it at first, then one day, that day I punched you, he told me everything. He took me into the caves, and showed her to me."

Shortly after he'd found her, Obadiah was informed by Victor of the existence of foul-smelling black liquid leaking through the ground at Adam Green's farm, where the little man had noticed it while doing some work there.

Obadiah was stunned by the coincidence of the news from the goddess and the discovery of black water, and he saw it as a sign of divine approval. But to get at the oil under Green Hill, Obadiah needed Adam and his family off the land.

After Walter and Henrietta turned down his offers to buy their farms, Obadiah hatched other plans to drive them off their property. He conjectured Adam was the one he could first target most effectively, and his family members would fall in line.

"So he stuck the magic box in the woods," explained George, his head bowed to the floor of the cold room. "He figured when you saw it, you'd think the land was haunted and be happy to sell. You know the rest."

Adam smiled sadly at his old friend. "Pretty stupid idea."

"That's what the Goddess said too."

"Looks like your Pa's great dream isn't going to come true."

"What are you going to do to me?" George whispered.

"That'll be up to the community. Don't worry, we're not going to treat you the way you treated me. I'm not going to let anyone stick you in a pillory. Christians don't torture."

George snorted. *"I'm* a Christian."

Adam didn't want to argue. From outside came the sound of approaching horses. "That's got to be the rest of them. Richard said he'd fetch folks over as soon as possible."

George brought himself to his feet and slapped dust of his pants.

"First stop for you, George, is Doc's, so he can stitch up your head."

They exited the building. George shut the door behind him and they rounded the side of the building. Adam was happy that George was cooperating. "Aren't you relieved this is all over, old friend?"

George sighed. "No, Adam, nothing is over. In fact, it's all just beginning."

Adam caught his breath when he heard a sound near his ear. A metal click. He turned and found a man pointing a gun at his head.

Other constables were pouring out of the main house by the dozens. All of them were carrying guns.

"Did you really think that was all the men I had?" asked George.

The man pointing the gun at Adam said, "Can I kill him now?"

Chapter Sixty-eight
The Language of Bears

Broke's man put the snout of the pistol close to Adam's ear and clicked open the hammer.

Adam stared at George. "We were friends."

"Yes, Adam, but these emotional things can't trouble real men."

With a snake-strike of his arm, Adam reached up and grabbed the gun, tore it from the constable's hand, and snapped the barrel across the man's head. He collapsed with a grunt and was still. When the gun hit the man, a solid crack shattered the air, and Adam felt the gun jolt from inside.

George Broke suddenly was on the ground, gripping his leg, his face contorted. Blood was pumping through his fingers.

"Oops," said Adam.

"You...you shot me!"

The other constables were moving toward him. From somewhere also came a buzz, a distant murmur of many voices, beyond the surrounding fence.

George was trying to crawl back to the stone house. Adam jumped behind him, crouched, and jammed a hand under George's arm. He lifted George up enough to shield himself. He pointed the gun at George's head.

He yelled at the approaching constables, "stop or I'll kill him.".

The men laughed. "Won't make any difference, because we're going to kill you either way, witch."

From behind the men, the buzz had grown louder and changed into the shouts of human beings. Adam saw them now, surging through the gates. It was the people of the town, Joss Hankers, who was in front of the crowd, shouted, "Where's George?"

"What do you want with him?" shouted a constable.

"We're going to take him to town and give him a trial. A real one."

Voice straining with pain, George called to a nearby guard, "tell them to make the line, like we practiced."

The constable nodded. He hollered, "Men, line up this side and back there! The gate!"

Without hesitation, the men spread themselves single-file, forming a straight line in front of the crowd. A couple of constables sprinted to the big gates, pushed them together and lashed them closed.

The line of constables pointed their guns at the crowd.

Joss understood and shouted, "Run! For the trees." A few people started off, but most stayed where they were, confused about what was happening.

George started to call out another order and Adam put a hand over his mouth. From his left, something slammed into Adam's head. The guard he knocked down earlier had snuck up and hammered Adam with a rock. He fell.

George Broke yelled, "Aim!"

The men leaned their cheeks against the end of their gun-barrels, sighting targets.

Adam was lying with his chin pressed to the ground. His head seemed engorged with hot, throbbing liquid. He was looking straight into the backs of the line of armed men. In stabs of comprehension pushing through the pulses of pain in his head, Adam understood all those people were about to be slaughtered.

Adam saw artisans from town, including George's own aunt, Wandabella, gawking around with her surprised, chicken-like head. At her side was Hildegard, hugging close to her mother, her wide eyes riveted on the constables. There were farmers Adam had known all his life, people he'd worked with in the fields, helped raise barns with, who'd helped him and his family through the seasons.

He saw Virginia staring defiantly at the troops.

He wanted to move, but his body wouldn't respond. His hands and feet had gone numb. The paralysis was spreading through his arms and legs. He was a half-lifeless thing, his awareness of being a physical animal limited only to his trembling torso and his throbbing head. It was becoming hard to breathe.

Adam saw a small, red-haired figure stepping away from the others. Daisy was walking straight across the open space between the crowd and the line of men. She was gesturing, forceful waves of a tiny arm. Virginia shoved through and ran for Daisy. She was followed by two others, Henrietta and Walter.

Madness. Daisy was looking at *him*. Her fists were shaking above her head, her voice was trickling across the distance, *Adam, do something! It was always you!*

Adam looked down. Sorry, sister. Sorry Merlin. Whatever you thought I could do, whatever you imagined I was destined for, it's not going to happen. I'm dying.

A constable belched and fired accidently. Flame spurted from his gun barrel. A chunk of metal hissed at head-level toward the crowd. Virginia slapped her hand to her eye and screamed.

Adam felt hot darts shoot through his body and a compressed mass, like a coagulated ball of blood, start to inch up in his throat.

Virginia fell to her knees, both hands pressed to her eye, her mouth open and Adam grappled for air.

Adam threw his head all the way back. From his mouth erupted a deafening string of bestial syllables.

The constables glanced around nervously for the origin of the horrifying, unearthly sound. The world seemed to hold its breath.

Then Adam's call was answered.

From the trees came the deep groan of an enraged animal. From the opposite direction, behind the factory, came another.

The constables began to move closer together. A third groan shuddered out of the forest to the south and then groans were coming from everywhere at once. The guards pointed their guns wildly at the surrounding forest but couldn't see anything to shoot.

All at once, from every part of the forest wall, bears exploded into the clearing.

In the space of a single breath, one bounded up all the way from the forest border to the line of constables. It rose on its massive haunches and, with a swat of a mighty forepaw, flung three of the guards high in the air and brought its open maw down on the head of another. The man's face vanished inside the bear's mouth and he was lifted whole by the neck. The bear tossed his headless body to one side.

The bears were everywhere at once and the terrified constables were trying to run away. Some were fleeing into the forest. Some tried to run into the factory buildings, but were caught in mid-flight. The bears killed them with brutal swipes of their claws and savage chomps of their jaws. A handful of men ran for the big family house. When they found the door was locked, they dived through the windows. The first bear to come after them preferred the door, smashing it to shreds with a blow, and shouldered in, cracking apart the doorframe and ripping bricks out the wall in which it was set. Another dozen bears roared in behind. Screams erupted and men came flying out the windows. Faces bloody, they stumbled to their feet and floundered blindly until the bears finished them off.

There were bodies everywhere, some gasping, some still, but most of the men went screaming into the woods, the bears not far behind. It wasn't long until all the constables who weren't already dead or dying in the clearing were gone, along with all the bears who followed after them. Tortured cries echoed through the trees.

Adam made it painfully to his feet and began to limp over to Virginia, who was still kneeling, with her hand on her eye.

The big iron gate creaked open. Adam flinched at the sight of it, anticipating some new species of monster to explode through, but when the halves separated, the horse-drawn wagon that appeared contained only four old people. The wagon stopped and Doc climbed down and immediately went to Virginia. Claire, William, and Anne followed him.

As Adam came up, Doc was bent over Virginia and peering at the wound to the side of her eye. He looked up at Adam and said, "she's okay. It just grazed her."

William said to him, "Where's George?"

Adam spun around, but there was no George Broke. Impossible. The bears, for some reason, hadn't gone for him. His leg was shot and he couldn't have made it to the forest. *Where was he?*

Adam ran back around the mansion to the gloomy, mysterious building containing the corpse of Obadiah Broke. It was there that he found George. He had crawled to the stone house and managed to get the door open. He was hoisting himself up by gripping the door handle. As Adam ran up, George twisted himself into the building and shoved the door shut. Adam heard the latch fall from within.

When Adam finally managed to break the lock, he rushed in, fists raised. He pirouetted, searching each corner of the room. A chill rushed through his body. Adam could see the magic box, the decaying corpse in the chair, and nothing else.

In no part of that stone cell was there any sign of George Broke.

Chapter Sixty-nine
Epilogue

The constables who ran into the woods were never seen again. Neither, in all the years afterwards that I lived in Arcadia, was George Broke.

After Doc confirmed that Virginia was not seriously hurt and that all the others were in good health, the people of Arcadia gathered as one and moved toward town.

They did not stop in the marketplace, but continued northward, like true People of God, to seek guidance from their spiritual leader. In the yard behind the church, they were confronted by the saddest of sights.

Clarissa Auberon weeping on her knees. Her baby was slumbering in the crook of one arm. The willow that sheltered the house dropped its tendrils low, almost to the ground, and seemed to be trying to conceal the two strange fruit hanging from its branches.

They must have done it together. They were completely naked. Reverend Calvin Branch had his eyes closed and his mouth open, as though in mid-snore. Little Victor wore the same startled expression he had had in life. The tall man and the short man swung gently, side by side, one hanging lower than the other. It was hard not to notice that one of the reverend's testicles was much larger than the other, and hung much lower, and that their arrangement seemed to mimic the size and configuration of the bodies of the two men dead in their nooses. Like a pair of unbalanced testicles, these polyps of Christ.

Daisy Auberon came up and stood beside Adam. A child shouldn't see such things, but Adam didn't try to drive her away. The small girl stood next to her tall brother and leaned against him, staring up at the bodies. "Adam?" she said.

"Mm."

"Reckon they can see better from up there?"

Adam looked down at her. "I hope so, Sprout."

Hildegard Shrenker returned to a household much changed, to parents who now understood the torment of losing what they loved most. Like the fairy tale about the evil stepmother who is cured of her wickedness when the enchanted duckling plucks the poisoned thorn from her toe, Wandabella returned to the way she'd been seven years before. She stopped designing clothing, stopped making catastrophes of baked goods, and ended her gossiping. James reduced his fishing hours. The curse was lifted and they became a family again.

Mayor William Gladford and Anne returned to the peaceful lives they were living before, as did Francis and Claire Midland. The many times I tried to interview them as I wrote this book, they were polite but aloof. If it were true that Doc could actually communicate with animals—as was insisted by many people in this story—or if he continued to do so after George Broke was overthrown, he never confided it in me.

Clarissa returned to her home with the Auberons. Agitated by grief and confusion, the move was difficult for her. However, Henrietta, Walter and, especially Richard, welcomed her and the baby back so unconditionally, and provided her wounded spirit such warm ministrations that within weeks, she was a member of the family again, and happier than she'd ever been. Even Daisy made an effort to be nice to her. When Clarissa finally brought herself to approach Adam to apologize, he was confused. "For what?" he said.

Not long after, Virginia and Adam were married. And soon thereafter, Virginia gave birth to their first child. The top of Green Hill was too damaged to live on, so the couple started a small farm on the plains, a few miles east of the Gladfords, in a region teeming with rabbits. The last time I saw them, Adam was building a chair for his little girl, who they had named Victoria. They took a couple of the pigs rescued from the Broke Ranch. Algie, who returned to Adam on her own from wherever she'd been hiding, hitched up with one, a handsome hog with keen eyes and firm jowls, and they'd already had two farrows together. Rosenlee returned too, and formed an easy bond with Virginia's horse.

Their fields were fully planted and the crops were going equally to support Hugh's Bakery downtown, the Green family in their new homestead close to the Grange, and the community stores. For the first few months after she married Adam, Virginia needed to take daily trips to the town to teach her father (who had indeed been hidden from George by the kind farmers at the Grange) how to bake and to assure herself he wasn't burning down the bakery because of some bumble or other, but eventually he made a competency of it. Hugh became better at everything when he and Dorothy Rivers married. A couple of years on, the Greens, the Auberons, and the Bakers had the healthiest competencies you could find.

I lived in Arcadia for three more years. I reconstructed this tale from the testimony of the people and the diaries most of them kept as a normal practice of their faith. Since the speech patterns of the Arcadians would be nearly incomprehensible to the modern reader, I have altered them to a kind of constructed accent that I hope captures some of the essence of these people without tearing them entirely from their unique cultural context.

Gradually it emerged, from many baffling conversations in a half-comprehensible dialect, that these people were American Puritans, directly descended from those who had settled New England hundreds of years ago. They themselves rarely called themselves "Puritans," a term I learned later was originally used to insult rather than identify them. During the 17th century, groups of early American settlers were branching through the north, settling in the wilderness, and this must have been one of them. I don't know how they came to this region so disconnected from the rest of the world, and neither do I know how I came there apart from the story I have already related. My car crashed. I wandered in the woods and somehow ended up there. I assume I and they stumbled upon it in a similar way. I don't know if the truth behind Arcadia was revealed to Adam by

Merlin that night in the grove, as he told me. But to comprehend an actual Utopia, Merlin's explanation makes as much sense as any other.

And Utopia it was. The reader no doubt is confused by such a designation after learning of all the horrors that occurred there. It is important to bear in mind that these events happened after the pivotal tragedies of seven years previous in the time of the narrative, the first and most important of which was the discovery by Obadiah of a very destructive chemical compound whose usage had certain egregious metaphysical consequences. Prior to that discovery, and the misfortunes it led to, Arcadia was as close to a real Utopia as any place could be. It was a land where intimacy between humans and earth, air, water, animals, and each other was uncontaminated by processed foods and revenge porn, by death metal and plastic bags, by celebrity gossip and automobile exhaust. It was a place of no crime, no poverty, and no disease.

#

A week after the town was freed from the Brokes, a public forum was held where I was interviewed by the community. The people were thunderstruck by the TV and videotape. I showed it at the Meeting House, explaining as best I could how the TV worked, and displaying the videotape scene by scene, with frequent pauses to describe what they were seeing and to answer questions. I was nervous about exposing the Arcadians to the images in it. After the disastrous inspirations the video planted in Obadiah and George Broke, what sort of Pandora's Box might I be opening?

The images frightened more than inspired the audience. They saw a speeded-up chaos of crowds zooming through train stations, enslaved in the mechanical cages of factories, tossed down smoke-filled rapids of luminous streets, and they were scared half to death. They saw nothing in these depictions of my world but threats to their own.

Obadiah Broke had wanted to alter this Eden to a dominion of molded metals and hissing factory smoke, to put into motion the engines he believed God had forgotten to create. The idea of peaceable Mill's Trail changed to a clogged urban freeway lined with tall buildings filled the Arcadians with dread. I filled me with horror too.

I moved in with Joss Hankers. I started working in her pub. Despite the fear provoked by the TV, and my complete foreignness, the Arcadians quickly accepted me as one of their own. Since my first experiences in there were so traumatic, the moment Hildegard got us free from the cage, I had run away because I was terrified about what they would do to me next. It was a stunning coincidence that I encountered the group at Green Hill, where the explosion occurred, and this was another of many incidents that makes me believe that nothing ever happens by chance in Arcadia.

During the next six months, I tried to escape and return to my world by venturing several times into the forest, but I got lost and needed to return. I once tried to use a boat, to travel northward on the Silver Stream, into the great valleys that I thought might lead home, but magic got into the water and my boat wound along toward the south, then all the way around until I was back at the place I started.

Having no choice, I settled in and began to live as they did. Only then did I realize what a miracle the place really was. The people were, almost without exception, remarkably happy and healthy, much more so than in any place I'd lived.

Food was plentiful. Everyone worked hard, but never too hard. There were festivals at least once a month, celebrating some aspect of our good lives. Some of these I later recognized, when I studied more about it, as remnants of the old Puritan beliefs these people brought with them, altered somewhat over hundreds of years.

Like the original Puritans, they did not celebrate Christmas.

The most striking quality of life in Arcadia was the balance people struck between community and individual labor. The first New England Puritans attempted something very much like the Community Grange of Arcadia, but far more weighted toward serving society. Their initial experiment with a social contract ended in failure. They found that labor done solely for the community caused workers to grow dispirited and reduced production of crucial food supplies. Women did not want to cook for men other than their husbands, and men wanted their crops to feed their own families. The Puritans went all the way in the other direction by changing their system to one of private ownership of land, which has remained more or less the same since, and while the literal and figurative fencing off of land and labor motivated citizens of the new "City on the Hill," they also lost a substantial portion of their community spirit. And the social contract, which still is alive and well in many happier, healthier countries, is dead in America.

The Arcadians appeared to have gotten separated from the other New Englanders before this change and instead of eradicating the notion of social responsibility instead modified it slightly, to better balance individual and community obligations. They developed a system of ownership where an even balance was set up between labor for the community and labor for one's family.

After a year or so of living in Arcadia, I decided to write about this strange and wonderful place. I of course first wanted to get down the details of the Broke debacle, because I had been at the center of all that, but I also began interviewing people about all the other aspects of Arcadia. Many kindly volunteered to talk to me and let me read their diaries. It was through these sources that I discovered aspects of Arcadia that were even more amazing than the things I'd already encountered.

Here's an example: Arcadians never became sick. I don't mean, like, they were pretty healthy. I mean, they literally never were infected with any kind of viral or bacterial disease. Neither were they ever afflicted by cancer. The whole idea of sickness was foreign to them. Two things caused death in Arcadia: age

and injury. Doc Midland, with the substantial help of his wife
(she was as capable an apothecary as he was a physician), had
little to do in the way of healing people. Their job was to heal
the injured and deliver babies. Most people knew how to do
these things anyway by themselves, so being the "doctor" of
Arcadia was an easy job. And freed up a lot of time to
experiment with extraordinary "medicinal" powders.

This was intriguing enough, but there was something else.
It kept jabbing at me for weeks, but I couldn't quite place it.
When the thing troubling me finally coalesced in my mind
sufficiently to understand, I felt stupid that I was missing
something so obvious, something the reader has certainly
already perceived. Here was a doctor, with substantial skills at
healing sicknesses, with a heritage of much knowledge of
apothecary cures, which he honed, as a hobby even now, but
there were no sick people.

Also, although in most people there was no knowledge of,
say, fever, there were still a few old people who remembered
having had a fever themselves, when they were children. I
borrowed Joss's wagon and rode out to William and Anne's,
because these two were among those who'd mentioned this
childhood experience. I'd grown to like them much, especially
Anne, who spent many hours patiently teaching me how to grow
tea.

As soon as they'd seated me on their front porch, I said, "I
have a question."

They nodded. They were used to my questions.

"By my thinking, you are all originally from the Puritan
settlements—the settlements of God's People, from the first
New England migrations. That would be in the 1600's, right?"

They nodded indulgently. They had only a hazy
comprehension of my reckoning of the years but had no reason
to disbelieve me.

"So, I figure this...um, lack of disease that you all have
here...comes from the time you moved to Arcadia."

"Yes," said the mayor. "That's how the story traces back. I was too young to remember clearly that migration, but I remember Calvin's father preaching about how we'd escaped the sicknesses of the old land."

I said, "You say you remember that migration? That you were alive then?"

Anne said, "Yes. I even remember as a little girl my father tromping us through a big town. It must have been ten times size of our town now—before he went along with the migration that brought us here. He called it Bow's Town, I think."

"*Boston?*" I said. "You were in *Boston?* You couldn't…"

"What, dear?"

"You weren't alive back then."

The mayor laughed. He jabbed a thumb toward his wife. "*She* was sure alive, because I remember her. Even when I was a little boy, I was smitten with her."

"But that…" I stopped and added in my head. "That was 350 years ago!"

To which the couple merely shrugged.

And that's the way it remained, whenever I asked anyone. The oldest people in the community maintained, and provided detailed memories to substantiate it, they were over 300 years old. Middle-aged folks were well into their second century of life. It was hard to get a fix on. Young people like Virginia and Adam were, indeed, only barely twenty. Hildegard was a little older than she looked, about eighteen, and Daisy was only ten. On the other hand, Richard was three decades older than Adam, well into his fifties, but he could easily pass for being in his early twenties. Daisy's mother had given birth to her when she was past 100 years old.

It took me a few more months to notice the problem the reader is also already noticing: if the Arcadians lived so long, why weren't there more of them? After again badgering people with questions came the simple answer: they had few children.

More exactly, they spaced their children more than what you or I would consider normal. An average family had about four children, but the age of siblings could range one to sixty

years in a single family. Was the cause of this low birthrate a
lack of sex? It was hard to get these old Puritans to talk about
their bedroom lives, but my experiences and observations push
me toward thinking the Arcadians fucked even more than we do,
but this fucking didn't make a lot of babies.

#

I gave up trying to return home. It was especially hard to
give up that dream, especially when I thought of the boyfriend
I'd left behind. He must have gone through hell because of my
disappearance. It was difficult, but in time the spurts of tears,
nightmares, and manic dashes into the forest dwindled and I
settled into my fate. I became a pub worker and an apprentice in
blacksmithing. Although I was (secretly) an atheist, I still had
enough respect for the neo-Puritan leanings of the community
that I became an eager participant in the social aspects of it. I
even went to church, which, since the death of Calvin Branch,
was presided over collaboratively by a group of interested
citizens. I became so acclimated to Arcadian life that my speech
patterns were changing; I spoke with the same lilting accent—it
always seemed a bit like Swedish to me—and altered my
vocabulary and inverted my word order when appropriate. If
someone from "my" country had stumbled onto Arcadia at that
time, as I had three years before, they wouldn't have recognized
me as different from the natives.

Then one day my life was again turned upside-down.

It was late autumn. Heavy clouds hung low in the sky,
churning masses pushing downward. I had traveled to the south
to deliver some barrels for Joss. The farm I was delivering to
was not far from the old Broke place, now defunct, a ghost town
of cobwebby buildings. I was passing the fork in the road
branching toward town, when I heard the snort of a pig.

I looked up and saw it, on that ugly, rocky path they called
Phagus Trail going into the mountains. It was looking down at

me. The pig scrambled up, peeked back, snorted, and rounded a boulder.

The storm was close to breaking loose. A luminous crack spread across the horizon and was gone. Thunder rumbled over the land.

"Come back, piggy, piggy," I said, feeling foolish. I didn't really believe pigs were intelligent enough to communicate with people, but the other strange things I'd encountered planted a seed of doubt, so whenever I saw a pig, and especially whenever I ate pork, I had a moment of uneasiness. Lightning crackled overhead.

"Come down from there, you stupid pig! You want to die?"

The pig peeked around the boulder, ducked away.

I got out of the wagon and started up the hill.

It was waiting at the top of the ridge. The wind was starting to howl through the rocks and whistle in the branches of the few stubborn trees struggling to live there.

I was within throwing distance of the animal when it started trotting toward me. I thought for a second it was coming all the way, like an obedient dog, but it took a sudden swerve to the left, straight between two rocks, and disappeared into a clump of bushes.

"Shit!" I yelled. I shoved my way through the bushes, scratching my arms. I heard my frock rip. I pushed through head-tall brambles and struggled upward. The wind was really shrieking. Another blast of lightning fingered across the sky, followed instantly by an earsplitting *boom!* Pushing hard with my right shoulder, I was breaking through the heavy patch of bushes. I could hear the pig just ahead. I shoved, felt the wall of vegetation give, and I was airborne.

It happened so fast that for a second, I thought the abrupt field of distant grey and green was another species of bushes, but they were, in fact, the tentacle feet of the mountain, dotted with trees, hundreds of feet below me.

There was an instant when all the writhing sparks of my fear came together to form an instant of recognition that I was about to die. Then came in my head a grinding, like an axe on stone, followed by oblivion.

When I came to, I was in a hospital bed, TV cameras pushing through the door.

#

You know the rest. There was a fucking media frenzy. A lot of lurid, hyped-up speculation about my whereabouts those three years flooded the airwaves and Internet. Social media lit up with all sorts of juvenile, mean-spirited nonsense, which seems to characterize everything about what is left of America. I received about five hundred death threats in a single month. An attempt to appear on a talk-show and explain everything only added gasoline to the fire.

I went into hiding. I spent six months finishing this book. I chose this narrative form because I thought it would be the best way to introduce the world I stumbled into. I'm not sure it really was. I'm not sure there is any good way.

My return has been much more difficult than I ever imagined. I learned my old boyfriend suffered much more than I thought possible because of my disappearance. He was arrested, held under suspicion of murder for two months before being cleared. My parents also suffered, because they not only felt the torture of thinking their daughter was dead, but of being hounded by the press camped out in their front yard.

My return brought all that back. My old boyfriend, now married, can't leave his house without being pestered by camera crews, and neither can his wife. He doesn't blame me for any of this, but we can't talk anymore. Even my parents, although they don't hold me responsible, don't really believe me. Can't blame them for that.

It is impossible to slow down, let alone stop, the strands of gossip which spread nasty speculation and lies about me, my family, and my loved ones. It's like trying to halt a disease with no cure.

Adjusting to Arcadian life was hard, but it has been much harder adjusting to my return "home." It's been so bad, in fact, that after two years, I'm less adjusted now than when I first came back.

I have to admit: it's too much for me. I have to admit: it's time for me to go.

Mama, Papa, please understand. It's not only the disruptions of my privacy or the attacks on my character. Things that used to make sense to me don't anymore.

I can't get used to the noise. The babble of people clamoring to buy shit or bragging about the shit they have, the trumpet of politicians saying one thing but meaning another, the constant barrage of flagrant bullshit and racist outrages from the leader of our land, the whine of the privileged about not having enough, the honk of cars under my window, the shriek of bombers overhead.

Time to say goodbye.

Last night, I finished packing.

I have good hiking gear this time, with a decent sleeping bag. I have enough food in my pack to last at least two weeks, more than enough for me to find them.

This time I won't take a gun. I will take nothing with me that will poison paradise. I don't feel a need for protection against the forest animals.

I'm not scared of bears anymore.

Did you like this book? If so, please consider writing an Amazon review, so that others might be encouraged to enjoy it too.

61007142R00257

Made in the USA
Middletown, DE
06 January 2018